BRADSTREET GATE

BRADSTREET GATE

A NOVEL

ROBIN KIRMAN

CROWN PUBLISHERS
NEW YORK

Published in the United States by Crown Publishers, an imprint of the Crown Publishing Group, a division of Penguin Random House LLC, New York.
www.crownpublishing.com

Crown is a registered trademark and the Crown colophon is a trademark of Penguin Random House LLC.

Grateful acknowledgment is made to Penguin Random House LLC for permission to reprint "I Knew a Woman," copyright © 1954 by Theodore Roethke; from COLLECTED POEMS by Theodore Roethke. All rights reserved. Used by permission of Doubleday, an imprint of the Knopf Doubleday Publishing Group, a division of Penguin Random House LLC.

Library of Congress Cataloging-in-Publication Data
Kirman, Robin.
Bradstreet gate : a novel / Robin Kirman.—First Edition.
pages cm
1. Friendship—Fiction. 2. Coming of age—Fiction. 3. College students—Crimes against—Fiction. 4. Murder—Investigation—Fiction. 5. Psychological fiction. I. Title.
PS3611.I7695B73 2015
813'.6—dc23 2014047554

ISBN 978-0-8041-3931-1
eBook ISBN 978-0-8041-3932-8

Printed in the United States of America

Jacket photograph: Dina Greenberg

10 9 8 7 6 5 4 3 2 1

First Edition

For Reuven and Emmanuelle

BRADSTREET GATE

Prologue

A young man stood on her stoop: tall, with lanky hair falling in his face, and thin, busy lips that he chewed while she studied him across the threshold. No one she'd met before. The sun was sharp; the maple outside her house was spiked with buds. Spring had arrived without her noticing.

"Georgia Calvin?"

She turned to check on Violet, in the dining room behind her, jabbering in her high chair.

"Miss Calvin? I'm Nat Krauss." He shifted his knapsack to offer her his hand. "I left a message I'd be coming."

There had been several messages, in fact, from a young man at the *Crimson*: she'd erased them all without playing them through. Only one matter ever brought reporters calling, though years had passed since anyone had tried.

This May, it would be ten years, exactly, since Julie Patel's murder. Georgia always marked the day, May 5, and made sure flowers were delivered to the family: *Mr. and Mrs. Barid Patel, 32 North Beatty Street, Pittsburgh, PA*. Nine bouquets and no replies. Nonetheless, she kept sending them, hoping that, if she hadn't been forgiven, she might at least be accepted as a valid participant in the family's tragedy, someone who'd been involved in those events the way they had: directly and against her will—unlike the many others who'd taken an interest in the murder out of some personal objective, the Nat Krausses of the world. "You're the Harvard reporter."

"Editor in chief, actually." His hand remained outstretched; she took it at last. The boy's palm felt sticky; his fingertips were stained with newsprint, black under the nails.

The oncologist had warned her again this morning: Mark could only be safely released to a clean, contained environment. No welcome home bouquets, no gifts of food, no guests.

"I'm sorry, this really isn't a good time."

A crashing noise came from behind her; she rushed back inside, relieved to find Violet strapped into her high chair, her bowl of mashed bananas spinning on its side across the floor. Georgia knelt to clean the mess; when she stood again, the young man was in her living room, laying his unwashed jacket over one armrest of her sofa.

"Ms. Calvin."

"Reese. I'm Reese now." She hadn't taken Mark's name when they'd married, but with the onset of his illness, she'd filed the papers. She would be Reese and remain Reese, whatever happened, from here on.

The clock in the living room read 10:15; by noon Mark would be prepared for discharge; Violet still needed her nap. Food lay scattered around the high chair; the reporter had tracked mud across the floor. "Look, if you'll just leave me your number—"

"One question. Please. Give me five minutes and I *swear* I'll get out of your way."

Despite the unkempt hair and rumpled bowling shirt, nods to hipsterism, the young man was clearly fanatically determined. The kind of guy that, ten years before, she'd have found easy to handle. These Harvard boys had not changed.

She was the one who'd changed. Her shirt was stained; her leggings had a hole in one knee; her eyes were ringed from lack of sleep and white hairs had multiplied among the gold. The past year had done the transformative work of a decade; just over thirty, she must seem far removed from anything to do with sex or scandal.

Violet let out a whimper of exhaustion.

"I need to get the baby to sleep first."

"No problem. I can wait." The young man dropped onto the sofa.

Georgia resigned—"*one* question"—and leaned down to unstrap the baby from her high chair. When she glanced up, Krauss was staring; her shirt gaped and, since she was nursing, she hadn't bothered with a bra.

Krauss turned away, to pull a notebook from his bag. But a moment later, from the stairwell, Georgia caught him watching her again: a more prurient curiosity shone in his expression.

It was a look that she remembered, encountered often after the murder, in the faces of strangers who'd linked her to the figure in the news. Rufus Storrow's student girlfriend. The seductress or the naïf, the betrayed or the betrayer, the partner of a killer: she'd been all these things to different people, might be any one or more of them to this Nat Krauss.

She shut herself inside the baby's room. Almost half an hour went by while she nursed and rocked and hummed; the presence of a visitor made Violet agitated. By the time Georgia laid the baby, sleeping, in her crib and tiptoed down, she'd allowed herself to hope that Krauss had given up and left. Instead she found him typing into his phone; his feet were propped up on the coffee table, beside a stack of unpaid bills: mortgage payments, insurance claims.

"Good to go now?" He sat up straight and pocketed his phone.

She took a seat across from him, inside this living room she'd scarcely used, furnished with items she and Mark had bought over the summer at local auctions: one way to introduce an element of chance, some playful chaos, into the seemingly staid business of setting up house—as if chance and chaos weren't already with them, as if she'd forgotten the lesson of ten years before.

"You can guess what's brought me," Krauss began.

"The memorial this May." Every member of her graduating class had received notice, and she'd been made aware of it much sooner, since Charlie and Alice had taken part in the arrangements. Over lunch, that winter, Alice had warned her that the ten-year anniversary of Julie Patel's death would have consequences: the media was taking renewed interest in the story and the investigation had been reopened; there was a chance that Georgia might be contacted by police or press. "You're covering the ceremony?"

"Also." Krauss shifted forward; the smell of cigarettes wafted from his clothes. "But my question has more, specifically, to do with Joe Lombardi—the officer who headed up the Patel investigation."

"I know who he is."

"Right, though maybe you're not aware he's Chief of Police Lombardi now. I don't know how much you keep up with Cambridge politics—there have been complaints of corruption, incompetence. Which must come as no surprise to you: given what went on with the Patel case."

That case had been mishandled in a dozen ways, but she'd never thought to blame officer Lombardi more than anybody else involved: the politicians who'd pushed the department to name a suspect quickly; the press that never clamored for a broader investigation. Everyone concerned, it seemed, had played his eager part in persecuting Storrow.

Storrow had been too perfect a target, after all: too well dressed and too well spoken, with a high Virginia drawl and the sort of fair, delicate good looks that called to mind outdated notions like breeding. A charmed, young Harvard professor, whose reputation she'd assisted in sullying forever.

Across from her Krauss brushed the hair off his pimpled forehead; he was sweating, talking on excitedly: "And not just any statements, potentially *exonerating* statements. I've already spoken with one witness who claims Lombardi completely disregarded what he told him: a classmate of yours. Miguel Santina. You might know him."

"Know who?" She rubbed her eyes; the night before she'd scarcely slept, woken by Violet twice and kept awake by her own fears that the day would bring bad news, that Dr. Poole would tell her Mark's immune system was still too compromised, that his release from the hospital would be postponed once more. *We can't be overly cautious; he's undergone a very serious surgery*, gravely serious, the name notwithstanding: Whipple—a word better suited to Violet's toys and gizmos than to a procedure to remove half of Mark's insides.

"Excuse me, Nat is it? I thought we'd be discussing the memorial, not the murder."

"Obviously, they're connected."

"Maybe they shouldn't be." A ceremony to honor a young woman's memory, to bring some comfort to her family: that was not an occasion for muckraking.

"I know these questions might make some people uncomfortable, but if Julie Patel was denied justice, that needs to come out. I'm sure the Patels would feel the same."

"Yeah? I kind of doubt it." On what should be a hopeful morning, she didn't need to recall death; and as unpleasant as returning to this subject was to *her*, it would have to be pure torture for Julie's family.

She studied the reporter, perched at the sofa's edge, knee bouncing; his pen ran, buzzing, up and down his notebook's spiral. A creature positively twitching with ill-contained ambition—as if he'd given a damn about Julie Patel or her family, until he'd seen his chance to earn some notice from Reuters or the *Times*.

"If you're here to discuss details of the case, I really doubt that I can help you; I said all I had to say to the police ten years ago."

"To Lombardi, you mean." Krauss looked down at his lap; he'd stuck his pen inside the notebook's spiral. He lifted the book, trying to shake the pen free without her seeing: a flush bloomed beneath the rash of tiny pimples; he was a child suddenly.

In spite of herself, she smiled. She supposed she was being rather hard on Krauss—too hard, probably, conflating him with the reporters who'd once assailed her, or with Alice, who'd been the one to expose her affair with Storrow, first to Charlie and then in the pages of the *Crimson*. Long ago, when they—she, Alice, and Charlie—were all really just children, too, self-preoccupied and reckless.

"Go on," she resumed, more indulgent. "Your question: there was a classmate . . ."

"Miguel Santina. The name came up in an old *Globe* article." Krauss abandoned the stuck pen and pulled a second one out of his knapsack. "Turns out the guy had phoned Lombardi to report seeing Storrow's BMW on the night of the murder. Fifteen to thirty minutes before—parked on Cowperthwaite."

The street adjoining Mather House, where she'd been living senior year. Back then she'd never have imagined Storrow would risk seeking her out in her dorm, that he could be so rash or obsessive, but subsequent years had made her less certain. "This is the first I'm learning of it."

"The first *anyone* is learning of it. Seems no one pursued the claim." Krauss repressed a grin: so pleased to have surpassed the achievements of the many adults who'd dedicated months to these same mysteries before.

"We weren't together, Storrow and me, if that's what you're wondering."

"No, I know. You were at a party. Kirkland House."

A detail she hadn't had cause to recollect, not since she'd been held inside a detective's office for three grueling hours of questioning. "So if you read the police report, you already know everything I know. I'd have mentioned seeing Storrow or his car."

"You're sure of that? Because Lombardi might have left it out."

"Of course I'm sure."

"Maybe there were other occasions; he'd come by another time?"

"Not that I ever knew of, no." No meetings on campus: foremost among Storrow's many rules. It had seemed the height of irony, really, that after all the disagreements they'd had about his precautions, bordering on paranoia—*Who gives a damn who you're sleeping with?*—in the end, every move Storrow had made in those months, including with her, had been scrutinized publicly, and judged.

Krauss chewed his bottom lip: it seemed this wasn't the answer that he'd hoped for. "I'm not here just on the word of Santina, so you know. There was a girl, on your floor in Mather, who also thought she heard a man's voice in your room."

"Well, she was mistaken." Not that it was necessary to defend her statements to this kid: Nat Krauss was not the police and she was no longer a guilt-ridden girl of twenty. "Look, I've told you what I can and now, really, I've got other things to do."

She rose and stood in front of Krauss; he remained seated, determined.

"If you don't want to help me, I get that, but I'd assume you'd want to help your friend."

"Storrow, you mean?" Even during their affair, she wouldn't have described him as her *friend*. Charlie was her friend. Alice, too, or so she'd thought. But not a man she'd spent the last decade avoiding, not a man she couldn't swear had been incapable of a brutal crime. "We haven't spoken in five years."

"Regardless, I'm sure you're aware of how he's been ruined: professionally, personally."

"So *Storrow's* your concern? I thought it was justice for the Patels."

"I'm concerned for everyone Lombardi's lies affected—and if Storrow had his reasons for keeping quiet then, it looks as if he has a different story to tell now."

"What story's that?"

"I hope to find out when we meet."

"You're meeting—where?" The last she'd heard from Storrow, he'd been living in India, where she'd hoped he had the good sense to remain. Doing penance, so he'd said, with deliberate provocation: the memory of that improbable encounter, inside a tiny Mumbai kitchen, made her jittery still.

"He's in Virginia. Great Falls," Krauss explained. "I'm driving down next week."

The news gave her a jolt: Storrow back on American soil, in contact with this kid who was now inside her home. "You know what he's doing there?"

"Visiting his mother, apparently, though I got the sense there might be more to it: government business."

When he spoke of Storrow, Krauss lowered his voice, and his tone became more knowing. That was Storrow's absurd effect, she recalled, on a certain kind of young man, even one as smart as Charlie. There had always been a bunch of them trailing Storrow across the Yard, enamored of his West Point lingo, entranced by his stories of the JAG Corps, suggestions of covert operations he was part of, the precise definitions of which always remained elusive. Whatever elite connections Storrow had once possessed had been severed long ago. A decade ago, come May.

"You don't think he's come for the memorial? For God's sake, he doesn't plan to use the occasion for grandstanding?"

"I can't guess what's on his mind."

But she *could* guess. A man like Storrow, so devoted to the perfection of his image; he wouldn't allow himself to be remembered as a villain, or to be forgotten either.

"He cannot be there. It would be a disaster for that family." Her voice was shrill. A small cry sounded from upstairs. She paused, waiting to be reassured that Violet hadn't fully woken. "The Patels must be allowed to have their day."

"I understand your feelings here."

"No, I don't think you do." Nat Krauss couldn't begin to understand what it would do to Julie's parents if Storrow showed his face again, what a horror it would be for them to see the man they believed had taken their child from them. Until Violet was born, Georgia couldn't have grasped it either: what it meant to care for a creature of such sweet defenselessness, from the soft crown of her head, to those feeble, immaculate feet—to tend to another body, its needs and pains, more thoroughly than to one's own. Even the ghost of a child was a mother's possession. Mrs. Patel ought to be left in peace at least with that.

"Storrow keeps out, or I'll take steps to make sure of it. You can tell him I said so."

"He does have a right to have his story heard, though, don't you think? He's suffered, too."

Suffering: what did this kid know about it? She wasn't about to discuss suffering with him, not after a year like the last one, spent watching Mark lose his hair and nails and so much strength he couldn't lift his nine-pound daughter.

She crossed to the sofa's edge to retrieve Krauss's jacket. He took it, blinking up at her. "I'm sorry if I've upset you, Ms. Calvin."

"*Reese.* And my husband is waiting."

From her stoop she watched Krauss unlock his car and drive away, the sun reflecting upon his rear windshield. The brightness hurt her eyes; she went back inside.

Soon Violet would wake and the house still had to be readied: meticulously disinfected. She had no time to spare on thoughts of Julie Patel now, to indulge in guilty musings of the sort that had kept her occupied for years after her classmate's death: imagining that she'd been sacrificed instead and Julie was living in her place. So it would be Julie with a child, a fitter mother, fitter wife, a better defender of the families of murder victims, more accomplished in everything and more deserving of existence in that parallel universe where she'd been the one struck down and Julie Patel lived.

Wallowing notions: such games just served to flatter, to convince us we had more profound consciences than we did. What good did it do anyone—Julie's family, or her own—to berate herself?

Still, once Mark was home and she was calmer, she supposed she should call Charlie and discuss this matter with him. Something should be done to prevent the scene she now envisioned: ten years since he'd been hounded from the campus, Storrow choosing this solemn event to surface once again.

He might just be capable of such a thing, a man who'd been mad enough, after all, to make an appearance at the vigil following Julie's death. Suspected of her murder, he'd dared to mix among the mourners, to stand before her family; he'd even dared to speak.

That was one more miscalculation that had ruined him: no falsely accused man could be ever so measured and so poised. He would shout and protest. He wouldn't give thoughtful speeches in remembrance of the victim. Such efforts to be proper, such measured dignity, especially for those who didn't know him, had only lent credence to the notion that Rufus Storrow was a monster.

Even she, who'd once lain beside him, couldn't quite muster certainty.

But why place the blame on Storrow? Who could hope for *any* kind of certainty in this life? Dr. Poole put Mark's chance of surviving the year at fifty percent. This was up from twenty; this was progress; it was the closest she could come to certainty. Human nature might not be designed to manage such odds—but life didn't care what we could manage, and death, even when it didn't hunt beloved husbands of forty, or strike down eager girls of twenty, was no kinder.

PART I

1

She could sense the officers' thrill at her arrival: heads were raised, pens lowered, even the phones seemed to have stopped ringing as Georgia crossed the station floor, beaded boots jangling, between the rows of interlocking cubicles where men in plainclothes sat in front of leaning stacks of files.

An older officer stepped forward to greet her: early fifties, graying, with fleshy, pockmarked cheeks; a high potbelly strained the buttons of his short-sleeved, collared shirt. Joe Lombardi, he reminded her; they'd spoken on the phone that morning, when he'd called to ask her to come in.

She followed him to a room set off from the main office: dusty blinds blocked the view inside; the desk was cluttered with papers, dirty coffee mugs, and take-out containers. Lombardi pulled out a chair for her, apologizing for the state of the place and for his own appearance: he was unshaven; his clothes were wrinkled.

"No one's slept much lately. I'm guessing you haven't either."

He wanted to get her on his side; she could see that, even before he offered his sympathy for what she must be going through: a girl in her position ought to be preparing for exams, looking forward to graduation. "We're all very grateful you've agreed to talk."

As long as her statements remained private, Georgia made clear at the outset, while Lombardi was still so mindful of his gratitude. Since Tuesday, Storrow had been featured in every local paper and news program. "You must have a form of some kind. For confidentiality?"

"Form?" Lombardi settled in behind the papers piled on his desk. "I don't believe we have anything like that. But you have my word.

Theresa will vouch for me." He motioned to a woman standing at the open door; her round, dimpled face looked gentle.

"You thirsty, hungry?" the woman asked her. "If you need anything, just let me know."

What she needed was assurance that her name wouldn't appear in the headlines the next day. Already she suspected she'd made a mistake by showing up here without a lawyer. "I really think I'd like more than a spoken promise."

Lombardi hunched forward, trying for an honest look, doing something complicated with his brows. "*You're* not the issue, Miss Calvin—no one cares about your affair, whatever went on with that guy."

Maybe not, though if what she had to say were so inconsequential, she imagined she'd be telling it to one of the more junior officers jammed into cubicles outside. And surely Lombardi wouldn't be taking so much time to reassure her if he believed her statements would accomplish what she hoped: to clear Storrow of suspicion.

Lombardi nodded to the kind-looking woman, who left the room, shutting the door behind her.

He paused to open a desk drawer and pull out a tape recorder. "Probably you think Storrow wouldn't approve."

She disliked this reference to approval and what it implied: a young girl in thrall to an older man. "Why wouldn't he? I don't have anything negative to say."

Lombardi smiled. "Good. I've been wondering when *someone* would stick up for that guy."

Of course this officer must be trying to unnerve her, Georgia thought: she couldn't *really* be the only person to come to Storrow's defense. Though it was true that on the news the night before, among all those students interviewed, no one had shouted at the cameras that what was happening was *crazy*, that the man they knew as a committed housemaster and professor could not possibly have done this awful thing. Instead she'd watched them, kids she'd seen around campus, in lecture halls and parties, relating their impressions of Storrow as "frosty" and "strange."

Where were the students who'd flocked to Storrow's classes or to the meals he'd hosted at the master's residence? Where was Charlie? If anyone ought to be on Storrow's side, Charlie should. Silently she'd observed the influence the professor had been having on her friend: the gingham plaid that Charlie decked himself out in now, those gestures he'd adopted—whistling as he walked, the rousing claps, and those Storrowisms—*that there's the max . . . bone up, spoon up, tie up . . . what's the skinny?* Such fidelity to the man's style should imply a deeper loyalty—enough to withstand even news of Storrow's affair with her.

They'd lied to Charlie, yes; but that didn't make Storrow a monster any more than it made her one.

Lombardi turned on the tape recorder and announced the date: "Friday, May ninth, nineteen ninety-seven." For the record, he asked Georgia to provide her name and address.

"Mather House, 10 Cowperthwaite Street."

"Any roommates?"

"I have a single." Though she supposed she ought to mention Alice: "A friend had been staying with me recently. Alice Kovac. But you've already spoken with her, haven't you?"

Lombardi faced her, deadpan: clearly information was meant to flow only one way.

"She must be the one who tipped you off about me."

"Why? She was aware of your relationship with Storrow?"

"I never told her what he was."

"Your boyfriend, you mean."

Boyfriend. Language adopted for her sake: the sort of naive designation Lombardi would expect from a young girl. "Nothing so conventional. Given our respective positions."

"Student and master?" Lombardi's lips twitched.

"Storrow was not *my* master, no."

She studied the officer from across the desk. Not much older than Storrow, she guessed, but his face was bloated and creased; his breathing was heavy and he smelled of stale coffee and rank sweat, whereas

Storrow—you could tell even from the pictures they'd run in the *Globe*—smelled of aftershave and fresh linen and strong health. A man who was meticulous in his habits and hygiene, who treated himself with care that suggested both optimism and self-importance. If Storrow could inspire jealousy even in his most privileged students, what sort of ire would he arouse in a man like this?

Lombardi was studying her, too. Her hair was wild—she'd neglected to brush it—and she wore the same cutoffs and peasant blouse she'd worn the past two days. Despite the recent strain, still she looked like herself, like what she was: the precocious, overindulged daughter of an artist.

"I'm curious, Miss Calvin. You mentioned your relations with Storrow weren't *normal*—"

"—Conventional was the word I think I used. And I don't consider that a bad thing."

"Nothing that bothered you?"

"Nope."

"Come on now." Lombardi smirked. "With women, there's always *something*."

There were no pictures on his desk, no smiling children or pretty wife. Possibly officers didn't risk displaying personal items, but she couldn't imagine, anyway, that such a man had acquired more in his romantic life than an embittered ex or two and maybe an angry, dispersed litter.

"Any difficulties we had were a result of circumstances."

"That you had to keep your affair hidden."

"Yes."

"And would you say Storrow was good at it? Hiding and pretending?"

"Apparently not good enough."

Lombardi laughed; his pen tapped, skipping, against the desk. "Good enough to hide something from *you*?"

"He wasn't sleeping with Julie Patel, if that's what you're getting at. She was his student: plain and simple."

"Maybe not so simple."

He was referring, she supposed, to the one weak motive ascribed to Storrow: Julie Patel had complained about him, repeatedly and publicly, taking offense at statements he'd made during his lectures. "Whatever their argument, he didn't get into that with me. But you've got Julie wrong if you think she'd sleep with her professor."

"So you *knew* Julie Patel then?"

"Not really. We were classmates, obviously. Sophmore year I started volunteering with her program, but it didn't work out." She'd had the chance to observe Julie closely only once: her practical, contained manner—hair done in a girlish braid and those dowdy clothes that didn't quite conceal the womanly body beneath them. For half an hour, one single afternoon, they'd sat alone in a room in Phillips Brooks House, the student community service organization, so that Julie could explain Georgia's unfitness for work with troubled kids: *How you dress, even your laugh—I'm not saying it's inappropriate in general; I'm not making a judgment or anything.* "We were different types, is my point. So nothing that went on in my case would be relevant."

"That may be. But I can't be sure until I know *what* went on in your case."

Lombardi's voice was low, falsely solemn, as if he meant to conceal from her the pleasure he was taking in this meeting, his readiness to hear from her a tale of abuse and depravity, to confirm the narrative already being composed round the clock, inside these rooms, among these officers, and with assistance from the press, to bring down a man whom his men instinctively disliked, just because Storrow had a striking résumé behind him and a bright career ahead of him and because he'd enjoyed the attentions of a young woman like her.

Lombardi and the rest might pretend they were above such temptations, but she didn't buy it. How many of the officers here would have resisted her the way Storrow had initially?

"He never pressured me. He actively tried to avoid me, if you really want to know." The tape recorder sat beside her, reels turning.

How odd it was: for four months she'd kept her secret, though she'd wanted, often, to confess, to share even one small, salacious detail. There were times she'd told herself the story of her affair, narrating it in her head, merely for the satisfaction of recounting the tale. But in all her fantasies—of telling Alice, or Charlie, or her father, or even a complete stranger—never had she pictured a first audience like this man across the desk.

One unseasonably warm October afternoon, she'd gone for a late-morning run along the Charles River with Alice; the pair of them had returned to campus starving and without cash, so Alice had suggested they stop at the Adams House dining hall to pocket whatever she could gather for their lunch. Alice had been a resident of Adams sophomore year, but had since moved out and skipped the meal plan. Georgia proposed they double back to her dining hall at Mather House, but Alice had no qualms about stealing, least of all from a university as well endowed as Harvard.

The pair easily followed a group in through C-entry and Georgia waited, stretching her legs, inside the dark, wood-paneled hall, while Alice went ahead to the dining room. Just as Alice was returning, booty hidden in her bag, a man entered behind them: midforties, with a wiry, athletic build. His hair was red and brushed back off a high forehead; his skin was softly freckled, his features refined: a long jaw and sharp chin, fine light brows above green eyes. He was carrying a squash racquet and dressed in tennis whites—pressed shorts and a gleaming polo. Like a vision of Harvard past he came striding between the slouching jocks in sweats and the alternative scenesters sporting stringy hair and Salvation Army flannel.

"Jasmine, Pam, Shawn . . . afternoon . . . afternoon." He spoke slowly, with a slight twang, addressing each student he passed by name. "Alice, nice surprise seeing you here."

As soon as he'd moved out of earshot, Alice turned to Georgia, cursing at the closeness of the call: "I was sure he was going to fucking search me."

The man (Sterling or Stern, something like that) was the new interim housemaster of Adams: a lecturer in both the Law School and the History Department, he was someone who'd aroused enough speculation that even Alice, who never set foot in Adams, except to pinch a fat-free yogurt or green apple, had heard talk about him among the students: *West Point, JAG Corps—rule freak of the first rank.*

They'd left it there, though Georgia remained curious: the man had struck her as both bizarre and somehow familiar. Was it possible she'd seen him before? Though if she had, hard to believe she'd have forgotten.

It was only after she and Alice had dispensed with their light lunch and parted ways that Georgia managed to place Storrow at last. He'd made less of an impression stripped of his preppy outfits, striking red hair tucked inside a swimming cap, merely one among the thin crowd of swimmers she'd seen often at the Malkin Athletic Center.

"The practice pool," she told Lombardi, "was where I first noticed him."

He was attractive: lean and handsome, in an anodyne way, though his body looked ghostly white inside the water and she found those pale brows of his unnerving; they made his gaze seem both blank and much too bold.

Each morning he stepped in from the changing room, goggles dangling from his grasp, dressed in flip-flops, white swimming cap, and matching white trunks. He kept to himself, likely choosing early hours, as Georgia did, to avoid the crowds. For forty minutes Storrow performed laps, crawl then butterfly, always the same routine. A man of routine generally, it seemed: he was there every Monday, Wednesday, and Friday at exactly eight a.m.

"Did it occur to you," Lombardi asked, "that his swimming when you did might not have been coincidental?"

"There were five or six others always there at the same time. Habits form, it's like that."

Not really true: she *had* wondered, feeling Storrow's eyes on her, whether their schedules had conjoined purely by accident. If she hadn't shared the same inkling as Lombardi, she'd probably never have been as forward with Storrow as she'd been.

"And when did he first approach you?"

"He didn't. I spoke first. Standard chitchat. Compliments on swimming. We didn't say much." There wasn't opportunity for long conversation while dripping at the side of the pool. During their most sustained exchange, they'd spoken about racing and she'd explained her lack of interest: when something is pure pleasure, why would you want to rush it? "Small provocations. To test his courage, I guess."

"And what was the result?"

"He disappeared."

Several weeks before Christmas, Storrow had stopped showing up at the pool: she hadn't given it much thought—too preoccupied with finals, and arrangements for winter break.

"So when did you next see him?"

"Just before vacation." He'd simply shown up again one morning, already in the water when she entered to do her laps. On the walk back to the locker room, she'd heard whistling behind her.

"He followed you?"

"Only to wish me a good holiday. And then I guess it must have come up that neither of us was going home. I mentioned I was staying with an old friend in New York." A solitary New York Christmas was preferable, she'd decided, to one in Mexico with her dad and whichever latest girlfriend was hanging off him. Her mother's invitation was no more tempting: two weeks at home with stepdad William, where she'd be subject to constant questions about her plans—or lack of plans—following graduation.

"So you led Storrow to believe you'd be on your own—and available," Lombardi said.

That was what she'd essentially done, yes; after her shower, once she'd fixed her hair and dressed, she'd torn off a scrap of notebook paper and copied down the number in New York where she could be reached. If Storrow were still lingering by the exit when she left, his presence would be invitation enough; and if he'd gone, or refused the number, or never called, no great harm. She would just swim at a different hour or, more likely, he would.

In the lobby she'd spotted him, leaning down to drink from the water fountain. He looked up just as she walked by and cleared his throat; before he could speak, she put out her hand and he took the paper.

"And you decided to do this," Lombardi asked her, "without encouragement?"

"Yes."

"He hadn't done *anything* to lead you to think he was open to a meeting."

"No."

"But you still thought he was."

"I told you he'd just vanished for two weeks. If you call that encouragement."

"It didn't strike you this might be a tactic? Playing hard to get?"

So far, Lombardi hadn't said a whole lot, but she'd begun to sense the impression he was forming of her story—not at all the one that she'd intended. While she'd flattered herself to think Storrow had been drawn to her, Lombardi must have assumed the man was tailing her, waiting for her to take what she *thought* was the initiative. Efforts that had seemed romantic began to look sinister when seen through the eyes of this officer: tricks Storrow had used on any number of women until one was dumb enough to fall for them.

Lombardi thought her dumb then—her fine education notwithstanding. When she continued, her voice was cooler, her explanations more exact. "I was a student; getting involved with me could cost Storrow his job. There were plenty of other women he could have who wouldn't be any threat to his career."

"Lots of women, in theory. But then—you were right in front of him."

"I'm not sure proximity was the most compelling criterion for him." In response to his judgment, she'd taken on a high tone, sounding like the cloistered, snot-nosed Harvard gal he no doubt thought she was.

"New York then." Lombardi dropped the matter and went on, efficiently. "Why were you going there, again?"

"Pursuing an internship. Visiting a friend who ran a gallery." More accurately the friend's son, Gabe, who'd offered her his roommate's bed for the holiday.

In fact it hadn't been merely a professional visit; Gabe had been a childhood crush and she'd been looking forward to their reunion, though her excitement had faded upon meeting him again: slicker, cologned, and less appealing than she remembered him, he'd shown her to the filthy room that was now hers. Men's underwear lay on the bed; he'd settled on top of them, kicked off his Doc Martens and lit up a joint. Almost immediately, the phone rang; Gabe, irritated, let Georgia know it was a man for her.

"I'm not disturbing you?" Storrow's voice sounded official. As if her welfare were his responsibility, he'd asked if she was comfortable where she was staying: "Because, as it happens, there's an empty apartment if you want it. It's been offered to me, but I won't be able to use it."

"He was giving you an apartment?" asked Lombardi. "Just like that?"

It *had* struck her as unusual, but Storrow had an explanation ready: "I've got a former classmate stationed overseas, still keeps a small flat here, in Manhattan, for when he comes through. Otherwise he lets us old grads use it. It's free now if you're interested."

An awkward silence followed as she wondered: Might he have gone to greater lengths to get this place than he'd let on, might he be providing them some kind of private pad? He was a stranger to her still, but she sensed a labored quality in the way he went about things, each task accomplished with the greatest possible effort, so that it wasn't inconceivable he'd gone to so much trouble because he couldn't make this happen any other way, couldn't make a simple proposition that they meet one night for drinks.

The address was in Hell's Kitchen, Fifty-Second and Eighth. Storrow was waiting for her there; he buzzed her in at the vestibule and, when she emerged from the elevator, he was standing at an open door. Crossing the hall, she'd been nervous, unsure whether to offer a handshake or a kiss. Storrow had removed the chance for either, backing up behind the door and waving with his free hand for her to come inside. He was dressed in a narrow, tailored, navy suit and a starched gingham shirt; she'd wondered if he'd dressed up for her, but this, she'd later discovered, was Storrow's standard uniform.

She'd come in and complimented the apartment: neat, spare, straight out of a catalog, lacking in any sort of character or personal detail. No photographs or ID cards or pieces of mail, no evidence about the tenant or signs of ordinary living.

Storrow gave her a brief tour, opening the bedroom door, but shying away from stepping in. The thought returned that he might have arranged this place for the two of them. She supposed she'd led him to expect that was what she wanted. Now she wasn't sure. When Storrow moved toward her, she stepped back, but he was only reaching to close the door.

"I'll leave you to it then." He clapped his hands and withdrew a set of keys from his blazer pocket. "Yours if you want them."

"That was it," she told Lombardi. "He showed me around and then he left."

"Just like that?"

She, too, had been surprised that Storrow had excused himself so soon, smiling and putting out his hand in that avuncular way he had, as if she were one of his Adams House wards and he were acting, merely, *in loco parentis*.

From the window she'd watched him step out into the street and hail a cab. Off to meet a woman? There must have been a woman, she'd imagined, observing his confident gestures and lean, strong back, and startled by the possessiveness she felt.

Alone, she'd lingered in the apartment, poked around a little. There was a stocked bar along one wall, a Bang & Olufsen stereo, a cable box, men's magazines. The bookshelves contained sober histories, political biographies: the sort of collection that bore out Storrow's story, which she was by then willing to believe.

"So you decided to stay?"

"I didn't see any reason not to."

It was a kick to have the run of a place like that—kept by men who did whatever they did without leaving any traces. Her presence there constituted a secret of its own; dressed in a man's sweatshirt she'd found inside one of the drawers, she sat on the leather sofa getting tipsy and flipping through X-rated channels. Not that Lombardi needed to know this, or to know that later, lying in bed, in the dark, in a room that smelled vaguely of aftershave and shoe polish, she'd listened for the door, imagined Storrow returning late at night, crawling into bed beside her. All the skittishness of the afternoon had fled her. If he'd come to her, she'd have welcomed him.

"Did he return that night?" Lombardi asked.

"No, he didn't."

When she woke the next morning, the phone was ringing. She'd snatched it up eagerly, but it was only Gabe. He'd apparently redialed the number Storrow had called her from the day before: tracking her down just to announce he'd left her bag out in his hall. She didn't bother asking about visiting the gallery. Her prior plans had been upended; the next weeks were cleared for whatever adventure might be waiting.

As long as she remained in the rooms Storrow had provided, she couldn't invite friends to come and visit, or explain her whereabouts to anybody, including her father, who'd called Christmas week to say he'd split from his girlfriend in Cancun. But rather than join him in sunny Mexico, Georgia chose to remain in Manhattan, strolling down slushy avenues under colored lights, wandering among tourists through museums, or simply lounging around the apartment like a bored housewife, occupied with idle daydreams. Each morning, in the shower, she'd picture Storrow drawing back the curtain; each time she stepped through the front door, she prepared to feel him grab her. As the weeks passed, though, she lost faith that anything would ever happen. If Storrow wanted her, he wouldn't have let this month—remote from campus, as free to meet as they would ever be—slip by without event.

On the last day of her vacation Storrow called to make arrangements to collect the keys. She'd planned to simply leave them in the mailbox, but he offered to drop in and see if she needed any help straightening up.

Storrow had arrived looking almost the same as when he'd left the month before: pressed gingham shirt and navy suit, not a hair out of place, nor any sign of an unbefitting motive. Seeing him there, relieved to find all in order, *looks good, all spooned up*, she couldn't understand how she'd ever imagined a different outcome: that this man could be lured into a messy affair. Possibly Storrow already had a girlfriend, or, for all she knew, a boyfriend; perhaps he was recovering from a failed relationship or even a divorce. She hadn't the faintest clue about his personal life, or any insight into his desires; it had been sheer invention to believe his interest in her had been anything but chaste.

Her bag was packed; she expected nothing more from Storrow than perhaps some help loading her things into a cab bound for Penn Station, and so she was caught off guard when he checked his watch and turned to her. "Do you need to rush off? Feel like some chow?"

He steered her to a restaurant on the next block, a place she'd never have chosen on her own, stuffy and pretentious: oversized flower arrangements, layered tablecloths, and crowded silver.

"So it was a date?" Lombardi cut in at last.

Markedly *unlike* a date: Storrow had refused to order drinks—just a ginger ale for him—and had begun by asking questions about her studies, her intentions after graduation. Precisely the sort of questions that might be asked over a dining hall meal: a housemaster getting to know one of the students.

Later, as the food arrived and Storrow grew more comfortable, he spoke about himself—a favorite subject, she'd discovered. He was evidently proud of his achievements and of the upbringing that had enabled and inspired them. The Warbers—his mother's line—could boast of six graduates of the Citadel, all gone on to become generals and public servants. As for him, he'd been the first in his family to head north to West Point, and the first to go to Oxford or have the honor of being a professor at Harvard.

While he went on, she'd watched him cutting his steak into same-sized pieces, observed the irritating order on his plate. Even his good looks began to seem drab, robotically symmetric, and its few peculiarities became unnerving: the small scars over one brow and at his chin, and that blue vein snaking down his forehead, ending just between his eyes. For weeks now, she'd fantasized about this face and this body; now she couldn't comprehend it: How could she have been caught up in a bizarre sexual stupor with this man at its center?

The whole impulse had been mistaken, from the moment she'd abandoned Gabe, who was far more her style really—artistic, cynical, and fun—to join a man for whom even a meal appeared a chore: all that slicing and chewing while supplying steady, bland conversation. When Storrow was finally through and the waiter came to take his plate, Georgia refused dessert and coffee; they would simply return to the apartment for her bags.

"And then," she told Lombardi, "that was when we became involved."

"You mean sexually."

"Right."

"You had sex. After what you considered 'not a date.' "

"Yup. That's how it was." They were scarcely through the entrance when Storrow gripped her by the back of the neck and pulled her to him; she'd been taken by surprise, equally by his action and her reaction, by the attraction that inexplicably arose in her again. He'd led her to the sofa, neglecting even to shut the front door behind them.

"Was he rough with you?"

"No." Though she had sensed some anger. At himself mostly, she thought, for submitting to desire. He'd retained a certain formality, held himself at a remove.

"You weren't scared or disturbed by anything he did."

"No. Maybe *he* was. He seemed more startled by it all."

"You mean to say he lost control?"

She sensed this was not a description to introduce in such a context. "We both knew what we were doing."

"So then, if he was deliberate, he must have brought you up there to sleep with you."

"Look, the man has urges like anybody else; if anything, it was harder for him to indulge them."

Afterward, Storrow had been mortified to see the front door still ajar; he'd risen from the sofa to shut it and hurriedly replaced his clothes.

"This," he'd said gravely, "can't become a regular event. You understand why. It goes without saying you can't tell a soul."

"Yes, it does go without saying." She'd been insulted that he'd think she'd imagine otherwise, that she was a child who would run and tell her friends.

"Not *anyone*." He persisted. "You can't hint, you can't imply. We say hello at the pool—that's all there's ever been. I just need to be sure."

"No one will know. And, don't worry, it won't happen again." She disliked this self-absorption. He might have paused to stroke her hair, to offer her a kind word before instructing her so coldly.

But then something changed in him; he peered up at her, cheeks damp and blushing, green eyes wide: "Please. I didn't mean to sound so harsh. It's just that I can't have a scandal. Truth is, I'm sorry: I like you so darn much."

Her anger subsided; someone who couldn't even utter the word *damn*, and she expected him to throw himself into an illicit fling?

They'd sat together on the sofa, close but not touching, she with her knees drawn up, he slumped over, head in his hands. This wasn't the kind of man to permit himself easy pleasure. Though she was no longer offended, she thought it would be best for their relationship—or whatever it was—to end right there. Storrow took life very hard, it seemed. Much too hard for her.

"So we both agreed it was to be a onetime thing."

But it hadn't been, Lombardi quickly reminded her: "Storrow tracked you down again on campus."

As if, to hear Lombardi say it, Storrow were some kind of stalker. To discourage that notion, she left out of her account how she'd tried to avoid Storrow by swimming in the evening, or how, one night, she'd exited the water and seen him seated at the side of the pool, reading a paper. A strange thing to do in a room choked with chlorine. He'd waved to her; she'd ignored him. If he wanted reassurance she'd act as if nothing had happened, he would have it. She'd done her laps, showered, and changed, and it was only once she'd stepped out into the frozen night that they'd spoken; Storrow was waiting for her by the exit.

"It's not safe, walking alone this late."

"I can handle myself, thanks."

"Right. I'm the one who can't." Storrow stood rubbing his hands against the cold. Even in the bitter chill, he wore only his navy blazer. "I . . . I've been wanting to speak with you . . ."

She'd pitied him then, this grown man at a loss for what to say next. Nervously he watched the building entrance, the students passing through: one among them waved at him. "We can't talk here. Can I call you?"

"To tell you he'd reconsidered?" Lombardi interrupted. "That an affair might be possible?"

"If we kept to certain guidelines."

"Guidelines?"

"You know. Precautions." She didn't wish to be any more specific, to have to repeat the many restrictions that Storrow had set out for her that evening. From here on, their relationship was not going to appear at all like she wished it would: as the story of a man of principle still susceptible to love. Storrow would not come off well, and Lombardi would never see her the way she liked to see herself: as a woman of sufficient maturity and merit to attract an accomplished, older man.

"The campus phones were untraceable, so Storrow and I set up appointments to speak on those."

"That will be our only means of contact," Storrow had said. "Under no circumstances can you come to my office or my house. I don't want you to be seen speaking to me in public after today. We can meet at the New York apartment on the weekends. You'll take a different train than I do and come up with a reliable excuse, a job or internship. Something, but not a boyfriend. No one can know that you've begun seeing anyone, and no one can ride into the city with you. I'll adhere to all the same constraints myself, of course."

What a creature, she'd thought: a man who could only permit himself to break the rules by creating twenty new ones. "Honestly, this doesn't sound like it's for me, so many restrictions."

"They're for me," he'd admitted. "I'm afraid with you I'll . . . lack restraint."

Through the line, she'd heard him inhale deeply, and that tense breath was what had overcome her reservations. She was attracted to this strain she sensed in Storrow: impulses at war with his monumental efforts at self-mastery. But she was reluctant to admit such feelings to Lombardi now.

"Nothing he did ever made me think that he was troubled or violent," she said finally. "I want to make that clear again."

"You've made your position very clear, Miss Calvin."

What she *hadn't* done, she knew, was alter Lombardi's view in the slightest. He'd obviously made up his mind about Storrow, and his suspicion was beginning to magnify those misgivings she hadn't even known she had, making her own assurance sound weaker than it should.

Four days earlier, she'd have refused to believe anyone who accused Storrow of the slightest inconsideration—of letting a door close on the man behind him, of leaving a woman without a seat on the train—yet here she was presented with this most vicious act, the murder of a girl, and suddenly she realized she couldn't banish doubt. Lombardi believed Storrow was guilty. He must know *something* to be so persuaded.

"I think I'd like to go now," she told Lombardi, finally; she'd been in this room for what felt like hours; she hadn't eaten since the morning. "I'm starting to not feel well."

Lombardi exhaled; above his belly, where the buttons strained, one freed itself from its hole. "I hate to put you through all this, I really do, but I feel obliged to point out—this isn't the first time you've defended a man whose behavior with you might not have been let's say, *conventional*."

"I have no idea what you're talking about."

Lombardi leaned back in his chair and pulled out an envelope from the pile on his desk. A manila envelope, like the ones she used to organize drafts of papers and class notes, a pile of them left in her living room, untouched for days. She thought of what her classmates must be doing at that moment: scribbling into blue books. Finals were in session.

"I came across an old charge on file in Colorado."

It took her a moment to grasp what Lombardi was getting at; she'd been just thirteen when she'd lived in Colorado with her father. The memory was hazy: officers waiting inside her home, asking questions about her father's photographs, suggesting that his portraits of her were improper. *Pornographic* was the word one officer had used. Stupid, brutal men, as she recalled these officers, pleased to torture her father—who was also young, handsome, and gifted—the way Lombardi was pleased to torture Storrow now.

"What can I say? The police were way off base then, too." She watched Lombardi rub his unshaved cheek. She'd had enough of him: those smug purple lips, the sweat stains under his arms. "You know, I came here because I wanted to be helpful, but I'm not in that mood anymore."

"Sorry to hear that."

"So I'm going to go now." She pushed her chair out and stood.

"In a moment you can, sure. But we still haven't gotten to the night of the murder. I wouldn't want you to have to come back in, when we could wrap all this up today." Lombardi raised his hand, beckoning her back to her seat.

"I have nothing to say about that night."

"You didn't see or hear from Storrow?"

"No."

"And that wasn't unusual, itself?"

"No, it wasn't." She and Storrow hadn't been speaking by then, but she wasn't about to be forthcoming with Lombardi: he'd overstepped, intending to upset her, obviously, to shake her into letting something slip. Well, she wouldn't—not a word about her final arguments with Storrow, the worst of them prompted by Alice—Storrow afraid of what Alice might have discovered, afraid of all that he might lose on account of Georgia's carelessness. *You risk my career, my peace of mind . . .* At the time of the murder, she and Storrow had been split up for two weeks, but that wasn't information for Lombardi, who would surely find a way to use it: to paint Storrow as wounded and unstable. "We only met in Manhattan on the weekends; the rest of the week I didn't know him. So if that's all."

"You mind telling me where you were last Sunday night?"

She grinned at him, joylessly. "Am *I* a suspect now?"

"It might help us, generally, with our investigation—if you don't mind."

"I was at a party, all right? Kirkland House. A swim team thing."

"The time?"

"Eleven to one, maybe? I don't remember. Ask someone from the team. Ask anyone but me, because I'm sorry, but I'm leaving."

"Soon, Miss Calvin. Something to drink?"

"I'm not thirsty."

"Hungry then? I can send Theresa for a sandwich."

"Do I need to call a lawyer? Are you keeping me against my will?"

"I'm not keeping you, Miss Calvin: I'm asking you to cooperate, out of consideration for Julie—a girl you knew—whose neck was broken five days ago. Think of Julie, think of her family."

And as soon as he'd said that, she was robbed of the desire that had been building—to tell Lombardi to fuck off. The moment she pictured

Julie Patel, with her smooth cheeks and neat braid, lying on a coroner's table—or was she already in the ground?—when she imagined the little sister mentioned in the news, lying awake at night, her mother sobbing in the next bed, into the rough sheets of some Cambridge or Boston motel—she'd given in, collapsed back into her chair, and let Lombardi start in on her again.

2

Even as a child, before he'd conceived of the ambition to become wealthy or renowned, before he'd grasped the route to such achievements, Charles Flournoy understood something about power—enough to know he'd been born precisely at its margins. His hometown, Garden City, Long Island, was a no-man's-land between the metropolis fifty miles west and the charming eastward towns that served as backyards for Manhattan's wealthy, a nondescript community not far from Mitchel Air Force Base: modest wood homes with trucks in the driveways and flags in the front yards, cheap restaurant chains, an aviation museum, a movie theater, a bowling alley, a library, and a putt-putt course.

Like most small towns, Garden City had its local notables—its politicians, its business owners, its coaches and sports stars—but none of these made much of an impression on Charlie. He seemed instinctively to grasp the limits of their influence, and was surprised when others failed to, and thus took umbrage at what they perceived as impudence or arrogance in him. Just the opposite, thought Charlie. It was humility that lay at the foundation of his insight: if he had hopes of avoiding the fate of his parents—scrounging and compromising, becoming bitter and angry like his father, or timid and defeated, like his mother—he must come to understand that the world wasn't centered around him, and whatever loomed in the foreground served as mere obstructions to the view of the big picture, of what and who *truly* held sway.

Charlie's father, Jim Flournoy, had spent over a decade as a technician at the air base, until, in the late '70s, not long after Charlie was born, he'd had a disagreement with a coworker, one bad enough to land the other man in the hospital and earn Charlie's father a lifetime reputation as a hothead. As Charlie knew him, his father could only hold a job working for himself, driving a van with his name and number on its side, doing repairs or making deliveries, carting furniture, lumber, and garden and nursery supplies up and down the Long Island Expressway. Charlie's mother, Margaret, worked as a secretary at the local high school he and his older brother, Luke, attended; on her summer break, starting when Charlie was five, she also began operating a small maid service for the Hamptons high season. This proved a shrewd and profitable enterprise; if she hadn't been marred by insecurity and bullied by her husband, Mrs. Flournoy might have built hers into a very successful business—among the ever-expanding Hamptons set, the need for housecleaners proved bottomless—but Charlie's father was forever upsetting her efforts, taking the van for his own use and vanishing when she had appointments. Jim Flournoy didn't like his wife's playing servant to the rich or, as he put it, *wiping Jewish asses.*

Such gripes grew louder when Luke began escorting their mother in search of odd jobs. While she cleaned, Luke checked around with neighbors to see if anyone wanted a lawn mowed or something heavy lugged around. "You'll make him think we're lower than those people," his father complained, forbidding the arrangement whenever he was around to stop it. "Luke works with me: if you want company, take Charlie."

For as long as Charlie could remember, his father was looking for ways to be rid of him; he seemed uneasy in the presence of his younger son. "The judge" his father started calling him when Charlie was just six, though Charlie had always been careful to keep his critical thoughts hidden, not to let his father catch him frowning at the mess inside the van after he'd used it, or at the bruises that, from time to time, darkened his knuckles. When his father was at home, Charlie kept to his room, reading mostly: Luke bought him books with some of the money he was earning here and there, and Charlie soon learned to let his gentle older brother stand as a buffer between his father and him.

Luke was four years Charlie's senior: popular, handsome and well-built, the state champion long-jumper and skilled at most everything he did, from telling a joke, to pulling off fifty push-ups each morning and night. In high school he announced his plans to be a pilot—which, in a town bordering on Mitchel, was a much-admired profession. Every afternoon starting junior year he spent an hour studying for the Armed Forces Qualification Test; upon graduation, he meant to join the air force. If he wasn't admitted to the officers program, he'd enlist as an engineering technician like their father.

Having grown up spotting soldiers emerging from the neighborhood bars and movie theater, Charlie was immensely proud to think that Luke would soon be among them. His big brother was already a hero in the mind of thirteen-year-old Charlie, and that belief persisted even when, one rainy summer day before Luke's senior year, their mother received a call from a client in Bridgehampton, accusing Luke of stealing jewelry from a neighbor's house. The neighbors claimed that they'd gone to the beach and had left the deck door open. Luke had been spotted in the backyard; they were threatening to call the cops.

Luke had been out when the call came, working a job in Hempstead, but his father didn't need to hear him say it to know his son could not have stolen. "Why not accuse their doped-up Swedish *au pair*, or one of those Mexican slaves out in the yard? No, they *want* to think Luke did it and I'll tell you why: because they're a bunch of thieving shits and the Flournoys are not. You're so clueless about these people, Margaret—how do you think they get their money? Being angels? And you're gonna believe them over your own son?"

"If he returns what's missing, they won't make an issue of it."

"He can't return what he didn't take. Tell 'em to go to hell; we don't need their money. You know what, I'll do it myself. Gimme their address."

Charlie had heard his father screaming, "gimme that fucking address *now*," while his mother's voice grew frailer, "Please don't, Jim, please," until at last the front door slammed, and his father left—to do what precisely, Charlie could only guess. All he knew was that Jim Flournoy came home later that night with a chipped tooth and a split lip. And still, in this one case, Charlie wanted to believe his dad was right: Luke must be innocent. He wanted to believe, but up in his room, he took down the books that Luke had given him, all of them never quite new, and felt the tackiness on the sides where library stickers must have been peeled away. As soon as Luke came home, he told his brother what he'd overheard, so that if there were anything Luke was hiding, he'd be smart enough to get rid of it in time.

"I didn't steal," Luke insisted.

"No, I know you didn't."

"Soldier's honor, Chief."

"I know, you wouldn't," Charlie said. Then he took down his raincoat and went biking in the drizzle, keeping his distance long enough for Luke to dispose of what he must.

The next summer, when Luke set out for Lackland Air Force Base, the threat of war was already being keenly felt by those in their town: Kuwait had been invaded, airmen and engineers were being deployed to the Middle East, reservists called up. The chance that Luke might see combat only added to the awe Charlie felt for him when he hugged his brother at the airport: Luke was at the very peak of his glamour: fit and tan and beaming, brimming with generosity. He'd given all he had to Charlie: his wardrobe, his music and magazine collections, his bat and barbells, mitt and cleats.

But try as he might to be like Luke—to don his clothes and lift his weights—Charlie's abilities and interests were distinctly different: books attracted him far more than sports. In English class, freshman year, Charlie discovered his love of poetry; there he learned the basics of meter and rhyme and read works by Wordsworth, Housman, Frost, and Whitman. It was the older styles he liked best: the antiquated ring of the words, evoking a time and place far away and far better than the one he moved in now. When the poets spoke of lust or disappointment or boredom, the predominant states of Charlie's youth, they elevated his experience; poets bestowed dignity. Each time soldiers came through town, Charlie would stand silently reciting stanzas in his head:

The street sounds to the soldiers' tread,
And out we troop to see: . . .

What thoughts at heart have you and I
We cannot stop to tell;
But dead or living, drunk or dry,
Soldier, I wish you well.

Over the next few years, as Charlie grew into a gangly teen, pale and prone to freckle, his narrow chest and slender jaw refusing to broaden like Luke's, he had to accommodate his dreams of military service to his peculiar strengths. Through his reading he encountered a different brand of hero, figures who served their country from behind desks: secretaries of defense, advisers in intelligence and national security. He learned everything he could about the most scholarly among them: James Angleton, Crane Brinton, and Henry Kissinger, men capable of expressing the most refined sentiments, while confronting the bluntest cruelties without illusions. Charlie became determined to emulate such men: to earn top grades and gain admittance to the universities that had fitted them for the highest ranks of power. Leading up to graduation, this was his principal pursuit and the subject of his obsessive reveries—this and girls of course. He was, despite his aspirations, still a lonely boy.

Pretty girls, in particular, fascinated Charlie, not just for the obvious reasons, or so he told himself, but because their ambitions more closely matched his. Among the dour, plainer faces in his mother's cleaning van, for instance, there were always a few pretty girls who saw, even in this demeaning work, the chance to rise, to mingle with the moneyed summer crowd. Beauty, Charlie observed, permitted them access to higher society; it stirred their yearning to belong. So these girls, not the plain ones he was expected to pursue, were on a course like him and thus his proper mates.

To be in their company, Charlie boarded his mother's van, too, each summer morning; he worked for her for three years, until he was sixteen and old enough to find legal employment: serving as a busboy at an exorbitant East Hampton steakhouse. He was sweeping up the crumbs left by CEOs, brokers and lawyers, standing by while their prep school sons poached the fetching waitresses he pined for. It was work his father made clear he found contemptible, but Charlie was happily free of his father's resentment, consoled by the knowledge that he'd be one among the blessed soon enough.

In the spring of senior year, when college acceptances came in the mail, Charlie was rewarded for his years of study: come September, he would head off to Harvard with the sons and daughters of the most privileged. While his high school classmates—bound for community college and local jobs—could spend their lives driving up and down Route 27 alongside the Manhattan elite, they'd never be *among* them. Harvard was a different sort of passage.

In the last week of August Charlie said good-bye to his parents at the dock of the Cross Sound Ferry; from New London on the other side, he'd catch the train to Boston's South Station and, from there, the red line to Harvard Square. He preferred to make the trip alone, without his father there to spoil his enjoyment. For years he'd been anticipating the moment when he'd step through Johnston Gate and greet the images he'd memorized from the glossy college catalogs and from pictures in history books.

Charlie's arrival on campus would remain, whenever he looked back on it, the most rapturous experience of his youth. It was an occasion—a lifetime might contain just two or three—when reality aligns itself so snugly to the contours of fantasy that the result is bliss. Harvard Yard hearkened to the spare and noble America of Emerson or Frost or Longfellow: neat paths beneath the elms, a harmonious assembly of white stone and red brick. Charlie's dorm room was in Weld, to his mind the most imposing freshman residence: arched entrances led to stairwells lined with clerestory windows. From his room in the left tower, he could hear church bells ringing and peer down at the statue of John Harvard.

On his first day at school, while Charlie's classmates hurried between placement tests or joined their parents for orientation meetings, he joined the procession of tour groups moving from quad to quad; soon he'd memorized the lore on every arch and gate and patch of dirt. Here, among the freshman dorms, were rooms once occupied by Kennedys and Roosevelts; five founding fathers once resided here, in Massachusetts Hall; and here, in Hollis Hall, Washington once garrisoned his troops.

Later that evening, the freshmen assembled in Sanders Theatre. The provost and dean stood applauding the entrance of their newest class; organ music swelled and the Holden Choirs welcomed the arrivals with the college hymn:

> *Thou then wert our parent, the nurse of our soul;*
> *We were molded to manhood by thee*
> *Till freighted with treasure thoughts, friendships and hopes,*
> *Thou didst launch us on Destiny's sea.*

Each phrase affected Charlie like the grandest poetry; he was dizzied by the scene—the tuxedoed singers, the vaulted gothic ceiling—all that gorgeous pretension that would have choked his father on the spot.

From his first week on campus, Charlie was determined to make his mark on this school, to meet as many of his extraordinary peers, and forge as many connections for the future, as he could. Each night of the week, he went out, moving among the different sets: from vegan dinners at the Co-op, to keggers at the Final Clubs. The name Charlie Flournoy was going to penetrate all circles, he'd decided, and mean something positive to one and all—call to mind a friendly wave, a clever joke. Already Charlie had an inkling that he might run for student office. To that end, he decided to affiliate himself politically on campus, and after exploring the various clubs and publications, soon fell in with the small clique surrounding the *Salient.*

The Harvard Salient was a journal of conservative thought; its staff was made up of debate team members and majors in political philosophy, kids who'd come to Harvard with romantic visions of youthful scholars smoking pipes and sipping brandy while discussing Burke and Hobbes. In the evenings, they gathered in the *Salient* office in the basement of Thayer Hall to approximate such scenes; the men donned button-downs and bow ties, the women wore cardigans and skirts. Aesthetics more than ideology were what attracted Charlie to the group—that and certain legends he'd overheard, tales of gifted *Salient* authors who'd been summoned by Republican advisers and speechwriters for afternoons out playing golf or yachting down the Charles.

While awaiting such an invitation, Charlie befriended another freshman *Salient* writer, a boy named Roger Waldman: Roger was from Cincinnati, Jewish, mild, and, even in his teens, fatherly. He wore suit pants and a beard and had arrived at school already decided upon a major in history and a career in contract law; soon he'd also set his sights on dating a rather plain Korean cellist, a freshman girl named Jasmine. There was a modest practicality to Roger that put Charlie at ease, helped relieve the pressure of his own grand aspirations. They balanced each other, Charlie felt, even if he couldn't comprehend the limits of Roger's desires. Had he never wished to be a celebrity or mogul or a hero? Had he never lusted after a girl far beyond his reach?

Tall with golden curls, high cheeks, and plush lips—she'd been among the marvels to strike Charlie during his earliest hours on campus. He'd spotted her for the first time during a tour: his group was stopped before Widener Library, while she was exiting the building, dressed in white upon the white stone steps. Among the Yard's several thousand denizens, here was the single creature, Charlie thought, equal to this glorious place.

Despite being outgoing with everybody else, Charlie hadn't dared speak to her that day or on any of the other rare occasions when he'd found himself in her vicinity that first year. But on a bracing afternoon in the fall of sophomore year, he'd seen her entering a lecture in

Emerson Hall and, feeling courageous, had followed her inside. This was during shopping period, when students were permitted to observe classes before settling on a schedule. The mood on campus was experimental, even boisterous. Students waved and called out Charlie's name as he moved through the aisle. Undergraduate Council elections were only two weeks away and his face was displayed on posters taped up to every campus kiosk: a good picture that maybe didn't make him look handsome exactly, but likable, hair slicked back to reveal his best feature, large, blue, expressive eyes.

For an instant, he caught his crush glancing his way, but she looked right back at her notebook and didn't seem to observe him settling in beside her. Nor did she notice his eyeing the page open on her desk, a list of classes she was deciding among for the afternoon. He tapped his pen beside Major English Poets.

"It's good?" she asked him. "You know something about it?"

"Beauty is truth. Truth beauty. All you need to know."

She'd turned away from him, before he could detect whether or not she'd caught his reference or found him charming or pretentious; the lecturer was at the podium. She listened for fifteen minutes or so (the class was on American art history, Charlie discovered) then rose and walked out, shamelessly, leaving Charlie to pity the young professor who'd left her so unimpressed.

English Poets met two hours later, but Charlie made up his mind not to attend; he didn't want to seem like he'd attempted to lure her there for his own benefit and, anyway, he preferred not to study poetry himself. Poetry was something approached privately, in quiet moments, a separate business altogether from the rules of governance and commerce that he'd come to Harvard to master. Only two weeks later, then, did he venture a peek into Lowell Lecture Hall, where lines of Edmund Spenser were scrawled across the blackboard. To his delight, she was there, in the front row, dutifully recording the words into her notebook.

Shortly thereafter, Charlie lost the UC election. The defeat hadn't come as much of a shock: on a liberal campus—Charlie had learned too late just *how* liberal—a guy affiliated with a conservative paper couldn't expect an easy time. The only person who'd shown faith in his campaign was Roger, now Charlie's roommate in Eliot House; optimistically Roger had purchased a bottle of champagne that stood on the mantel in their common room. The morning his defeat was announced, Charlie suggested they take the bottle and make off for a picnic at Fresh Pond—it was a clear, blue autumn day, too beautiful to waste inside a lecture hall. But Roger wasn't one for skipping class, so Charlie set off alone, riding his bike to the reservoir's edge to spread his blanket on a wide patch of grass.

He'd popped the cork and was pouring his first glass when he spotted her, his dream girl, jogging up the path. Just a few yards away, she paused to catch her breath, sweating in high red running shorts and a white ribbed tank. Her legs were still tan from the summer; stray ringlets of hair clung to her neck.

He waved to her from where he sat and she started over, out of politeness, he guessed. Despite the apprehension they inspired, most pretty girls, he'd found, were unfailingly polite.

"Are you celebrating something?"

"My opponent's landslide." He invited her to join him in a consolation drink. Politeness, pity—any cause of her remaining would do. "Please. I've already been rejected once today. I'm Charlie, by the way."

"Georgia."

"Georgia," he repeated, as if he didn't know, as if most every male classmate hadn't lingered over her photo in the freshman directory. "Have a seat, Georgia, quench your thirst."

"I'm not sure I meet the dress code." She raised an eyebrow and Charlie quickly regretted the outfit he'd picked out that morning—a yellow shirt and white bow tie. He stretched out his blanket for her and she plunked down, cross-legged, on the cloth, her bare knee brushing his, beads of sweat gathered in the crevice above her lip. He drank a full glass before he dared to speak again, waiting to have his courage strengthened by champagne.

He'd need to take more care proceeding: Georgia's remark about the dress code was a warning that, already, she found him a little silly. Bow ties were a *Salient* affectation and not the only one he'd picked up in that company. *Quench your thirst.* Had he really said that? What an ass he could sound like. He shouldn't require an election to tell him that elitism was out among his peers. A girl like Georgia especially, a queen in peasant blouses, was just the type to harbor guilty reverence for a working-class background. The smartest course, he decided, was to let her know the real him. But this must emerge naturally, in the course of conversation and after he'd put up, for a time, with her indifference.

What had drawn her to the park that day, he'd asked, and luckily the champagne came to his aid; dehydrated from her run, she drank more than the promised sip and was tipsy within minutes, unable to jog away and, instead, ready to share with him her mood.

"I woke up restless."

"The change of seasons," he remarked. "Spring and fall are the worst."

"Fall for me. It's the first one in years when I've returned to the same place."

"Diplomat's daughter?"

"Opposite, really; a provocateur's." Jethro Calvin was her father, she informed him, as if Charlie ought to be familiar with the name. He was a famous photographer, apparently, and a lifelong rover; she credited him with inspiring her own need for an ever-shifting vantage, so that she'd very nearly transferred to a different university after freshman year.

"My dad was cool with it, but my mother insisted I stay put. Four high schools screwed me up enough, she thinks; she always hated it when we moved. Eventually, she just stopped coming along. . . ."

Such openness so early on in their acquaintance: more than champagne was required to explain it, though Charlie didn't flatter himself about the reason; probably it was because Georgia didn't expect they'd speak again. And then this was also the way with pretty girls: rambling on with a sort of abandon that only people automatically exciting could permit themselves. What was there to hide when your skin was tawny smooth and your thoughts free of envy? Later, he considered there might have been more to it than that; she must have known from the start that he'd forgive her every fault, and so he made the perfect receptacle for her confessions.

"Honestly, I'm not sure I want to be at Harvard—in any college for that matter. My father says the whole educational system in this country is an excuse, as much as anything, to coddle and isolate the rich, distract them from what they'd learn about America if they actually had to deal with some hard reality."

Her father said: the man's opinion held too much importance for her, Charlie thought, certainly given how little he esteemed his own father's. Both men, in their way, disapproved of universities like theirs, bastions of privilege. But for Charlie, this was cause to smoke a pipe and drink champagne, whereas Georgia needed to resist her advantages somehow, to show allegiance to her dad's radicalism, and so she'd sought out contact with the most desperate examples of "hard reality" that she could find.

"At-risk youth, juvie types, you know. I'll be volunteering with them Saturdays starting tomorrow. What I wanted was to work with prisoners at Jamaica Plain, but there's some security issue. Of course, a girl like me, I've got to be protected at all costs." Fully drunk by then, Georgia railed on, objecting to the fortunes paid—another two million for campus security that year—to prevent any one of Boston's poor or homeless from brushing up against tomorrow's future leaders. "My dad would say: fuck our protections. Open up the damn gates, let the city's underclass pour into our classrooms, slap some truth into us Harvard kids."

"On that point your dad and mine would agree—except my dad would rather do the slapping part himself."

From there, it was simple enough to let her lead him into speaking of his own childhood, to mention that his father hadn't known that Charlie had even applied to private colleges, how he'd arranged his own scholarships and loans and jobs. As he went on, he could see her studying him afresh, revising her impression. His teeth were clean but crooked—was that because his family couldn't afford braces? Whatever she was observing, her lids dropped, her expression became softer, more compassionate.

They'd been talking for over an hour when Georgia announced that she felt woozy from champagne and needed to eat. It was already nearly four and, by the time they got back to campus and she showered and dressed, the dining halls would just be opening for dinner.

He tagged along, unsure whether she meant to include him in her dinner plans; when they reached her room in Mather House and she invited him up, he couldn't quite believe his luck. Her room was in the low-rise, a single duplex; he waited in the living room while she visited the shower. The walls were hung with art posters—photographs; rows of art books sat on her shelves, mixed in with the ordinary college reading. The cover of one book read *Jethro Calvin: Portraits*. Charlie asked Georgia about this when she returned, dressed in a towel; she took the volume down.

Slowly, she turned the pages, revealing figures tired by life, not unlike the people from Charlie's hometown, only these had been stripped nude and placed in classical poses.

"This series is a bit grim. After my mother and father split."

She lowered a second book from the shelf then; this one contained images exclusively of Georgia: dozens of pictures of her as a child. In some she was nude, too.

"And those?" he asked. "The reason for the split?"

She laughed, a throaty laugh, not girlish at all, and leaned against the stairwell.

Did she know what she was doing to him, showing him those pictures, lingering on the stairs up to her bed, with just a towel wrapped around her?

She knew. She must, of course: a girl capable of stealthily supplanting her mother in her father's life. She knew her power perfectly well, and he, who thought he was schooling himself on all there was to know about power, discovered something new that day: the ecstasy of laying himself and all his future happiness or unhappiness at the mercy of a girl with a throaty laugh and honey hair who would never, he saw even then, take proper, loving care of him.

Later, as they stepped side by side through the Mather courtyard, Charlie had a fateful feeling: that he was already a different man than he'd been that morning when he'd set out across the campus alone:

Let seed be grass, and grass turn into hay:
I'm martyr to a motion not my own;
What's freedom for? To know eternity.
I swear she cast a shadow white as stone.

3

They were going to a dinner with the new housemaster of Adams. Roger sprang the news on Charlie one gusty Thursday evening in the fall of senior year. Charlie had dawdled on the way home, taking a long walk across the leaf-strewn quads.

"You'll need to change into a suit," Roger instructed. "Jasmine says the master likes to keep it formal."

Charlie had planned to stay in, maybe catch a late movie alone—the Film Archive was playing *Gilda*, and Rita Hayworth caught something of Georgia in that role—but Roger claimed this dinner was a chance he couldn't miss. "We're lucky a few students got sick; these dinners are just for Adams residents and there's an invitation list."

Apparently the new Adams housemaster—Storrow was his name—attracted interest: he'd arrived only that fall, to act as interim master while the man that he'd replaced was on sabbatical. Storrow wasn't the typical old married professor usually appointed such a role; he'd served in Washington and in the JAG Corps where he'd received the Bronze Star Medal. The man was worldly; he was sportive; and he'd gone out of his way to be social—coaching intramural men's squash and rugby and replacing the traditional stuffy and crowded Thursday master's teas with more intimate dinners in his home.

Jasmine, Roger's girlfriend since freshman year, lived in Adams, and was on the guest list for that night. She'd been the one to arrange for Roger and Charlie to tag along.

"You can't miss this," Roger urged him. "The guy was at the Pentagon, chief of the International Law Branch. This is precisely the kind of man you need to know."

Roger, better than anyone, was privy to Charlie's professional goals—aware that he still wavered between pursuing a career in business or national service, and hadn't yet abandoned his admiration for his childhood heroes, men whose résumés bore significant resemblance to Storrow's.

Back in his room, Charlie studied the three suits he kept hanging in his closet. The invitation to meet this young housemaster *was* tempting, he had to admit: the most tempting offer his friend had come up with until then. All that fall, Roger had been hounding him with extra tickets to the New College Theatre and Bach Society concerts, requesting a fourth on dates with Jasmine and some next single friend—anything to get Charlie's mind off Georgia and wrest him from his solitude.

It was depression, Charlie supposed; this gloom had been plaguing him, along with a seemingly incurable flu, ever since the summer. Disappointment over Georgia was at least in part to blame (about that Roger wasn't wrong), but what had undone him, really, was the decision to spend his summer vacation at home. Since setting off for college Charlie had avoided staying more than a few days in Garden City, but he'd been lured back by just about the only thing able to accomplish such a feat: his brother's return.

In June, after six years of active duty, Luke had left Eielson Air Force Base in Alaska and moved, temporarily, into his old bedroom. It was an extraordinary chance—maybe the last the two brothers would have—to share a room again for three months, to get to know each other now as men. Without hesitation, Charlie had canceled his prior plans: the past two summers he'd forgone the prestigious internships in Washington and Wall Street to rake in thousands as a live-in tutor for wealthy families in the Hamptons. Now, he meant to sacrifice the hefty paycheck and focus these same energies on helping his brother. To qualify for a commercial pilot's license, Luke would need a college degree: Charlie meant to prep him for his tests and guide him through his applications.

Over the phone, Luke sounded game, but once Charlie had come to join him, he found his brother more disposed toward sunbathing than study. Luke seemed to want to spend his days just like their father generally did now, working small jobs for small money and mostly sitting and drinking beer on their front lawn.

"A little break," Luke told Charlie, "if that's okay with you, Chief."

Sure it was okay with him: *everything* was okay with him: his beloved brother was back. "Go easy, melt off that Alaskan frost."

Three weeks later, Luke still hadn't approached a single one of the study guides that Charlie had saved for him, nor had he, or anyone in the family, made any mention of college. Eventually Charlie became afraid to raise the subject, concerned that Luke might be ashamed to accept help from a little brother who had, in a certain regard, surpassed him. On outings in town, people remarked more on Charlie's achievements—*Dean's List, your mother says*—which left Charlie to wonder why his mother hadn't bragged to them about Luke. It was his parents' fault that a bigger deal wasn't made of Luke's homecoming. For his part, Charlie tried to compensate, but this—like everything he did that summer—only seemed to grate on Luke.

Each time Charlie came to join his brother and his father on the lawn, the pair would grow quiet—leaving off the idle talk of everything they planned to do—*bet we could put in a pool here, do the whole job ourselves*. A new reserve would grip them, as if Charlie really were "the judge" his father once made him out to be. That old, loathsome nickname echoed in Luke's increasingly acerbic "Chief."

By July, when Luke and his father began talking about starting a business together, Charlie felt he couldn't sit by any longer. Maybe his dad didn't give a shit whether or not Luke got his pilot's license, whether or not he made good on his dream—he was perfectly satisfied to have his elder son stuck home along with him—but their mother was not so selfish. Charlie made up his mind to speak with her.

"Better not to pressure Luke just now." His mother's tone was hushed and nervous, the same she'd used over the phone to neighbors these past weeks: *We're just glad Luke's back and safe; we don't need to make a fuss.*

"Is there something you haven't told me, Mom?"

She'd refused to admit it right away—*your father would be*

furious—but finally, after Charlie pledged not to let on to his father that they'd spoken, after he'd threatened to walk out if she didn't say what was the trouble, his mother confessed.

"There was an incident in Fairbanks. A fight with a fellow soldier. This soldier, it seems, was a homosexual. Luke had seen him harassing some local boys. He was only trying to protect them and then, well, he lost his temper. He went too far. The soldier had some, I guess, pretty serious injuries."

Charlie could hear his father's voice in hers, his father trying to make the facts flatter Luke rather than incriminate him. "Are you saying Luke was discharged? Was there a court-martial?"

"I don't think it got that far. The only thing we need to know is that Luke's home now and needs our support and our respect. You have to believe he was trying to do right."

When Charlie returned to campus that fall, Roger asked if he'd been sick. Skinny to start with, he'd lost another ten pounds. He no longer put care into his clothes and he'd stopped attending *Salient* meetings. Georgia was the only one who could roust him from his room, but when he went with her, he went in a spirit of defeat. Their relationship would never amount to more than a friendship, clearly. He'd missed his chance to make her see him as a potential boyfriend, a mate, a *man*; he'd been too timid, afraid of losing her completely, and duped by her efforts to keep his desires in line. "I mean, who the hell wants to be pounced on?" she'd announced (speaking of some other foolish boy's mistake). "Longing is all about deferral—don't guys understand this?"

So he'd suppressed every urge to touch her or otherwise make his feelings known, and he even believed—because she meant for him to believe—that his patience would be rewarded: her arm began winding around his waist as they walked back from dinner, her head dropped against his shoulder as she read beside him on his couch. Such gestures were required to compensate for his frustrations, but as those frustrations multiplied, and Georgia's encouragements with them, the tension grew too great. At the junior year spring formal she'd sat lounging on his lap; her thighs parted above his knee, her hair swept to the side, baring her shoulders. As she'd rocked backward to say something, he'd kissed her neck, and she'd laughed, shaking her hair, as if some strange object had accidentally brushed against her: a passing moth, a falling leaf.

Of course he understood her intentions (decided in an instant) to behave as if what she'd felt hadn't been his lips. The reflex expressed their lie so plainly, he couldn't keep pretending any longer. For Christ's sake; he wanted Georgia and she didn't want him. *Face it and move on,* he'd told himself that spring, and still, almost two months into senior year, he couldn't resist meeting Georgia when she called, nor could he muster enthusiasm for the other girls that Jasmine kept bringing around. The latest was Pam, Jasmine's roommate, a petite chemistry major with a short top lip and nasal voice.

Charlie would be joining Pam that night, Roger informed him, at the last possible moment. The two of them were already dressed in their suits.

"Hang on. You didn't mention that part."

"She's a resident of Adams; you're there as her guest; otherwise you can't go."

"Maybe then it's better if I don't."

Roger ignored this: crossing to Charlie's closet, he removed the hanger draped with Charlie's ties. "Pick one, and do it quickly."

In fifteen minutes they were due to meet their dates at Apthorp House, the master's residence.

When Charlie and Roger arrived, Pam and Jasmine were already waiting for them: early, as only girls hopeless about seduction would allow themselves to be. Under her open jacket, Pam wore a long, pink cotton dress that Charlie didn't consider the least bit stylish. Too sweet on shapeless, sexless Pam—though, on Georgia, worn with her loose curls and boots and buttons opened at the top, it would have had appeal.

Jasmine and Roger had dressed up, too. She was in floral print; he, in tweed. How unfortunate. At least Charlie thought he looked all right: he'd selected his tan suit for the evening, along with a blue shirt and coral tie. His outfit was more suitable in warmer months, but it was the only one he had that befitted a dinner with someone of Rufus Storrow's reputation.

Apthorp House was an imposing, yellow-painted, three-story home, far too large for a single tenant. Jasmine rang the bell and a man came to the door: in his forties, with red hair and green eyes. His posture was precise; his proportions, elegant—lean torso, narrow nose, and pointed chin. A blue vein divided his high forehead, a mark of distinction, Charlie thought.

"Gentlemen, welcome. Ladies, please." Storrow's voice was deep, with a faint, gentlemanly southern drawl. He shook hands with the men and bowed to the young women, who seemed unequal to his graciousness. "Don't you all look sharp."

Storrow was the one, though, who looked sharp, dressed in navy trousers and a red and white gingham button-down. Bright and sporty—a style perfectly suited to his lithe frame: this *was grace*, Charlie thought, watching Storrow, full of easy vigor even while hanging up coats. A permanent ruddiness shone in his cheeks, as if he'd just risen from doing push-ups.

"Fantastic. Feel at ease. The others are in the sitting room." Clapping his hands, Storrow led his guests from the foyer.

The house was prefurnished, with heavy mahogany and leather chairs fixed with gold buttons; an equestrian painting hung on one living room wall, a football banner from the '20s on another. A different tenant might have been oppressed by the stale pomposity of the arrangement, but Storrow seemed right at home. All he'd done was add his books, a big black box of a TV, and a set of barbells that occupied one corner of the room.

The students were strewn across two couches, sipping ginger ales. Charlie knew only one of them by name: Gerry with a *G*, thin and pale, with black hair long in front, so that every few seconds he was forced to sweep it, wearily, out of his eyes. Gerry had a show on the campus radio and a small-time drug operation, dealing in pot and coke out of his off-campus apartment. An odd figure to turn up at such a dinner, but he'd lived in Adams sophomore year and maybe he'd seen a chance for fun in a meeting with the new straitlaced housemaster. Gerry had brought a friend along, it seemed: a redhead girl with cat-eye glasses, whom Charlie recognized from the offices of the *Perspective*, the liberal journal just across from the *Salient* in the basement of Thayer Hall.

The rest of the guests were strangers. It always surprised Charlie to come across students he didn't know, when he'd dedicated so much time at school to acquainting himself with all of his classmates. Anybody who'd escaped his notice must be well under the radar, which these remaining three appeared to be: a heavy-set Hispanic boy who stared down at his feet; another boy in a ponytail and army jacket; and the Goth girl draped around him on Storrow's couch, her legs in torn fishnets.

Storrow introduced the couple first. "This is Troy. And Sandra, his drag."

The girl jerked upright. "*What* did you call me?"

"'Drag.'" Storrow hastened to explain. "It just means the young woman you're with." He went on with introductions, recalling every name with the tense determination of someone taking an exam: "Rebecca, who prefers to be called Becca, and, last but not least, Adams's own chess champion, Miguel Xavier Santina—did I say that right, Miguel?"

The chubby boy gave a tense nod and Storrow clapped, excusing himself after a moment and jogging off to finish preparations in the kitchen.

Gerry watched him go: once he was sure their group was safely unsupervised, he rose and made for Storrow's bookshelf. The redhead followed, and Pam occupied the open spot left alongside Charlie. While she chatted him up—after the dinner, she and Jasmine were going for

Scorpion bowls at the Kong—Charlie listened in on Gerry at the shelf, reading off the titles, seeking out the more embarrassing items: "*Expert Expat, Training for the Iron Man, Becoming Your Own Hero.*"

"He could be back any minute," Roger warned, but Gerry wasn't listening; he'd spotted something higher on the bookshelf: a framed photograph, color, from the '70s, to judge by the faded ink, showing ten or so men in swimsuits, arms enlaced. The men looked close in age to those gaping as Gerry took the picture down, but unlike that motley set, each of these was white with short-cropped hair. Storrow stood at the center, rounder in the cheeks than he'd become and smiling wide. Stripped of the carefully pressed clothes, pale torso pink from sun, he looked somehow vulgar, too healthy.

The redhead pointed to the bottom of the picture. "It's signed here: 'Riefenstahl.' "

The sort of remark, thought Charlie, expected of someone whose closest glimpse of soldiers was in screenings in Film Theory.

His associations were different; in the photo were boys like the ones who'd walked in uniform through his hometown: the same shorn hair, the same mixture of obedience and aggression, of arrogance and innocence. Was that the Hudson behind them? He thought it might be, which would make Storrow a West Point man.

He didn't bother to reveal this knowledge, doubting it would impress anybody here but him. Certainly this photograph hadn't warmed these kids to Storrow. In a community that valued uniqueness above all, such a scene of homogenous camaraderie could seem unfashionable, even a little poor.

Whistling sounded from the hall; Gerry replaced the photograph just as Storrow reappeared, coming to stand before his guests. His glance darted from one student to the next. After a nervous moment, Charlie realized he was counting.

"Well, friends, looks like we're it," Storrow concluded. "Flu going round, you know: more food for us. Hope you're all hungry—sorry for the delay."

"Maybe you could use some help?" Charlie stood to join him before

Storrow made off again. The man was doing all the work for the meal himself, while his guests lounged in his home and idly snooped; Charlie wanted no further part in their behavior and had more interest, anyway, in getting to know his host.

He and Storrow entered the kitchen, its countertops crowded with bowls of cherry tomatoes, pearl onions, button mushrooms, cubes of tofu, meat and fish. Skewers sat inside a glass at one end: a do-it-yourself dinner, from the looks of it. Probably that had been Storrow's vision: all hands together.

If so, he wasn't complaining; the man seemed pleased enough to have Charlie along for company, there to keep him from feeling he'd shirked his social duties.

"Take your jacket for you, Charlie?"

Storrow fitted each of their blazers, neatly, over adjoining chairs, and both men came to stand at the sink, folding back their cuffs. They washed their hands, Charlie's freckled wrists alongside Storrow's. The man kept his nails clipped and clean, like Charlie did, in contrast to most of his schoolmates, who might be scrupulous when it came to translations of Latin or physics problem sets, but often neglected to brush their hair or change their socks.

It was becoming clear to Charlie what a rigorous sort of man Storrow was, how disapproving of sloppiness or half measures of any kind. That his party was a few guests short seemed enough to disturb him: he clearly put effort into these meals. Another housemaster would have boiled up vats of pasta, but Storrow had invested time, shopping, dicing, and setting out these items to be placed, one by one, onto skewers. Those guests outside might not appreciate it, but that wasn't the point, Charlie thought. Men like Storrow lived by their own standards.

"Where you from, son?" Storrow began their chat straightforwardly, displaying an adherence to etiquette.

"Long Island. Garden City. I doubt you'd have heard of it, it's small."

Storrow considered, his thin brows knitted. "Isn't that near Mitchel?"

"Right."

"You're not an army brat?"

"My dad used to work on the base, and my brother just left Eielson."

"A zoomie?"

"Engineering technician."

"Important work," said Storrow, nodding. "The planes wouldn't take off without them either."

It was the first Charlie had spoken of his brother since the summer, and the first he'd thought of him without a knot forming in his stomach.

"My family's also got a history of service," Storrow said. "Three generals and a field marshal."

"Long gray line, huh?" This was a term for West Point grads, a phrase Charlie was grateful to have picked up from his reading.

Storrow set down the skewer in his hand and looked across at Charlie, grinning. "Actually I'm the first from Hudson High—how'd you make me?"

He preferred not to admit the truth, to allude to that photograph passed around in the next room. "People talk."

"Not me, on my honor." Storrow raised his palm. "Oxford taught this country boy some manners. Don't want to sound like a ring-knocker."

And what was a ring-knocker meant to sound like? No doubt just like Storrow: tossing out institutional slang, taking every chance to allude to those illustrious academies that had produced him. It seemed the man was still rather in awe of his own progress, still living out an ideal he'd defined for himself: a striver like him, Charlie thought, and also in his way, probably a romantic.

The two men went on chatting for some time, lingering together over their work in the kitchen, while other guests came traipsing through, on occasion, asking for a napkin, or more ice, or making perfunctory offers to assist. Finally, Jasmine appeared to coax Charlie back outside. He'd been neglecting Pam, and Jasmine meant to put an end to it, even if that required leading Charlie by the elbow.

"My drag," Charlie quipped on his way out.

Back in the living room, he found the others absorbed in hushed conversation; he asked Roger what he'd missed.

"Stupidity, that's all."

Apparently, Gerry had managed to scope out the house and discovered that several upstairs doors were locked. A man didn't do that unless he had something to hide, right?

"Or else," suggested Roger, "he just doesn't want a bunch of strangers poking around his underwear."

And what exactly did everyone imagine a middle-aged Law and History professor would be hiding?

But Storrow wasn't any ordinary professor—not in the minds of these Adams students, anyway. According to the kid in the army jacket, Troy, Storrow had done his military service in the late '80s in Afghanistan and Pakistan—so obviously that meant covert work with the mujahideen. After law school, he'd specialized in the law of war-based detention—still, the Pentagon routinely sent him to bases around the world to advise on special cases involving military prisoners. God only knew what sort of things the man had seen—and been required to keep quiet—though if Storrow really did have things to hide, Charlie thought, then he was doing a pretty lousy job of it.

So much speculation—Storrow must be contributing somehow to the rumors. Certainly it was a provocative choice to appear at once so open and so closed, to invite students into his home and then lock doors. If Storrow wasn't actively *trying* to get people to talk about him, at least the way he announced his entrance into a room, loudly whistling, stood as a sign that he was in on the game.

As Storrow strolled in, his guests grew silent.

"Chow's on," he announced, holding up a steaming tray.

Dinner was served at a creaking, circular wood table. Storrow waited for the guests to help themselves and took his own food last, lining up three skewers. He fitted his napkin at his neck and sat very straight, chair pulled in close. For the next half hour or so, he ran the conversation like he ate the food off his plate, dutifully making his way around. One by one he addressed his guests, focusing his interest on a single pursuit—Jasmine, orchestra; Miguel, chess; Gerry, radio—as if he'd challenged himself to memorize a fact about each student. *Good stuff, well, isn't that the max.*

Not far into the meal, the discussion was already threatening to falter, when Troy turned to Storrow with a question.

"About your military service."

"If you think that's of any interest." Storrow smiled and rolled his eyes; in an instant, he'd grown playful, overcome his rigidity. "What's on your mind, son?"

"You were in Kuwait during the war?"

"No—Kuwait, no. Saudi Arabia, that was all, only for a few weeks. And strictly in my capacity as a legal adviser to soldiers on the base—whatever else you may have heard." Storrow chuckled and hunched forward, at attention. "I'm afraid to even ask."

It took Troy a moment to realize that Storrow *was* asking.

"What I heard? That you were there to oversee aspects of detention, deal with POWs."

"Deal with how?"

"You know, interrogations."

Storrow's hand went to his chest, in a weak gesture of shock, while his eyes shone, inviting conjecture. "Nothing so exciting, I'm afraid; I was just the stiff quoting Geneva regulations."

"All about the rules, right?" Gerry put in sharply. Until then, Charlie noted, Gerry had been uncharacteristically reserved. "Geneva, Hague, *Georgetown Student Handbook*."

The remark seemed to catch Storrow off guard; his smile fell and he turned, with all the rest, to look at Gerry, who sat with his chair tilted, so that it rocked on its back legs.

"A friend of mine knew her well," Gerry continued. "Suzannah Bell. The girl you had expelled."

Storrow untucked the napkin from his collar and dabbed at his chin. "Not that I intend to get into it here," he said sternly, "but if a student is going to come to my class high on drugs, if she's going to flaunt illegal behavior—"

"She claimed you went out of your way to follow her."

"She *claimed*. All right she *claimed*. A girl like that." Abruptly, Storrow left off and rose to begin collecting plates. "Anyway, I think we've talked enough about me. What say we move onto dessert? I can't offer you coffee, I'm afraid, just cheese and fruit. House rules: no caffeine, no booze, no boodle."

Storrow's tone was breezy, but sweat had broken out across his forehead; arms stacked with dishes, he quickly escaped into the kitchen. From the next room came the sound of drawers opening and closing; the students sat shooting each other looks. Charlie considered going into the kitchen to check on Storrow, but just then the man reentered, apparently rallied. In one hand he held aloft a bowl of fruit; in the other, a stack of notecards and several pens.

"Let's have a game, friends. Something we lawyers used to do in the corps."

The rules were simple. Everyone would be asked three questions—two to be answered truthfully, one with a lie. Storrow's job would be to spot the lie. But to be kind, to spare his guests any discomfort, he'd allow their answers to be written, and the results to remain a secret between each person and himself.

Storrow distributed the cards and pens among the group: "Relax, I'll go easy."

True to his promise, his first inquiries—to Pam, Jasmine, and then Roger—were perfectly mundane: "Have you ever owned a pet? Number of siblings? What sort of profession do you see yourself in?"

Moving on to Becca, Gerry's friend, Storrow's questions grew a bit more pointed: "What do you fear most? Have you ever lied to hurt somebody?"

Gerry was next in line. Storrow smiled at him benignly and asked after his favorite musician and the name of the street on which he'd first lived. Gerry scribbled his answers on his card, while Storrow leaned forward to select an apple from the bowl before him. He rubbed the apple on his shirtsleeve as he considered his last question. "Any reason you—Gerald Laverne—would be especially concerned that I exposed a student's drug use?"

Charlie felt Pam kick his shin under the table. In the silence, he could hear the noise of Storrow chewing. Gerry wrote down his final answer, trying, unsuccessfully, to appear nonchalant; his hands were shaking slightly as he set down his pen. Storrow looked ebullient.

The next guest to play the game was Miguel. Storrow turned to him, distractedly. "So, let's see, let's see . . . what's the worst thing you've ever . . . stolen?"

"*Excuse me?*" Miguel looked up and crossed his arms above his large stomach; his movements were slow, his voice monotone. "What was the question you just asked me?"

Storrow rapped his knuckles on the table, apparently oblivious to any misstep he had made, beaming still from his small triumph over Gerry. "Now, don't let Gerald's nonsense scare you off, son. No trials, no penalties, you have my word."

"I'm not *scared* to answer you. I don't *wish* to answer because I don't appreciate the question."

Storrow shrugged, still trying to make light of this refusal. "Fine then. I can ask you a different one."

"But you didn't ask me a different one: of all the things you could have asked me—about chess or math or any of my interests—instead you asked me *about stealing*. You assume I've stolen. As a *Latino*, I have to wonder why."

Storrow took a deep breath and exhaled hard, puffing out his cheeks. "Honestly, Miguel, I meant no offense by it. Look, I just asked Becca about lying—was that because I don't trust redheads? I'm a redhead, right friend? Hand to heart, Miguel, the thought of your ethnicity was nowhere on my mind."

And probably this was the truth, thought Charlie: Storrow seemed strangely unaware of the care a man like him must display in less privileged company. He wondered how much Storrow grasped of this new, liberal campus culture he was facing: the mistrust of the sort of old-fashioned white, entitled male he couldn't help but represent.

"Let's just move on," Charlie suggested, but it was too late to salvage the evening; even Storrow made no further efforts to revive the game or find another. He sat sunk into his chair, folding his notecard over and over, into an ever tighter square.

Roger was the first to announce his departure: the others followed suit. A line formed at the front door, Storrow at its head, distributing the coats. For politeness' sake, he struggled to summon a last burst of gaiety: "Button up, friends, October chill . . ."

Out on the lawn, Roger and the girls waited for Charlie to join them. He was the last of the guests to exit Apthorp House; in the foyer, while Storrow kicked a few stray leaves from the threshold, Charlie took his time fixing his jacket, fitting his scarf around his neck. He felt the urge to shut the door after the others, to stay behind with his host and offer comfort.

Whatever his faults, Storrow was a good man, Charlie believed. He might even turn out to be a great man—and this, Charlie wished to say, was difficult for people to acknowledge, especially where comparison revealed their own deficiencies.

In that one evening, Charlie's sympathy was united to this professor he'd only just met; he felt Storrow's sadness where others perceived blithe arrogance. There was a tragic element to the man: in his outmoded brand of dignity. Looking back, it was strange that he'd foreseen this even when Storrow was at the height of his achievements, before anything to do with tragedy had touched him.

4

Master language, master fate. That was the lesson Alice Kovac received from both her father and her mother, who'd never seemed to agree on anything but this in all the years they'd spent together as immigrants from Belgrade to Wisconsin. Alice's father, Radovan, was the one who'd insisted on the move. A gifted engineer, he'd worked hard to earn an American professorship and was immensely proud of the life he'd arranged for his wife and children: the ordered, spacious streets of Madison, the manicured lawns of the campus, his private office with its modern equipment, new beige computers and boxes fitted with knobs and dials and wires, whose purposes Alice, as a little girl, could only wonder at. Wonder was what her father wished to inspire on outings with him: to instill in Alice the same appreciation he felt for this world he'd discovered, one marked by rationality and optimism and so utterly unlike that barbaric land he'd left behind.

In this regard, Radovan and his wife were at odds; Senka Kovac had never admired American culture or envisioned any life for herself outside of Serbia. Unlike her husband, she hadn't chosen to study English in school and so, while Radovan settled into his American life easily, following American news, chatting with his American colleagues, she spent her first years in isolation, daunted by her surroundings and kept at home with two small children. Once the children were of school age, Senka's situation only worsened. She watched her little girl and boy grow more and more independent and incomprehensible; they no longer needed her, and her own poor English barred her from pursuing any meaningful career. In Serbia she'd briefly worked at a news station, but here no such career was possible for her: she felt trapped, confined to menial housework, to stuttering crude formulations, robbed of humor and grace. Only those who knew her in her native language knew her at all, she insisted; and if she must live in a nation of strangers, at the least her own children should understand her.

From the age of five Alice had been forced to spend long afternoons sitting at the kitchen table with a dismal Serbian language book that her mother had saved from her own school days. She'd detested that book—its faded cover colored orange, yellow, and brown—and those hours studying while her mother cooked up pots of paprikash and goulash, filling the kitchen with heat and pungent smells. Each lesson in Serbian felt, to Alice, like a betrayal of her father, whose wish for her was to become fully American. He took great pride in Alice's advanced abilities in English—several levels above her grade—and he was convinced her mother's lessons only slowed this progress.

"*You* should be the one to study English," her father told his wife. "You're unwilling to do anything to get along here." And it seemed to Alice that he was right; her mother preferred to submit to depression, refusing to pretend she could have a proper future anywhere but in Serbia, refusing to see this country, even if it represented freedom for her husband and children, as anything but a jail for her.

Throughout those first years in Madison, Alice's mother made regular threats to return to Serbia. What finally put an end to this was the arrival of her older brother, Vasily. Uncle Vasily, as Alice knew him, was bald and massive, not less than three hundred pounds, with a mole on his cheek and a neck that sloped from his earlobes to almost the middle of his shoulders. Before he'd gained weight and lost his hair, though, he'd been remarkably good-looking, with thick black curls and catlike eyes. (Alice's mother proudly displayed pictures of Vasily and herself in their teens, when they were still a striking pair.) After decades spent cavorting with various women, Vasily had charmed his way into a marriage to a wealthy American tourist: they'd traveled together for a time before settling down in Broadview Heights, a Serbian community in Cleveland.

The year Vasily finished construction on his new home, he invited Alice's family to come see it, an outrageous McMansion with sculptures in the front yard and a basement bowling alley, where Alice's younger brother, Peter, had played for hours on end.

Alice's father was appalled. He and Vasily were opposites in every way, physically and philosophically. Radovan was lean and mild, while Vasily was inflated and preening; Radovan believed this country rewarded hard work while Vasily maintained that the immigrant dream was entirely a sucker's game: all that slaving so that one's children could enjoy a better life. He'd preferred to skip the slaving and the children, too; Vasily lived unfettered, doted on by his wife, waited on by their maid, happily an object of envy in that small Cleveland enclave inhabited almost exclusively by other Serbians like him.

After only a few hours, Alice's father insisted upon cutting the visit short and leaving Vasily's. Alice left with him, but her mother stayed behind and wouldn't be lured away for another week. Nor could she, after she'd returned to Madison, forget the life she'd glimpsed in Broadview Heights—Serbian churches and Serbian restaurants and shops, windows displaying Serbian delights—pindjur relishes and plum brandies, semolina cakes and baklavas—and everywhere her lovely language: on the signs and menus, spoken in the house with her brother and among their countrymen out on the streets.

From then on, during her usual arguments with her husband, "I'm moving back to Serbia" was replaced with "I'm moving to Cleveland," a threat that she was able to make good on much more quickly than expected because, six months later, while preparing his 3:00 lecture, Radovan Kovac suffered a fatal stroke.

That November afternoon, Alice and her brother were picked up from grade school early and gathered at the kitchen table by their mother. There, Alice learned the news that she'd lost her father—the gentle, clever father that she'd loved—and it was there, in this moment, that she knew her chances of happiness had vanished with him. She'd cried for days, refusing to leave his room, face smothered in a shirt that still smelled of him, while the house that he'd chosen for them and that still bore his imprint—the maps he'd taped up to her bedroom walls, the constellation he'd painted on her ceiling—was emptied around her.

Madison would be home to the Kovacs no longer: Alice, her remaining family, and their belongings were crammed into a moving van bound for Broadview Heights. Her father's body was shipped separately, to be buried a mile from Vasily's mansion in the most garish style, with live musicians and a tearful, histrionic eulogy from her uncle, delivered in Serbian to baffle those well-mannered American friends her father was so proud to have acquired. For this insult to her father, for this disregard for all the man had valued in his too-brief life, Alice would have liked to slap her uncle's fat and oily cheek. Instead, she'd hugged and thanked him: not because her mother told her to, but because she'd understood her situation had changed and that she must now look to Vasily for her support.

Her father's death marked the division between Alice's mostly sunny childhood and her wretched Cleveland adolescence. Until age twelve, she'd lived in her father's tidy universe; now, under the auspices of Vasily, the family regressed. Her little brother turned from a shy boy to a thug; he and his friends were forever punching and kicking each other over nothing, or else in Vasily's basement knocking pins down with a ball. Her mother embraced a protected helplessness. She settled into a house less than two blocks from her brother's, grew obese, like him, and also primitive and paranoid: the world beyond Broadview was treacherous; everyone was stealing from her—the cable and electric companies, the tax authorities—sending her bills she didn't owe, so that Alice was eventually required to run the household for her.

As for Alice, in the space of two and a half years, she grew from a slight, pretty child, to a hulking creature of six feet. Black hair sprouted on her underarms and between her legs, creeping up almost to her belly button. Twice a week she shaved not just her legs, but also her abdomen and the small of her back. She developed broad shoulders, fleshy thighs, and pointy breasts. Boys in her class stared but didn't dare approach her: the majority stood only to her chin. Girls, who first ignored her, later learned to make use of her, dressing her up with lipstick and powder, like a drag queen, to serve as their guardian for R-rated films.

She was, she knew, at best an object of curiosity among her Cleveland "friends." At slumber parties they would strip her naked to expose a body so much more developed than their own, gawking at her like they did the slides in health class. Among them she'd lie awake, gripped by the first stages of a lifelong insomnia; to try to sleep, she'd imagine being young again, and small again, and on her father's lap.

Meanwhile, during the days, Alice came crawling onto Vasily's lap, even when she was too big to avoid raising eyebrows. An egomaniac, Vasily was easily persuaded of her adoration, and she needed him persuaded because she needed his money, most immediately for electrolysis. During her twenty treatments of electric shocks, Alice discovered she possessed a great tolerance for pain. Anorexia taught her another lesson: she could survive on almost nothing. Refusing her mother's food, she subsisted on carrots, popcorn, chewing gum, and bottles and bottles of Diet Coke. If she were to drop dead, as her mother insisted she would, she couldn't think of a more American fate than to die of Diet Coke.

Having mastered her own rebellious body, Alice turned her ambitions toward controlling those around her; here, her gift for language served her well. Nicknames she devised for her new classmates proved surprisingly adhesive. Lovely Carol, who in seventh grade began rouging her cheeks, Alice dubbed Clairol. Her next victims were Priscilla Tucker, Tyra Anne Clark, Shawna Lamb; all the pretty little girls with their pretty little names soon became Pucker, Tranny, Shanks.

In order to be spared the worst of her wit, even the cheerleaders sucked up to her, and by sophomore year, she'd made pets of the most popular girls and come to dominate the manipulable society of her high school. Armed with a fake ID, she became a source for alcohol and cigarettes. Being on her good side brought important benefits, and being on her bad side brought worse risks: dull facts were no match for a lively fiction, and adolescent Alice was expert, already, at telling a story.

It was the one she'd framed about herself—of her family's heartbreak and perseverance, set against the distant, tragic landscape of her war-torn homeland, and peppered with droll Serbian proverbs she'd invented—that convinced Harvard's admissions to accept her. Persuading Vasily to pay her way through private college was tougher.

Vasily claimed to see no use for education: he'd never finished high school and had still acquired every emblem of that vaunted American prosperity. Not *every*one, not *yet*, Alice had made him understand; in this country, the ultimate symbol of success was to have a child (niece would do as well) enrolled at one of its exclusive universities. A name like Harvard, dropped among his neighbors, would dazzle them more than all the jewels on his fingers or the statues in his front yard. Vasily was curious enough to test her theory; so their neighbors had their expectations set, and, come the next fall, Vasily had no choice but to ship Alice off to Cambridge. In this way, she'd turned her uncle's vanity to her advantage and never once let on the true motive for her efforts; namely, that her admission to such a campus would have made her father fiercely proud.

Already, Alice understood that she'd mostly disappointed her father's hopes for her. Her spirit was too black for her ever to become one of those rational, benevolent, and blessed creatures he'd wished for her to be. But at least she was clever enough to find her way among them, to escape the backward isolation of her uncle's Cleveland, and to stride onto manicured lawns of the sort that had so pleased her father once.

Arriving with her freshman class that fall, Alice was prepared to maneuver once again for her social position. She "comped" the *Crimson*, figuring this would give her an overview of what and who mattered in the campus scene. While other first-time writers were covering sports matches, the freshman formal, or auditions for the a cappella groups, Alice proposed a who's who of the school's fifteen hottest freshmen. The editor let her move ahead, as a lark, and not only was that item the most talked about that fall, Alice had been happily surprised to find her own name among the nominees offered by the paper's staff.

Unlike at her high school, where petite blondes were favored, here tastes ran toward the more exotic and high fashion. Tall and starved thin, Alice could pull off the heroin chic then in vogue—she cropped her kinky black hair Linda Evangelista short and went around in clinging tanks and low-riding fitted pants and skirts (designer ones, paid for by Vasily). Girls thought her cool, and men, especially artsy types who pursued obscure degrees, prided themselves on appreciating her androgynous beauty.

Whatever value others might place in her appearance, though, it was conventional, American good looks that Alice envied. Delicate bones and full lips, a narrow waist, a tanned calf: such features never failed to rivet her and, for this reason, she felt her pulse quicken on that morning in the fall of sophomore year, when she entered her art history section and spotted Georgia Calvin.

Like most of her classmates, Alice already knew who Georgia was: her second day in the Boylston dorm, when she'd met the boys who shared her floor, she'd seen a photo of Georgia, torn from the freshman directory and tacked up to the wall—dappled sunlight highlighting her smile, brightening her curls. The photo looked professional, something torn from a magazine, leading Alice to assume the girl must be an actress or a model—as it turned out, Georgia *was* a model, though only for her father, a well-known photographer. About a month into the school year, someone among Georgia's male admirers came upon a book of Jethro Calvin nudes, including photographs of his only daughter. That book made its way around the Yard, and Georgia became a kind of campus celebrity, while other freshmen still had to remind one another of their names.

Over the next months, Alice picked up several more bits of gossip about Georgia: that she'd never lived in any place more than a year or so, that she hardly knew her own mother, that she'd lost her virginity to a high school classmate's father. Alice was familiar enough with the workings of rumor to greet these claims with skepticism. Georgia Calvin was the rare girl in possession of a potent beauty, the kind that guaranteed her a place in people's fantasies, whatever those fantasies might be.

For Alice, her desire was clear: to share in that attention which Georgia inspired, to harness that power. This was the wish she'd formed while observing Georgia from a distance: studying in the reading room of the Fine Arts Library, or jogging on the path along the Charles, decked out in tiny red retro shorts, an outfit hardly appropriate for the routes Georgia took through urban streets, sometimes after dark.

Almost always, Alice noticed, Georgia was alone. She appeared to have trouble finding her social niche; she'd quit the swim team after only one season, and, following a few weeks of volunteering the next fall, she quit that too. Though she kept a few friendships going with some swimmers, by sophomore year Georgia's only truly close friend seemed to be an awkward, skinny kid whom Alice recognized from UC election posters. For an entire month, his picture grinned from every campus kiosk—bow tie, slicked hair, and crooked teeth—Charles Flournoy, running his campaign like he ran after Georgia, blind to his own clownishness.

Unlike Charlie, Alice wasn't one to make a show of her pursuit. The first time she spoke to Georgia was in an official capacity, as a reporter for the *Crimson*, when she'd invited her to appear among the "15 hottest freshmen" in her story. Georgia had refused to participate—*I'm not really into drawing attention to myself*—and Alice hadn't pressed the matter. If this wasn't to be the occasion for their meeting, another would present itself; so patiently she'd waited until sophomore year for her path to cross again with Georgia's—as classmates in the Monday/Wednesday section of The Female Icon in Contemporary Art.

Every other Wednesday their class paid visits to the Fogg Art Museum, and there, Alice imagined, she and Georgia were bound to find themselves drawn together, finally, attracted by the same object, standing close until conversation was inevitable. But at the first visit, she'd waited in vain for Georgia to appear. The second visit was the same—nor did Georgia show up for the third or fourth.

One afternoon as the semester was drawing to a close, Georgia strolled up to Alice's desk beside the window; she wanted Alice's opinion, she said, on a collection of photographs, works by a Balkan artist, that were to be the subject for her final paper. Lambert, their section TA, had suggested she speak with Alice, "as a woman of Serbian descent."

Later that night, after dinner, Alice stopped by Georgia's room.

Georgia was living in Mather House, in a single that shared a door and bathroom with a blunt-featured, muscled girl from the swim team: Gillian went by Gill—"a swimming joke," Georgia explained, introducing Alice to the girl doing crunches on her floor.

Georgia's bedroom was up a flight of stairs; it smelled of chlorine and lavender. A bra was dangling from the beams of her bed, bottles of lotion sat on a shelf below a mirror. Georgia took one bottle down, rubbing lotion on her legs and neck; then she reached behind Alice to lift a folder from her bedside table. As she laid the photographs out across her bed, she explained how they'd come to be in her possession.

She'd been twelve, traveling with her father for the Venice Biennale, when they'd paid a visit to a local art dealer. The dealer had led them into a back office, where twenty or so photographs were strewn across one corner of the floor. While the men discussed their business, Georgia had studied the pictures, all portraits of the same young woman (the artist, it turned out), dressed in shiny clothes and a ridiculous blond wig. Each frame contained a picture of Marilyn Monroe somewhere in the background; the woman in the foreground was made up and posed in precise imitation of that picture.

By then Georgia was modeling frequently for her father, though she hadn't yet begun to think about what her image meant, nor could she appreciate yet the political dimension of these self-portraits: "the artist's critique of the West's proprietary power over the feminine ideal." Still, she'd been affected enough by the work for the dealer to take notice; in an effort to coax her father into doing business with him, he'd offered the photographs to Georgia as a gift. The only extant copies, as far as Georgia knew. Recently she'd thought to examine them again and still held them to be an extraordinary find, however little the Venice dealer had esteemed them. She was curious to hear if Alice found them as powerful as she did.

The photographs, black and white, the size of Polaroids, crowded the length of Georgia's comforter. Each displayed an intelligent-looking young woman posed inside the same gloomy room; taken together, especially, the mood was claustrophobic, monotonous, hopeless. Alice thought of those snapshots kept by her mother, those of her and Vasily, from a time when Senka Kovac had been a charming creature, not yet deformed by loneliness and disappointment.

Georgia went on, rearranging the pictures, filling the gap left by Alice's silence: "I'm thinking of showing these to some gallerists. My father has a good friend with a small place in New York—the son and I used to play together, and now I hear he's curating. Wouldn't it be amazing if there were an exhibition? Twenty years ago a woman in a slum of Sarajevo picks up a camera, not believing anyone will care. I wonder what she'd think to see us taking interest now?"

Alice looked from the photographs to Georgia—this pretty, happy creature so very pleased with herself for her discovery—and was seized with irritation. As if the artist should be *grateful*, Alice thought, as if it were her fucking *dream*, as she sweated under that cheap blond wig, to end up splayed across the bedspread of some spoiled, honey-haired American. "I guess before you make your plans, you might want to ask the artist what *she* wants."

"Yes, of course." Georgia's reverie was ended; she let go of the pictures and crossed her arms over her chest. "Obviously I would try to contact her, ask permission. Though I can't imagine she'd object."

"I can." The anger behind her outburst took even Alice by surprise.

A small flush brightened Georgia's cheeks; she pulled her hair up over her neck. "I may not know this particular artist, but I've met my share, okay. No one ever stands in the way of having work shown."

"Well, probably the issue's moot in any case. With what's been going on in Sarajevo, with any luck the woman's dead."

Georgia stared across at her, refusing to be shocked. "Frankly, since you bring it up, the political situation only makes this work more urgent. Sorry if that sounds crass, but the way I see it, good art should have an audience, regardless of what the artist thinks, or even, believe it or not, what *you* think." She let her hair fall again at her shoulders and stepped away to open the bedroom door. "Anyway, I appreciate your coming over; and I really didn't mean to piss you off."

In fact Alice wasn't angry any longer: her annoyance had dissipated as quickly as it came, replaced by a reluctant admiration. Georgia had shown mettle.

Leaving the door open, Georgia stepped away to gather the photographs into a folder. Alice remained beside her; she had no desire to leave, nor, she sensed, did Georgia really wish for her to go. Their argument had left them both less embittered than enlivened, curious where the encounter might lead next. Alice suggested they head out for a drink.

There were several bars around the campus, noisy ones frequented by undergrads, but Alice escorted Georgia past these, to the upstairs room at Charlie's Kitchen. A dive with colored lighting, a dartboard, and a decent jukebox, the spot was frequented by young professors and grad students mostly, since the staff there made a point of checking each ID. On their way in, Alice simply nodded to the bouncer, who waved her on; upstairs, she paused to order two vodka cranberries at the bar, then coaxed Georgia into one of the brown Naugahyde booths.

"They don't even card you," Georgia marveled.

Looking old was one of her talents, Alice said. "On the first day of our section, two students came to me with questions; they thought I was the TA."

"I thought you were his girlfriend, maybe."

"And I thought the same of *you*." She hadn't, not really; pretentious Lambert, with his goatee and turtlenecks, wasn't up to Georgia. Still, Alice took the opportunity to address a question that had been bugging her these last weeks. "You skipped out on all the Fogg trips; I figured without sex he'd have flunked you."

"No, it's not like that. Actually, I'm not allowed inside Fogg anymore." An embarrassing story, Georgia claimed, which made Alice urge her the more forcefully to tell it.

"Just so we're clear," Georgia began, a finger raised to her lips, "I was only trying to do good."

"Doing good," meant volunteering, Georgia went on to explain: that fall, she'd signed on with a campus-run program called Inspire Youth. Each Saturday, volunteers would pair off and escort groups of troubled teens to various university attractions: usually a play or musical performance. The group leaders organized these trips according to their interests; Georgia's first proposal was a tour of the major works at the Fogg Art Museum.

From the start, she'd feared her choice was a poor one: the kids were rowdy, their voices echoing through the hushed halls and disturbing the other visitors. Complaints were made, and a guard warned that if she and her partner couldn't control their group, they'd need to leave. As a compromise, Georgia moved the kids down to the central courtyard, where she purchased a poster of Van Gogh's self-portrait from the gift shop and offered up the story of his severed ear.

The kids perked up: *They got the ear stashed here? Let's see it. Ear. Ear. Ear.*

Laughing, horsing around, the kids were all moving much too fast for Georgia to notice that one of them had pulled out a switchblade. A girl shouted; the kid with the knife was holding it to the side of her head. Before Georgia knew what was happening, a security guard was upon the boy, seizing the knife, pushing him up against the wall. The boy was taken to the police station; the others were sent home, forbidden, along with Georgia, from returning to the museum. A week later, Georgia was called in to speak with the head of Inspire Youth, a fellow sophomore named Julie Patel, who suggested Georgia was better suited to working with the elderly or blind, anyone other than children with impulse disorders: "Apparently I was responsible for the incident; I'd been sending provocative signals."

"So now," Alice observed, "you're trying to make yourself sound exciting, is that it?"

"To you?" Georgia let out a laugh, pleased, it seemed to Alice, to be spoken to so boldly. "I wouldn't presume."

Georgia leaned toward her, tipsy and languid; her hair tickled Alice's arm. Others in the bar were watching them, a dozen pairs of eyes turning their way. Alice and Georgia, a beautiful pair, united, newly inseparable—the pleasure in that arrangement was enough to induce Alice to keep Georgia's company from here on, even if she hadn't found Georgia more interesting than she'd imagined. Behavior that Alice had before ascribed to naiveté—running through dark streets in skimpy outfits, volunteering with delinquents—she'd come to see, that night, another way. Here was a girl, thought Alice, who was looking to be shaken, seeking out some misadventure, and *that*—the warped, irrational core in the smooth, harmonious package—Alice *did* find exciting.

5

She didn't know who he was, but a man had entered Georgia's life: Alice was sure. Just as their college years were drawing to an end, years in which Georgia had enjoyed only rare and furtive flings and shown no sustained interest in any of the campus guys but Charlie (and then, strictly a platonic one), Georgia was finally involved in an affair. At least this would explain her weekend visits to Manhattan, trips that Georgia claimed were for an internship in Soho. It was to work at a gallery, supposedly, that she rode four hours each way by train, toting lingerie inside her duffel—Alice had searched the bag once, back at Georgia's place after a run, while Georgia, in the shower, shaved her legs and washed her hair with her swanky Parisian lavender shampoo.

From what Alice could tell, the affair had started sometime after Christmas; Georgia must have met the man in New York over winter break. At first Alice suspected the gallery owner's son, Gabe, whom Georgia claimed she stayed with each Saturday night—only that wouldn't account for Georgia's secrecy. No, whomever she was seeing had to be married or famous—someone so desperate to keep their relationship hidden that Georgia hadn't dared to share the news even with her, her closest friend.

One Sunday night, after Georgia had returned from Manhattan, she and Alice were hanging out in Alice's new place on Inman Square. Draped across Alice's bed, Georgia pulled a joint from her jeans pocket; Alice rarely smoked—pot made her paranoid—but that night she'd joined in, feeling bored and craving new sensations. Later, she'd promised to drop in on a party at Gerry's. Gerry was the only friend Alice had made in Adams House during her year there; since then, he had also moved off campus, where he could throw better parties with better drugs and an edgier crowd than could normally be found around the Yard. Still, tonight the prospect of a night at Gerry's didn't tempt her; even the most outrageous displays had grown old: the same meltdowns and hook-ups, the same ecstasy-fueled fumblings, observed by her and Gerry with the same wry commentary, before she returned home with the same cigarette stink in her clothes, to climb into bed alone. As always. Meanwhile, Georgia was off enjoying some wild, forbidden, alternative existence.

"What are we doing here?" she asked Georgia, out of the blue, it must have seemed, that cold February night. "I should have met you in New York. We should be at a club right now, making out with indie actors, fleecing brokers." Why were they spending these—their most fuckable years—lying on Georgia's bed and staring at the ceiling?

"I'm perfectly satisfied," said Georgia lightly.

Alice propped herself up on her elbow: there were no marks of sex on Georgia's body that she could see; no dark patches on her neck; no rashy skin around her mouth left behind by a man's stubble. Her lips were puffy, though, and curled into a slight smile. She looked like somebody savoring a secret.

"And *how* are you so satisfied? By this sexless marriage you've got going with Charlie?" They'd been over it a dozen times—the stultifying effect of Georgia's friendship with Charlie, her fear of hurting him by letting down his hopes, or by demonstrating an attraction to any other man—not that Alice wished to concern herself so very much with Georgia's sex life. The only reason she'd brought the subject up again this evening was to provoke Georgia into making a confession; if Georgia was hiding an affair, Alice meant to let her know she understood her motive.

In any case, Georgia wasn't lured into the trap; she chose to steer the conversation in a different direction.

"I'm not denying there's some sexual component there with Charlie. But so what? Attraction is the basis of all friendship."

"You *would* think that."

Georgia was lying on her back, her hair fanned out around her on the covers; her legs were dropped toward Alice, brushing her side. "And what do you think?"

Alice peered down at her: Georgia with that dewy skin that never had a blemish and those curves which would have made almost any girl feel mannish, even one who didn't stand six feet tall with shoulders wider than her hips.

Georgia began to laugh her throaty laugh—and a thought struck Alice with the force of a revelation: Georgia was purposely keeping her affair from her—not out of concern that Charlie would find out and be jealous, but that *she* would. *She* was the one who couldn't bear to know her friend was loved by some man unattainable to her. She, even more than Charlie, was the frustrated one. Wasn't that why Georgia was laughing at her now? What else could it be? Why else would Georgia lounge across her bed that way unless she was trying to taunt her?

Rising from the bed, Alice crossed to the chair where she'd left her coat. "Gerry's expecting me."

"It's cozy here. Why not stay a little longer?"

"Let yourself out then. I'll go alone."

Georgia sat up, dazed, and brushed a curl from her eyes. "Are you upset or something?"

Alice buttoned her coat and stood at the wall mirror to fix her hair. In the reflection she caught Georgia looking at her, her pretty face contorted with confusion. But Alice was feeling sharp, taken over by a fierce and clarifying anger. She strolled out the bedroom door, leaving Georgia kneeling on the mattress and calling after her: "You're just leaving? Alice, stop. Come back here! What the fuck just happened?"

Gerry's place was on the other side of Inman Square, a three-bedroom shared with two local kids who ran a music store. Despite the distance from the main campus and the falling snow, the apartment was packed. Bodies crowded the entrance: standing, seated, sprawled. On her way in, Alice stepped over a pair of giant feet, laces untied. The man attached to them was large, with a round face and brown hair starting to go gray. Alice couldn't decide if he was handsome; he had bulbous features that could be considered either sensuous or barbarous.

After half an hour, she noticed the same man approaching Gerry, apparently to say good-bye. Gerry told her later who he was—a German grad student named Torsten.

"He asked me about you."

Ten days elapsed before Torsten called her—not to invite her on a date, as she found herself hoping, but to request a delivery. He needed pot for his migraine, which was so bad he couldn't bring himself to stir from bed. Gerry wasn't feeling well himself, so the story went, and had suggested that Alice, in his stead, might bring the package by.

"I don't do favors," Alice said.

"I wouldn't call it a favor," Torsten replied. "You caused this headache. All week I've been banging my head against the wall, trying to remember exactly how stunning you are."

Torsten was fond of giving compliments, the more outsized the better: this was one of the first qualities Alice observed about him. If not for her argument with Georgia, it was doubtful she'd have been taken in by such gross charms, but she was feeling eager for both a distraction and male admiration, and so she'd promised Torsten she'd come by.

When she'd arrived at his apartment, a cheap basement flat in Somerville, Torsten continued to fawn over her: she made him tongue-tied, he claimed—Gerry had warned him the only thing more devastating than her beauty was her wit. To relax, he rolled a joint, but she refused to share, afraid she might say something fatuous to spoil his impression.

"I dislike drugs, too," he assured her. "I smoke only for the migraines." He apologized for feeling sick and failing to entertain her. Otherwise he'd have cooked for her or at least put on some music. His music collection was enormous—hundreds of CDs—stacked between expensive speakers and stereo equipment. Apparently this was where all his money and attention seemed to go—the apartment was otherwise neglected, smelling of mold.

She asked him if he studied music.

"Physics. It's my second Ph.D."

"What was the first?"

"I'll tell you another time."

Another characteristic of Torsten's that Alice soon observed: he enjoyed being elusive, especially when it came to the most innocuous subjects. At the same time, matters that another man would have felt compelled to hide were open territory for him, like the fact that he was married and his wife had refused to join him in Cambridge, preferring to remain in Paris with her many lovers.

"You resemble her," he told Alice, "a black version." This may or may not have been the case, hard to tell from the one blurry photograph he'd shown her of a tall, strong, square-jawed blonde. "Not in the features, so much," he amended, "but in essence."

Alice wasn't sure what to make of such remarks, or of the fact that Torsten called her again, that evening, scarcely after she'd left, to ask her to keep him company the following day: "You're magical, you know; you made my headache disappear."

By the week's end, she'd been to Torsten's place four times; never once had he made the trip to hers. When she raised the issue, he pleaded a mild case of agoraphobia; he only left the house to visit the local food shops or for the single class he had no choice but to attend. Thankfully, he was sure Alice's magic would soon cure this condition, too: "You make me feel at home," he claimed, referring not to Paris, his wife's domain, but to what he called his *true* home, the extinct East Germany (thus uniting himself and Alice as children of the Soviet catastrophe). They were like siblings, sharing a common soul, he said—all very grand, but could soul siblings fuck? Still Torsten hadn't so much as tried to kiss her or in any way suggested the possibility of sex.

One night, when Torsten had fallen asleep on the sofa, Alice stripped off her clothes and went down on him. He'd been just hard enough, just long enough, for her to climb on top of him for several minutes and, from then on, they kept up a practice of occasional, usually abortive encounters. Each time, she had to be the instigator and the incident was followed by Torsten leaving her in bed and going off to sit alone for the next hour, sifting through CDs. When she pressed him on the problem, he attributed his inhibitions first to his migraines, then to his loyalty to his wife, and finally to his wife's destructive effects.

This was progress of a sort, Alice believed, and soon Torsten was comfortable enough with her to instruct her how to touch him and what stories to tell him while she did: there was a rigid formula that he required—her and another woman, him as the observer. After fifteen minutes of such encouragements, Torsten was able to perform on his own, albeit briefly, which seemed to leave him gratified. Not her, it was true, but she'd never much enjoyed sex anyway, the few other times she'd had it: once in high school, with a college boy whose only attraction was the fact that he was taller than she was, another time with a persistent admirer who'd cornered her at Gerry's. Before Torsten, she'd had to be drunk even to get naked with somebody; since puberty her body had been a source of anxiety, not pleasure—a place where terrible failures might take place. At least with Torsten she didn't feel ungainly; he was big and clumsy enough to render her comparatively dainty. She liked how small her hand felt in his, how slender it looked at the wrist, and there was something in his foreignness, and loneliness, that touched her and bound her to him.

Torsten, for his part, declared her his perfect woman—at least she might be, once she'd shed certain conventionalities. He urged her not to hide her height, to wear clothes that bared her wide shoulders, to dress in heels—not little kitten ones—but platforms like the leopard print pair he brought home for her one evening. He didn't want her slouching and softly padding in her flats; he didn't approve of her efforts to be sweet. He liked her humor best when it was cruel, found her darkest, most suspicious insights most intriguing. He'd followed her pieces in the *Crimson*, most recently, the *Playboy* Ivy models search, and he believed she could become a tremendous writer if she could just purge herself of that American restraint; in this cause, he was prepared to help her.

"You can only become your true self with me. The same for me, with you."

What sort of true selves he meant, she wasn't sure; but he'd begun speaking of a "him and her," of a future together, and Alice had been surprised to feel that she, perhaps, desired the same.

During Torsten's next migraine attack, while he was confined to the sofa, his landlady appeared. An older black woman, she stood at his door yelling, threatening to call her son to collect the rent, which was three months overdue, if it wasn't paid that day. Alice wrote out a check on the spot and, when Torsten was well enough for her to tell him what had happened, she suggested he come to live with her. Torsten groaned at the prospect of a move, but approved of the idea of living together: Alice could sublet her place on Inman and the proceeds would more than cover his rent and afford them dinners out, taxis to campus, a life of relative luxury.

Of course it occurred to Alice that he was taking her money, but it was Vasily's money anyway and a small price to pay for getting what she wanted: power over Torsten. She'd discovered a passivity in him—not only in bed—and, the more he needed her, practically, financially, the better positioned she'd be to make demands. In the end, if it was what she wanted, she'd get him to leave his wife for her. Already she and Torsten shared a home and a routine. In the mornings she attended classes while he slept, in the evenings he attended class while she did school work, and in the middle they met near campus to shop for dinner on Harvard Square.

While Alice and Torsten were stepping out from a bakery one afternoon, Alice saw a young woman jogging toward them, blond hair bobbing at her neck, dressed in a wife-beater and skimpy red shorts.

She turned away, hoping that Georgia hadn't seen her or would sense that she wished to avoid her. But whether out of cluelessness or out of decency, Georgia called her name. Or maybe neither cluelessness nor decency explained it; Georgia was eyeing Torsten, curious to observe the man behind her friend's recent disappearance. Six weeks had passed since she and Georgia had last met.

Immediately, Alice could see how taken Torsten was with Georgia: the sexy outfit, the fluffy blond hair, lifted off her neck like a pom-pom. For all he mocked that plastic American aesthetic, he, like Alice, was evidently fascinated by this instance of its perfection. She supposed she'd known he would be and had kept him from Georgia not by accident.

"I've been wanting to meet Alice's friends," Torsten effused, the first Alice had heard him utter anything of the kind. "Come by tonight, Georgia. We'll buy a cake. Angel food. Do you like angel food?"

With one glance in Alice's direction, Georgia seemed to understand she must decline. "Another time maybe."

On the walk back home, Alice felt her jaw aching from tension, the effort of not shouting. Since when was Torsten so eager to entertain—their universe seemed to happily include only each other—and what was this sudden enthusiasm for pastry, let alone one so specific? "Angel food cake. What the fuck was that?"

"Your friend inspired me. She's like a frothy, yellow cake."

"And you want that, that's the idea?"

"Not for me: for you. You're the one who denies your appetites."

He'd grinned down at her, his fleshy lips repulsive. Cars were moving past them; she felt an urge to shove him into traffic, to hurt him terribly for what he was likely imagining.

As soon as Alice and Torsten returned home, she went to her closet and retrieved the pair of platform shoes he'd bought her. Drag shoes. She threw them across the room: one struck him in the chest, another at the knee.

He shouted at her: "Are you crazy?"

"You are. You can't even admit that you don't want a woman, do you?"

"Alice, I have no idea what you're saying."

Torsten, who'd before extoled the perceptiveness in her most paranoid musings, now dismissed her suspicions about him as utter nonsense. "I refuse to talk with you until you're rational again."

Fine with her: he wasn't the one she wished to speak with in any case. There was only one person, she believed, who could help her out of her confusion—she had to get in touch with Torsten's wife. That night she locked herself away inside their bedroom and waited for Torsten to fall asleep on the sofa. When she was sure he wouldn't hear her, she crept out and found his wife's number listed on one of his old phone bills.

"I've been living with your husband," she told the French voice on the answering machine. "I'm not calling to upset you; it's hardly sexual. It might seem strange my turning to you, but I must ask. Did he ever suggest you do things with other women? Did he ever ask you to pretend to be a man?"

She made several such calls. Maybe more than several. She began to lose track of what she'd actually said and the things she'd just imagined saying, lying in bed half sleeping.

The next day she didn't attend class, she didn't leave the bedroom even to eat. Torsten went about his business, shouting at her sometimes through the walls. Time jerked along—both quickly and slowly—before her subletter called to let her know that people had been leaving messages for her: students, the senior tutor of Adams House, and her concentration adviser. She told him not to give out her new number and not to bother her again. Finally, one afternoon, Torsten threatened to kick down the door if she didn't get up.

"This has gone on long enough. You've been in there five days. Let's take a walk."

"I'm not going anywhere with you."

She sent him away and then emerged from the bedroom, dressed in sneakers; her running shorts gaped at her stomach.

She'd run as far as four blocks before she started to feel dizzy, another four blocks before she blacked out.

When she awoke in the University Health Center, she was being fed through an IV. The nurse informed her that she was suffering from dehydration and malnutrition. She was down to a hundred and five pounds, severely underweight. A psychiatric consultant was brought in: an easy mark, Alice believed, a student doctor not yet out of her twenties, with a mild voice and cow eyes.

"Physically, you're well enough to be released, but I still have some questions. On admission, you were disoriented. Do you remember how you got here? I need you to help me understand what happened."

"I let myself fall for an asshole, but it's not fatal, I think." Alice was making an effort to appear lighthearted and lucid, not to ask anything that might raise flags: whether Torsten had been informed of her collapse, whether he'd been by.

"I'd like to schedule you for a meeting with the head of my department. And we also need to get you into treatment for your eating disorder."

"I don't have an eating disorder. I had an argument with my boyfriend; I couldn't eat because I was upset." Whatever would get her out, Alice was prepared to say; for appearance's sake, right there in front of the counselor, she'd even taken several bites of the greasy hospital meat and slushy mashed potatoes left for her on a tray.

"Loss of appetite?" That could be a symptom of depression. "Any history of mental disorders in your family?"

"They're from Serbia."

The resident refused to join her in a smile, to alter in any way that earnest expression of concern. "Are they in Serbia now? Because I'd like to speak with a parent to discuss some treatment options."

Finally, Alice let her have it straight: there was no one in her family capable of such a conversation—her father was dead and her mother, even if she could understand what was required, had a hard enough time looking after herself.

"There must be somebody I can call. Any relative. A friend. Someone you can stay with until we're confident you're stable."

"It's really not necessary."

"It really is," the resident insisted. "I'm afraid I can't release you until I have the name of a responsible adult."

At five p.m., Alice signed her discharge papers and left the hospital for the Au Bon Pain on the ground floor. She was expecting to find Georgia, in whose custody she'd placed herself for the next few weeks; instead, she spotted Charlie Flournoy rising from one of the plastic chairs. Georgia was in New York, he explained, but she'd gotten Alice's message and spoken with hospital staff. "Everything's fine. I'll just be with you until she comes; she's catching the next train."

"Is today Saturday then?"

"Sunday—which means I've got all day to help you get squared away." He clapped his hands, a new habit he'd picked up; he was different from when last she'd seen him: dismal that fall, losing weight. Today he looked healthier, even sporty, dressed in navy pants and a pale blue gingham shirt, sleeves rolled up to show off forearms grown more muscled. He was pleased to be in charge; his tone was surprisingly commanding. He'd told Torsten to go out, he said, so she'd feel at ease while they packed up her things, and then they'd sneak them back to Mather House; Gill would let them in through the bathroom and Georgia would meet them there.

Around seven, as Alice and Charlie sat waiting in Georgia's living room—she, smoking; he, reading a library hardcover, *Arts of Power*—Georgia bounded in, with a flurry of apologies. "I'm sorry I'm so late: just missed the one o'clock and then the next was local . . . Are you tired, Alice? Do you want to lie down?" She led them up into the bedroom—clothes strewn across the bed, items she'd chosen not to pack, lacy underwear, heels (for her internship, yes, of course). "Huge mess—wasn't expecting anybody. Such bad timing, but I'm so glad, so grateful, Charlie could be there for you."

Was it about Charlie, this frenzy, fear that he'd discover where she'd really been that weekend? But if Charlie noticed anything strange, he didn't show it; he only turned modestly away as Georgia snapped up a bra, a pair of stockings.

"We'll figure out where to put everything later," Georgia rambled on. "I've got two floors, plenty of room. And no one in the dorm will make an issue. They all let their boyfriends stay, right?"

Georgia looked up at her, finally: Alice, alone, sickly, and sad. Only for an instant, but unmistakably, pity flashed in Georgia's eyes. Alice felt a surge of rage then: at Georgia's health and beauty, at her rosy cheeks and winning smile, at her delight in her secret affair, one as thrilling as Alice's had proven agonizing.

The hardest part of that humiliating afternoon was hiding her discomfort at seeing her friend again, the girl who, Alice felt, despite Georgia's concern for her, was the cause of her breakdown even more than Torsten. A girl to whom everything came easily and whom she wished, then, to see suffer. Merely for existing, Georgia should suffer, since her mere existence had become, for Alice, a source of pain.

6

Georgia's happiest childhood memories were of swimming, particularly during that year when she was twelve and her parents, together still, had first moved to Santa Cruz, into a weather-beaten yellow house just two blocks from the ocean. Each afternoon that year, in all conditions except lightning storms and raging fever, she went to the beach, after school, for swimming lessons with her father. Lessons, now that she was growing tall and lean and strong, were of a very different sort than she'd had when she was small; now they were not to learn the proper form of basic strokes, side and back and freestyle, but to tackle the waves and current, to navigate through forces much stronger than herself, to dart and glide through tumult.

The summer before these lessons started, she'd waded out into the waves on a choppy day and was caught up by a massive one, dragged across the sandy bottom, her knees and chin scraped upon the pebbles; when she'd finally been spit back out onto the shore, coughing and trembling, she was convinced that she'd brushed right up against death and had only just escaped.

Afterward, she was afraid to enter the surf again, until her father took it upon himself to venture out with her. Clinging to him, she rode piggyback like a child, or else floated beside him, rising on the rollers and diving into the breakers, all the while clutching his hand.

Her father was just forty then, enjoying the first of his fame. Jethro Calvin was a name that the right people had begun to recognize. His photographs sold at shows; his presence was requested at celebrity-strewn parties in L.A. Tan and strapping, clever and handsome, hair burnished by the sun and curly like Georgia's own, he seemed to have sprung from the pages he'd read to her out of *Bulfinch's Mythology* when she was a girl: stories of gorgeous, gifted heroes desired and envied by both gods and mortals—maidens punished for their beauty, men driven by violent passions, women by consuming jealousies.

Even after her dread of the ocean had subsided, Georgia went on feigning fear to keep her father at her side; some days, she'd hold him with her for so long the tides would carry them down the beach until they'd lost sight of her mother's red umbrella on the shore. Georgia's mother never set foot in the water—rarely, even, into the sun, which burned her delicate skin. She preferred to sit and read in the shade of her umbrella while the salt air wrinkled the pages of her books. She read all the time then, an earnest new professor preparing her first lectures. It was clear she found these trips outdoors an inconvenience, and Georgia wondered, sometimes aloud, why she even had to come.

After that happy year in Santa Cruz, Georgia's father was offered a teaching fellowship in South Dakota. As a family, they'd always traveled, her father moving between teaching positions, or on photo assignments, or simply chasing inspiration. Jethro Calvin—the artist and the man—had an interest in tiny towns with obsolete shops, quaint poverty, and quirky residents. He was fond (her mother claimed) of any environment where he was able to feel big. Her mother hadn't objected to this lifestyle as long as she was still at work on her dissertation, on the anti-Romantic politics of Mary Shelley, but that fall the manuscript had been accepted for publication and, in the spring, she'd been appointed a tenure-track position at UCSC. Georgia's father passed up South Dakota, but such compromise was not for him; halfway through their second year in that beachside yellow house, he claimed he needed new scenery and Georgia was left to choose: Santa Cruz with her mother, or her heart's fancy, with her father.

She and her father didn't wander far during their first year of living alone, just to a town with a jaunty name that grabbed her: Texico, New Mexico. Her parents' separation hadn't struck her then as either permanent or threatening. Every few weeks they'd go back to stay with her mother, or else her mother would come and stay with them. Only after Georgia and her father had moved a second time, following a teaching job at the Christian University in Windsor, Colorado, did her mother begin to ask that Georgia visit on her own. During that Thanksgiving, which she insisted Georgia spend with her, her mother introduced her to a friend named William. William was ten years older than her father; Jewish, like her mother, and a math professor. He specialized in something called "operations research," which was described to Georgia and which she, in turn, described to her father as "the pursuit of optimal solutions."

"Well," her father said, "looks like your mother's found a new one."

Her father didn't appear angry, nor did he think that Georgia had reason to be; her mother's new partner would make the dissolution of the marriage painless. Life would go on even more smoothly than before.

A month after they'd moved to their cottage in Windsor, though, Georgia came home to find her father shouting her mother's name.

"Judy Steiner, she made this complaint, didn't she? Didn't she?"

Her father was seated in the living room with two policemen. One had a mustache and was leaning aggressively over her father; the other, younger, looked discomfited by her entrance. A book of her father's photographs lay open on the coffee table. Seeing her hesitating at the door, her father dropped his voice and turned to wave her in.

"It's okay, sweetheart. Don't be upset. I just need to speak with these men for a moment."

"What's this about? Mom did something?"

"Mom's fine. Everything's fine. I'll explain later. Go on into your room."

Through her bedroom door, she'd heard him defending himself to the officers. "Of course she's wearing a bathing suit. No, I know you can't tell. I blurred it out; the image is meant to be obscure. It's precisely *not* erotic. You can't even see what kind of body this is: male, female, child, adult."

"Looks like a young girl to me," said one officer, the one with the moustache, Georgia was sure.

"All right, enough." Her father seemed to be struggling to keep his tone light. “Now why don’t we acknowledge what’s really going on here. Even my own students don’t follow my work—I should believe the Windsor Police Department does? Clearly my ex-wife called you. You’ve got to see why she’s doing this. Neither of you has an ex?”

“I think I do see. I see a young girl without clothes.”

“Maybe we should move this to the kitchen,” the younger officer suggested.

Georgia couldn’t hear what happened next; after what seemed like ages, she caught the sound of footsteps approaching, and then a knock. When she opened her door she saw her father slouched between the officers, abject, shaking his head. “I’m sorry, baby; they just need to ask you one small question.”

The elder policeman turned to address her: “Has your father taken any photographs of you recently?”

“He’s a photographer; he takes pictures all the time.”

“Has he taken any *inappropriate* photographs of you?”

“*Inappropriate* how?”

“You don’t need to upset her, please,” her father said, but the officer ignored him.

“Has he taken any nude photographs of you? Pornographic pictures.”

“Who gave you that idea? I was wearing a bathing suit, for God’s sake.” She knew to act shocked and was pleased to see the younger officer grow nervous and mumble something to his partner.

Her father’s confidence returned; he came to her side and put an arm around her. “You want to know what child abuse is? *This* is child abuse. Right here. My wife is the abuser. And if you don’t leave my daughter alone, I’m going to the station and file a charge against *you*.”

The officers left soon after that and the visit marked the end of the harassment from police. It was not, however, the end of the trouble. Word got around of the accusation and, after his first semester, Georgia’s father was relieved of his position at Christian University. Again he and Georgia packed their things and started out on the road, bound next for Balfour, North Carolina. This time they seemed to be moving on less by choice than by necessity, though her father would have denied there was much difference. Behind every action there was *will*: nothing so rational as choice, and nothing as helpless as need. In general, he believed most language was used to escape accountability or soften reality. That was the way with most people, though he and Georgia weren't the kind for such evasions. If they lied, it wasn't to fool themselves, but to elude the narrow-minded judgments of others.

Facing the world beside her father, Georgia came to share his cautious view of strangers. Teenage girls, especially, must be approached with care—not only because they envied her looks and her talent as a student, but because none of them had been permitted to see as much as she had—they hadn't vacationed in Europe or been to gallery openings in New York; their fathers weren't friendly with Rod Stewart or Julian Schnabel or Susan Sontag. Though Georgia kept such details to herself, her classmates felt the difference in her outlook: that the places and lives they took to be significant, were for her, merely stops along her way.

By the time Georgia arrived in Balfour, halfway through her junior year, she'd entered four schools in four years and had devised a survival strategy. Boys were to be avoided, so as not to inspire competition from the girls, whose allegiance, such as it was, could best be earned by joining whichever team would have her. In Balfour, swimming was in season when Georgia started school that winter, and so she'd joined the team and made special efforts to befriend its captain, Mindy Mayhew.

Each Saturday, Mindy invited the varsity swimmers to her house for lazy afternoons around the Mayhews' overchlorinated backyard pool. Mindy's was the first local family that Georgia had been invited to meet: Mrs. Mayhew, blond with black roots, smoking on the deck and palling with the girls, Mindy's younger brother finding excuses to wander out to the back deck. Mr. Mayhew was the only one who maintained distance; he rarely loitered at the house, preferring to set off alone by bike, escaping for hours. Georgia had caught sight of him a few times, wheeling down the driveway. The sort of man her father might have photographed: handsome in an authentic way, something arrogant and stubborn in his eyes, the set of his jaw.

One afternoon in March, just after the successful close of the swimming season, the team gathered to celebrate. They blasted the usual crap music—Tiffany, Taylor Dayne—and downed spiked Mountain Dew, which made Georgia's head hurt. Several of the girls were drunk enough to lie topless, provoking Mindy's little brother to stand gaping out the window.

Finally Georgia went into the house to grab some quiet shade and a cold glass of water. She was in the kitchen, at the sink, when Mr. Mayhew stepped in to empty a bottle he'd just filled up for his ride.

"Tire's busted." He pointed out the kitchen window: the bike lay, dejected, against a tree. "Guess I'm grounded."

He stared at her, looking just about the way she felt: utterly remote from everything around, bristling with energy, and bored.

"Where do you go?" she asked him.

"I try to do it different each time; my goal is to get lost."

"Pretty hard to manage that if you're from here."

"Like most things, if you're from here, it's pretty hard to manage unless you're a fucking moron." He splashed cold water on his face, then headed out through the side door.

Later that week, she was going for a run, out about a mile from her house, when Mr. Mayhew pulled up in his car: "I can take you to a better spot. A place I like to bike."

He dropped her about three miles out, giving her instructions on how to make it back.

"You're just going to drive off?" she asked him. "You're not worried I'll get lost?"

"There's a motel along this road if you have trouble; anyone can point you to it."

"A motel, huh?"

"I'll come and check there in an hour, just in case you need a ride."

She hadn't waited for him at the motel that day. She hadn't dared meet the man again, in fact, until she had just one month left in Balfour. That was all, if the worst happened, she believed she could endure.

It was a warm day in early June. Mayhew had come by bike and arrived sweating, insisting on a shower as soon as they'd entered the motel room. He'd run the water, pulled off her dress, and coaxed her into the hot stream.

Not the scene she'd had in mind for her first time: she hadn't imagined standing, or clutching a rusting spigot for balance; she hadn't imagined the squeakiness of wet skin, or the numbness that set in from the heat, the blurriness of feeling—if there was pain, she didn't know it; if there was blood, the water washed all traces away. The next time she and Mayhew met, opting for the bed, there were no stains on the sheets, nothing to force any admissions—and by the third time, she'd been able to appreciate his steady, precise touch and deft avoidance of burdensome emotion—gifts she wasn't going to encounter again, certainly not among boys her own age. With Mayhew, there was no need to mull over lost youth or innocence, or address the fact that what went on in that hotel room was technically a crime; no need to discuss the fact of Mayhew's marriage, or of his being the father of her schoolmate. That motel shower had been her baptism into sin, a secret pleasure that endured three weeks, exactly, before news spread of their affair.

When she and her father picked up and switched towns again, Georgia still hadn't learned how she and Mayhew were discovered, whether someone had spotted her in his car, or an employee at the motel had spoken up. All she knew was that she, unlike Mayhew, was blessed with the ability to disappear, and that she'd come to share with her father—who'd borne the news and its consequences without judgment or resentment—the elation of such departures. Her father's philosophy had become hers, too: the perspective from a rearview mirror was the freest, the most enlightened.

Throughout these years, as Georgia moved from one high school to the next, her mother voiced complaints that her father wasn't allowing her to develop stable relationships with anyone but him: "if any relationship with that man could conceivably be thought of as *stable*." Georgia defended her father, insisting she was doing fine, socially and academically, too: notwithstanding the many upsets in her studies, she was graduating as the valedictorian of Oregon's Oceanside high school and had been accepted into Harvard.

At the graduation ceremony, Georgia's mother and father appeared together for the first time in years. That afternoon, after three glasses of white wine, her mother took her aside. She'd worn a dress with roses on it, completely out of keeping with her usual no-nonsense style. Wobbling on heels, she'd held Georgia by the arms, which was also out of character, her mother never much given to touching. There were tears in her eyes and she was agitated. She'd been working herself up to this moment; there was something she felt the need to say.

"I owe you a tremendous apology for what I've done to you. I was angry and I was selfish—every bit as selfish as your father. I should have protected you from him."

Why should she require protection from her father? "Please don't start on Dad. Not today."

"He hijacked you and I let him."

"Well, I don't see it that way."

"That you can't see it is the worst part, and it's my fault. It's the regret of my life—letting that man take you."

Jealousy, that was all this was: how else to explain her mother's choice to insult both her father and her on this day when they had every reason to be proud? Who could fault her father for the woman she'd become?

It was thanks to him that she'd grown up to be energetic and curious and strong; thanks to him that she'd been saved from being confined within one town or school or one idea about learning or living. Her father's lesson was to fear only safety and stasis; ever since those days out by the ocean, he'd taught her to crave more from experience than an even surf.

At Harvard, Alice Kovac was hard to miss: six feet tall and rail thin with short black hair and clever, dark-rimmed eyes. Though she looked older, Alice turned out to be a sophomore like Georgia, which left Georgia to wonder if this wasn't the same Alice who'd called her room her freshman year, in connection with a story for the *Crimson*: *I'd like to learn more about you, Georgia.* But if this were the same girl, she'd either lost interest in Georgia or kept it well hidden: she sat on the opposite end of the room, at a desk pulled by the window, exuding such sly confidence that even the TA seemed to seek her approval, directing his various asides and jokes her way.

Lambert was the one to suggest that Georgia speak with Alice. Georgia's final paper was on a Sarajevan artist, and Alice, who'd been born there, might offer unique insights on the work. In fact, Alice expressed no reaction to the photographs Georgia had shown her—just what felt like a visceral antipathy toward her. An unusual beginning for a friendship, but Georgia supposed it was Alice's unorthodoxy, in general, that attracted her. Alice was never boring, and there was no false courtesy with her, nothing hesitant to slow the progress of affection once it started.

Alice's childhood offered a partial explanation for her bluntness: her mother was a miserable lunatic, to hear Alice tell it, and her father hadn't lived past forty.

Georgia's father, then forty-seven, was still completely vital, without a wrinkle or gray hair. "Forty's so young," she'd remarked.

But Alice was without pity: for her father or for herself. "I think it's old enough. I don't plan on lasting too much longer."

A comment intended to provoke, as so many of Alice's remarks were, and yet there were times when Georgia really could see Alice driving herself to an early grave; there were full days she spent in Alice's company without seeing a morsel of food pass her friend's lips. Meanwhile, Georgia never felt more likely to drop dead than during their runs, despite her strong heart and lungs from swimming. Alice always had to stay a step or two ahead; she grinned each time Georgia was compelled to stop and catch her breath, and she wouldn't quit until Georgia announced she was exhausted. Once, Georgia noticed blood on the back of Alice's sneaker. A blister must have popped or a scab opened; the cut was deep and Alice had run their seven-mile loop without a word of complaint.

Not even among the most ambitious athletes she'd known had Georgia encountered a girl as fiercely competitive as Alice, and soon this quality infected other facets of their lives. Georgia would catch Alice peeking at her papers when they studied, silently comparing marks; when they dressed to go out, Alice would ask to try on Georgia's clothes, never to wear them, in the end, just to be certain that they fit her more loosely. When they walked down the street, Alice noted each gaze that trailed them and seemed to count out which of the two girls attracted more. If a man showed interest in Georgia at a party, by the end of the evening, she would be sure to find Alice speaking with him, her head tilted back, her shirt slipped over her shoulder.

Such displays were nothing new to Georgia; in high school she'd developed tricks for managing envy: putting herself down, offering compliments and the occasional gift. "Take this," she'd tell Alice, handing off a new skirt, a tight pair of pants. "It doesn't fit me anymore." If such acts of generosity didn't dispense with Alice's accumulated irritations, then Georgia would vanish for a few days, let Alice work them off herself, until they could greet each other with fresh enthusiasm once again.

What might have seemed like fickleness Georgia saw, rather, as proof of Alice's intense attachment, so strong it sometimes pained her. Alice wasn't easy—Georgia understood that—but her affection was sincere and could be maintained, Georgia believed, if she cared for it the right way: as long as their bond was now and then relaxed, as long as they spent the odd weekend and holidays apart, as long as summers came to burn away bad feelings, giving scrapes time to heal.

Charlie didn't get Alice's appeal. The girl was unreliable and selfish, in his view, and Georgia hadn't wished to insult him by explaining why she chose to overlook such faults: whereas Charlie made her feel accepted and at ease, Alice kept her divinely off-balance, a sensation that, somewhere in her travels with her father, had become pleasurable to Georgia. She counted on Alice to keep her alert and honest, and it was Alice who pointed out, toward the start of junior year, that Georgia's social life had become a snooze. Charlie was to blame, obviously. Alice was tired of witnessing the same pathetic scenes weekend after weekend, tired of being dragged along to all the same parties with her and Charlie—there to help Georgia through any awkward moments: Charlie drinking too much and touching too much; his hands on Georgia's knees or in her hair.

It was time Georgia let the guy down firmly; otherwise, she and Charlie were both going to miss out on the string of sexual misadventures college life was all about.

"Unless, that is, you're *looking* to miss out. Unless Charlie's not the reason you skip sex, he's the *excuse*."

Georgia might have drawn attention to Alice's *own* shortage of sexual experience, but she didn't wish to provoke an argument and, anyway, she had to admit Alice might have a point. "Why would I be avoiding sex?"

"Because there's just two ways it can go with you: disappointment or disaster."

"Why not satisfaction? Why not ecstatic delight?"

"Sweet Georgia." Alice leaned in to kiss her cheek. Her lips lingered a moment—too long, perhaps—and then she shrank back, shaking her head. "What do you think disaster *is*?"

7

Outside the train window, yellow cranes loomed over heaps of metal and stretches of dust. The Big Dig was under way: roads shut down in all directions. Only a month before, Georgia had enjoyed the sense of flying above the endless mess, leaving bogged-down Boston for her weekly Manhattan jaunts.

But not today. Today, she'd have preferred to stay on campus, to devote the weekend to her several final papers. A draft of her thesis was due Monday and she ought to be spending her weekend absorbed in the work of Cindy Sherman, not in the latest inane argument with Storrow. Ever since she'd packed her bag that morning, she'd had a sense of dread about this visit, and her mood wasn't being helped by the images she'd brought along, from *The Untitled Film Stills*, the subjects of her paper: women alone in strange bedrooms and hotel rooms, each caught in her own drama, trapped.

"I promise," Storrow had told her, "I'll be nothing but nice."

So he said, but there was no predicting his behavior lately. In one moment he'd be kind, then impatient with her, rough and then remorseful. He'd insisted nothing was wrong, but he looked tired and had begun dozing off in bed after sex; his sleep was troubled, and sometimes he made noises, muffled cries and moans. She'd woken him, finally, one afternoon, to ask if he'd had a nightmare.

"Chest congestion maybe, might be fighting a cold."

"You sound like you're in pain."

He'd smiled, red hair ruffled, and kissed her forehead. "How could I be in pain when I'm with you?"

That was the sweet Storrow, but at their next meeting he'd been foul-tempered again. She'd arrived late, held up by a problem with

Alice, who'd failed to keep a hospital appointment. The psychiatric resident had notified Georgia and she and Alice had argued about it; as a result, Georgia had missed her train, and Storrow had greeted her coldly: "If I can make the time to be here, with all that I have on my shoulders, I'd expect as much from you."

"I have a friend going through something."

"Was it really so important?"

"I don't know—is *anybody's life important besides* yours?" She'd begun to resent his self-absorbed intolerance; maybe she ought to turn around, maybe, she had said, she should not have come at all.

"Please; I'm glad you did." He took hold of her, nuzzled his nose into her neck. "I'm just all eaten up. You can't imagine the sort of pressure I've been under lately."

How could she? Storrow shared almost no details of his life with her. Truthfully, she wasn't sure she minded the strict limits of their relation; nevertheless, she hadn't stopped him when, that afternoon, seated on the sofa—the first Saturday they hadn't headed straight into the bedroom—Storrow finally opened up to her about his problems.

All that semester, he'd been facing a conflict with some of the students in his senior seminar. "It was a mistake to try to teach colonialism and the law; the only thing anyone wants to talk about is Western oppression, Eurocentricity—to them there's no such thing as justice, no perspective beyond a shallow relativism."

One student in particular had been causing a disturbance: "I'm hardly able to get a word out before she interrupts; I can't even approach the subject I came to teach, unless, of course, I want to be dragged before some disciplinary committee, kicked off campus. That's what she hopes to accomplish, it seems, before graduation. The woman has it in for me."

"I'm sure that isn't true." It was all a bit melodramatic, even for him, she thought. And yet it wasn't hard to imagine how Storrow could inspire dislike—through those very qualities that had attracted her and could as easily repel her: his vanity, his self-righteousness.

Desire and hatred, she felt, were often related, and certainly when it came to feelings for a man like Storrow. As she sat there on the sofa, seeing him more excited by his enemy than he was by her, she couldn't help but wonder if their roles had been confused. Perhaps it was this other girl who was in love with Storrow, really; and she, the one who wished to make him disappear.

Nevertheless, she did her best to show compassion: "You obviously didn't mean to, but maybe you said something to offend her?"

"It's not anything I said—it's that I presume to speak at all about people with darker skin than I have. Of course, she's the official voice of the subaltern. Never mind that, unlike her, *I* actually spent years on the Indian continent."

An Indian girl, from the sound of it: a fellow senior, outspoken and obstinate, concerned with matters of social justice.

"Are we talking about Julie Patel?"

Brusquely Storrow stood and shook his head: "I can't tell you that; I shouldn't even be discussing this with you. This is just the problem I'm describing—lack of respect—and it's my fault too, obviously—for not insisting on it."

From there he quickly changed the subject back to her, *her* inconsideration and irresponsibility, her coming late to meetings, her failing to show up to receive his calls. The last two evenings he'd phoned her room, she'd been out. "You mind telling me where you were?"

"With Charlie, not that it's any of your business."

"Actually I think it is." Charlie was another problem, Storrow let her know. It really wasn't prudent for her to be so closely involved with one of his students. Not to mention that Charlie was obviously in love with her. A weakness on her part, this endless need for adoration, for some young man always traipsing after her. Every time he chanced to see her, she was with another guy; just the other day he'd passed by Widener Library and seen her speaking with a young man on the steps.

"Dirty-blond, tall, nice-looking. Who was he?"

"No idea. There are just so many, according to you."

"None of whom you've ever been attracted to, or slept with?"

"I wasn't a virgin when you met me. Would you have wanted me to be? To have that on your conscience too?"

"Were you in love then?"

This was the first either of them had mentioned love. Storrow's question—let slip without his thinking, revealing some insecurity or hope—might have softened her toward him again, if not for the bitterness of his next remark.

"Or do you just go to bed with men you don't much care for."

"I certainly don't fuck men that I *dislike*, I can tell you that. And I don't like you much the way you're acting. I didn't come here to be chastised."

In the beginning of their courtship such arguments had seemed a mode of foreplay—the way to get Storrow past his inhibitions was to anger him. But lately the sex hadn't seemed worth the longer and longer lectures that preceded it; what had begun as teasing had become tedious.

If she weren't stuck inside this train, she now thought, she'd turn around right then, tell Storrow she simply had too much work to make the trip. In fact, it wasn't too late; she could get off at the first stop and buy a ticket heading back; the train had only just pulled out from South Station. Behind her, the compartment door slid open and a man in uniform came through checking tickets, marking new ones with his hole-puncher. From the corner of her eye, Georgia saw his wide torso moving down the aisle and then, behind him, a slender body, stopping at her seat.

"Alice." She tried to smile, to hide her alarm at her friend appearing this way. Back at the room, Alice had said nothing about taking the train, herself: they might have shared a taxi to the station. "Why didn't you tell me you were coming?"

"Gerry phoned last minute." Alice hoisted her bag into the rack overhead. "He's housesitting for a friend in Chelsea."

Not, her tone implied, that she owed Georgia any explanation. Since Alice's release from the health clinic, she'd been living, in effect, under Georgia's "supervision"—an arrangement Georgia didn't cherish any more than Alice did. But what choice did she have? She couldn't turn her friend away in the state she'd been in: frighteningly thin, her skin sallow, her eyes ringed with purple. Someone had to keep an eye on Alice, even if the longer she stayed, the more likely it was that Storrow would discover her or that Alice would discover Storrow, and the whole thing would blow up.

The next three hours dragged on. Alice read a sociology textbook while listening to her headphones; Georgia busied herself with her notes, which was merely a show of work, at this point. She couldn't possibly think about her paper now; all she could think about was whether she'd given Alice reason to believe she was having an affair or that these weekend trips weren't what she claimed. Alice *had* been regarding her suspiciously—or so Georgia sometimes thought, catching a sly or bitter look come over her friend. But it was impossible to keep track of Alice's ever-shifting moods and Georgia believed that she'd been careful, adhering to most of Storrow's various precautions.

She hoped to God that he was, too, that Storrow wouldn't be waiting for her at the platform when the train pulled in. Their meeting spot was meant to be the Blarney Rock Pub, an old dive bar on Thirty-Third, but lately, at least when they were in New York, he'd started to relax his vigilance. On her last visit, to show he could be spontaneous, he'd snuck up on her right inside the Penn Station main concourse.

The conductor announced the last stop, and the train moved through a dark tunnel before coming to a halt. Georgia and Alice exited the car together, heading up the steps and as far as the subway escalators. Alice was looking for the downtown 1 train, so Georgia claimed her destination (Gabe's place) was walking distance. She said good-bye and waited for Alice to vanish underground, then she went off to find a bathroom; despite the filth, she lingered by the sinks until she felt sure Alice was long gone. Out in the concourse, there was no sign of either Alice or Storrow; she stepped through the doors into the sunshine, making her way toward the Blarney Rock down Seventh Avenue.

The place was largely empty at this hour: a few shabby men were slumped over stools along the bar, gaping up at a baseball game that played on the TVs. Storrow sat alone, at a table in the back; posture straight, elbows off the plastic tablecloths, he was drinking ginger ale through a straw. After two weeks apart, she was reminded of his crisp, good looks—he seemed to shine in the dim room—and yet his fustiness among these men slugging their beers served to confirm her recent feeling: Storrow was much too square. Not at all the sort to chaperone her through her first light steps into unfettered, adult life.

"I wasn't sure you'd come today," he said, his voice drowned out by the men at the bar, cheering at some play. Storrow frowned, and she began to wonder if she'd picked this meeting place, from the beginning, precisely to make him uneasy.

Leaving his glass full, he dropped a few bills onto the table, grabbed his blazer off the chair back, and took hold of her arm. They were heading for the door when, through the window, she caught a glimpse of Alice, stopped on the street out front to light a cigarette.

"Outside," Georgia stuttered. "Alice."

Storrow seemed instantly to grasp the situation and what it required; he took Georgia's hand, shaking good-bye. He was smiling, steady, calm. "You leave first. I'll wait for you at the apartment. Just be easy. Say hi to her on your way out."

"What if she asks about you?"

"We ran into each other. You saw me through the window; you know me through Charlie, and from the pool."

But Alice would never buy it. Georgia felt certain: there was nothing innocent or accidental in Alice's appearing here today.

"Well, it doesn't matter, anyway," she heard Storrow say. "She's moved on."

Georgia turned to face the window; outside, there were only strangers passing by. The whole encounter—if it was even that—had lasted but a few seconds. Storrow had handled himself well, but Georgia feared she hadn't, that Alice had seen her looking stricken, and her face had given everything away.

"What do we do now?"

The safest thing, Storrow instructed, was to take separate cabs to the apartment.

"The apartment. After this?" She didn't wish to go with Storrow or have the argument she knew was coming. This was all her fault; Alice had been her guest this month and she'd concealed the fact from him. "I should just get back on the train."

"You and I need to talk about this, Georgia."

"We do; we will. But later, please."

"I'm getting you a taxi; just go to the apartment."

"I told you: I want to go home."

"Why should I give a damn what you want?" Storrow inhaled sharply; his fist thumped against his chest. "*I'm* the one who stands to lose here. This is *my* job on the line. *My* life."

Angrily, he pushed through the front door and stood at the curb to hail a taxi. She watched him through the bar window, thinking of that first day in the apartment he'd arranged, when she'd peered down from the third floor and seen him stepping out, arm raised, into traffic. His elegant frame, the assertiveness in the gesture; she'd felt her attraction keenly. That moment seemed far off now.

Storrow was beckoning her toward the waiting cab. She stepped out and he gripped her arm, guiding her, a bit too roughly, to the far edge of the seat. He got in with her. Apparently he'd rethought the idea of taking different cars, maybe he no longer trusted her to go where he instructed. Inside the cab, he slammed the door, gave the address, and then sat with his head in his hands. She could hear his breathing, thick with the emotion he was struggling to control.

"Don't be mad," she said softly. "I swear I never told Alice anything."

He didn't raise his head; his voice was muffled by his palms. "Just give me a minute, okay? Just please sit there and don't speak."

When the cab pulled up to the building, Storrow shoved a twenty at the driver. Georgia followed him into the narrow, empty vestibule and watched as he searched for the keys. His hands slapped at his jacket pockets; his face was red; he yanked his blazer off.

"Are you all right?"

"No, I'm not. Before I met you I was, now I'm not." He found the keys in his pants pocket and, cursing, turned the lock.

"Sorry, but I'm not going upstairs with you like this."

He looked flustered, annoyed, like he was losing patience with a child. "Stop this. Get inside."

"No. I don't feel safe with you."

"*You* don't feel safe with *me*?" With a crash he threw the keys down onto the tile. "*You* push me into this affair. You reassure me, promise me, and now, after your carelessness puts me in danger, you act like you can't be bothered with it all. You risk my career, my peace of mind, and you say *you* don't feel safe?" He'd come to stand between Georgia and the exit; when she took a step, he raised his fist against the door and held it there.

"Let me out of here right now," she whispered, "or I will scream."

"Why?" his voice was rising. "What are you afraid I'll do to you? What can I do that's worse than what you've done to me?"

His arm blocked her way. She could see the muscles tense, pressing at the fabric of his neatly pressed shirt. His lips were pursed and bloodless.

"All right, calm down and we'll talk, okay? I'll come with you once you calm down." She waited for him to withdraw the arm that barred her in and then, when he bent to reach the keys from the floor, she darted past him out onto the street.

"Georgia. Come back. I'm sorry."

She heard him calling, not far behind her. She jogged ahead, reaching the corner. A taxi stopped before her and she hurried inside. The window to her door was open and Storrow stood leaning above it.

"I didn't mean to yell. I'm upset but not at you. Don't go; don't blow me off, not now."

His expression was gentle, at once boyish again, wounded, but she thought back to the image of him standing over her, minutes before, his knuckles against the door.

"Please, let's go," she told the driver and the car lurched forward, leaving Storrow panting at the curb.

The next time she encountered Storrow was a week later, at his office on the fourth floor of Robinson Hall. She'd come by late enough to slip in unseen: the receptionist was gone for the day; the other professors' office doors were closed. Only Storrow's was left open a sliver; he was seated inside, his back bent over his desk. He turned at her entrance and rose quickly to pull her inside. His hand lingered on her arm; he kissed her cheek, then hesitated, confused whether to chide her or embrace her.

"I know I'm not supposed to come here."

"It's fine, fine. I'm glad to see you." He studied her expression. For all his stiffness, Storrow wasn't without sensitivity. He must have seen she wasn't also happy to see him, that her need to come here wasn't motivated by desire. "Though, to be honest, now isn't the best time. I'm expecting a student at seven."

"I'll be quick."

He sighed and dropped into his chair. He stared ahead, at the thick piles of books and papers; the strain she'd sensed in him, and which, at times, had made her tender, now made her more certain of her decision.

"I tried calling you," he said. "To check you were okay."

"I am."

"And your friend? Anything from Alice?"

"Not a word about New York." Since returning to Georgia's, Alice had behaved as if nothing had happened, if not for her sake, Georgia thought, then out of self-interest; after all, until graduation, Alice was reliant on her hospitality.

"She probably didn't even see us." Storrow smiled dryly. "It was a fuss over nothing."

He seemed oddly serene on the subject, suddenly, Georgia remarked. "You were worried enough last week."

"Last week I was not myself." He leaned forward, to take her hand in his broad pale one. "I need you to understand; it was the stress that I've been facing."

"Really, you don't have to explain."

But Storrow insisted on it: "A bloody cabal against me: they drafted a letter, you believe this? To the head of my department. But to heck with them, what's the worst they can do, get me kicked out of here? So fine, I'll go; a few more weeks and we can *both* get out of here. This will all be behind me and I'll be different then, you'll see." He squeezed her hand and smiled brightly. "After graduation, it will be like a new beginning for us."

"After graduation? I have no idea where I'll be."

"You'll be in D.C. with me." Scooting his chair out, he pulled her close, against his knees. He'd been working on it, he said, a way for them to be together after she left school. This trouble with his students had made clear he wasn't suited for a university career; he had other, better options, in government and at law firms, among his many contacts in Washington. As for her, he'd put in a call to someone he knew at the National Gallery; she'd have to start in fund-raising, but from there, his friend claimed, she could move into acquisitions.

"You found a job for me?" She had no idea Storrow could prove so devoted, or so delusional.

"You don't have to take it," he put in, fearful, maybe, he'd overstepped. "There's plenty you can do there."

She didn't see herself in Washington, with or without him. She belonged among artists and musicians in a loft in DUMBO or a bungalow in Venice Beach.

"It's just a chance for a fresh scene. That's all we need, Georgia. I'm convinced of it."

She wasn't convinced in the least; on the contrary, the very circumstances Storrow blamed for their troubles were also the basis of her attraction: she couldn't envision them as an ordinary couple, not in D.C., not anywhere.

"I'm sorry," she told him, drawing away. "None of this is going to happen."

"Listen to me: you and I deserve a proper chance."

"We've had three months."

"Three mad months. I've never faced such hostility in all my life. It's been really more than I can take. After all that, I can't handle your leaving me, too. I'm serious. I can't." He sat with his hands clasped; his sinewy forearms were downed with those red hairs she'd found charming once. "I'm in love with you."

"Let's not . . . exaggerate."

"How can you speak—how can you treat me this way?" He rose sharply from the desk and took a few steps toward her. When she recoiled, he stepped back, palms up. There was a knock at the door.

"Professor Storrow?" A woman's voice.

Storrow closed his eyes. "Just a moment."

"It's all right; I should go." The interruption had come at precisely the right time. Georgia moved to the door, passing on her way out the petite Indian girl waiting in the hall. Julie Patel.

Storrow admitted her, then turned to address Georgia, his tone professorial. "I don't think we've quite finished yet. If you'll give me a minute or two."

He shut the door behind him; Georgia could hear his voice, muffled, on the other side. "I'm afraid you've caught me at a bad time."

"You're the one who called *me* here," Julie replied. "Though I don't see what good it can do; it's a bit too late to start apologizing."

"You think I called you to apologize? You think I'd stoop to that?"

After just seconds, Storrow was on the edge of shouting. Georgia had begun to walk away, but now she stepped back again, held by the tension of the exchange behind the door.

"Why would you be *stooping*?" Julie's tone was the same Georgia recalled from their meeting in Phillips Brooks House: gentle, feminine—and yet there was something dauntless behind those soft manners. "Am I so low to you or something?"

"Oh, it's all a trap with you—every word I say becomes a problem."

"Maybe because there *is* a problem. Maybe *you're* the problem, and I'm just pointing it out."

"You have no idea," Storrow snapped, "what sort of problem I can be."

A man appeared across the reception desk, another instructor locking up his office. He held the elevator for her and Georgia joined him, darting between the closing doors. Her heart was beating hard; she fixed the strap on her shoe so that the man wouldn't notice her frenzied excitement, then hurried out through the main door, jogging on toward Sever Gate. She felt the same wild relief she had years ago, setting off inside her father's car, leaving behind her latest hometown, the site of her last catastrophe. All she wanted then was distance from Storrow, to turn this man she'd been intimate with into a stranger again. What else should Rufus Storrow be? Not her boyfriend, not her friend, not her concern—nothing to her, finally, just some other girl's problem.

8

The visit took Charlie by surprise: professors didn't go showing up at students' homes, not even professors as sociable as Storrow. Yet here the man was, standing in the hallway of Eliot House, on an otherwise ordinary late April evening.

He knows I know, thought Charlie. At least Storrow had to be wondering if it was mere coincidence: Alice spotting him with Georgia in New York and Charlie's absence from his lectures ever since.

Skipping class was irresponsible, of course, a move bound to arouse Storrow's suspicion. If Alice found out, she'd be angry; she expected Charlie to maintain appearances. She'd made it very clear she didn't want Georgia, whose room she shared, learning what she'd told him, and so she'd put him in an impossible position: smarting from this betrayal, he couldn't confront the two people responsible, not Georgia and not Storrow, both of whom he'd been clumsily avoiding.

"Come on, son. Let me in."

Charlie hesitated at the door, peering at the room around him: its mismatched, thrift store furniture trimmed in empty soda cans and chip bags. If he'd known Storrow was coming, he'd have cleaned up and made a point of putting away the more juvenile items, Roger's mostly: the Smashing Pumpkins poster, those dopey pictures of his parents and his dog. He felt embarrassed in advance, then annoyed: *Storrow* was the one who ought to be ashamed, a man invading territory meant for a boy. Charlie hadn't realized how angry he was until this moment.

But as soon as he opened the door and looked Storrow in the face, he relented. The professor was pale, his eyes puffy and red. Pity and, even more, *curiosity* trumped indignation: Charlie stepped back and

Storrow crossed the room and took a seat on the cheap, lumpy sofa, ignoring the litter around him.

"I tried phoning first, but no one answered." Storrow sat forward, elbows on his knees. His navy jacket was rumpled, and there was a small wine stain beneath the collar of his shirt. The impossible seemed to be happening: Rufus Storrow—spotless even on the muddiest of days, a man who wrestled even with a sneeze, never yielding to impulse, whose meticulousness and self-control had fascinated Charlie—was unraveling.

No doubt the man was under pressure: from the first week of the spring semester, Storrow's class had inspired controversy. The subject was a touchy one—Law and the Colonial State—made more so by the fact that *he* was the instructor. A man in his position must show special sensitivity; he must know better than to repeat the sort of anecdotes that Storrow had from his time on the Indian continent: a description of his trip to the High Court of Bombay, a building of "colonial splendor," with thirty-two sitting judges and no one, apparently, to clean the toilets. On the subject of Pakistani law, he'd quoted one local with whom he'd discussed the phasing out of jury trials—*If your American peers were as stupid as ours, you'd hardly wish to be judged by them.*

One simply could not say such things—not in 1997, not at Harvard, in front of a classroom filled with men and women many of whose ancestors hailed from places other than London or Amsterdam or Zurich.

After class, students began to gather outside the room, in the corridors of Sever Hall, to voice their disapproval: just a few in the first month, but their numbers multiplied with Storrow's gaffes. By March, almost half the class stood whispering as Storrow nervously brushed by. The discussion moved to the lobby and then to the Quincy Junior Common Room, where a formal meeting was hosted by the student most critical of their professor: Julie Patel. Charlie didn't know her well. Julie was a fellow senior, serious, subdued: she'd sat quietly through Storrow's first lectures until, one afternoon, she'd objected to Storrow's suggestion that British common law was more advanced than the ancient Hindu law it had replaced.

Storrow had responded with an anecdote. Arguments for cultural relativism were hardly new, he'd told the class: Hindu priests had likewise criticized British authorities for banning their practice of *sati*—burning widows alive. "We British also have our customs," one commander had famously replied. "When men burn women, we hang them."

And what was the point of such a story? Julie had asked him. "Indian women should be grateful to Western men?"

"Not to men. If gratitude is due to anyone, it would be to the English Queen."

Storrow's cool response had earned him smiles from his admirers, but, in the long run, done him damage. In the days that followed, Julie claimed his remark expressed violence against her and all women of color—*if you were just going to bitch, Storrow had implied, we should have let you burn*. But Charlie believed Storrow never meant any such thing. Julie, he felt, was taking matters much too far. When she went further still and began to press for a formal complaint against Storrow, Charlie showed up to her meeting in Quincy to argue for lenience. So maybe their professor was a bit smug and tone deaf, poorly attuned to the subtleties of campus lingo, but that didn't make him the sort of brutal bigot Julie and her supporters made him out to be. There wasn't anything that Storrow said which others among his colleagues weren't thinking.

Before you go on record accusing him, just keep in mind, this is a career you could be ruining. A man's whole life.

He'd stood up for Storrow then, not only because Storrow had been good to him, but also because he sensed that behind such attacks stood a resentment of privilege—of the same sort displayed by his own father. Sure, Storrow had his faults, but if people were eager to go after him, it was because of his background, because—here was the irony—*they* were intolerant of *him*.

Well, they could string Storrow up for all Charlie cared now. He hadn't been to class for the last three meetings, not giving a damn what befell his former mentor. Nor was he moved to hear the man insisting from his sofa how he'd been fretting over Charlie's absence and what it might mean.

"I was worried you were sick."

"You can see I'm not."

"Look, I'm not here to catch you out. I'd hate to see you fall behind; you're a superior student and your grade ought to reflect that. Whatever the reason you've missed class, you can confide in me. I hold you in special regard, I think you know that; I consider you a sort of protégé, and more than that, a friend."

Charlie snorted.

Storrow ignored this. "Just make up what you've missed; bone up for a few days, take the test, and we'll get this squared away. Otherwise, if I don't penalize you, we could both get into trouble."

"Is that what you've come to talk about? *My* getting into trouble?"

Storrow looked down at his fingers, laced together over his knees. The knuckles were white from his tight grip.

He wants to ask but he's afraid. Afraid of what I know. Afraid of what I'll do.

"Are you going to stop seeing her?" Charlie demanded gruffly. He hadn't planned on confronting Storrow; it would come back to Georgia now, and then to Alice, that he'd failed to keep their secret. Well, so what? To hell with them: Why should he be false because they were all such liars? "Are you through with her? Just tell me."

"I'm going black here, Charlie. Going black." Storrow left off, unable to say more. His silence was empty: not a defeat for either of them, nor a victory. "You're angry and I don't blame you. I suppose I failed to live up to your idea of me."

An arrogant remark, Charlie thought, *and a stupid one*. Didn't Storrow realize he'd matched Charlie's ideal exactly? He'd gotten Georgia; he'd done precisely what Charlie wished to do.

"You might not believe me," Storrow continued, "but it hurts me a great deal to know I've disappointed you. You matter to me, and your opinion of me matters, too."

In fact Charlie *could* believe that. For a few lovely months, he and Storrow had shared a mutual desire to believe in Storrow's myth and in the existence of such grand and exclusive circles to which he belonged and to which Charlie was about to be admitted.

Now, seated across from Storrow in his own living room, Charlie saw him as unworthy of his veneration. For the first time, he saw Storrow, with his elegant looks and manners, the way his father saw the privileged summer renters on the Island, and he understood Jim Flournoy's refusal to consider such people—however educated or accomplished—nobler than himself. What was nobility, really? It wasn't behaving as if the whole world belonged to you; it was a demonstration of proper conduct and restraint, of not taking more than one was due.

Georgia had not been this man's to take.

"I want you to know," Storrow went on, sternly. "If you were to inform the administration, I wouldn't blame you. In your position, that's probably what I would do."

"So why don't you inform them then. In *your* position. Go ahead, do the *honorable* thing."

Storrow sighed, defeated. "You're right. I've been a smack, haven't I? I'll do as you say."

But truthfully, it wouldn't bring Charlie any satisfaction to see Storrow suffer.

"What I want is to forget this," he told Storrow, finally. He would return to class for the few sessions that remained; he would complete his assignments and finish the term without incident. All he asked from Storrow in exchange was to respect the boundaries: "Just stay away from Georgia Calvin and stay away from me."

Charlie appeared in class, as promised, and chose a seat in the back row beside Julie Patel. Storrow must have taken note of him, and of his new location in the room, but if he had, he didn't let it show. The man's attention remained fixed on the dais: he was reading from his lecture—a new approach: perhaps meant to prevent further inappropriate, off-the-cuff remarks.

Charlie glanced over at Julie. A button was open on her blouse, the lace of her bra peeking through. A pretty girl, sexy in her demure way, though he hadn't paid her much mind until then. To think she'd been in this classroom all semester and it hadn't occurred to him to ask her out. A campus full of young, attractive, clever women—he'd never be surrounded by such abundance again—and he'd wasted this chance, just wasted it, on Georgia. What was the sum of his college dalliances? A few awkward nights with the girl across the hall of Weld his freshman year and, in all the time since he'd met Georgia, nothing but one rushed revenge screw, after the junior formal, with a snub-nosed blonde from the *Salient*, an episode that had left him feeling guilty and regretful.

Georgia wasn't stupid: she must have surmised the reason he'd held himself apart from other women. She must have known it and chosen to ignore it. Had she once, while in bed with Storrow, given a moment's thought to him, felt a single pang of regret for what *she'd* done?

She hadn't, of course, and now only a month was left before graduation and all he could hope for was a hookup, to share in a last grab with others like him, seeking small compensation for experiences missed. He wondered if Julie might be among them, if she were also single and susceptible to a last orgiastic impulse.

Sleeping with Storrow's adversary—that might offer consolation. And why only sleep with Julie? Why not become involved with her, develop a commitment based on trust, a love founded in mutual respect? Julie was thoughtful, courageous, and responsible: with her he might have a relationship like Roger had with Jasmine, one far more adult than Georgia's with a man twice her age.

Childish creatures, both her and Storrow, Charlie had decided, because they'd both somehow belonged to *his* childish fantasy, creatures of a world dreamed up during Hamptons summers of some golden aristocracy. A bygone world, a narrow one and a boring one, besides—how flat in comparison to the actual, multifarious reality he'd been refusing to appreciate. On that day in Storrow's classroom, Julie Patel came to represent this new reality and all its possible allurements, all the beauty he'd failed to see that was everywhere around him, only waiting to be noticed by him to come, fully, to life.

9

The last morning of exams: students came rushing past, a nervous blur of bouncing ponytails and baseball caps. Alice looked on, squinting against the sun. She wasn't sure which exam she might be missing; she'd lost track of which papers were due when. The typed pages that she carried weren't meant for some professor's desk. She was headed to the office of the *Crimson*.

Her temples throbbed: too many cigarettes and cups of coffee, too little sleep; she'd caught maybe an hour between the time she'd finished writing and when she was awoken by Charlie's roommate—Robert, Roger, whatever the fuck his name was—his beard-trimmer buzzing in the bathroom at six. Unbearable, that guy, with his geriatric schedule, but she would have to bear him, and whatever other inconveniences she faced as Charlie's guest. Like it or not, she was stuck there until graduation: someone had to vouch for her with health services and there was no going back to Georgia's now. No going back to how things were. Not in a hundred ways.

A classmate was dead. Her life had been stopped short, and for those she'd left behind, events plunged forward all the more quickly.

Within hours of the murder, the news was everywhere, spread during the night via the victim's boyfriend, Lucas Parker, who'd been called in by police to identify the body. By dawn a group of twenty or so students had assembled on the Quincy green outside Stone Hall. Gerry had passed by on his return from a late night, so Alice had learned the first bare facts from him: Julie Patel, a fellow senior, had been murdered on campus around one a.m. that morning.

From then on, Alice kept up with every mention of the murder appearing anywhere: on the TV networks and in the papers, local and then national. Reports were sketchy in those first days; police weren't yet releasing details of the crime, out of concern for the investigation and for the grieving family, so they said. But by the following Wednesday, when the chief of police held a press conference, attended by reporters from Reuters and CNN, among others, a more thorough account of events was provided.

May 4 was a Sunday, the last day of reading period, the week preceding finals, and Julie Patel had spent the afternoon and evening, like many of her classmates, studying in Lamont. At seven, she was due to meet her boyfriend at his dining hall in Winthrop House; however, she called him just before to cancel, claiming, curtly, that she needed the time to study for a final in the morning.

At around 8:15 p.m., Julie Patel was next observed, by two students, exiting Adams House on Linden Street. Neither of these witnesses spoke with her, but one did note that she appeared distracted and upset. Her mood had apparently improved by the time she called her boyfriend again, around 8:45, to say that she'd finished her work and would be coming by Winthrop after all.

The last person to see Julie Patel alive was her boyfriend, who reported nothing unusual about her behavior that night, and who said good-bye to her outside his dorm around eleven. Julie was then heading back to her room in Quincy House, just around the corner, but it was on the northeast edge of Harvard Yard, between Robinson Hall and Memorial Church, that her body was discovered two hours later.

So far, the investigation hadn't determined any motive for Julie to have proceeded to this location; Robinson housed the History Department and was, according to the cleaning staff interviewed, otherwise deserted at that hour. Julie's roommates couldn't account for her detour, and there were no witnesses who'd observed Julie in the old Yard past sundown. One student, however, stepping out for a smoke by Sever Gate at half-past midnight, claimed to have noticed a slender white man in a dark suit walking out through the gate, head down. Neither this witness, nor any other, reported seeing or hearing anything else remarkable that night—not an argument, not a single scream—until, at one a.m., a member of the Harvard Police Department came upon Julie's corpse.

The homicide, police determined, resembled a professional execution more than a simple street crime. There was no evidence of a struggle or of sexual assault or robbery: Julie Patel was found fully dressed, in a corduroy skirt and button-down blouse. Her backpack, left behind with her, contained twenty-seven dollars. A gold necklace, a present from her boyfriend, remained hanging from her broken neck.

Experts determined the cause of death was asphyxia. The break was neat; the attacker had come from behind and employed a technique likely taught in military training. None of the assailant's DNA was discovered on the body; no traces—not a footprint—were left by him at the scene. It seemed whoever had done this was also familiar with forensics methods.

Based upon these facts, the chief investigator had issued an announcement, on the morning of May 6, that the department was focusing its attention on a certain Law and History professor, a man with a military education and an acquaintance with the victim. The suspect wasn't named, but Alice wasn't the only one to recognize Storrow's description.

The *Crimson*'s office was on Plympton Street, less than a block from Quincy House. Plympton was quiet now; just a few students trickled from New Quincy and Stone Hall where, in the week since the murder, crowds had stood gaping at news vans. Sometimes two or three vans had been parked there at a time, and Alice had been among those listening in as reporters questioned passing students. The day after Storrow's picture ran in the papers, one local reporter managed to get hold of Lucas Parker, a neat boy with even features, attractive in a sexless way. The sort of boyfriend, Alice thought, who must have been sick with guilt after his first timid fumbling down Julie's pants—*Can I? Is it okay?* The sort who stood as further proof of Julie's virtue—that virtue which everyone seemed so eager to establish—*Julie had so many friends; she volunteered!* As if the real tragedy was that Julie Patel was lying dead and not someone a bit less nice and inclined to public service, someone who could lie and cheat and fuck.

"Julie was just this amazingly good person," Lucas had announced before the cameras. "She stood up for what she felt was right; she wouldn't be intimidated—which was what Professor Storrow tried to do. Julie was the only one who saw him for what he was: a racist and a bully. In the end, I got the sense she was even a little afraid of him. But she wouldn't let that stop her; and I mean she couldn't have thought—how could anybody think that this . . . something like this . . . ?"

The reporter—tan brunette, shining orange in her makeup—patted the boy's shoulder as he left off, his voice strained by the effort not to cry.

Inarticulate, confused, pitiable—the way Lucas appeared that afternoon was how a man *ought* to seem under such circumstances. Had Storrow managed a similar performance, Alice believed, he might not be facing the mess that he was now.

Storrow's *60 Minutes* interview had aired four days after the segment with Lucas made the rounds of weekday news shows. Alice had watched it that Sunday night, alongside a small group of mostly Adams seniors who'd assembled for the event at Gerry's. The interview was staged in Storrow's office. Seated at his desk, spiffy in his navy suit and checkered shirt, the man exuded a false freshness: only someone truly dirty would contrive to look so clean.

Julie had been his student, nothing more, Storrow insisted. They'd had a few lively debates in class, but he'd always appreciated her intelligence and verve. In words that seemed rehearsed, Storrow went on to address each of the reporter's queries: yes, Julie had threatened to make a formal complaint about him, but ultimately, she had not. An understanding had been reached between them; the calls that had been discovered by then, from Julie's dorm room to his office and spanning the last month, were a part of these efforts at reconciliation.

The last he'd had any contact with Julie was in class as usual, said Storrow, ten days before her death. He couldn't comment on reports of her leaving Adams House on the night that she was killed; he certainly hadn't crossed paths with her, not there at seven and not later, either, outside Robinson Hall. Whatever conservatively dressed white male had allegedly been spotted near the murder scene, it wasn't him—surely he wasn't the *only* man at Harvard to fit that broad description. As for his keeping an office in Robinson, he only used it to meet students and preferred to do his solitary work at home. That was where he'd been the night of Julie's death, his only company the draft of the final exam he was preparing.

Storrow had concluded his remarks by quoting the Harvard motto—*Veritas*—as if he hadn't yet come off as pretentious enough. *Truth,* he'd told the interviewer, *truth will prevail.*

Alice could have forgiven him his lies—petty stuff, considering—but not that colossal arrogance. Watching Storrow on TV, she'd been reminded of her own meeting with him inside that same Robinson Hall office; a few days after she'd caught him with Georgia in New York, he'd called her in for a private conversation.

"You've missed some work recently, Ms. Kovac, and I've been informed you may not graduate with the rest of your class. That seems a shame. You were a member of Adams House once, and I'd like to advocate on your behalf; I understand that you've been sick."

Storrow had addressed her as a concerned housemaster, merely, showing no signs of culpability, making no reference at all to the real reason she was there, to *his* misdeeds. Whatever nasty ideas she'd contrived about him were *her* invention, his tone made clear: symptoms of *her* sickness, which he, in his munificence, was prepared to pardon.

That afternoon, she'd looked across at Storrow, at his proud, immaculate features and depthless gaze, and felt as if this man was every man she'd ever hated. He was Torsten; he was Vasily; he was every brutal narcissist who lived to impress his distortions of reality upon souls weaker than his own—which Storrow had, misguidedly, taken hers to be.

A red door led to the offices of the *Harvard Crimson.* Alice stepped inside, jiggling the lock that had never quite worked; pizza boxes and old issues were strewn around the newsroom, and each desk was occupied. Most editorial staff were in already; many had no doubt stayed the night.

The editor in chief was upstairs, hunched up in a leather chair stained with newsprint and beer; he was drinking black coffee from a beer stein and reading over copy. Alice knew him only slightly; she hadn't written much for the *Crimson* since the start of junior year, and she had never been involved in the politics or weighed in on the election that had earned him his post. He raised a finger and went on reading, caught up in his own importance at this moment—*this* being possibly the biggest story he would ever oversee. Alice pulled another chair across from his, and sat down, awaiting the moment he would notice the pages she'd placed between them, on her knees.

Not one among the professional journalists out there had anything like she had on Storrow: those that mentioned his argument with Julie attributed it to cultural insensitivity, a consequence of the man's conservative upbringing. Storrow was either described through institutions and accolades—West Point Cadet, Rhodes Scholar, Bronze Star Medal winner—or with recourse to a few oft-recycled adjectives—"disciplined," "aloof." This was as far as anyone had probed into the man, all everyone but Alice seemed prepared to let him be.

10

Ms. Kent was Mather House's senior tutor: a pear-shaped, short, dark blonde with a gap between her top front teeth. Her smile was wide, overly friendly; until now Georgia had met the woman only publicly, at Mather House functions.

"I want to thank you for coming in." Touching Georgia lightly on the back, Ms. Kent guided her inside her tidy, book-lined office. "I wasn't sure you'd be up for meeting me today."

"Today?" What was today? For her, it had been a day exactly like the one before it, and like the one before that. Since she'd been questioned by police on Friday, Georgia hadn't left her apartment but once, for the nearest grocery to buy bread and sleeping pills, nor had she spoken to anyone except her parents.

At first she'd just confessed her situation to her father, less prone to judge her than her mother. But the madness of those days soon left her craving her mother's cool, practical advice. "I'm getting you a lawyer now," her mother promised; meanwhile her father vowed to catch the next flight to Boston. He was supposed to reach the campus later that afternoon.

"I looked for you at the vigil this morning." Ms. Kent took her seat behind the desk. She was wearing a black dress; chalk smudges showed around her elbows.

"I haven't really been following . . ."

Ms. Kent gripped her hands together and made a perch for her chin; she was watching Georgia, thoughtfully. "I'm sure that's best, keeping distance. Press was there. Bit of a circus, honestly. I don't know if you heard, Professor Storrow chose to make an appearance."

The reference to Storrow startled her. Of course, she reminded herself, Storrow was in the news now, his name—along with Julie Patel's—must be on everybody's lips. If Ms. Kent happened to mention him, that didn't mean Georgia's fears were realized: that officer Lombardi had notified the school of her affair.

After all, there were other reasons Ms. Kent might have called her in this afternoon: she'd missed two exams; she hadn't turned in final papers or been answering her phone. Likely the school was on alert, following up with anybody whose behavior was affected since the murder. It wouldn't do to have students breaking down, especially not during finals; no one wanted outraged parents, more bad press. This was Harvard: a cautious and thorough institution.

"Georgia, I want you to rest assured: you're not in any trouble. You've been a fine student and you have the full support from your dean and your professors. No one wants your academic record to be affected or your future to suffer. No one blames you. You're also a victim in this case."

"How am I a victim?"

"He was the adult, after all . . ." Ms. Kent left off, alarmed. "You *do* know why I called you in? I was sure someone had shown you." Her stubby finger tapped on a newspaper on the desk.

There was a picture on the cover page, but it took Georgia a moment to recognize what she was seeing upside down: her image from the student directory, her friend's name at the byline: Alice Kovac.

The last she'd heard from Alice was before the murder; returning home from a party, Sunday night, Georgia had found Alice's drawers emptied, the girl and her belongings gone. A curious exit, but Alice had been acting strangely since her hospitalization, if not before, since meeting Torsten. Probably Alice had gone back to him, sneaking off, without warning, to avoid having to hear what a huge mistake this was. Under ordinary circumstances, Georgia would have tried to track her down, or informed the psychiatric resident that she was missing, but the next days had been anything but ordinary.

The pages of the *Crimson* were crumpled from her grasp; she'd clutched them tightly on her way, resisting the urge to stop and read on the Mather quad or stairwell, awaiting the privacy of her own room before she dared confront the damage that Alice had done. All around her, on her tabletops and sofa, lay manila folders containing notes for exams and drafts of papers: everything was almost exactly as it had been before the news of violence had yanked her out of her routine. She settled down with the *Crimson* on the floor.

> *Police are now inquiring into a pattern of sexual misconduct involving Professor Storrow and several female students, among them senior Georgia Calvin . . . Calvin, it seems, was not the only undergraduate toward whom Storrow made advances: "A second student, who preferred to remain nameless, alleged she'd also had a sexual encounter with the man."*
>
> *According to the chief investigating officer, Joseph Lombardi, "Certain facts revealed by the investigation calls to Storrow's office, vague excuses made by Julie to her boyfriend, a personal animus in her complaints against Storrow all of these details, taken together, could suggest either an affair or its aftermath."*
>
> *Police have yet to establish a sexual motive regarding Ms. Patel, or to charge Professor Storrow in connection with her death. Still, there will be consequences if these allegations of sexual misconduct are confirmed: at the least, Professor Storrow will lose the right to insist with indignation on his innocence, even if, on the greater charge of murder, the law falls short of establishing his guilt.*

The phone was ringing. A male voice—not, as she'd hoped, her father's—began to speak through the answering machine: "Murphy again, from the *Globe*. If you could spare a moment, just to comment on these statements."

Georgia stood and climbed the stairs to her bedroom; she pulled a suitcase from the closet and shoved her clothes haphazardly inside. The clock on her bedside table read two thirty; her father's flight ought to have landed. She hoped that at this moment he was speeding toward her, down the highway; when he arrived, she'd crawl into the rental car beside him and ask him to drive, as far and as fast as possible.

Just a few more hours, she told herself, and she'd leave it all behind: the course work she'd never finished and didn't give a damn for now; the so-called friends who clearly didn't give a damn for her—Charlie, who still wouldn't speak to her, and Alice, who'd proven more devious than even Georgia, who'd believed she could handle the hazards of their friendship, could have guessed. A few more hours and she'd have them all relegated to her rearview: the reporters and the gossips, the meddlers both malicious and benign, like Ms. Kent.

You're also a victim in this case . . .

A victim how exactly? Unharmed and unhindered, she was escaping once again, into a future that remained as blessed as before. She could have everything she wanted: adventure, a grand career, marriage, children. She could be rich; she could be envied, she could die old, painlessly, surrounded by her comforts.

It was Julie Patel who would never have these things. Julie, with her prim clothes and fussy braid, whose memory for Georgia would always be the lecture she'd offered her following the Fogg Museum incident, inside a stuffy room of Phillips Brooks House, a place that smelled of cheap food and crayons and ammonia and virtue.

Violence just has no place in what I do, Georgia. I don't want ugliness; I don't want scandals.

Responsible, decent Julie Patel, whom Georgia had scarcely known and mostly scorned; a young woman utterly unsuited to the horror that befell her, more worthy of a bright future like hers, Georgia thought, than she'd ever let herself pretend to be.

The phone began to ring again; Georgia dragged her suitcase down the stairs, toward the front door, past the answering machine.

"Sorry if I'm disturbing you, Miss Calvin, I'm with the *Boston Herald* . . ."

She yanked the phone cord from the wall.

11

A breezy, cloudless morning in May and Harvard was going forward with graduation ceremonies. At Tercentenary Theatre the scene was as it had been for decades: crimson banners, hundreds of folding chairs in rows across the lawn. Johnston Gate was open for the academic parade, and a stage was set out on the steps of Memorial Church, from which the university president would confer degrees en masse before the students dispersed to their residential houses to receive their individual diplomas.

The afternoon program had been altered only slightly on account of the recent tragedy. In Adams House, there would be no master to assist the senior tutor in the proceedings and, on the Old Yard, there was to be a special evening program for Julie Patel's family and friends and any others who wished to view the new memorial and pay their respects.

For the rest, the many thousand family members come to witness this proud day, they were determined to have their pleasure untainted: they'd paid their fortunes and were entitled to shed only happy tears at seeing their grown sons and daughters honored in a grand setting. The students, too, had spent the night before as they'd earned the right to do, enjoying, first, some solemn admiration from mom and dad over expensive dinners, and then escaping early for a final night of revels at the dozens of parties spilling out onto lawns and rooftops in and around campus.

Charlie had joined his classmates, staying out till dawn; at six he'd been woken by the noise of bagpipes. Alice slept on, in Charlie's bed, while he and Roger dressed in their suits and set off for their last Eliot House breakfast. After the meal, replete with bowls of strawberries and bottles of champagne, Charlie stopped back in to check on Alice. Her two suitcases stood, packed, inside the entrance; she'd left without a word about her plans. Possibly she'd gone to Adams House, to proceed to the Yard with her former housemates; possibly he'd see her at morning exercises or the luncheon that followed—or as likely not—Alice tended to skip meals, and was no keener on ceremony.

It surprised Charlie to find that, on this particularly wistful morning, he was craving Alice's company, which he'd frankly only endured these last few years for Georgia's sake. When Alice had shown up at his door, two weeks earlier, he hadn't exactly welcomed her arrival. He'd been drinking that night—Roger on his back about this change in his habits: *You used to find even the smell of alcohol depressing.* He still did, but a few shots of Jim Beam at bedtime helped him fall asleep; he'd just begun to doze when Alice woke him with her knocking.

"I'm going to have to stay with you now," she'd announced, not asking permission, as if they'd both known such a moment had to come. Eventually Georgia would surmise the cause of Charlie's coldness; she'd guess that Alice must have told him about Storrow.

"You had a fight? She threw you out?" *Something* had obviously happened; Alice was agitated, and her cheeks were flushed, her black eyes bright.

"I just need to sleep right now, okay?"

He'd agreed, yielding his bed, and intending to broach the matter again in the morning. But the events of the next day had rendered such details inconsequential. Charlie had woken around ten, surprised to find himself sprawled on the sofa, and then Alice in the kitchen speaking on the phone with Gerry: she'd been the one to let Charlie know that Julie Patel was dead.

A week later, Alice's article ran in the *Crimson* and there hadn't been peace in the room since. The phone rang day and night; angry Eliot dorm mates complained that Alice had no right to be there and even Roger, who'd been patient with her until then, wanted Alice gone, out of respect for his girlfriend's wishes. Jasmine had been friends with Julie Patel and was appalled by what Alice had implied about her in her story: "As if anybody who actually knew Julie," Jasmine claimed, "could believe she'd cheat on Lucas." Around that time, Julie's boyfriend showed up on the lawn below Charlie's room; Charlie hadn't even known Julie *had* a boyfriend until he'd seen the kid railing against Storrow on the TV news: Lucas Parker, a boy whom Charlie was acquainted with vaguely from an econ lecture sophomore year.

Let me in, man, Lucas had called to him, trying to keep his tone calm, though Charlie could see from how the boy couldn't stop moving that he was worked up, in a rage. *You don't need to defend that bitch.*

No, he didn't, it was true: nor could Charlie endorse what Alice had done: and yet, while keeping her as his guest, he'd felt some protective instinct had been triggered. More than that, a part of him was relieved that she'd announced what they both knew: she'd exposed Storrow's guilt and, in the process, exposed Georgia as well.

While Lucas stood on the grass, cursing, Charlie went into his bedroom to check if Alice was all right.

"I can call campus security, but they might wonder why you're here."

Alice was in his bed, reading a magazine, dressed in the tights and cropped hoodie she'd been wearing both to sleep and on her brief forays out. She stood then and came to stand before the window, where Lucas could see her and address his insults directly to her.

"Lying, vicious, cunty bitch . . ."

She let him shout, while others in Eliot shouted back at him, until two large boys from down the hall came down to draw Lucas away. Then Alice closed the window and returned to the room that she'd made hers, to climb back into bed.

Don't take off without saying good-bye.

Charlie left the note for Alice on the largest of her bags, then he descended to join the raucous crowd out on the lawn. Residents of Eliot and Lowell Houses were already lining up together, according to house tradition, for the procession to the Yard. Charlie took his place among them, locking arms, whistling and singing like the rest, doing his best to appear cheerful. Inside the Yard he doffed his cap to the statue of John Harvard and bowed deeply to the alumni escorts dressed up in tails and top hats. On the march to his seat, he waved at Roger's parents as if they were his own. Mrs. Waldman was squealing with excitement, hair like a poodle's; Mr. Waldman, stooped and balding, remarkably like his son, stepped forward to hug both boys in turn, taking pride in Charlie in his father's stead.

Though they had been in town since yesterday, the Flournoys were nowhere to be seen. Maybe it was just too much for them, thought Charlie, which was fine, better for everyone if they didn't show at all today. Certainly he hadn't urged his family to attend graduation, but if they felt obliged to come, he refused to be bothered by anything his father or brother did. If they arrived late, or deliberately underdressed or talked too loud and put off the other guests, he was prepared to ignore it all, as he'd ignored their misbehavior at the restaurant where they'd dined the night before.

Months in advance, he'd booked a table at Harvest, one of the best restaurants in Harvard Square. He'd made the evening out to be a gift, though, admittedly, it wasn't for his family so much as for himself. On this, his celebratory evening, he didn't feel like wolfing down a burger somewhere because his parents hadn't made any arrangements. For once, he didn't feel like pretending he demanded less from life than he was able to take from it, and he didn't care if his family viewed this as a reproach, as one more reminder of the distance their son had moved beyond them.

Both his father and his brother had sat sullen at the table. Only Charlie's mother was able to express satisfaction at being taken to a proper restaurant.

"Can I order anything, really? It all looks so good."

"Just order, Margaret," his father grumbled. When his entrée arrived, he refused to eat more than a few bites of his steak—the sauce was off—and he nearly lost his temper when the waiter explained the dish was meant to taste that way.

"So now you mean to school me?"

Charlie's mother changed the subject to dessert: "I think I saw someone eating cheesecake. Should we order some of that?" She seemed to be asking Charlie's permission now, as he'd once asked his father's at Howard Johnson's, hoping for a hot-fudge sundae or a slice of apple pie.

"Everyone get what you like," Charlie offered, but his father and his brother balled up their napkins and tossed them on the table.

"We're full up, Chief," his brother said.

On their way out, after Charlie had left the abused waiter a large cash tip, he noticed Luke slipping the money into his jacket pocket. *Perfect*, he thought; at least he had no lingering illusions what sort of man his brother was: the generous and dazzling figure of his boyhood had clearly been his own youthful invention. Every younger brother made a hero of the older at some point and he'd been especially prone to hero worship. But Storrow had rid him of that particular condition.

The hard lessons of the spring had forced Charlie to do some quick growing up. He was through wavering, as he had been, about what to do after graduation—whether to start work or continue his studies, whether to stay east or go west—waiting for Georgia to figure out her plans. Now it struck him as ridiculous that he'd ever thought to compromise his professional future based on the whims of a girl. The path he'd settled on was the one that he believed would offer him the most success most quickly; he was enrolling in Columbia's MBA program and, from there, he'd be poised to take full advantage of the boom economy, to join the growing numbers of twentysomething CEOs.

That evening, Charlie walked out of Harvest belly full, unrepentant: from here on, Charles Flournoy was letting no one and nothing stand in the way of his achievement; if that should cause his father or his brother pain, then pile it onto the several tragedies to emerge from Harvard Yard in the spring of '97.

The Flournoys did turn up for commencement, finally, arriving at Eliot House for the midday ceremonies, albeit twenty minutes late. The first of the young men and women were already being called up to receive their diplomas—"Burnheart . . . Cahill . . ."—robed students marched forward, while the Flournoys piled into the seats Charlie had saved. His father sat on the aisle, his mother beside Charlie, her expression flustered and contrite, her dress spilling off her seat, a floral print with shoulder pads. Her eyes were hazy; she was in shock, he could see it, at the wealth and scale of the campus. Only now, when Charlie was leaving, had it dawned on her exactly where her son had spent the last four years.

More names were called; parents cheered. Charlie's mother squeezed his hand in her moist one and dabbed her eyes with her sleeve. From time to time, she muttered under her breath. He could imagine the blur of associations she must be bringing to these elegant buildings, the green courtyard, and the iconic white bell tower. Here was a setting for grand romances and elevated musings, for an enchanted life like she'd never experienced. Her tears, he suspected, were mostly for herself.

He remained dry-eyed and steely; two weeks from twenty-one, he was already a grown man, making his own money, deciding his own future. He felt at a remove from his classmates, many of whom sat clutching their parents' hands, daunted by the prospect of years ahead without the protections they'd hitherto enjoyed; some, already nostalgic, sensed that their time in this place—their excitements, intellectual and sexual, the depth of their discoveries and the lightness of their responsibilities—would not be equaled again.

Not him. The last weeks had spared him such sticky sentimentality. Harvard was over for him; he was ready to get out.

When his name was called, Charlie stood up and took the short walk down the aisle. He accepted the tutor's handshake and his diploma without looking back to see if his father or brother were among those applauding.

Charlie hadn't planned to stop in on the ceremony for Julie Patel, but after the Eliot House luncheon, and the president's and class speaker's addresses, his father complained of feeling tired; he wanted to sit somewhere quiet and get a drink. Charlie announced he would catch up with his family later, and then he left for the Old Yard.

Press circled, but no reporters had been let inside the gates. University police checked his ID. Several hundred people were gathered on the green, alongside Holworthy Hall, the dorm where Julie had resided freshman year. A small podium had been erected near the street exit, in front of Bradstreet Gate, the newest addition to the yard. Next fall that gate would be commemorated in honor of the twenty-fifth anniversary of women living on these grounds. Until then, it was to be kept closed. But this afternoon it stood wide open; a small square of white cloth covered what must be Julie's memorial, now installed on one of the gate's brick columns.

Charlie kept to the back of the crowd, studying the faces; he hadn't come to look for Georgia, though their most recent exchange seemed too sour to be their last. During those first weeks he'd avoided her she'd left him messages, which he'd ignored; but after Alice's article, the news of her and Storrow, Georgia had stopped phoning. He hadn't even been sure she was in town until, by chance one night, exiting the Star Market in Central Square, he'd spotted her waiting in the parking lot, seated inside a parked car. When she saw him, she stepped out; she was underdressed for the cool May evening, her bare arms wrapped around her body.

He'd had the impulse to offer her his coat, but resisted.

"My father's shopping for me," she'd explained: "So I don't have to be seen. I've been staying in New York; just came back for graduation. My mom insisted."

It was more information than he needed; he no longer wished to be a witness to the details of Georgia Calvin's life. "It's good you have him to help you get through this." *Him*, he wished for her to hear: *your dad, some other man, anyone but me.*

Georgia watched him; her eyes narrowed. "And I guess Alice has *you*."

She'd been the one to end their exchange that night, returning to her father's car, and leaving Charlie to head alone down Green Street, loaded with bags too heavy for the long trek home.

Well, if he hadn't come to the Old Yard this afternoon to see Georgia, still he couldn't claim that he was shocked to find her there. She was lingering at the opposite edge of the crowd, hiding behind her hair and leaning upon her father's arm. Georgia's mother was there too; this was the first Charlie had seen her: a sturdy, attractive woman dressed in tan. Georgia's father he knew well enough for the man to offer him a wave, but Georgia must have cautioned him; briskly Mr. Calvin swiveled, leading his daughter off in the opposite direction.

The university president began speaking, explaining the choice to remember Julie here, at this newest entrance to the Yard: "a passage that stands in honor of the brilliant young women who have enriched this campus and who represent the future of this university, women like Julie Patel.

"Julie didn't come from privilege; she made the most of her talents, without ever letting her personal ambitions stand in the way of her concern for others. Each and every day she graced this campus, Julie helped us to remember what the soul of this institution is: an ideal of scholarship, humanity, and progress."

Politics, thought Charlie, politics and bullshit; the president is using even this opportunity to flatter his institution. If Julie was the soul of Harvard, what, then, was Storrow?

From the first mention of Storrow in the papers, Charlie had kept informed of everything that befell his former mentor (there was really nothing more that he could do, he told himself, even if he had been inclined—and he hadn't—to offer Storrow support or come to his defense). Alice's article had resulted in Storrow's official suspension from his position as housemaster, but in fact he'd already been urged to absent himself from campus. The president had expressed his concern that Storrow's presence would be a distraction to the students during finals week, which was *not* to say, he made clear in his statements to the papers, that anyone presumed his guilt in Julie Patel's death. Still, it was critical at such a time to recall one's duty to the students, to minimize the trauma caused by these events.

Obligingly, Storrow had vanished: a proctor had administered the final for his class. But on the day exams were returned, Storrow had made a last appearance in Sever Hall; he'd dropped the stack of blue books off at the history office and then proceeded to his former classroom with a bouquet of white lilies. Several students, Charlie among them, had looked on from the doorway as Storrow laid the flowers at the desk where Julie once sat. In fact, he'd been off by a seat, but no one was going to tell this to the man who staggered, glazed eyed, out of the room.

Already, Storrow must have known he was a condemned man: his office and home had been combed through over and over again. These searches had all turned up empty, but no matter: it was surmised that a man of Storrow's intelligence and military background could have removed any incriminating evidence ahead of time. The very lack of evidence, more paranoid voices rumored, was all the more proof of his guilt. Without DNA from the attacker recovered from the crime scene, it seemed Storrow would be neither convicted nor cleared; he was either fantastically lucky, or hopelessly ill-fated.

And then there were his public appearances. His first had been unplanned; a reporter had caught him walking hurriedly down Dunster Street on Tuesday night, two days after Julie's murder, the same day Storrow's name and photo made the papers. Caught off guard, possibly drunk, he'd struggled to account for his being on campus: he'd merely stepped out to get air and hadn't noticed where he was. He wasn't looking for anything or anyone, just trying to find some space alone. All he wanted was to be left *the hell alone.*

Exasperated, he'd raised his voice at the reporter, and under the harsh camera lights, his eyes looked bloodshot, his skin white with angry splotches of red; he'd come off as menacing, unstable.

The next time Storrow showed himself on TV it was carefully arranged: a *60 Minutes* interview on Sunday, a week after Julie's death. It seemed Storrow meant to correct his previous impression: he'd combed his hair and shaved, applied Visine to his eyes, used any tricks at his disposal to resemble more or less a tenser version of the neat, dashing figure who'd so impressed Charlie at their first meeting. His remarks had been prepared: he would not let his sentences falter; he would not lose his train of thought.

His performance was flawless, and the results had been disastrous. If Charlie hadn't known Storrow before, he too might have thought what tens of thousands of American viewers must be thinking: this is the face of a stone-cold killer.

But he *had* known Storrow, at least he liked to think so. Even Georgia likely hadn't observed the details of Storrow's nature as Charlie had. Where others saw severity, he saw adherence to a code of personal integrity. A man so upstanding could have nothing to do with the violence the papers had described. During the day, Charlie was certain of it; only at night, lying in bed, he'd find himself with a different, yet equally vivid and convincing picture of Storrow in his mind—those strong arms with their red-blond curls, hooked around a fragile neck.

Across the Yard, Georgia was standing with her head upon her father's shoulder. Mr. Calvin was nearing fifty, but he remained vain and virile, with his dark blond beard and long legs in tight jeans. Of course, thought Charlie, he should have foreseen long ago how things would end for Georgia: running off with Daddy once again.

In a few hours, he imagined, she'd get into her father's car and start the drive to wherever she was moving. These might be the last images he had of her, and so, despite himself, Charlie gathered them up like photographs untaken: golden hair, black cap in her hand, white sandals that laced up the back of her brown calves.

From a distance Charlie watched Georgia view the memorial, the white cloth now removed, and leave the yard beside her father; then he took his own place on the line. A plain bronze square, with Julie's name, stood at the left of the gate; Charlie paused before it briefly, then stepped out onto Cambridge Street. Up ahead, twenty feet or so from the Bradstreet exit, stood a young woman. She was dressed in black, her hair slicked back; her robe and cap lay on the ground. Alice.

Understandably, Alice hadn't dared to join the ceremonies, but it seemed she couldn't quite stay away either; maybe it was more than curiosity that had lured her. Maybe she'd wished to pay respects or felt genuine regret for what she'd written. Charlie never assumed he had access to what Alice was thinking. Always she kept some secret for herself, some corner of her mind to curl up into, even while she shared the space under his roof.

"Gerry's driving me into the city," she said. "Supposed to pick me up here." As if that explained her presence in this spot. "We'll swing by Eliot, grab my bags. If you're not there, I'll leave the key under the door."

This was good-bye then, Charlie thought, though neither of them chose to say it. He preferred to believe it wasn't really, that he would see Alice again, in Manhattan, where he would soon begin his studies and she would launch her magazine career. Along with the abuse she'd received for her writing came plenty of attention and more than a few job offers.

Such willingness to benefit from others' suffering was, according to Roger, Jasmine, and almost anyone Charlie spoke to about Alice, further proof she had no conscience. Maybe so, but Charlie had come to admire Alice's toughness. Pity, regret, longing—some of his once-favorite emotions—simply had no hold on Alice and, thanks to her influence, had lost some of their power, also, over him. Fine for lovelorn boys and poets, but of no use—Alice alone helped to remind him—to the man Charlie Flournoy was setting out into this world to become.

PART II

12

No breaks between, no year abroad to muse and booze and bumble: from college, Charlie moved on to business school and then straight into his first job. The new millennium was here, and these were thrilling times for a fresh MBA keen on success. Start-ups were forming daily; venture capital firms that had declined in the 1980s were rising again, stronger than ever, and Charlie was in a hurry to get working and to establish the sort of accomplished, adult Manhattan life he'd always aspired to have.

His apartment made him proud each time he crossed its threshold: a one-bedroom rental on Riverside Drive with high ceilings and hardwood floors and a view of the Hudson. While most of the young bachelors he knew were drawn to trendy lofts downtown, to the company of models and Eurotrash and streets crowded with bars, the past two years had taught Charlie to appreciate Morningside Heights. The domain of the good students was how he thought of it—decent, rational, hardworking people who earned advanced degrees and married campus sweethearts and were already saving for their infants' educations. Each morning, Charlie walked to the subway alongside pretty mothers on their way to Pilates, and he returned each evening among fathers who were equally at ease reading *Barron's* as they were *Winnie-the-Pooh*.

There was nowhere else he wished to be, he told himself—and told his friends, as well, whenever one of his business school pals tried to induce him to move out west. Silicon Valley was where the truly fantastic entrepreneurial feats were taking place, where it seemed any kid with a dream could stick a "dot-com" at the end of it and own a company worth millions. Such things did happen, though far less often than the Bay Area advocates made out. In any case, Charlie didn't feel he could afford to put in months or years on speculative projects, nor could he cash in options on hypothetical IPOs when his student loan payments were due. He had debts, substantial and pressing, which required him to find some sort of salaried employment.

When he'd been hired, just out of school, by Warren Welch Equity, he'd considered himself lucky. VC jobs were hard to come by anywhere, and in Manhattan, they were almost unheard of; at Warren Welch he could survey the field of start-ups on both coasts and do it while collecting a steady paycheck and maintaining his Upper West Side apartment. Moreover, he could justify taking a safer career path on the basis of numbers: out of the thousand-plus business proposals he and the other young hires reviewed in his first year, each passed about fifty up the chain so that Welch and his partners could finally invest in, precisely, four.

Three of the chosen four that year proved to be Charlie's recommendations; from then on, Terrance Welch began approaching Charlie for his opinion rather frequently. In April of 2001, Welch made a formal proposition that Charlie work exclusively with him. "You'll research only my projects; you'll be my guy now."

"It would be a privilege, sir."

Welch, as Charlie saw it, was the real brains of the firm: he'd launched and sold four companies by the age of forty-eight. In their interactions, Welch had always been decent with him, though it was true he had a reputation for egomania.

Only after he'd accepted the offer did Charlie realize what sort of servitude he'd signed on for. Welch would call him up at any hour, any day, usually from an unknown or blocked number, to send him searching for some information on his desk—not because Welch actually needed it, Charlie was sure, but just to confirm that Charlie was in the office as he claimed to be.

There was no excuse for missing work: not religion, not family, not illness and not, certainly not, a toothache, like the one Charlie suffered from most of that next July. As a result, he neglected the problem for so long that he developed an abscess and then sepsis. He had to be hospitalized for five days and made to rest another five, during which time his main concern was whether his job would still be waiting for him when he returned.

To make up the lost time, he canceled the vacation he'd been planning with some business school buddies in the Hamptons and spent all of August, while his colleagues were baking on the beach and boiling lobsters, stuck behind his desk.

Monday evening, Labor Day, he received a call from an old friend: Udi Epstein, his roommate for his first year at business school.

Hyperactive, foulmouthed, and conceited, Udi had managed to alienate most of his teachers and fellow students in the one year he attended Columbia, but Charlie had always liked him and never doubted his brilliance. Udi had grown up in Israel, on a moshav, with little interest in the farm life he was born to, or in much of anything besides his big sister's computer. By fifteen he was such an able hacker that the Israeli army had gotten wind of him; they'd offered him a position in intelligence and employed him from the age of eighteen to twenty-three, working with some of their most advanced computer systems. From the IDF, he'd moved on to pursue studies in computer science at the Technion, the most prestigious science university in Israel, but hands-on engagement suited him much better than the classroom. He claimed he'd enrolled for his American MBA merely to improve his communication skills, but he'd given up on those efforts after a year and skipped off to Palo Alto to take a job with a place called Cardcom, heading up its antifraud team.

"What the fuck's taking you so long?" Udi asked him. "I sent you my proposal Thursday."

The papers stacked on Charlie's desk stretched a foot high. Welch, he let Udi know, got about a hundred packages addressed to him each month.

"This one's not addressed to him. For your eyes only. *Nu?*"

"So what? You want my take on it first?"

"Read it," Udi instructed him. "Then we talk about what the fuck I want from you."

Over the next few days, as his colleagues returned to the office, tanned and refreshed, Charlie reviewed the materials Udi had sent him. The project they described was some kind of data-mining tool, but the proposal was rough, marred by the faults of its author—imperfect English, impatient explanations, and a tendency toward bombast. The claims being made about the potential for this software struck Charlie as unrealistic: no comparable system could cross-reference information from three distinct formats—from video images, to spreadsheets, to cell-phone records—but that was just what Udi insisted his would do. Nor could available technologies handle anything near the volume of data Udi was proposing.

Very early Monday morning, while Udi was still up working late on the West Coast, Charlie phoned him to discuss the matter further.

The idea had emerged during his two years at Cardcom, Udi claimed, while he'd been working to identify patterns of fraudulent conduct among users. He and his partner, another engineer named Doug Fincher, had come to realize just how adaptable—and valuable—the system they were developing could be; they wanted to strike out on their own, submit patents, raise capital, build a company. Such efforts, Udi and Doug agreed, would require a third partner to cover the business side—someone who knew how to persuade people and understood the culture of VCs—while they managed the technical one. They were interviewing candidates out in Palo Alto, but Udi already had his choice in mind.

"I told them how a good talker you are—and you did worked at a VC."

"I do work at a VC." One grammatical error Charlie felt obliged to correct; he had a job, at present, a job that was more or less reliable, as anything involving Udi could not possibly be.

"You need to come now. Doug expects to meet you for lunch tomorrow."

"In Palo Alto?" A call was coming in; he checked the phone: a blocked number. "I need to take this. Could be my boss."

"Could be your boss. *You* could be your boss. *You*, you stupid asshole."

Udi was still cursing him when Charlie switched onto the other line.

"Thank God, you're at the office. I've been trying your home number. I wasn't sure I'd reach you."

A familiar female voice, a voice that collapsed the last four years into a single moment.

"It's me, Charlie. It's Georgia. Alice might be in trouble."

Hours later, on the cab ride to the hospital, Charlie called Udi to apologize for having cut their conversation short. "Personal emergency," he told him, his excuse made more credible by the sirens in the background. His cab was slaloming between the cars on the West Side Highway, struggling to keep up with the ambulance ahead. Probably the ambulance driver was just impatient with the traffic; at least mental illness didn't seem to Charlie to require special haste, let alone adding to the mad clamor of the city. He wondered if the noise was distressing Alice, feeding into whatever fantasies had taken hold of her. Though by then she was probably so sedated that nothing could perturb her, the wail of sirens lulling her to sleep.

"She thinks the police are after her," Georgia had reported, "because she's hurt someone—I don't know if she really has. She was disoriented. Maybe she was on something. I hope that's all it was: in any case, she seemed very much out of control."

That Alice had called Georgia—this alone was proof she was unwell. In possession of herself, Alice wouldn't dare display an enduring interest in the friend whom she'd disowned.

"I'm so sorry to foist this on you," Georgia went on, "but I'm stuck here in D.C.; and I couldn't think who else in New York to contact. I'm afraid what she might do."

He'd offered to check up on Alice, which was what Georgia clearly expected from him, even though he wasn't sure where Alice was living now or how exactly he would find her. Over a year had passed since he and Alice were last in contact. When they'd first settled in Manhattan, they'd tried to establish an intermittent friendship; she'd invited him to a few parties in Tribeca and Soho, pleased to have someone from her past stand as witness to her inclusion in The Scene, and also, perhaps, so that they'd be safely surrounded by loud music and crowds—the better to avoid difficult subjects. But finally he and Alice had little in common except the things they preferred to forget; each took turns canceling plans, and then, in tacit agreement, they fell out of touch.

Now, just as Georgia claimed, Alice wasn't answering her cell, nor was any address listed for her in the White Pages. Charlie checked the Ohio listings and found an S. Kovac on record, but all Alice's mother could tell him was that her daughter was living on a street with a "very boring, American name." Alice's colleagues could no doubt be more specific, but Charlie was reluctant to announce Alice's troubles to them and risk her blaming him for the indiscretion later. Finally, he came upon a captioned photograph of Alice online: at some red carpet event she'd attended with her boyfriend, a TV producer named Nick Slakey. Nick wasn't at his office that morning, but his partner offered Charlie his cell number.

"I'm an old friend of Alice's," he told Nick. "I don't want to alarm you but I'm concerned she might not be well."

"You talk to her?"

"I'm trying to—to get hold of her."

"So if you do, you let me know. Because I'm looking for her too."

"Okay . . ."

"And you can tell her, when I find her, I'm going to run her down. I'm going to drive my SUV up and down her fucking face."

Not the response he'd been expecting. "Okay, obviously she's done something to upset you, but I'll make sure she's held accountable if you'll just help me find her. Can you do that for me, Nick?"

At close to ten, Charlie reached the address that Nick had provided: a brownstone on Jane Street with potted daisies on the stoop and a tricycle inside the gate. He rang the bell and a man came down to meet him, a jittery guy in his late forties: Bernie, he said his name was; the building belonged to him, and Alice was his tenant.

"Can you get her out of here? She won't answer me. I was about to call the police again." According to Bernie, the cops had already been by once, the night before, while Alice was still out. "They waited a bit then left. She must have snuck inside just after. I've been trying to get in—I've got a key, but she's wedged a chair or something under the knob."

Standing outside Alice's apartment, Charlie heard a German opera blasting within. He shouted to Alice, though he had little hope of being heard, then he continued up to Bernie's to call the paramedics. A half an hour later, while Bernie and his wife nervously looked on, two large men arrived and broke down Alice's door. Charlie waited at the entrance: the music was shut off; he could overhear fragments of conversation—Alice shouting, the EMTs trying to calm her—until the noise stopped and the men finally escorted out into the hall a numbed and frightened approximation of the sharp woman he'd once known.

"Where to, which hospital?" one of the medics asked him. They'd searched Alice's wallet for an insurance card and, having found none, asked Charlie if he knew her doctor's name or where she might prefer to receive treatment.

"I don't know. Columbia Presbyterian, I guess." It was the hospital closest to where he lived—most convenient if, as the past couple of hours seemed to suggest, he was going to be the one to oversee Alice's care.

Now here he was inside a taxi, trying to keep pace with an ambulance careening ahead, sirens blaring so loudly he'd failed to notice that his cell was ringing. Georgia again. “She’s safe,” he reassured her, “but we’re on our way to a psychiatric hospital. Police are en route, too.”

“Police? Jesus.”

“She’ll be all right. I’ll stay with her and, if need be, arrange for a lawyer.”

“It really shouldn’t fall on you. Isn’t there somebody else?”

“The boyfriend doesn’t seem inclined to help. I’ll try her mother.”

“She won’t be much use either. Maybe I should come up.”

“It’s really not necessary.” Already he could feel the danger: four years’ progress undone. A crisis like this had the power to achieve such a feat: he and Georgia intimately intertwined, when the week before, neither had anything to do with the other. “I think it’s better you don’t come. Let’s not, you know, make this into something.”

“Isn’t it something already?”

“Between us, I mean.”

“Oh. I see.” The softness drained from her voice; he felt relief and regret at once. “Okay, Charlie. You say you’ve got the situation covered; I promise I won’t bother you again.”

Later that evening, while Alice was examined by the psychiatrist on call, Charlie went down to wait at a nearby coffee shop. It was a cheerless place: Naugahyde seats with stuffing showing, encyclopedic menus, placemats with advertisements for florists and funeral homes. Such joints were always lurking in the shadows of hospitals, providing meager sustenance to those expecting lab results or with a loved one in surgery. The atmosphere was less like a restaurant than a waiting room, a mixture of harsh lights and queasy stomachs, of boredom, and dread.

Charlie’s belly growled. He hadn’t eaten since seven a.m.—half a bagel at his desk—nor had he given any thought to the work he’d left behind. Welch was expecting to hear his opinion on some new GPS software; he should have brought the relevant materials with him, but he’d forgotten them, as he’d forgotten about his suit at the dry cleaners, and about a dozen other details that helped make up the ordered, mature existence that he'd believed to be so solid when he'd woken up that morning. From his booth, he watched the city lights flash by in the windows of passing cars. His meal arrived: grilled cheese already cold, congealing into plastic.

13

The old shit Vasily was dead. Departed from this world, but still not quite done with her yet: now, from the beyond, Alice imagined, he meant to drag her to hell with him.

In a matter of weeks everything that had been under her control suddenly was not, as though Vasily had spent each of his last breaths on curses—against her, especially, his most ungrateful niece. Not that Alice shared her uncle's faith in curses. What she believed in, what life had taught her to expect, was that disasters refused to face her singly, so that she might, one by one, slap them down. No, instead for her, they stalked and hunted in packs, assaulting all at once and from all sides. Thirteen years ago it was the same: father dead, the move from Madison, puberty striking her like a disease. Then it had been farewell neat bright house, farewell to anyone who cared, farewell to a cute lovable body and a self she could just about endure, farewell childhood, farewell contentment.

This time, though, it would be different; no longer an innocent of twelve, she'd more than doubled in age and strength and she would hold on to it—this elusive thing called happiness—until she, like Vasily, was swallowed by the grave.

They were to bury him today at three o'clock. At Sacred Acres Cemetery in Cleveland, the same cemetery where Vasily had interred her father, two dozen Serbians would gather to mourn ostentatiously that most ostentatious man. Alice wouldn't be among them. What was to mourn? Vasily had outlasted her father by more than a decade, and he'd deserved to enjoy not one cool breeze or birdsong or glimpse of sunlight more. So while, at this moment, relatives and assorted neighbors were gathering around what must be a grotesquerie of a casket, she was at a salon on Hudson for a wax.

Rosy, the woman slathering the hot mixture on Alice's most tender skin, didn't speak English well enough for chatter. This was one of the reasons Alice went only to her: twice a month, without exception. Nick had also preferred hairlessness (no longer a preoccupation of her own, it seemed, everyone now wanted women childlike below the waist).

She doubted Nick could expect as much from Mary, his new Amish sweetheart—nice Christian girls, at least, must still maintain their pussies in God's image.

And yet who could say for sure? Standards of innocence—like media platforms—were fast evolving lately, and it was impossible to trust in morals even among members of extreme religious sects—expecially a type like Mary, who'd test her faith, for fame and money, on a Rumspringa reality series Nick had line produced for VH1. That was how the pair had met, just another romance to emerge from reality TV—if not to spawn a spin-off, perhaps, Alice dreaded, a few mortifying lines in *US Weekly* or Page Six.

Rosy ripped away the first cloth strip; Alice gritted her teeth against the pain. The room was cold and smelled of rubbing alcohol. She pictured her uncle, lying prone on a table like this one, while some poor creep prepared his body. Dead or alive, most bodies were vile, though few were as gruesome as that one in far-off Cleveland, waiting to be covered up with dirt.

Farewell obese, brutish Vasily with the mole on his cheek, and, it turned out, a Ping Pong–sized growth on his kidneys.

It must have been in March that Vasily had learned about his tumor, and about his limited future, if he had any, of illness and dependence. That would explain why he'd chosen such a moment to phone Alice, outraged at the neglect her mother suffered.

"My sister can't be safe to take care of herself. You need to be living at home."

"Peter can stay with her," Alice had suggested. Out of community college for almost a year, Peter still had no job, whereas she was a contributing editor at three major magazines. Few writers had risen so far so fast: the death of Princess Di had occupied her talents from graduation until Monica, and in '99 she'd been working on a profile of Carolyn Bessette-Kennedy, when John-John's plane went down. "Our Last Aristocrats" ran as the *Vanity Fair* cover; from then on, most every story that she pitched was guaranteed the go-ahead.

Vasily, however, didn't bother with such details: "Peter is the boy and you are the girl; it is for you to stay at home."

No, she told her uncle, it was definitely not for her; she was her father's daughter, finally, and meant to live as he'd intended her to: American and free. Americans didn't abandon their lives to care for aging parents. They didn't yield their twenties, that precious, most selfish decade, that brief time in which her ambitious countrymen must accomplish so much: build a career, attract a successful and stimulating yet reliable spouse, and, in the meantime, rack up experiences sufficient to console them through the next several decades of at least relative monogamy, part-time parental obligation, and whatever professional and personal stagnation would inevitably assault their impossibly high expectations. A satisfactory twenties was an inoculation against midlife crisis, and if Uncle Vasily had the first clue about the particular perils of affluent, modern, Western life, he'd have understood that her years of immersion in superficiality were in fact the most responsible course of action she could take.

But Vasily was a chimp, like her brother, and instead of admiring her foresight, he'd cut her right out of his will.

Three hundred thousand dollars was what Peter had been bequeathed, half of which would have been hers, had Vasily failed to call his probate lawyer after their little family spat. If only she'd known to indulge her uncle one month more—but she'd been unaware of Vasily's affliction and irritated by her own: Amish Mary. So with Nick, as with Torsten before him, Alice felt she'd paid an absurdly high price for letting herself give a damn about a man—not including the money for her wax and manicure and what she'd shelled out at Scoop for the dress she planned to wear that night.

At least her uncle's meanness had settled a scheduling conflict for her—his funeral was on the same day as a party she'd been looking forward to, at the Mercer Hotel, hosted by the network that had bought the rights to her Bessette-Kennedy story; that project, stuck in development two years so far, had one thing going for it—Nick was attached as a producer.

That Nick hadn't backed out of the job, that he'd agreed, moreover, to swing by the party later, suggested he wasn't quite lost to her yet. From this cold table she would rise, therefore, to don her six-hundred-dollar Dior dress and reclaim a share of the happiness that had been stolen from her: Let the dead rest and, for the living, as she'd learned from Torsten, *Das leben geht weiter.*

Alice's Jane Street apartment was on the lower level of a privately owned brownstone. The upstairs family was a nervous, meddling bunch—the husband, Bernie, often remarking on Alice's late nights, the wife standing as a shield between her children and Alice whenever they crossed paths in the hall. Alice would have told them both to fuck off long ago if the rent weren't quite so low and the space quite so charming, with its western view onto a patio and private garden. This evening, the colors of the sunset shone upon her walls as she kicked off her shoes and pressed the play button on her answering machine.

Four calls, all from her mother, her tone increasingly strident. "Ingrate, sinner": Alice could guess what her mother must be saying, though the words were Serbian and mostly incomprehensible. Leaving her mother's voice babbling in the living room, she hopped into the shower to scrub the last bits of wax from between her legs. She spent the next three hours getting ready: taking a run and second shower, straightening her hair, applying makeup, and finally slipping into her dress and three-inch heels to teeter to the corner for a cab to Mercer Street.

Walking alone into a party was a disagreeable experience: she hadn't realized how much of a comfort it had become leaning on Nick, tall handsome Nick, towering together over the assembled guests. Tonight she spotted no friends in the crowd, though there were plenty of people she was obliged to greet: fellow writers and editors, a handful of producers she'd met through Nick, minor celebrities from indie films and stints on *Law & Order*.

She searched among the glossy, perfectly tousled heads for Nick's. After two turns about the room, she ran into Carter, Nick's partner at their production company.

He ordered her a drink, without her asking—*vodka cranberry for the lady*—trying to be suave, though she could see that he was nervous to be around her. Carter knew everything—he must have been Nick's confidant in the last weeks, audience to the same romantic slobber that she'd been subjected to in their final conversations: *Mary's taught me so much. She's helping me to appreciate, like, the meaning in everything.*

Well, if it was an education Nick was after, Alice could oblige him, too. The quantity of knowledge she had over Nick could occupy them for a lifetime. He couldn't name ten U.S. presidents (once she'd dared him to try on the ride up to Bridgehampton: "Think of money, holidays—those are both favorites of yours"). The first love note she'd read from him had made her wince: *Deer Sexy*. But that "Deer" had quickly been excused for the Sexy that followed, as every subsequent stupidity, great and small, was forgiven as soon as he'd kissed her ear or pulled her up onto his lap. Enjoying sex was one thing Nick *had* managed to teach her. His style in bed—athletic, uncomplicated—might have seemed too vanilla for her before her time with Torsten but afterward, she'd found it a relief. After Torsten, frankly, she'd have forgiven Nick just about anything simply for calling her "Sexy" and appearing to mean it, rewarding her with a hard-on each time she searched his pants.

———

Her breath caught as she spotted him, her beloved, in skinny jeans and rumpled blazer, surveying the room from the entrance. Nick waved toward her and Carter. She clutched the railing of the bar; he was coming over, friendly, dimpled. Carter clapped him on the back, promising to catch him later, and she and Nick were left alone.

"Those shoes look painful," Nick observed. "Why don't we go find a seat."

Putting her out of her misery: a promising start.

They spent the next five minutes searching for an empty leather cube where they might get half comfortable, before giving up and leaning against the whitewashed brick wall.

"You and Cart were talking before. Did he say something to you?"

"That's the gist of talking."

Nick hunched his shoulders and dropped his head, hair falling in his eyes; that gesture of embarrassment was one she'd seen a thousand times. Had she been too hard with him, mocked him too often—was that what had made him run away? She could smell his shampoo, the same scent that used to linger on her pillow. If only he would kiss her, she would not, not ever, make fun of him again.

She smiled at him sweetly. "I'm sorry, I'll be nice. Go ahead."

He tucked a lock behind his ear; his hair had grown longer since she'd last seen him, five awful, lonely weeks. "It's about our show."

Alice held her smile; she didn't want to discuss work. There was music playing, an open bar, colored, swirling lights. She studied Nick to see if he was high; then it would be easy to lure him off into the stairwell and from there, up to a room.

"Thing is, lately Carter and I have taken on an awful lot and I'm feeling like it's time to, you know 'take stocks.'"

She bit her lip, not to correct him. "Right, uh-huh."

"I've got to consider what our company stands for, what our reputation's gonna be. Like, this whole Bessette thing, profiting from a person's tragedy, I've got my qualms about it, ethics-wise."

This was all coming from Mary—obviously—the girl afraid of what might happen if Alice's project ever actually got rolling, if Nick and Alice were to spend long hours side by side. "So what's her plan for you, exactly, if you don't mind my asking? Abandon all your projects that have issues—ethics-wise? And what's left for you then, TBN?"

"It's not like that—though, for the record, Christian programming is booming."

"*God* no." Stupidity she could abide, but not sanctimony, not prudishness, not from blissfully unrepressed Nick. "Listen, you want off the project, fine. I don't give a damn about the project—what I care about is you, the free-spirited, perfect you that this girl seems bent on destroying."

She'd dared to stroke his arm as she uttered these last words; Nick scratched his elbow, knocking her hand away.

"Alice."

Alice, he called her. No longer "Sexy." She'd never felt such hatred for her own name.

"I don't want to fight," Nick continued. "I know the kinds of stories you tell yourself so you can live with what you do. I was there, too, once . . . before."

Before *her*. She could feel the bile rising. Nick, her friend in fun, had come to join the ranks of the moralizers, strangers who, from the Patel story onward, felt the need to lecture her, to concern themselves with the state of *her* conscience. "You know, I missed a first-rate funeral for this."

Nick laid his hand on her bare shoulder. "You're a good person: I really think so, you just haven't figured out, you know, what's like, intended for you—"

"*Intended?* By who? Don't start with all that, Nick. That shit's too dumb—even for you."

Nick took a step back and slouched again, defensively. "I realize spirituality isn't your thing, okay, but I don't think it's dumb to believe that we're meant for certain destinies, or certain people."

"Is *that* the story she's got you believing?"

"Like I said, I know spirituality isn't your thing."

"Yeah, okay, but enlighten me: I want to understand your girlfriend's metaphysics. So is it that God intervened to bring you two together? In Mary's universe, *the divine being* is like some giant reality TV producer?" She was speaking sharply, rapidly; Nick's eyes began to glaze over. He never could handle a proper argument. Once the words poured from her, he'd do his best to wrap it up.

"I didn't come to fight, okay? Carter's waiting for me at the bar."

"So Carter—was he part of God's plan, too? Inspired to conceive his Amish schlock just so that you could be saved from sin by your messianic twat?"

"Please don't call Mary that."

"What, *messianic*? I lost a fortune 'cause of you. My whole fucking inheritance." People had begun to stare; she was shouting, louder than was required to be heard above the music. "Was that also God's fucking idea? For God's fucking entertainment?"

She peered up at Nick, into the charming face that she'd once trusted; red lights swirled across his cheeks and down his torso, scuttling off across the floor.

Maybe faith *was* what she needed then: not in God or heaven, but in an existence at least less trivial than this party at the Mercer, free of tormenters like Vasily, Torsten, and now Nick, who'd taken turns pummeling her wounded spirit.

"What about *my* soul?" she shouted, as Nick began to walk away. "What if you and all these other assholes and this whole bullshit spectacle have been arranged merely for the purpose of *my* redemption. Maybe I'm the one God's really hot for—ever fucking consider that?"

A week later, she phoned Nick to recover the possessions she'd left strewn around his places in Bridgehampton and Tribeca: her old laptop, clothes, perfume, CDs. "Just throw them into a suitcase," she instructed, and she'd do the same with his things. Her outburst at the Mercer had alarmed her; after Torsten, she'd resolved never to lose her balance over a man again. Just walk away, she told herself. Chances were Nick would come crawling back to her one of these days, anyway, just as Torsten had tried to do two years ago, and chances were, she would find Nick's offer equally ludicrous. Once the spell was broken, she couldn't believe she'd ever gone for Torsten, a brooding agoraphobic like her mother; soon she was bound to settle on a similarly unflattering view of Nick. Not hard to picture how she'd groan to remember those subliterate love scribbles of his.

They'd arranged to make an exchange of suitcases the following Sunday. To remind him, she left a message on Nick's cell, letting him know that she'd drop by around five. When she arrived and no one answered, she used her key. Inside Nick's doorway, Mary was standing there wide-eyed, in the rumpled green shirt Alice had bought for Nick at Barneys. She turned, darting away from Alice, flashing her bare ass and a thong.

"A thong, now that is a surprise."

"Nick," Mary called; her voice was small and choked. He emerged from the bedroom, in his boxers, scratching his bed head.

"Alice, you completely slipped my mind."

She ignored him, addressing the half-naked girl crouched behind the sofa. "Forgive my ignorance, but I want to get the rules right. I thought the Mormons are the ones with the magic underwear, but is there an Amish thong version too?"

"Mary, be cool," Nick advised her. "She's just trying to upset you."

Staring straight ahead, Mary rushed across the room, ass tiny as a child's, to shut herself inside the bedroom. Nick went after her, calling across the door, and Alice headed for the kitchen to pour herself a glass of water. A moment later, Mary stepped out in her own clothes, a floral dress and sneakers.

Keds, just like Alice had worn in the sixth grade. "Jesus, Nick, do you fuck her in her Keds?"

"Shut up, will you? Just shut the fuck up." Nick had begun to shout; he checked himself, continued more civilly. "I don't see why you need to degrade her. This isn't her fault."

"Me? You film this girl on the toilet, and *I'm* the one degrading her?"

The front door slammed; Mary was gone.

Cursing under his breath, Nick hopped into a pair of pants, grabbed a shirt, and jogged out to the hall.

Alice was alone in the apartment; slowly she sipped her water, calming down, then strolled into Nick's bedroom, averting her eyes from the tangled sheets. A suitcase lay open in the corner—packed with her things, though not all of them. Never mind. She didn't want to be here when the two returned; she didn't want to risk an even nastier display. Nick was still in a position to hurt her if he wanted: not just personally but professionally, too. She had her share of competitors and enemies, people who would thrill to read of her humiliations. The cachet she'd established over the past four years could be lost in as many days. Already she'd begun to feel her confidence was slipping: she'd contacted one of her editors that morning and he hadn't yet returned her call.

Paranoia. She must fight it off, hop in a taxi, and go home. Get in the bath and take a Valium and, in the morning, call the therapist she'd gone to for antianxiety meds a few times before.

She dragged the suitcase to the elevator; Nick hadn't thought to provide her one with wheels. Outside the building entrance, the doorman whistled for a taxi, but few ever ventured down Nick's narrow, cobblestone block. Finally, Alice chose to lug the bag up to West Broadway.

A woman was standing at the corner: blond hair, floral dress, Keds. No sign of Nick nearby. Mary was alone, apparently; her face was tear-streaked, her expression dazed. She seemed oblivious to everything around her: a random man peering at her with concern, then looking her up and down; Alice, dropping her bag and coming up beside her; the rushing traffic, the van barreling toward her.

Just a small shove—Alice was sure she'd hardly touched her—until she heard the thud and saw Mary staggering back. The man standing at Mary's side came forward to catch her arm.

"Miss, my God, miss? You okay?"

Dragging the man down, Mary crumpled onto the gutter. Her mouth was open; she was in shock. A deep cut crossed her cheek and a flap of skin hung down like a page.

If she'd wanted to, thought Alice, she could have shoved her harder—another few newtons of force and Mary would have collided with the windshield, not just had her face slapped by the rearview. She would have been joining Vasily that week. It was a matter of restraint on her part—that was what Alice told herself as she wandered the streets for the next hours, afraid of going home. When she couldn't walk anymore, she returned to her apartment: a notice from the police had been taped to her front door. She went inside, wedged a chair against the knob, took the two remaining Valiums in her bathroom, and then sat down at her desk to call a lawyer. She did make calls that night—a few stuck out in memory—to her mother and Vasily's wife and Peter, insisting she'd need money right away; there were other calls, too, maybe many others. By morning she'd lost track. The next thing she knew, Strauss's *Salome* was blasting and two large men in uniform were holding on to her, dragging her out of her apartment to the hall. There, inexplicably, Charlie Flournoy stood waiting for her, dressed in a suit and assuring her in a steady, adult voice that everything was going to be all right.

14

Charlie had never seen the city so empty, so still. Walking through Times Square, to his office, he'd paused to stand on the island between Broadway and Seventh, under the flashing ads and lights, to stare out at sidewalks free of tourists and vendors peddling Big Apple souvenirs, closed his eyes, and heard not a single shout or honking car.

Many had simply fled Manhattan; those who remained ventured out only for work and then burrowed away at home. All the presidential speeches and all the mayor's imprecations couldn't make the city buzz again, and though word was that the terrorists would win if we abandoned our capitalist habits, and shopping sprees and sushi dinners were deemed small patriotic acts, for this brief time, the crowds could not be roused onto these streets, and Charlie could step out every morning into this strange, desolate, concrete island.

A few people he knew (one of his neighbors, a secretary at the office) had gone, in the weeks following 9/11, to visit what was now being called Ground Zero, but Charlie didn't feel that he needed further proof of the horror. With his apartment window open, on days when the wind blew from the south, he could smell the chemicals and smoke. At night, looking out from his office, he could see the lighter patch of sky from the fires that still burned at the site.

In the halls of Warren Welch, no one dared speak about anything else: *I was this close to taking a job at Lehman . . . My buddy's roommate got out just in time.* During two companywide meetings, Welch offered the firm's official statement on the matter. The world had changed, though business, it seemed, would go on much as before; the only salient difference for Warren Welch employees was a new focus on investing in security technologies. Welch had asked Charlie, in particular, to seek out projects relevant to the moment: *x-ray systems, retinal scans*.

Such projects—though doubtless poised to turn huge profits in the coming months—seemed to Charlie to have very little to do with what had gone wrong that gruesome Tuesday in September. Udi's take on the disaster felt far more pertinent: 9/11 was the result of an intelligence failure—specifically a failure to *synthesize* intelligence. They'd talked about it, for long hours over the phone, how big data-mining systems, as ambitious as those Udi wanted to implement, could be a central line of defense in what was being called "the war on terror."

Now was the time to think on a grand scale, according to Udi; and Charlie, shaken by the events of that fall, craving a change, couldn't help but be stirred by his friend's boldness. To balance it, though, he proposed bringing Roger in as a fourth partner. After Harvard, Roger had gone on to law school in Chicago; he'd trained in contract law, which would prove useful to them in negotiating future deals, and he could offer what Charlie felt he and Udi needed most—a cautious perspective. If Charlie were to give up his job at Warren Welch, he told both Udi and Roger, he needed Roger on board with him. He would await his friend's decision.

But whatever the outcome in this case, Charlie already sensed his days at his firm were drawing to a close. He'd lost his enthusiasm for the work and, especially, his patience with Terrance Welch and his demands; flouting his boss's instructions, he'd taken to leaving the office early or slipping out for several hours at lunch. Either he went walking through the quiet Midtown streets, or else he took the train up to Washington Heights to visit Alice, who'd by now spent almost the last month in the hospital.

Those hospital visits became points of respite in his hectic week. Once he'd passed into the psychiatric unit, it was as if there had never been any national catastrophe; no one chattered about the city's most vulnerable targets or stammered ingenuously about the cruelty of the world. Nurses kept the TV tuned to the Disney Channel; the patients hummed and muttered and moved slowly; their focus was soft and drifting. Those white ward halls really might seem a quiet refuge—if not for the dreadful door that barred the exit, the sort of heavily secured, elaborate contraption worthy of being financed by Warren Welch.

During his first meetings with Alice, Charlie made a point of sitting at a distance from that door—for her sake, not to insist upon the fact of her confinement. But it turned out Alice didn't miss her freedom all that much: the ward suited her, she admitted, and her appearance bore this out. She looked healthier, cheeks plumped up by hospital food.

"There *are* certain advantages to being here," she said, though she refused to be specific until Charlie's fourth visit, when she had a reason to confide. She'd been writing again, she let him know: twenty to thirty pages every day. In less than a month, she'd already filled every page—front and back—of the three notebooks she'd had her mother bring her. She'd hidden them under her bed, but one of the nurses had found them and confiscated them, and so she'd raised the subject with Charlie in order to ask him to sneak in several more.

"You'll need to do it quietly. Dr. Baum disapproves. Apparently, he should be the only one permitted to have thoughts here. That I might be able to reflect on my own personal history—on things he doesn't know and might not see—it drives *him* crazy. To be honest, I think he's even intimidated by me."

She laughed, gleefully, and Charlie suspected she wasn't altogether wrong.

"Notebooks, okay; I'll get them."

"And if you could do me one more favor." She paused, looking right and left, making certain none of the nurses was in hearing range. "When I'm done, if you could slip the completed notebooks out, hold on to them for me. But you have to swear, you can't read anything I give you, and you can't show it to anyone—especially not Georgia."

He agreed, refraining from asking the question that nagged him: *What* were these subjects that Alice was so determined to keep private, from her old friend above all? To ask about such things would be unfair, he felt, with Alice so confused, and she *must* be confused if she imagined he still kept up such close contact with Georgia.

It seemed as though, for Alice, the friendships between them were unchanged since college, as if she'd simply erased the last four years of their estrangement. Perhaps such details were of no interest to the mad imagination, Charlie thought, which struck him then as the most faithful kind: a place where relationships that mattered could never come to an end.

The next week, when Charlie dropped in to see Alice after work, the nurse at reception told him he'd have to take a seat: Alice was occupied with another visitor.

"Are you sure?" To his knowledge, Alice never had any other visitors, not since her mother and her brother had vanished back to Cleveland after just a few days in New York. He checked the sign-in sheet, set out on a clipboard and tied in place with purple ribbon; two lines above his own was a signature he recognized: Georgia Calvin.

"I'll come back another time." He signaled to the desk nurse to let him out and was waiting for the steel door to unlock and click open when he heard a woman's voice.

"Charlie."

Georgia was unhappy—that was his first reaction to the sight of her, though he couldn't have said precisely why; she was smiling and composed, dressed in a womanly beige linen skirt and with her hair cut to her shoulders. She stepped toward him, leaning in as if she meant to touch him, then she stopped short: "I should have called to tell you I'd be here."

"Why *are* you here?" His tone was rough, but Georgia had caught him off guard; it was an aggressive move, he felt, turning up here, breaking her promise to him, intruding on what had become his business, thanks largely to her.

Georgia dropped her smile and crossed her arms: "I am the one Alice chose to call."

Though not in her right mind, he might have pointed out, and this still didn't explain why Georgia had chosen to respond. Presumably her friendship with Alice had ended the night Alice had shown up with two suitcases in tow at his door. Now, despite whatever argument they'd had then and despite all that came after—Alice's article and the hurt it must have caused—Georgia had made this trip to visit: there must be *some* motive behind it. Loyalty to an old friend in distress was the generous interpretation, but Charlie hadn't yet resolved how generous he meant to be.

Regardless, he didn't want to get dragged into the past—or into anything—with Georgia now. "Fine, you've come all this way, go ahead. I'll visit her another time."

He didn't wait for Georgia to reply: signaling the nurse to get the door, he exited the ward. After a moment, the door behind him opened, and Georgia stepped out again, to stand beside him at the elevator bay.

Alice was napping, she explained; the orderly in charge had recommended returning in an hour. "Is there some place nearby to grab a bite?"

Charlie led her to the same coffee shop where he'd sat waiting for Alice her first night in the ward. He had every intention of depositing Georgia there and leaving, but when, outside the entrance, she inquired if he'd had dinner, he found himself agreeing to sit down.

Fleeing her would be cowardly, he thought, and at least this coffee shop was a kind of announcement that he didn't mean to make a fuss out of their meeting; otherwise, he'd have suggested they walk a few blocks farther in search of cooler music, better lighting. To make his lack of commitment clearer still, he kept his order limited to just a Coke, though he was actually hungry, and though Georgia was having split pea soup and a large side of coleslaw. She hadn't eaten, she told him, since she'd gotten on the train.

She studied him across the table; he was embarrassed by the intimacy of her gaze: *Finally a proper tie and not a bow tie, finally a suit that isn't from the Salvation Army.*

Georgia had changed in small ways, too. Her cheeks were sleeker;

in place of the berry gloss and blush she'd used at school, she was made up in subdued browns, gold swept under the brows. The plainer clothes she wore now—no beads or embroidery, not showing as much skin—were even sexier than the girlish cutoffs and open-necked blouses of her college days.

"It's really so good to see you, Charlie."

He nodded, afraid of offering her encouragement, afraid she might say something to shrink the distance between them he was at such pains to sustain. In the halls of the mental ward, he might have just told her good night; one of the doctors should have stopped him. It was *his* sickness: sitting here with Georgia once again.

"So then," he began, trying to sound disinterested. "You've been living in D.C.?"

Since graduation, she said, despite her distaste for the city; she'd moved down for a job at the National Gallery of Art. "I'm sort of a fund-raising geisha; also not what I planned. But sometimes things just happen, don't they?"

Already Charlie felt the gaps in her explanation. *Storrow* had worked in D.C. once and, back at Harvard, had bragged about the many opportunities that awaited him there still. "Four years is a long time to spend somewhere you don't like for no good reason."

She offered him a sideways glance, one he knew well: *Can't keep anything from you.*

"You're right, of course. And I've asked myself a hundred times why I'm still there. Maybe I've been hiding; maybe I've been stuck. At one point, I almost came up here; there was a position at the Soho Guggenheim, but I was—am—having problems with my dad. He's living over in Williamsburg now. Considers the city interesting again—especially since the towers." She pressed her lips together, a bitter expression Charlie had never seen on her before, certainly not while speaking of her father. "I doubt you'd know about it, but he's had a resurgence; it started with a show three years ago—some old photographs of me—I think I showed you once, maybe you've forgotten."

As if he could have forgotten: those perfect nudes, that perfect mix of sympathy and desire she'd managed to arouse from the first day of their acquaintance. He supposed she was up to the same game now, going on about the show in Chelsea, the family argument over those pictures being exhibited again.

"My mother was appalled, but my father wasn't going to miss his chance. This was the year of Monica, mind you, and any artist with a prayer of succeeding has to have a genius for timing, my father says, mistaken by us laypeople for luck. One year later, no one would give a shit about those pictures, but I'd just been in the news and there was interest in the whole scandal, still."

It was the closest they'd come to acknowledging the events at Harvard, and the effects Georgia had endured in their wake.

Her food arrived; she stirred her soup in large circles and stared out of the window. An old woman was passing by, dragging along a grocery cart.

"I thought about you," Georgia said, "when I heard about the towers. Where your offices were, if you were okay."

"I'm okay."

"Yes, you clearly are." Another close-lipped smile.

His first impression had been right, he thought. Georgia was unhappy.

But so what if she was? Why should that matter to him? Twenty minutes with her and he felt himself getting drawn back into the old familiar drama: battles between her indignant mother and her self-indulgent father—a man for whom Charlie felt no pity, less even than he felt for Storrow. The longer he and Georgia sat together, not saying Storrow's name, the more Charlie's thoughts went to him, and to what he still didn't know about Georgia's feelings for the man: if she'd loved him and suffered with him—if she'd feared him and avoided him, if Storrow had anything to do with why she'd come here to see Alice and was sitting with him now.

Alice had exposed her and Storrow. Perhaps Georgia felt this gave her the right to do some prying of her own, to take advantage of this moment when Alice was doped up and confused enough to give Georgia what she wanted. Explanations. Remorse.

Charlie's cell began to ring; one of the nurses was calling from the ward. He waved to the waiter for their check and hurried, more than was necessary, to stand and button his coat. Their time was up, he told Georgia: Alice was awake.

Alice came down the hall shuffling, puffy socks bunched at her ankles, hospital slippers on her feet; her robe was too short, reaching up above her knees. Sheet marks streaked her bare face. Georgia winced. Alice stopped a few feet ahead of her and stood, squinting and smiling—as if her friend's appearance constituted some sort of a shared joke.

Charlie offered to stay with them, but Georgia muttered that they were fine and joined Alice on a bench along the wall. Charlie crossed the room, hiding out on the sofa in the lounge. A young man sat beside him, tapping time on the sofa cushion, watching a pair of children singing and dancing on TV.

Every few moments, Charlie cast a glance across the room. Alice seemed to be doing all the talking; she sat hunched forward, gesticulating, absorbed in intricate explanations. Georgia listened beside her, politely nodding, evidently baffled but indulgent, like she might be with an overexcited child.

This went on for twenty minutes until, abruptly, the demeanor of both women changed; Charlie peered over to see the pair seated in silence. Georgia's hands played in her hair, a nervous gesture; Alice was motionless, staring at her fingers clasped tightly in her lap. At eight thirty, visiting hours ended and an orderly called Alice back to her room. Alice retreated down the hall and Charlie stepped up to join Georgia.

"You all right?" he asked.

Georgia blinked up at him, dazed. "Fine. I'm fine."

On their way out, Georgia was so hurried that she forgot the suitcase she'd stowed behind the reception desk; a nurse came running to the elevator to stop her. Charlie carried the bag down to the street, where Georgia hailed a cab. Before he let her go, he asked after the address of her hotel.

"Anywhere in Midtown's good. There are several places I can try."

"You don't have a reservation?" Forget it, Charlie told her; he wasn't going to have her searching for a room, not in the addled state that she was in. "I'll take the couch; you can stay with me."

"Really, Charlie, I couldn't ask that of you."

"You didn't ask me. I'm insisting."

Charlie entered the apartment first, moving ahead of Georgia among the light switches, illuminating the built-in bookshelves and tiger oak paneling, the original moldings and restored hardwood floors—all those details the real estate broker had felt obliged to report, though she'd assumed a young guy like Charlie couldn't give a damn. *Your girlfriends will love this space*, she'd said; it was full of charms to catch a woman's eye, to make her feel she'd found a peaceful spot to rest.

Georgia observed the rooms with a half-teasing gasp: "This is all just you?"

She circled the sofa, pausing at the wood-burning fireplace, and went to stand beside the window. The George Washington Bridge cast blinking trails of light across the Hudson.

Charlie moved to the kitchen and poured Georgia a vodka and orange—the closest he had to the vodka cranberries she and Alice used to drink at school.

"I guess you've had a shock," he began, settling beside her at the window. "Seeing Alice like that, hearing her go on the way she does now. She certainly broke the silence between you two."

Georgia nodded, reticent, by contrast. She took a slow sip of her drink.

"Anything you want to talk about?" He would have liked to confront her more directly, to inquire what exactly had passed between them to leave Alice looking so frozen and Georgia so unsettled. But Georgia shook her head and roughly set her glass down on the sill, splashing its contents on her wrist.

"She's confused, obviously—paranoid, delusional, and you know Alice, even when she's sane, anything she says should be viewed with skepticism. That used to be your view once, too, before."

"Before?"

"Before you became buddies, roomies, before whatever went on between the two of you." Her tone was blunt now; one thing the meeting with Alice had apparently accomplished, it had banished the hesitance Georgia displayed in the coffee shop before.

"She needed a place; I was a convenience. What do you think went on?"

"Some convenient fucking maybe?"

The suggestion startled him, flattered him as well: that Georgia should be so preoccupied by such a matter, these many years later, enough to need to ask him. "Nothing like that," he heard himself explaining. "And however it looked, I never took her side against you."

"Let's just forget it; I shouldn't have brought it up." Georgia left the window for the sofa, curling one leg beneath her; after a moment, she took a deep breath and sighed. "You were angry; I know—not without reason."

"I don't think *reason* ever entered it—or into *anything* to do with me and you."

She smiled at this and then grew thoughtful, staring at him from the sofa. Her skirt, the same color as his couch, billowed where her boot kicked back and forth.

He turned away again to face the window; across the highway, the dark line of trees dropped off at the shore. For the first time since he'd moved here, he felt his loneliness: Why had he chosen this spot to make his own, on the island's edge?

"Charlie?"

Footsteps sounded behind him; a hand brushed his shoulder. He was absolutely still, not even breathing as Georgia came around to kiss him; it was *her* breath, cool and steady, that he felt on his lips.

No, reason hadn't entered into it: not four years earlier, when he'd been embittered against Georgia by jealousy, and not that night, when he'd let his gentler feelings take hold of him again. Afterward, he was better able to be sensible. He wasn't an idiot, for Christ's sake: he recognized a fleeting impulse, had already felt Georgia's excitement giving way to numbness before the night was through. He hadn't expected her to stay with him, to quit her job and D.C. and move in here; he hadn't imagined that they'd spend Sunday mornings taking walks in the park or waiting on endless lines at Barney Greengrass or Sarabeth's for brunch. He wasn't even surprised when she called three weeks later to announce that she was going abroad for a while—to India of all places, as if anywhere on the same continent as him wouldn't be far enough.

Good then. At least there could be no doubt; this wasn't a beginning but an ending, a chance to put to rest whatever illusions still gripped him. Since their night together he could assault his dreams with facts: Georgia's ass was square and muscled; her toes were long; he knew the color of her nipples; he'd tasted her mouth.

After the many times he'd imagined her body, the reality hadn't disappointed him, and yet he'd felt a sadness while he held her—finally held her—knowing that she wasn't quite there with him. She was exhausted; that's what she'd told him, anyway—too tired even to keep her eyes open, too tired to do much but lie back and utter small moans and touch, now and again, his cheek or meet his kiss.

Of course he knew the true meaning of these gestures and knew that Georgia had just turned up with him again because she was lost and lonely—nostalgia only took root in barren ground. He knew better than to let his hopes be raised when she had pretended otherwise that night, speaking of a future that might make up for the past: *I don't know why I couldn't let myself be with you before. I was young; I was confused.*

You're still young and confused, he'd told her, and of course knowing this didn't change the fact that he was, too.

15

The sky outside Chhatrapati Airport was brown; the air smelled of smoke. The result of unchecked industrialization, Georgia assumed, until Sanjay, the man sent by the orphanage to collect her, provided another explanation for the smell: it was not the by-product of thousands of poorly regulated sweatshops, but rather of the staggering numbers of home-cooked meals, of Mumbai's many million humble hearths.

"That's forever been the smell of my city," Sanjay told her on their walk through the airport parking lot, displaying neither pride nor shame. He was about her age, with slightly yellowed brown eyes and a scar across one cheek, and had appeared outside the baggage claim holding a sign bearing her name, or almost: *Calvin George*. His voice was gentle, though he was stubborn about fulfilling his orders and had to be cajoled into letting her carry even her smallest bag out to the lot herself.

The car waiting for them was a beige minivan, new or almost new, and kept spotlessly clean, unlike the mostly rusted vehicles around them. A boy was standing by the driver's side. Sanjay must have hired him to keep watch; he handed a coin to the boy, who took it and ran off.

Sanjay slid open the door to the backseat, but Georgia moved instead to the front passenger side. When she rolled down her window, Sanjay rolled it up again and turned on the AC.

"Until you get used to the poor air."

The van entered the main road into Mumbai, lined with drooping trees, clusters of small ramshackle houses, and long stretches of fencing—"construction sites," Sanjay informed her. The city was ever expanding to keep up with its population. Closer to the city center, housing became denser and climbed to two stories: ladders stretched to second floors, and many of the openings were without windows and doors. Women sat in shadow inside; children peeked their faces into the sunshine, peering out across the road.

Soon the traffic became clogged, and the honking grew continuous. Small, yellow-roofed black taxis nosed into each gap in the lanes. Women in saris beeped past on mopeds; men on bicycles wove, shouting, between the cars; and, without regard for crosswalks, pedestrians dashed into the rush. Each time she saw another body dart out from the curb, Georgia held her breath. Never, not even in the worst reaches of D.C., where kids chased balls into traffic and drunks stumbled down highways, had she seen chaos like this. There must be some hidden method to it: moving through Mumbai couldn't be the perilous mayhem it appeared to be. No one could take life quite so lightly.

But wasn't that just what she'd hoped to discover? Wasn't that why people came to India? To feel lighter—not to find meaning, in the Western sense, but to disappear, to relax into one's own insignificance?

After less than an hour on this new continent, though, she had clues that it would not be as indifferent toward an American—let alone a tall, blond one—as it was toward its own people. Passengers in nearby cars were staring; children in backseats pointed and waved.

"You're like the movie stars for them," Sanjay explained. Several times now, she'd caught him watching her, too, from the corner of his eye. "You have a husband, miss?"

"Fiancé," she remarked, a simple lie to spare her future awkwardness. "Back in New York." She found herself thinking of Charlie, though not only *wasn't* he her future husband, he was likely out of her life altogether. Had she been more cautious with him those two days in Manhattan, she might have managed to revive their friendship; instead she'd acted on impulse and then panicked: waking in the morning in his bed, she'd seen his freckled chest rising and falling, ingenuous, exposed. She'd covered him up with the sheet and rushed to the other room to dress.

Never go backward, her father had told her, by way of explaining why he'd not once been tempted to reconcile with her mother. Such reversals were inevitably a search for comfort that ended in pain, and after the relief that came with Charlie's forgiveness, Georgia had already begun to sense the gloom stalking them both. They'd done their best to delay it, avoided all references to the horrors of their last weeks at school—*they* had, but not Alice.

"*You* must see what's happening," Alice had chattered on, excitedly, as though Georgia alone might grasp the sense where others just saw chaos, as if Alice had been waiting all month for her to appear inside that mental ward. "Everyone thinks I meant to kill that girl. I'm the murderer now. That's his idea. It's his revenge."

Georgia had assumed—or wished to assume—Alice was talking about Nick, her recent ex; Charlie had told her the guy was furious. Still, some doubt prompted her to ask: "*Whose* revenge?"

Alice frowned at her impatiently; the old arrogance persisted through her madness—as if *Georgia* were the one whose thinking was impaired. "Storrow of course."

The fluorescent bulb flickered above their heads; across the room, from the sofa, Charlie was watching. Georgia did her best to maintain her composure. "No one's taking revenge here."

"You're not seeing the whole picture. I hadn't expected to find Mary; I'd come by looking for Nick, just like Storrow came by looking for you."

Looking for her? Had Storrow really done this or was it merely part of Alice's delusion? Even Georgia, who'd held on to sanity in the last years, had fallen prey to such imaginings: Storrow tracking her down.

She'd tried to press Alice for more details—*when* had Storrow come looking for her, back at school or recently?—but such questions just heightened Alice's paranoia. Her lips curled into a tense and eerie smile, her black eyes seemed to retreat behind her swollen lids. *I must be confused,* Alice said at last, and then she'd turned away, to sit staring at the fingers locked together in her lap, until an orderly came by to lead her back to her room.

What, exactly, had she hoped to get out of meeting Alice? Some insight into why her friend betrayed her, or some understanding of her illness that might allow her to forgive her? What Georgia *hadn't* expected was to feel the past suddenly crowding in on them. She hadn't expected to feel Storrow so much with them he might have come striding down that bright white hall.

That visit had given Georgia the shove that she required.

Movement heals the soul, her father said.

"We're entering Malabar Hill," Sanjay informed her, pointing over the hood. "Like your Fifth Avenue." As they drove past, he indicated Mumbai's most Western attractions: its tallest skyscraper, its Mercedes dealerships and department stores. Many of the fancier buildings were barricaded, their fences hung with the laundry of families living on the streets. Young men lay sleeping on piles of sheets, their pretty wives beside them. Up above, the many billboards featured pale Indian girls; the advertising copy was written entirely in English.

"Are we going to the orphanage?" she inquired.

"First to the office. Another fifteen-minutes' drive. There you'll meet the orphanage owner, Mr. Nandi."

Leaving behind the glamorous avenues, they came to a more cramped neighborhood; painted billboards stood amid tangled electrical wiring above open-air shops, tables heaped with clothes spilled out onto the pavement, and carts crowded the curb, bearing vegetables and fruit, shaded by umbrellas.

They passed a shop with a large sign: PATEL GROCERY.

Patel, she reminded herself, was the Indian equivalent of Smith or Jones. In a country of over a billion people, she was bound to shop in at least one Patel grocery, or be waited on by at least one Mr. Patel at the bank, or chat with one Mrs. Patel at the laundry. And yet the sign still gave her pause, made her think about what she was leaving behind, and the complex of motives she hadn't wished to examine that had led her to this place in particular.

India, however, had hardly been her choice. Volunteer opportunities had lately fallen into short supply; she wasn't the only one in the wake of 9/11 to seek out a more worthy occupation, or a free flight out of the country. Global Aid was the sole organization that had found any use for her, and the options they'd presented her numbered exactly two: the Mission of Hope orphanage in Mumbai or a hospice in Kenya. The company of children sounded like the less dismal prospect.

But already, she'd begun to fear she lacked the stomach for her role. At every stoplight, children waded out into traffic to beg at her window. They sold balloons, beaded purses, bracelets made of flowers; some merely held their palms outstretched.

"Don't open and don't give," Sanjay warned her. "These children will only be robbed by their parents. As long as the parents can make money this way, they will send the children out into the streets."

When the children, encouraged by her glances, became too aggressive, Sanjay honked his horn. It wasn't done with malice, nor did the children appear either frightened or offended. They simply backed away, hard little businessmen already, and moved on to the next car.

At last Sanjay pulled over to the side of the road; he came around to let her out in front of a shop selling cheap dishware.

"On the second floor you will meet Mr. Nandi. I'll wait with the car."

Nandi's office, at the top of a narrow, crooked flight of steps, was very plain: one small room with a desk and a man squeezed in behind it. He stood when Georgia walked in and offered his hand; he had a pointed belly and round eyeglasses, cracked in the corner of one lens.

"You met Sanjay all right then?"

"Yes, thank you. Though it really wasn't necessary to send a driver." She took her seat opposite the desk. On the walls were posters of sunsets and mountaintops. "Magical India" was written across the top of one.

"It's our pleasure, Ms. Calvin. We're very pleased to have you here. Ms. Roy has sent me some information about you. We don't get many of your kind."

"My kind?"

"With your qualifications."

None of which prepared her for the work she'd come to do, she thought. "Well, I'm eager to get started, to settle in at the orphanage."

Tomorrow she would do just that, of course, Nandi promised, but since the previous volunteer hadn't yet vacated her room, Georgia would need to spend the next night or two as a guest of a personal friend. "Mrs. Chandar lives very near here, on Cardinal Gracious Road."

Georgia heard a thudding noise from the hall: Sanjay was hauling her suitcases up the stairs.

"Better you leave the larger parcels here," Nandi explained. "Mrs. Chandar's house is neat but small."

Georgia consented to this much—she could do one night with only her essentials—but when Nandi asked her to leave her passport with him, too, she refused.

"It's for the authorities, you see, Miss Calvin. I'll need to get you registered. Things can be slow here, you understand, and you must want to rest."

"I'm in no hurry; I'll come with you." Years of travel with her father had taught her a few lessons at least: she would be polite, she would be patient, but she would never let her passport, not for a moment, out of sight.

"Another day then," Nandi relented. "Registration can wait. Sanjay will take you to your room now."

Georgia's temporary home was a ten-minute drive from Nandi's office: a cramped, ground floor flat with a rusting toilet and just one sink for the apartment—in the kitchen area, surrounded by exposed pipes. Mrs. Chandar was waiting to show her in: her face was thickly lined, and she squinted like there was some trouble with her eyes.

The room she pointed Georgia to was barely large enough to hold a cot and a small desk; on the desk sat a plastic fan, a lamp, and an old miniature television, with dials missing.

"It's perfect, thank you," Georgia said.

After unpacking the few items she'd brought with her, she lay down on the cot. Out in the hall, a phone began to ring; Mrs. Chandar answered and then came to knock on Georgia's door. Georgia followed her into the kitchen, where an old rotary phone sat beside an electric kettle.

Mr. Nandi was on the line. "I want to invite you to join me and a friend for dinner this evening."

"Tonight?" She hadn't slept but an hour on the flight and jet lag was making her light-headed. "Honestly, I'd planned on just collapsing into bed."

"Oh, but you must eat. We'll make it early. Sanjay will pick you up at six and deliver you again at home."

She agreed; if Nandi meant this dinner as a gesture of welcome, she didn't wish to seem ungrateful. After a short rest and a rinse with cold water at the kitchen sink, she dressed in her only change of clothes: a button-down and linen pants. Sanjay called to her outside the door.

"We must leave now, miss. The roads can be slow this time of day."

They headed north, back on the highway, crossing again over fields of low, congested housing; sturdy tile-roofed homes gave way to hovels topped with aluminum siding or simple sheets of plastic, held down with stones. Soon the city center was behind them and they were back on the dusty highway: roadside shops sold maps and gum and trinkets for tourists. Above one, an electric sign blared: LUXURY SURPRISES.

She had the urge to tell Sanjay to turn around; she hadn't bargained for an hour's drive each way. But Nandi and his friend were waiting. It would be too rude to stand them up; better to use the drive to catch some sleep. She closed her eyes and when she opened them again, at Sanjay's honking, she saw muddied, skinny bovine haunches, a tail snapping; they were in the country, waiting for a cow to cross the road.

Not long after, Sanjay pulled up to an impressive wrought-iron gate under a freshly painted sign: HILTON MUMBAI.

The gate opened and the car moved down a driveway to where three men in white uniforms lined up to open Georgia's door. Sanjay instructed them where she was headed and two different men, in different livery, appeared to escort her through the lobby, past other white tourists and under chandeliers, to drop her in the dining room. The hotel restaurant was frigid and low-lit; the walls were painted with frescoes of dancing elephants. Mr. Nandi waved to her from a front table. He was dressed in a brown suit and pink shirt, beside a fat white-haired man in a well-cut gray suit.

Mr. Nandi performed the introductions. "Mr. Sadiq Gupta."

When Gupta put out his hand to shake, a gold watch jangled from his wrist. He handed Georgia a business card and she slid it into her pocket.

"Mr. Gupta is one of our largest donors."

She took her seat between the men. The waiter laid her napkin on her lap; he brought no menu.

"Allow me to do the ordering," said Mr. Gupta. "I come here often; this is among the best restaurants in Mumbai."

"I told you the man was generous," said Nandi, smiling across at Gupta.

Generous, maybe, but she was starting to suspect that it wasn't for her benefit that she'd been kept from bed after two sleepless days and carted miles away from her new home. These men wanted something; it was only the substance of their desire that eluded her. She had nothing to offer, nothing but the company of a fair-haired American—could that be all they sought?

Mr. Gupta began making small talk, asking how she found his country so far.

"On first glance, it's a culture of extremes." A polite way of saying one marked by shocking inequality. Already, this dinner had begun to feel oppressive—she was recalling her unpleasant work back in D.C., the many meetings she'd endured with potential museum donors, feigning interest because they were, like Gupta, reputed to be "generous men."

"A culture of extremes, exactly," Gupta agreed. "Both very foolish and very advanced. India has a long tradition of this. My father was educated at Oxford. My brother's son studies now at MIT. It's a fine school, they say."

"Yes, it is."

"And you, too, Mr. Nandi tells me, studied at a fine school. Harvard, am I correct?"

It surprised her to hear the name of a place so far away repeated here, though the explanation was simple enough: the volunteer agency must have sent Nandi her CV.

"I have a son, seventeen now," Gupta explained. "He would very much like to attend Harvard himself."

"Well, I'm sure he can if he works hard and if he's smart."

"Oh, he is certainly smart. Smart enough to choose a rich father."

Mr. Nandi laughed loudly at his friend's joke. A rather cynical take on the principle of karma, Georgia thought, but it must be hard not to grow cynical in a city where children begged on the streets outside designer shops.

Mr. Nandi turned to her. "I suggested to Mr. Gupta that perhaps you could be of help."

There was a lull; the men were waiting for her to speak. "I'm sorry," she said finally, "but there seems to be some confusion. I came to work in an orphanage. And you look healthy to me, Mr. Gupta, so, until your son qualifies . . ."

Nandi coughed and wiped his forehead with his napkin. Despite the cold air blasting from above, he'd begun sweating.

"Naturally, you'd need to meet the boy first," said Mr. Gupta. "You'll visit us in Malabar Hill. You'll see Dhanesh is a very special child."

"She will," insisted Nandi. "She'll meet the boy tomorrow."

Georgia fiddled with her silver, growing nervous. She disliked how freely Nandi spoke of what *she* would do—none of it implied by their previous agreement. She'd come to aid the deprived, not to dine among men in Bermuda shorts and loafers, women stuffing their rings into purses before they dared to step outside. An American couple sat bickering at the next table: "For God's sake, Sue, it won't make you look fat. The guide said *money belt up front*."

She must remember though, that beyond this hotel, she was not among her countrymen; she knew no one in this place so far but Sanjay and these men, and so she refrained from speaking her mind. She must better understand Nandi's intentions and her options. In the worst case, if she were the victim of fraud, then she'd contact Global Aid and lodge a complaint. She could demand her bags back, take her things, and go. She was here by choice, a volunteer, she told herself, though, seated between these strange men, she'd begun to feel more like a prisoner.

Four waiters arrived to parcel out three heaping plates of food.

"These are just the appetizers," offered Gupta. "You must try one of each."

"You see," said Nandi, "how very generous Mr. Gupta is."

16

Back in her room at Mrs. Chandar's, Georgia lay awake; the fan clattered madly but scarcely stirred the air. She was too full and hot to sleep. After a restless hour, she considered getting up and asking Mrs. Chandar if she might use her phone.

Her father was her first thought, the obvious person to turn to for advice in such a situation. But relations between them had grown strained. Her father's show in Chelsea had caused a storm within their family. Her mother had been outraged: it was vile enough that her ex-husband had taken those pictures in the first place, but to display them again at that moment, to profit from their daughter's ordeal, and from her public humiliation—this was a level of selfishness and depravity too low even for him. Georgia chose to disengage; she'd skipped the opening, pleading sick, and though she sensed her mother went too far in her anger, privately, she'd agreed with her.

The argument had only added to the stress of her first year out of school. Most of Georgia's memories of that time were of fear and isolation. Strangers recognized her from her photo in the papers; the story of the Patel case refused to go away. Storrow remained in the news, depicted as a drifting victim or a monster on the loose: trying to escape recognition, he'd moved from Boston to D.C., then to Cincinnati. Finally, he'd been hired by a Cincinnati law firm under a false name, and then summarily dismissed when the lie was discovered. Around the time Georgia discovered these facts, from a *Washington Post* story published a year after the murder, she began receiving strange phone calls. The number was blocked, and the caller usually hung up after a few seconds; he never spoke, but once she'd heard him cough "excuse me" and, based on this alone, this reflexive courtesy, she came to believe the man was Storrow.

To this day she didn't know if it really had been him; after a few weeks, the calls had simply ceased and nothing like them had occurred again. A year went by without incident and then another. The press moved on to other stories of other alleged murderers, and even she was beginning to forget about Storrow and Julie's death—or to think of them without fits of anxiety—until her visit to New York.

Alice's fantasies, Charlie's loneliness as thick as hers. Charlie's was the voice, Georgia realized, that she most wished to hear then, in Mrs. Chandar's dark, sweltering room, but she wouldn't allow herself to call him. She'd already abused what kindness he had left to show her, and anyway she couldn't risk letting the dread she'd felt with him, in New York, catch up with her here.

The next morning, when Mr. Nandi called at nine, Georgia inquired when she would be paying her first visit to the orphanage. Today was not a good day, Nandi said, because the orphanage director was ill, but Sanjay would be by to collect her around noon to show her the Mumbai sights.

"Actually, I'd prefer to go around on my own."

"I would discourage that. Until you become more familiar with our city." It seemed that Mr. Nandi meant to look after his valued property. Closely. But Georgia was insistent; the events of the day before had made her all the more determined to assert her freedom here, and Nandi's reluctance to take her to the orphanage that morning only deepened her suspicions. She decided she didn't need to wait for him; among the paperwork that she'd received from Global Aid was an address for Mission of Hope.

According to the guidebook map, the trip was short: the nearest train station, Andheri, was just a few blocks away, and a few stops on the Western Churchgate line would get her almost to the orphanage door. She packed her rupees and her passport—after Nandi's efforts to take it from her, she didn't trust leaving it behind. To keep people from staring, she wore her hair twisted up inside a cap and an Indian print scarf draped over her Western clothes. Experience had made Georgia confident on foreign soil; she was adept at navigating even poorly marked roads and at picking up local habits. On the streets, she moved swiftly with the crowd and, at the crossings, ran alongside other Mumbaikars, slipping nimbly between cars.

Traveling by train appeared much simpler and safer than by foot. She found the Andheri railway station and was relieved to see that the Mumbai trains didn't look like quite the death traps the guidebooks made them out to be. Parked on the platforms, they appeared sturdy enough, though the entrances were without doors. She moved deep inside the full car; the human stench was potent. Before the train had even left the platform, a child approached her, hand outstretched.

Her guidebook had warned her not to give—once tourists started doling out rupees, they would find themselves swarmed by children. Georgia gripped a rail and held her purse close, with the straps wrapped around her arm. Stoically, she shook her head over and over; it did no good. Within minutes she was surrounded: these children knew their trade; the motions and noises, even the costumes seemed arranged for effect. A boy began to whimper. His face was streaked with dirt. A girl pressed a flower into Georgia's palm, her hair was done in braids.

"Please," Georgia found herself pleading back at them, "a little space; I'll give you something when I'm getting off, okay?"

At first Georgia thought it was the tug of a child's hand she felt; but when she looked down to check her purse, just the straps were left dangling, neatly cut. In front of her, a man leaped out the open doorway onto the platform. The train was still in motion; she waited for it to slow and jumped down next, shouting for somebody to stop the man racing ahead.

People pushed against her, entering and leaving the train. Georgia watched the black head dashing through the crowd, and then lost sight of him; the thief and her purse—with her money, her passport—were gone.

Inside the station, she found a man in uniform who led her to another station employee, seated at a desk in a small office; a plastic fan turned in one corner, flypaper hung from the ceiling. She explained what had happened, and the man made out a note for her to show the conductor: her fee would be waived for her return trip.

"That's all you plan to do? What about police?"

"You want police?" the man asked, rubbing his nose; clearly he found money for a return trip the better choice.

She reconsidered. "I'd like to call the U.S. embassy."

The man at the desk said something in Hindi to his colleague and then returned to her. "Police can take you to the embassy. If you'll just wait a few minutes, madame. The police will come."

She waited, thirty minutes and then an hour and then two; the police were occupied, the station official told her, or else they must be coming from another station. Sometimes, he admitted, there were problems with the trains. She watched a fly trapped on the flypaper buzz and then grow still, buzz and stop, buzz and stop. She was sweating terribly.

"Maybe I should just call the embassy directly," she told the man at last. He shook his head. He didn't know about the embassy, he said; his duty was to notify Mumbai police and keep her there until the proper authorities arrived to file a report.

"You're saying I can't leave?"

"No, madame. Police are coming; they expect to find you here."

The time was nearly twelve. Soon, Sanjay would be arriving at Mrs. Chandar's to collect her; he and Nandi would worry at her absence. She ought to get word to Nandi somehow—but his contact information had been inside her purse. In the pocket of her pants, though, the same she'd worn the night before, she discovered Sadiq Gupta's business card.

It was Gupta's secretary who answered her call and realized at once the mess Georgia was in: "If the police ever arrive, you'll be there all day and evening." After consulting with Mr. Gupta, the secretary assured Georgia that the situation would be handled now: "Whoever seems to be in charge there, just put him on the line."

Twenty minutes later, Georgia was ushered to the station entrance, where a silver SUV waited for her outside. A man in a clean white jacket beckoned her into the backseat.

"Thank you so much," she told him, finding herself suddenly close to tears. "I'll be fine now, thank you, once I reach the embassy."

"Embassy, miss?" The driver locked the doors and honked at a beggar who leaned over the hood. "Mr. Gupta has instructed me to take you to his home."

Three more servants greeted Georgia at Gupta's apartment, leading her into a plush living room where, among the marble tabletops and upholstered divans, a boy and a strikingly pretty woman were seated. The woman rose to take Georgia's hand; she was dressed in Western style in a deep red blouse and skirt, makeup flawless, if a bit heavy. She looked far too young to be either Gupta's wife or the mother of the teen boy who sat with her, but it appeared that she was both.

"My son and I are very grateful that you've come today, with all your difficulties. Rest assured, my husband deals directly with the embassy. You don't need to worry, Ms. Calvin. Dhanesh, say hello."

The boy mumbled his greeting. He was a mousy type, with a narrow face and long-lashed eyes. Mr. Gupta had claimed his son was seventeen, but this boy seemed several years younger.

"Dhanesh is very eager for his first lesson."

"I'm sorry? What lesson?"

"I suppose an introduction," Mrs. Gupta offered. "You could start by describing the expectations you encountered at Harvard, or with the application process."

She could hardly stand: the cold air of the car on her sweat-dampened clothes had given her a chill. What she felt, along with relief at the sight of such pleasant surroundings, was a desperate desire for a warm shower and a rest. "I'm not in any state, I'm afraid, to have a lucid thought right now."

"Of course." Mrs. Gupta smiled, not acknowledging the distress in Georgia's tone. "In that case, you're welcome to simply get to know each other then, until my husband returns to help you with your passport. Have a seat. He should be back home shortly."

Mrs. Gupta excused herself, leaving Georgia with the boy, who sat staring at his feet. He was just a child, shy and protected; his world, she imagined, consisted of these rooms, these servants, and his parents. She tried to recall a time, if such a time ever existed, when her own life had felt so small and safe.

"You must be hungry." Mrs. Gupta had returned with a servant, an old woman, who laid down a tray piled with mimosas, pastries, apricots, and figs. Georgia hadn't eaten since the tea and toast offered by Mrs. Chandar in the morning, but she was wary of accepting more of this family's gifts.

"Mrs. Gupta, I think there's some confusion here; I don't know who came up with the idea that I can get your son into Harvard."

"I don't expect that of you," Mrs. Gupta said plainly. "That's the sort of thing I rely on my husband to do. But I think there are things that you can teach him, to prepare him. Mr. Nandi told us about you. We've discussed your helping out. It's quite all right with him."

"That may be. But I'm still not sure this will work."

"Has my son done something to discourage you?"

"He seems perfectly nice. But I came here to do a different job."

"Maybe you want private compensation."

"That's not it either." There was a steeliness to this soft woman, a practicality behind her refinement that encouraged Georgia to try to negotiate. "I'll tell you what. If the same assistance I give your son could be provided to others, if we could somehow arrange a class to include more children, from the orphanage—"

"Ms. Calvin, be reasonable."

"I don't see what's unreasonable about that. I understand your husband is a patron."

Mrs. Gupta cocked her head, contemplating the young woman before her. "You don't have children, do you?"

"I don't see how that's relevant."

Mrs. Gupta nodded. "Once you have a child, then you'll understand."

No arguments, Georgia sensed, would serve to alter this woman's need to improve her son's chances at happiness, even by a sliver. And just because Georgia knew, firsthand, that acceptance into Harvard would not guarantee him health or peace or satisfaction, still she wasn't going to lecture this woman about life's contingencies.

It must have seemed obvious to Mrs. Gupta, standing in her calm, elegant home, that if Georgia knew half as much about contingency as she did, she wouldn't be wasting these few years while her looks remained and her status afforded her entrance into the highest circles wandering through third world nations. She would be finding a man like Mr. Gupta who would provide for her in her old age and send her children out into the world as well prepared as they could possibly be.

How foolish she must seem then, Georgia thought, clinging to ideals of public service, while she clearly lacked the capacity to look after even herself. Her limbs were aching; she felt feverish. A thief had hold of her passport; Nandi had possession of her luggage; and she—without one rupee for a taxi, or one friend to call, or any home to stay in but the one Nandi was providing—was in no position to give voice to her scruples. If the Guptas wanted a tutor, who was she to wax indignant? Until she'd figured out her next move, until she was *at liberty* to move, perhaps she ought to agree to go along with whatever her hosts were asking.

"My husband will settle everything, don't worry." Mrs. Gupta laid a hand on Georgia's arm and gestured to the tray of food again. Georgia picked up a pastry, soaked in honey, and sank onto the cool sofa to wait with the silent boy for his father to return.

17

Two hours later, when Mr. Gupta finally appeared, Georgia was released and driven back to Mrs. Chandar's. The old woman met her in the hall, informing her there had been a call for her. An American. "He says he comes here."

"From the embassy?"

Mrs. Chandar nodded and wiped a cloth across her neck; there was sweat gathering in the wrinkles; she'd been cooking. The smell of oil and spices filled the narrow rooms, and the temperature had risen to above the heat outside.

Georgia washed herself with a hand towel at the kitchen sink, then lay down on her cot. The news from Mrs. Chandar gave her relief enough to sleep a little, despite the honking cars outside her window: the incessant bleat of traffic. When she woke, mouth dry and limbs aching, the light in the room was dimmer, and a man was speaking with Mrs. Chandar in the hall. The words were Hindi, the accent American. His voice was familiar, deep and formal, though he was making an effort to sound buoyant.

She stepped outside, and the man turned and gave a clap: "Georgia Calvin. What on earth are you doing in this place?"

The visitor was brown haired and freckled, dressed in an off-white high-collared linen shirt. A jacket was thrown over his shoulder, with affected casualness; his eyes were hidden behind a pair of Ray-Bans, which he lifted, slowly, as Georgia took a step back.

"It's me, yes."

Her legs trembled. For an instant, she thought this figure must be a product of some fevered hallucination.

Rufus Storrow: darker, more weathered, aged—but nevertheless it was him. Somehow he'd materialized here, in Mrs. Chandar's rotting Mumbai flat. It wasn't possible—she'd never been further out of reach from her past; no one from home knew where to find her. Not even her father had this address yet. And yet, this man whom she'd successfully avoided for four years, had appeared at her new home as simply as if he'd strolled from Harvard Yard onto Cowperthwaite Street.

"I didn't mean to take you by surprise," Storrow said, smiling, with deeper creases now at the edges of his mouth. "I called earlier; I left a message that I'd be coming."

"That was you? *You're* with the embassy?"

"Not directly, no. I've been consulting on a case though, involving an American ex-soldier, and it's involved some cooperation with the embassy. I've made friends over there, let's say. That replacement passport, it's being seen after, by the way. Is there somewhere we might sit?"

Storrow peered around the rooms before starting toward the kitchen, where he took his seat at the small table. Though there was scarcely space for three, Mrs. Chandar slipped in behind him to offer him something to drink: "Tea, beer, sir?" Georgia caught the woman eyeing her and smiling: Storrow was still handsome and, seemingly, capable and friendly—the sort of man a young woman would be pleased to receive at her home, especially when she was in trouble. To Mrs. Chandar, Storrow must have seemed someone whose presence should soothe Georgia, rather than inspire the panic that was visibly overtaking her.

She stood at the doorway, unable to move. "What do you want?"

"Plain tap water would be grand," Storrow remarked calmly. He turned to address Mrs. Chandar in his American-inflected Hindi and pulled out a chair for Georgia.

She took her place in a different chair, across the tiny table; she couldn't bring herself to sit alongside Storrow—this, the same man she'd once spent afternoons in bed with, studying the freckles that dotted his forehead and shoulders, the small scars by his brow and the bottom of his chin, all the details of that body still much the same, despite the different clothes and that dyed brown hair.

She supposed she had been staring because Storrow grew self-conscious; he peered down at his shirt, worn more loosely these days, with a hint of slovenliness that was completely absent from the starched Storrow she'd encountered at Harvard. He ran his hands through his hair, which she observed was now receding at the temples.

"To blend in better, I colored it finally. You must have noticed how it is here, if you're fair. All that unwanted attention. Well, I'd had enough of that back home."

He smiled up at her, a different smile, too, than the one she recalled seeing, if not often, in the past: this one trickier and shakier. The smile of a man who'd faced plenty of stares, yes, and the question behind them: Am I looking at a killer?

"How did you find me? Nobody knows I'm here." She wasn't about to pretend, even if Storrow meant to, that this was any sort of ordinary meeting. "You still haven't told me how you got this address?"

Storrow paused to thank Mrs. Chandar, who set his water glass before him and exited the room. "I happened to have some business in the embassy this morning. A friend there had come across your name on a request form. 'Could it be the same Georgia Calvin?' he asked me. He's one of the few here who knows about my past, our history."

Their history.

Storrow was watching her; there was a new gravity to his face, apparent once he'd stopped smiling—a raggedness around the eyes. He was still attractive, she couldn't deny it, but he'd grown more battered and more bloated than the elegant sportsman she'd once admired from poolside. He'd begun to look like what he was now: a man approaching fifty, whose great energies had been spent. She knew something of his failed attempts, covered in the press, to avoid living under constant suspicion; even now he seemed to grow more tired as he took note of her alarm. Perhaps he'd hoped to be spared the task of persuading *her*, at least, that he wasn't someone to be feared.

"Of course," he said, with that laborious good cheer. "I don't blame you for being shocked. It's quite a coincidence, both of us ending up here."

"Is it?"

"Unless you've followed me," he said, forcing a laugh. "You're the one who's just arrived; I've been here over a year already." He took a gulp of the tap water, which was poison for newcomers, not that this stood as proof he'd spent the year here as he claimed.

"You can imagine it's been easier for me abroad," he went on, since Georgia remained quiet; she could hear, behind his voice, the rush of blood in her ears. "I still have my old pals, from my time in Pakistan. Work isn't a problem for me here. Just had to bone up on my Hindi and then, well, I've found myself settling in."

Storrow withdrew a handkerchief from his front pocket and patted his face slowly, until she'd had ample time to observe the thick gold band on his left hand.

"You're married."

He glanced over at his fingers, looking as if he was surprised to glimpse the ring himself. "Recently engaged."

Employed and engaged: Storrow welcomed back into society, albeit not the society he'd once worked so hard to impress. Could he have come today just to make his progress known to her? Was he vain enough to put them through this strenuous encounter just for that? Perhaps it was the spite of the rejected behind his boastful grin: the pride of having discovered satisfaction—even love—before she had.

"You're here alone?" he asked her.

"With a volunteer program." She didn't know how much this alleged embassy friend had told him, but she wasn't feeling eager to admit her isolation.

"And out of all the places in the world, you've arrived in Mumbai." Storrow tapped the table beside Georgia's arm. He'd have preferred to touch her, it seemed, but this was as much as he'd permit himself. "It can't be a fluke."

"What is it then?"

He looked off at the small window, with that intensity she'd found in the past by turns oppressive and magnetic—as if the grapplings of his soul, his desires, his aspirations and regrets, were of such greater consequence than for the rest of us. "You've come for the same reason I have. To do penance."

Storrow's face grew grim. In the harsh glare of the kitchen, she could see the sun and pollution had toughened his complexion, turned his delicate pallor to a mottled, unhealthy red. His features, now that his skin was rougher, looked more brutal. His green eyes settled on her, cold.

"I'm not saying I killed that girl," he remarked sharply, breaking the silence in the room, shrinking it around him, until she became aware of his strength, of the implicit threat he posed.

"*You* said penance, not me."

"You're right, I did. I did." He clapped and laughed, a loud laugh that seemed to rattle the weak walls. "It's good to see you, Georgia. Still the same spirit. Giving hell. Really, it's good to see you're well."

"And you, too," she replied, though in fact, she wasn't sure the man was *at all well*.

He nodded, gratified. "Hasn't always been that way, but I've come to accept what's happened. Never considered myself a spiritual man, but when something awful happens to you—it does inspire reflection. Not at first; the first reaction, that's plain rage. What did I do to deserve this? But the second reaction, which takes time, you start to ask, in earnest, *did* I do something to deserve this? Did I—somehow—bring this upon myself? That's the beginning of self-knowledge and reform. Humility, let's say."

But Storrow did not look humbled to her. He seemed to be gloating, rather, and to recognize that she was now his captive audience. This most unfortunate man—or so, in the press, he claimed to be—had finally caught a bit of luck: he'd managed to find her at her most vulnerable, in the one corner of the globe where he could present himself as an authority again.

Even she couldn't help seeing him that way a little, reminded of the mysteriously connected man who'd once rescued her from Gabe's apartment in New York. Some small voice in her still wondered if he might rescue her again—from Nandi and Gupta, these people who'd lured her to Mumbai under false pretenses, and now meant to take advantage of her. She didn't let this small voice speak, however, because she couldn't be sure that Storrow wasn't worse: that he hadn't come, somehow, to take advantage of her, too.

What could he want from her? After so many years, their affair should be behind him, but Storrow's ordeal might have locked him in the past; how could she guess at the compulsive workings of his mind? Or, for that matter, her own?

He'd come here to do penance Storrow said. And so, he said, had *she*.

A thousand times her thoughts had circled back to that afternoon, four years ago, in Storrow's office: maybe Julie had known they'd been having an affair. Or maybe, by coming by to break things off with Storrow, Georgia had caused him to lose his temper and say something foolish to Julie, something he'd come to regret so much that he'd gone after the girl—just to talk, *just to get things squared away*—later that week, late at night.

"Georgia," Storrow's voice startled her. He wore a far-off expression, as if he'd been lost in contemplation of his own. "I really can't quite believe we're sitting here. Us. Again. On the other side of the world."

"Anyway, I won't be staying," she put in quickly. "Once my passport comes, I'm leaving India."

"Are you really?" His manner remained cool, but something desperate flashed in his eyes. "You might give this place a little bit more chance than that."

"It's just that my position here hasn't worked out."

"Maybe I could help you find another."

"No, no, thank you. I'm looking into other options, elsewhere." Storrow's apparent need for her to stay—this was enough to drive her out, even if all her plans hadn't gone horribly awry thus far.

All at once, Storrow grinned and lightly waved his hand: "Sure, India isn't for everyone, I'll admit. They do make a mess of things here—squirrelly people—though the country has its marvels too."

And really it would be a shame for her to fly off, he continued, before she'd taken in the Taj or the Ganges—or witnessed one of the charming local ceremonies. An authentic Indian wedding, for instance, was a spectacle that shouldn't be missed. "Arpana's and mine is just three weeks away—a two-day event at her family's country estate." Storrow fished through his wallet and withdrew a snapshot of himself alongside a young Indian woman, with smooth light skin and wide, dark eyes, her hair in a single braid.

An Indian beauty. One with an obvious resemblance to Julie Patel.

Georgia rose to her feet.

"Are you all right?"

"I'm sorry, but I . . . I haven't slept and I'm not feeling very well."

"Right, right, of course." Storrow stood and lifted his jacket over his shoulder; he was doing his utmost to remain calm, to insist upon his normalcy and this seemingly decent life that he'd constructed—work, a home, a fiancée—which struck her then as confirmation of his madness.

At the exit to the kitchen he stopped and turned; he filled the doorway, his arms stretched out to touch each side. "Maybe I'll be seeing you again then. If you're still here in three weeks, before the wedding—who knows how long the embassy will take to process your paperwork."

"In an emergency, I expect they're quick."

"And I do have friends there," he reminded her. He offered her his hand, then rethought himself and waved, stepping out to the hall and leaving her to wonder if he meant to assist or impede her departure. The front door closed behind him and, for a full minute, Georgia stood there waiting to make sure it would not open again, that Storrow was finally gone. Her whole body shook as she took the few steps back to her room, where she imagined she might wake to find this had all been a fevered dream. Only the logic of a dream could explain Storrow's finding her again: her, his erstwhile accomplice, lost like him beneath the Mumbai smog.

18

What awaited Alice beyond the mental ward on the day, two months into her treatment, that she was elevated to the status of outpatient would be enough to send anybody back behind those sterile walls. Enough, she thought, to send the sanest souls banging at that steel door, begging for readmittance, just to avoid the troubles that descended upon her sluggish, lithium-soaked frame.

The messages from the lawyer alone: Mary Wittmer's lawyer. Mary, who Alice had wished was, and at times convinced herself had been, an invention of her subconscious, a figure from a bad dream who teased her and tormented her but who surely couldn't—not legally—file suit.

Unfortunately, Mary was all too real, as was her lawyer, Andrew Kleinman—their existences were documented on legal stationery in three letters presented to Alice by Dr. Baum on the day of her release.

"You should know the authorities have been in contact with me; I told them you were in no state to talk. If you need me to offer a medical opinion, that's something you should have a lawyer get in touch with me about. Meanwhile, if you feel overwhelmed by any of this, I want you to call me right away. And I think it's obvious, given what you're facing, you'll need to be vigilant in keeping up with your outpatient care. You have someone to take you home?"

Today, as on the occasion of her first hospital discharge, four years earlier, she was to be escorted out by Charlie. He'd taken off the afternoon from work, he let her know, once they were out on the cold and humming street. She maintained this wasn't necessary, that she could get home on her own, but Charlie insisted on riding downtown with her, and in fact it proved a good thing that he had. When she arrived at her apartment, she discovered that her key no longer fit the lock.

She banged at the door, and a paunchy stranger came to answer, dressed in boxers and a yellowed undershirt.

"You must be Alice. I'm Sam, Bernie's cousin."

"What the fuck are you doing in my place?"

Charlie stepped between them then, urging her to calm down, and the stranger to go back inside, while he climbed to the next floor to have a word with Bernie. From below the stairwell she could overhear their conversation: Charlie lecturing Bernie about tenants' rights, speaking with a mature, informed authority he hadn't been able to pull off back at school. Bernie was scrambling to defend himself.

"Look, I'm not some rich landlord. I've got one floor to let and I rely on that income. She's four months overdue on rent—and it's not only about money. Whatever she's done, Sam tells me there have been some pretty screwy messages on her machine. Lawyers, cops, some guy making threats. We've got kids, you understand. And, besides, Sam's not really a tenant. He's my cousin."

Like she gave a damn who he was, Alice thought, this creep listening to her private messages. She had to grip the banister to keep from charging up those stairs to tell Bernie that she'd have police come by again, have *him* and his fucking cousin arrested for trespassing.

But the mention of the problems awaiting her was enough to give her pause. She'd need to ration out her anger if she had any shot at holding on to her hard-won sanity.

Taking a deep breath, she knocked again at her front door. "Sam," she told the baffled, half-dressed stranger, "I've got business here; go put on pants and take a walk. Please."

Among the sixteen messages that filled the tape on her machine, five were from Nick, spread across several days. Furious rants, typically inarticulate: "a severe *lazeration*, damage to the zygomax . . . zygomatimax . . . the fucking smile muscle, you fucking crazy bitch . . ."

Another five messages were work-related—from editors and from her agent—she'd missed deadlines on the stories she'd been writing:

one about a strangled socialite; the other, a prep-school prostitution ring. The second had been destined for next month's cover of *New York Magazine*, but no longer—both stories had apparently been pulled.

Three other calls were from the bank and a collection agency, and the rest were all from Kleinman, Mary's attorney, urging her to present herself to the police, and then apprising her of notices she'd receive by mail. Kleinman's final message, left just the day before, was to congratulate Alice on her discharge.

"I trust you've had a good recovery, Ms. Kovac; maybe you still need a day to settle in, review the documents I sent you. We've been patient, but you may hear from officers today; I suggest you retain counsel."

Alice's next move that afternoon was to contact a lawyer: Larry Skinner. She'd seen Skinner's talents displayed the year before, after a publicist friend of hers had tossed bleach onto gate-crashers at P-Diddy's white party. Skinner hadn't just kept the offender out of jail, he'd managed to keep her name out of the press.

Over the phone Skinner's voice was gruff and imposing, precisely how a bulldozer lawyer ought to sound, and so she'd expected him to be roused to battle when she showed up at his Midtown office the next day, after spending a sleepless night on Charlie's couch. In person, though, Skinner proved disappointing: short, with narrow shoulders and a grim disposition on the depressive side of the two poles it was her fate in life to shuttle between. His professional approach was risk-averse, if not outright defeatist.

There had been eyewitnesses, he pointed out, after reviewing the materials sent to him by Kleinman. West Broadway had been well lit and crowded at the time of the incident: one man claimed to have been standing right by Mary and to have observed the entire thing, up to and including Alice's fleeing the scene. The charge would be aggravated assault. Jail time was probable if she were found guilty, and even with her insanity defense, that result couldn't be ruled out. Opposing counsel would argue that her manic episode was brought on by the stress of what she'd done, and Nick would testify that she'd seemed perfectly lucid earlier that evening. If the matter went to trial, Mary would make a sympathetic witness, more sympathetic, frankly, than Alice. A jury conviction was a risk that Skinner didn't advise she take and, even if the verdict went her way, a trial would be long and costly, too, and emotionally draining. She needed to consider her mental well-being, to get on with her treatment.

The good news, or what he considered good news, anyway, was that Ms. Wittmer was open to a fair settlement, which she and Kleinman estimated at four hundred thousand dollars.

"For a scrape? That's the rate now?"

"Depends on the scrape." Seven stitches had been required for the wound on Mary's face. A cosmetic surgeon had been called in and, still, there would be a scar. Kleinman was claiming that Mary's deformity was easily worth a million in lost revenue, and, if they went to court, that was what they'd demand: after all, she wasn't only a beautiful woman, she was a TV star.

"Let's not go that far."

"Look, she was on TV. That's a statement of fact. And I gather there was talk about another series; seems she had hopes of a career in entertainment."

"Everyone has hopes of a career in entertainment."

"You came to me for my opinion, Miss Kovac, and I'm telling you: four hundred thousand is reasonable given what the girl has suffered."

Reasonable or not, she didn't have it. She didn't even have enough money to pay off her medical bills or her back rent. Bernie had moved a bed for her into his attic, crammed between a broken Exercycle and bags of his wife's prepregnancy clothes. A temporary measure, Bernie said, until Alice could become solvent again. How was she ever going to do that now?

More good news from Skinner: he'd negotiate a billing schedule so that, if need be, she'd be paying off Mary Wittmer for the rest of her indentured life.

Alice needed money, urgently, and so, ready or not, she meant to throw herself back into work. Her first calls—to her agent and two editors—were to apologize for the deadlines that she'd missed: she'd been sick, she said, avoiding details; the people in her circles had ways of picking those up on their own in any case. The point was she was back and eager to resume where she'd left off: nothing at all had changed.

Her colleagues, however, were of a different opinion; since the events of that September, *everything* had changed.

Surely she was aware of what had happened downtown?

Yes, she was aware: Baum and his minions couldn't keep news of the attacks out of the ward forever. As time went on, new patients came in with wild reports and Baum had to organize special group sessions to address "the national trauma and its implications for recovery." But nowhere in Baum's remarks was there anything about how it would affect local print media and Alice's career: no warning that readers had lost interest in socialite victims or scurrilous youth. That news came later, most directly from her agent, once Alice finally caught her on the phone: the city didn't need more dirt—only stories of brave widows and intrepid first responders.

Apparently America, and New York especially, would never be the same—or not, at least, before the next news cycle. The diagnosis from the trend watchers: the city was postcynical, posttrivial, and thus post-Kovnc.

After two weeks spent chasing an assignment—there must be some scrap somebody could give her—Alice couldn't even get an assistant to call back. Finally, in a fit of irritation, she hopped a cab to the Condé Nast building. She was apprehensive about showing herself among her former coworkers. Force-fed shitty hospital food, she'd packed on fifteen pounds; the dozen pills she took daily ruined her for exercise; they slowed her movements and, worse, hobbled her wits.

Only such dullness could account for her mistake: as soon as she'd seen the pity in her colleagues' faces, she'd realized she was finished. The next day, she received a call from Les Soroty, her editor at *Vanity Fair* and closest professional friend: "I'm speaking on behalf of everyone when I tell you, you should take advantage of this chance to look after yourself. Forget about your career right now, step back, reassess. Do you follow me?"

She'd been put on meds, not *lobotomized*.

It was all enough to make her long for the asylum, and her old cohort: the dim patients and dimmer orderlies, presided over by unit chief Dr. Baum. Not that she'd ever cared for any of them in particular; least of all Baum, whose egomania she'd glimpsed clearly enough through the fog of medications he administered to her—a drop more Lithium, a pinch more Depakote, until she began to feel like a meal he fretted over, like the carcass he was seasoning to impress a date. No, it wasn't that self-important prig she missed, only this: the sense of being looked after while she was free to write, whatever struck her fancy, and for as long as she could stay holed up inside her bright, clean room.

The mood that had gripped her while her fingers cramped around her marker—a round-tipped Crayola was the only implement she was allowed inside the ward—wasn't what she felt when she sat down at her computer to compose an article. That, her professional writing, was always a task fraught with a mixture of contempt for her subject and for herself—there wasn't one page she'd penned *outside* without the assistance of coffee and cigarettes (drugs that had served to keep her motivation outpacing her disgust). Always, her mind was on what her editors would want—Les Soroty the paradigm for all those that followed; "Les" she'd thought, a fitting name for a man determined to fit prose neatly below an ad for Prada—and for a man who wanted her, *expected* her, to make people who were already so very small look even smaller.

But in the ward, there was no editor to keep her from embracing the vastest of subjects from the loftiest perspectives: love, envy, violence. The things she'd written during her two-month confinement were more honest, she believed, than anything she'd dared express before; still she couldn't forgive Dr. Baum for the disappearance of her notebooks. She'd planned on giving them to Charlie, for safekeeping, but Baum had instructed the nurses to confiscate them first. Her writing was interfering with her treatment, he maintained, and when a nurse threw the notebooks out, he refused to see the loss as anything substantial: it was de rigueur, during a manic episode, to imagine that one's insights were far greater than they were, and better for Alice, anyway, as she prepared to rejoin society, to move beyond such distractions and focus on the practical concerns that she would have to face.

Her bank account was overdrawn; the hospital was sending bills; already she'd heard Bernie's wife complaining: "Why are *we* stuck with her? Doesn't she have a family?"

Three weeks after her release, Alice gave in and called her mother, asking for a portion of Vasily's inheritance. Magazine work had dried up and she was entitled, despite Vasily's deathbed caprice, to a share of the family money. Her mother replied to her in Serbian, though she knew Alice could scarcely understand her. Had Alice cared to retain those language lessons so important to her mother, perhaps the woman's response would have been different.

"Find other work," her mother told her. She had every advantage: youth, education—what was the problem?

"Think of it as a loan, to cover me until I do."

If she couldn't support herself on her own, her mother told her, then she could always move back home.

"I can't leave the city now; I'm still in treatment. Dr. Baum needs to monitor my medication."

Her mother pointed out they had telephones and doctors, too, in Cleveland.

"I can't handle a move now, okay, Mom? No shocks, no anxiety. Do you understand me? I need to do everything I can now to stay calm."

"So calm here."

"I could never *calm* there. *There* is the last place I could *calm*."

Alice's next call was to Charlie: Bernie's wife had left an empty suitcase at the entrance to her room. "I've already started packing," Alice let Charlie know.

If it was money she needed, Charlie offered to lend her what he could, but apparently staying with him again wasn't an option. "Thing is, I've started seeing someone and I . . . I don't think she'd appreciate it, appreciate *us*."

Us: as if he interpreted her turning toward him as a come-on—which it wasn't. She was almost sure it wasn't. And since when had Charlie become involved in a relationship? He hadn't mentioned anything about a girl before, nor had Alice observed the signs: evening plans he must rush off to, calls answered in a muted voice.

He was lying to her; he must be. Even if she couldn't identify the reason—not simply to avoid an inconvenience, or insist upon boundaries—such concerns hadn't bothered him till now. It hit her then, the one explanation for his acting so strangely. "This isn't about *Georgia*?"

"Georgia? No, of course not." Georgia had gone back to Washington, he stammered, and then on to India; "It can't be. Couldn't be."

He paused, exhaling heavily; Alice burst into laughter.

She went on laughing, drawing out his humiliation. She meant to hurt him: he was refusing her when she most needed him and without the decency even to be honest. On top of everything, she was sure he was doing this for Georgia, even after all she'd done to free him from Georgia's power, after she'd helped him to become a little less pathetic for a spell.

"So like I said," Charlie continued, straining to sound cool, "if you need a loan I'll be more than glad to help."

She hadn't bothered to reply.

The next day, Alice did the unthinkable: she registered for New Horizons outpatient care in Broadview Heights and boarded a bus—a fucking *bus*, to save a hundred bucks—bound for Cleveland.

"Home" was a brown brick house on Wallings Road, even dingier than Alice recalled from her last visit, two years before. The wall-to-wall carpeting was stained, the shower curtain fringed with mold. Plants—indoor varieties and others brought in from the porch for the winter—cluttered the kitchen and living room; it was a new development, her mother's penchant for gardening. The house smelled of wet soil and dog food.

The dogs were not new, or not two of them; the third one looked familiar but was the doppelgänger for a schnauzer mix that had died three months before. Poor Mother: beloved brother Vasily and beloved mutt both dead within weeks of each other, and Alice thought that *she* had problems.

It didn't come as much surprise to Alice that her mother wasn't dripping with sympathy for what she'd suffered; the woman's concern seemed reserved for her nonhuman charges. Senka exhausted half her time between walking and feeding and watering and weeding; the rest of her day was occupied with cooking, huge vats of food, more than even she and Peter, at a combined weight of over four hundred pounds, could consume. A few dishes she sold to a local deli or took to Vasily's widow. By five p.m. she was tired enough to reward herself with an hour's reading: novels in Serbian. She spoke to the dogs in Serbian as well, which might account for her intimacy with them: they indulged her by responding to a phrase or two.

For responsiveness, in general, thought Alice, the dogs seemed ahead of the people in that household. Peter, who still hadn't left home after Vasily's funeral, was so out of it that she first assumed he'd gotten into drugs. As it happened, Peter wasn't even curious enough for that; he was content just to spend his days working in a bike repair shop and his nights hanging out in her old room with his ugly girlfriend. Alice could hear them groping and giggling through the walls.

Yet who was *she* to criticize Peter or her mother for the vacancy of their lives? Since she'd come to join them, she'd accomplished nothing—despite her vow to start working on a larger project, like she and her agent (assuming the woman *was* still her agent) had once discussed: maybe a more personal account of her college days, centered—of course—on the '97 murder: *I mean, if you feel comfortable tackling all that.*

Inside the ward, Alice had felt more than up to it, unafraid of this or any subject. She'd had so much to say back then; the fullness of her being threatened to break her at the seams. In Cleveland, however, it was her emptiness assaulting her each time she sat down at her desk. Torturous enough that she even looked forward to the interruption, three times a week, when she was obliged to join her group at New Horizons.

There, she took her place in a circle of depressed housewives—not even one manic spirit to liven things a little—for sessions led by a therapist who wore leg warmers under skirts. Alice had asked her about them, finally, those repulsive flops of fabric. She'd meant only to be cruel, but after that, the therapist wouldn't shut up about it: "Do you hate all women? Are there *any* women you admire?"

"Dora. Anna O."

The therapist looked puzzled.

"Pop singers," Alice said flatly, "from the eighties."

But as much as she abused her, the group leader wouldn't let it go. "I'd like you to answer the question, if not to me, then to yourself. Can you name a single woman you like or trust, or, God forbid, might even love?"

Several days later, Alice received a postcard from Georgia, forwarded from Jane Street by Bernie and postmarked, two weeks before, from Mumbai.

On the front was a picture of a male silhouette against a steamy, silver riverbank. On the back, Georgia had penned just a few lines: she was leaving India for Africa and was sorry not to have written sooner; she hoped that Alice was recovering swiftly. *If you're getting this, you must be home already, feeling better. In which case there's something I'd like to speak with you about. Something you started to tell me at the hospital.* This seemed to be the main reason she was writing: *Storrow, you said, had come by looking for me.*

All that day and then at night, lying awake, Alice thought back upon her meeting with Georgia in the ward. Their conversation had been charged—affectionate at turns, also fraught—she'd evidently made some sort of admission about Storrow—but the precise details eluded her. Her memory of those weeks in the hospital was clouded; she'd been too medicated to think clearly or to censor herself.

And wasn't that the point? Why else had Georgia dropped in after four years? An aggressive thing to do: to take advantage of a person so exposed, to go fumbling among private thoughts without adequate permission. Vengeance masked as concern.

During the next of their biweekly phone sessions, Alice brought the matter up with Dr. Baum. Had she ever, by chance, talked with him about a visit from an old college friend?

"Is this the friend you wrote about at Harvard?"

"You know about that?" She was almost certain she'd never mentioned her *Crimson* article to Baum, but evidently, he'd done some research, taken what seemed a personal interest in the events of her past. Now, rather than answer her question, he was using this opportunity to address a few related questions of his own.

"We never spoke about your involvement in that story."

"Because I *wasn't* involved." She hoped she'd never given him a reason to think otherwise, not in their sessions and not in her private writings in her notebooks, which, after all, he might have read without her knowledge, too.

"You must have been close with the girl you wrote about, since you knew intimate facts about her and that man. There were certain facts I wondered how you even *could* have known."

Already she regretted asking Baum for help. She was tired of his hectoring, monotonous voice. Why couldn't they all leave her alone—first Georgia, and now Baum—prying into details that shouldn't matter anymore? "*Certain facts*: you're playing investigator, is that it? I thought your subject is the soul or whatever you chemists like to call it. Desires, fantasies, those are what matters; facts aren't supposed to."

"Do you believe that? Isn't one lesson of your illness the importance of holding on to reality?"

"No," she told him. "Guilt is what matters. And guilt isn't out there. It only exists *here*." She raised her finger to her skull, as if Baum, or anyone, were with her in her bare Cleveland room to see.

19

The Patels were living in East Liberty, a suburban neighborhood of Pittsburgh. 32 North Beatty Street. A pleasant house, split-level, newly painted, shining with that earnest immigrant effort toward middle-class American respectability.

Alice had come across this information almost by accident; Storrow's whereabouts were what concerned her after she'd received that postcard from Georgia. She'd done a search online, but rather than find any recent references to Storrow's activities, she'd instead turned up a small piece on the Patels in a local Pittsburgh paper—"Victim's Family Fights to Keep Case Open." A photograph accompanied the story, the family posed before their home. Mr. Patel was trim and balding, a technician at a research lab, a man of science like Alice's own father had been. Mrs. Patel was pretty, with a round, clever face and a graying braid. The girl, Darlene, was harder to make out: tall and hunched, dark hair shielding her eyes.

The Patels' address was listed; it was just a two-hour drive from the Kovac home in Cleveland—so Alice discovered, the next week, after she dropped Peter at the bike shop and borrowed his car to make the trip. She arrived at eleven when no one but Mrs. Patel was home; Alice glimpsed her taking out the trash, dressed in a red parka, moving slowly in the snow.

On the phone, the woman sounded every bit as sad and gentle as Alice had imagined. Her voice was slightly accented; it made Alice want to close her eyes.

"I'll be glad to meet you," she'd said to Alice. "I'm always pleased to hear from Julie's friends."

Mrs. Patel had prepared lunch: yogurt with mint, spiced potatoes. She was dressed in a cream tunic, neat and simple, like the sunny kitchen that she bid Alice enter. They ate together at a table beside the patio: much too cold to sit outside, but they could see the fresh snow on the lawn through the glass. Mrs. Patel took only a few bites, occupied with listening to Alice's idea, the excuse she'd given for her visit. With the five-year anniversary of Julie's death approaching, Alice had come to suggest a means of honoring her memory: a fellowship offered in Julie's name.

"We might start reaching out to alumni for donations now; take advantage of the reunion this spring. The idea would be to pay extra for the reunion, and that money would go to cover Harvard tuition for one student who best embodies your daughter's spirit."

"Did you know Julie well?" Mrs. Patel asked her.

"I knew her, but I wish I'd known her better."

It was enough; Mrs. Patel was a warm woman, evidently pleased to meet someone with even a slight connection to her daughter. Over the phone, Alice had given a false name: Shawna Lamb, the most innocent-sounding appellation among all her Cleveland former schoolmates. She'd been sure that Mrs. Patel would remember the name Alice Kovac, the aspiring student journalist who'd written so coldly of her daughter's death, questioning the virtue of a young woman held to be beyond reproach. Such a person wouldn't be welcome in the Patel home, unless, perhaps, she meant to offer an apology. Well, if she'd come seeking forgiveness, Alice thought, then lying to Julie's mother was a strange way to begin.

"My sense of Julie is that she'd have wanted some good to result from her passing."

Mrs. Patel agreed. "I'd like to move forward with this. Especially if Julie's sister could be involved somehow." She stood then, to replace the dirty lunch dishes with clean teacups and a plate of sliced spice cake. "Darlene is a senior now; she'll be attending college next year."

Ordinarily, this would be a plain enough remark, but given the fate of the woman's first daughter, and the stillness that descended over Mrs. Patel then, Alice understood that there was a complex motive for her mentioning this now.

Mrs. Patel went on. "After what happened to Julie, Harvard administrators made clear that they would waive tuition if Darlene ever decided to attend. There wasn't much else they had to offer; and they wanted to make it up to us in any way they could."

"As if there *were* any way."

"No, of course not." Mrs. Patel looked at once grateful and abashed to hear her say it. "There can be no reparation. Even to suggest there could be . . . But, my own feelings aside, as much as the idea of it disturbs me, I need to think about what's best for Darlene. Harvard is an opportunity for her. She's not the student Julie was. Money aside, her other options won't compare. We've left it for her to choose what she will do, but it's December, college applications are nearly due, and she hasn't started any of them. I had her guidance counselor and the school psychologist try speaking with her, but, as I say, Darlene isn't like her sister. She can be stubborn, and I don't always know how to reach her."

"It can't be easy, the whole subject, for any of you."

Mrs. Patel looked down at the table, brushed away nonexistent crumbs. Neither had touched dessert. "But maybe, if we could come at things another way, if you could interest Darlene in this scholarship of yours, then she would have to think about the chance that she's been given, too. She'll be home from school soon. I hope you don't mind, but I mentioned you were coming. As long as you're here, might you wait and have a word?"

Less than ten minutes later, a girl came through the entrance, clomping in wearing combat boots that looked like they weighed as much as the rest of her. Her hair was long and loose and not very recently washed; her pants were camouflage print, cut low enough to display a brown belly with a ring through the navel. She wasn't as pretty as Julie had been; hips and chest flatter, face longer.

"This is Shawna," Mrs. Patel informed her daughter. "I told you about her. She was a classmate of Julie's. She was curious to meet you."

"Why's that?"

"Be polite, Darlene. Shawna came all this way. Maybe you could show her your room?"

Darlene dropped her knapsack on the floor and continued down the hall. Mrs. Patel bent, sighing, to pick up the bag, and Alice trailed the girl to her room. Its walls were painted slate gray, bare, but for two tempera paintings of Ganesh, likely chosen for their kitsch value rather than their cultural significance. The bed was neatly made—her mother's handiwork, no doubt. Darlene plunked down onto the mattress and kicked off one boot. "So, let's have it. *Shawna*, is it? Why are you here, really? What's your deal?"

"My deal?"

"I've never heard of you, and then you turn up in my house."

Alice took her seat at Darlene's cluttered desk; school work and college informational booklets lay buried under CDs: Green Day, The Ramones, The Offspring, Jimmy Eat World. "What did your mom say?"

"You're planning some scholarship for Julie—maybe I'd like to be involved, which I wouldn't, which she knows, so that's all bullshit." Darlene kicked off the second boot and sat against the wall. There was a hole in her sock at the big toe; she stretched the hole further, picked lint out of the space between her toes.

Seventeen now, Darlene must have been twelve at the time of Julie's murder: studying herself for hours in the mirror, memorizing every pimple and unwanted hair and looking to her poised and pretty sister with admiration and probably a dose of spite. People couldn't shut up about Julie, perfect Julie, proud to excel and to satisfy her parents' wishes for her. A joy as a daughter and, almost certainly, a misery as an older sister.

"This is about Harvard," Darlene said at last. "Has to be. That's all my mom can think about—that I don't miss my one chance not to be a fuck-up."

"You can go to Harvard and still be a fuck-up, trust me."

Darlene eyed her skeptically, her chin buried in her knees. "So what, then, you're trying to act like a bad ass, get me to like you? That's what she's hoping: you'll be like some kind of example?"

Alice faced the girl, her angry, unbeautiful stare: "I doubt your mom wants me as your example." Reaching into her purse, she withdrew a vial of pills: Lithium, 600 milligrams, to be taken with lunch. She popped a pill and tossed the rest of the bottle onto Darlene's bed.

Darlene fingered the bottle, then sat, head cocked, not sure what to make of the strange woman who'd appeared, unbidden, inside her home. "You don't seem the type Julie would have hung with."

Alice laughed; it was a fact obvious to anyone but a mother desperate to believe. She took the bottle back from Darlene and returned it to her purse. Darlene watched her, unblinking, refraining from asking, again, the question that had begun their meeting: What *was* Alice doing here then?

There was a knock on Darlene's door and Mrs. Patel stepped in, looking sheepish. "Anything I can get for either of you? Soda? A snack?"

"Actually, I think we're finished here," Alice said. "I should probably start heading back."

"So soon? Are you sure?" Mrs. Patel looked nervously between Alice and her daughter. Darlene was quiet; her black-painted nails scratched at some tape stuck beside her on the wall.

The next morning, Mrs. Patel called to ask if Alice was free that afternoon. "I don't know what you said to Darlene, but it seems she'd like you to stop by again."

Alice was only too happy to accept the invitation, to skip out on group therapy and make the drive to revisit that house, and the family it contained. The Patel home suited her: the absence of pictures or childhood drawings on the walls, of holiday cards or vacation souvenirs along the mantel. There was no silly clutter, just a sober neatness.

Remembering the anarchy her own home had fallen into after her father's death, she found Mrs. Patel's efforts to keep domestic order an admirable feat. It might just be an illusion that chaos could be held at bay, still, it might have been the illusion she'd required at age twelve.

Thanks to such a mother, Alice thought, Darlene would pull through fine; whatever brief rebellious efforts she was making to distinguish herself from her lionized dead sister, in a few years Darlene, too, would be sensible and self-possessed. She would not make the same mistakes that Alice had. She would steer clear of creeps like Torsten; she wouldn't hold herself above her more sincere and decent classmates, the sort of people toward whom Alice had only shown contempt. How arrogant she'd been, to consider these others naive when, in fact, they were far ahead of her, further along in building balanced, satisfying lives than she'd ever be.

It was, Alice knew, a little early for regret: she was only twenty-six, a child by most standards, but not on the scale of her father's life, ending at forty. With all that she'd endured, she did not feel young. What she felt, above all, after her drive and with the medications heavy in her blood, was tired.

When Mrs. Patel welcomed her, Alice made a strange request, which, equally strangely, Mrs. Patel granted. She asked if, while she was waiting for Darlene to return from school, she might take a rest and lie down in Darlene's room.

Inside that cool, gray room, the college catalogs had been collected, stacked, and set out prominently on the desk: Harvard's featured at the top. It was clear that Mrs. Patel's true wish was for Darlene to accept the school's offer, that her youngest might resume the course Julie had begun, and bring her parents some share of that pride they'd been denied and maybe even, if such a feat could be accomplished, by stepping back onto that campus, cleanse those grounds of horror. Darlene could inherit the many hopes her sister had carried with her to the grave; she could also, her mother must imagine, go on to become a more successful and happier person, and all she had to do was decorate a dorm room, register for classes, and set up home a block or so from where her sister had been murdered without explanation by a killer still at large.

From the kitchen came the sounds of dishes clinking, running water. Alice crawled onto Darlene's bed, resting her head on the two plump pillows, fluffed up by mom each morning, smelling of fabric softener and the slightly greasy scent of Darlene's hair. *The Great Gatsby* lay splayed open on the nightstand. There was a drawer below; Alice slid it open and reached inside. Pens, batteries, junk: if Darlene kept a diary, she wasn't careless enough to leave it here. The most intriguing find was a series of shots taken inside a photo booth. Darlene and another schoolmate, a girl.

Alice studied the pictures: Darlene's friend had half her head shaved; in one shot, she was biting Darlene's ear.

The sound of running water stopped: Mrs. Patel was speaking on the phone. The conversation lasted only a moment, and then Alice heard timid steps outside the door. Unhurriedly, she replaced the photos of Darlene. Though Mrs. Patel might have been tempted to walk in, to check on the stranger she'd left among her daughter's private things, Alice knew she wouldn't dare to. It was too essential that the woman maintain her trust in her, this guest she'd placed such faith in, hoping Alice might achieve what the guidance counselor and school shrink could not.

"Shawna? Are you sleeping? Am I disturbing you?"

When Alice stepped out, Mrs. Patel was standing in the hall, gripping a dishtowel; she looked more nervous than when Alice had left her in the kitchen. "I have a request to make, if it's all right."

"Of course."

Mrs. Patel twisted the cloth and cleared her throat. "I hope it won't annoy you what I've done, but I went ahead and discussed your idea with a few of Julie's closest friends. Some of them have kept in touch, over the years. It seemed appropriate to include them."

Appropriate and inevitable, thought Alice, that a moment such as this would come. One of Julie's friends would grow suspicious: *Shawna Lamb you said? I don't recall a Shawna Lamb.*

"People seem to like the idea," said Mrs. Patel. "And someone already asked if he could speak with you about it."

"Oh?"

"You remember Lucas Parker?"

Not the face so well, but the voice, quaking with anger outside Charlie's window: *cunty bitch. . . .* What sort of curses would he shout to find her here, inside the Patel home? "Julie's boyfriend."

"So you *do* know each other then." Mrs. Patel looked relieved. "The whole family has been very supportive. Lucas especially; he'd like to join us, he said, for our next meeting."

"He's more than welcome." Alice offered a thin smile; Mrs. Patel folded the dish towel and checked her watch.

"I'm so sorry Darlene's keeping you waiting."

"Never mind. I'm the one who should apologize," said Alice. "I'm afraid I'm going to have to talk with her another day."

"No. Why? But you drove all this way."

"It's the drive back that concerns me; the roads are icy, and I'm a bit worried about my focus. I should have said something before, but all morning I've felt a migraine coming on." She didn't put too much art into the story; this episode with the Patels was over, anyway. Even if she'd begun to imagine she might, in fact, like to assist them, might really like to play the sort of charitable role that she'd assumed, there was no chance of that. This was the last time she'd set foot inside this house.

After another round of protests—Darlene would be back soon, Alice might lie down again—Mrs. Patel stepped away to retrieve Alice's coat. At the door, she paused. "I shouldn't have called those other people."

Her tone was so forlorn that Alice was left to wonder: Might the woman have other motives, separate from Darlene's interests, for wishing she would stay? She recalled her first glimpse of Mrs. Patel, before they'd spoken, when Alice had parked her car across the street and watched her carting out trash, standing on the snowy lawn alone.

Perhaps Mrs. Patel had never believed the lies she'd told her, Alice thought. Perhaps, Mrs. Patel had always known her for precisely who she was: a woman who'd lost her way, a woman like herself.

20

The trees along the National Mall were red and gold. This D.C. trip had offered him, thought Charlie—whatever did or didn't happen next—his first glimpse of a *true* autumn since his move to Palo Alto. He rolled down his taxi window to breathe in the bracing air. The cold felt familiar to him; it helped to still his nerves and clear his head.

He hadn't slept but a few minutes on the plane. His midnight flight had been delayed, and by the time he'd reached his hotel, close to morning, he was too excited to lie down. Anyway, sleep was something he'd learned to do without in the last weeks, while he was preparing for this meeting, his second one with In-Q-Tel's vice president, Mike McCraw.

Ten months before, back in 2002, McCraw had offered Charlie a lesson in how things worked in this town. He'd been around Washington awhile, it seemed, a man already well into his fifties, with a square face and the slicked-back, salt-and-pepper hair favored by politicians. His manner was cool and blunt: In-Q-Tel couldn't invest a cent in Charlie's project unless one of the intelligence agencies took an interest first—which wouldn't happen without his providing the relevant introductions, which he wasn't yet inclined to do. McCraw admitted he found Udi's model intriguing, but he had also pointed out gaps in their proposal and concerns he knew would be raised in future meetings, meetings he meant to delay until Charlie could put on a better show.

"To fix this will take money," Charlie told him, but McCraw hadn't been offering.

"Go track down a rich uncle."

That exchange had taken place while Charlie was still living in New York. Not long after, he let go the lease on his beloved Riverside

Drive apartment and boarded a plane bound for Palo Alto, planning his pitch and jotting notes in his in-flight magazine.

The greatest intelligence failure of our time: entirely preventable. It was by now public knowledge that before 9/11, the government had been in possession of all the information needed to identify the hijackers. Agents had known Atta and his men all hailed from nations harboring terrorists and had arrived on temporary visas, trained here to fly airliners, and purchased one-way tickets, each for the same day. Had the defense department been able to rely on a system like the one Udi and his partners had devised, government staff could have cross-checked such data in seconds, foreseen the attacks, and taken steps to prevent them. "With *your* help," Charlie planned to tell investors, a tragedy like this would never be permitted to occur again. Here was a chance to contribute to the most vital national interest, and, in the process, he would make clear, turn a considerable profit. It was also by now public knowledge that the Bush administration would be investing in technologies like this one, and contracts worth hundreds of millions would be up for grabs in the near future.

Over the next months, Charlie delivered a similar speech forty times, to execs from every VC firm on Sand Hill Road—none of whom reacted the way Charlie had hoped. Though they shook their heads in sympathy for the 9/11 victims, that sympathy didn't extend to the government. Bin Laden's strike on innocents might have been evil, but it was Bush and his assaults on civil liberties that got them really heated.

Have you read the Patriot Act? In the hands of this administration, big data means Big Brother.

Charlie listened and assured these men and women he took such concerns to heart. That summer, he called a meeting with Udi and the two other software designers on the project. The four men sat down together: skinny Udi, all limbs and Adam's apple; Doug Fincher, the eldest of their group, thirty and already bald; and Philip, the prodigy, an African American kid with bulbous hazel eyes. Surely with all the talent assembled in this room, Charlie announced, there must be some way to equip their software with solid privacy protections: the searches on their system should be targeted—no arbitrary fishing expeditions—and there should be audit trails to hold agents accountable and lockouts to control leaks of information.

In September 2003, Charlie returned to Sand Hill Road to offer investors a new pledge: their system would defend the nation from both terrorists *and* from an overzealous government willing to trespass laws to stop them.

Still, the millionaires of Menlo Park were unconvinced: for all their revolutionary optimism about technology, they proved to be cold skeptics about people. Privacy protections sounded nice enough, until the guys at the NSA found a way to circumvent them. Whatever Charlie's intentions, the government would take the tools he gave them and continue to do what they'd been doing—trampling the Constitution in the name of some bogus war.

Bogus war? Maybe, as far as justifications went, but it was also a very *real* war, Charlie thought. Missiles had struck Baghdad in March and since then, *real* men and women were risking their *real* necks; his technology could save their lives.

While these young financiers sat there in their air-conditioned offices, playing video games and sipping bubble tea, kids like them were standing in blazing dusty heat trying not to get blown up. This was what Charlie felt like saying, each time he was thanked for coming in and told that the partners at "Who and What" weren't quite ready to invest. Instead he shook their hands and smiled. No good would come from arguing; national security was an abstraction to these people, none of whom, he imagined, had a brother like his who'd ever donned a uniform—and might again.

It was while Charlie was settling down in Palo Alto that he'd gotten word from his mother that Luke was petitioning to reenlist. Two months earlier, Luke had filed an appeal with the air force board of corrections and he'd performed favorably at subsequent hearings. Despite the unpleasant events that marked the end of his service at

Eielson, Charlie's brother was determined to find a way to serve his country again.

"I've got family in the service too," Mike McCraw informed him, when Charlie phoned again, that October. "A nephew—you remind me of him, really: stubborn kid."

McCraw sounded considerably warmer than the last time they'd spoken. Recent history had done a great deal to improve his attitude toward Charlie and his partners: terror alerts hovered between high and elevated; the NSA had just put together a consortium on data analytics; Boeing and Booz Allen were competing over contracts worth almost three hundred million. All this inspired Charlie to be bolder with McCraw this time: "Enough stalling; you need to make those agency introductions for me now."

He'd get back to him, McCraw promised: a scant two hours later, he called again to schedule a next meeting for the end of November; there would be other people joining them, he said, though he hadn't mentioned who, or from what government branch these people hailed. He'd only left Charlie with one piece of advice: "Come prepared."

The meeting lasted just half an hour. It took place in McCraw's Arlington office, a brief cab ride from Charlie's hotel, past the National Mall and across the Potomac. The room was spare: a couch and a desk with a statue of an eagle perched at its edge; a screen had been set up for Charlie's presentation. Two men were waiting with McCraw: one young with shiny skin and round glasses; the other older, with a high belly and bristly neck. They wore not black suits, as Charlie had imagined, but gray flannel ones, and introduced themselves as NSA agents, Price and Marshall, which had to be a joke. In the company of this pair, even the name Mike McCraw rang false.

For the first twenty minutes, Charlie ran the prototype that Udi, Doug, and Phil had been toiling away at these last months: a simulated counterterrorism exercise, and a sharp demonstration of what their software could accomplish. After that, McCraw took over, speaking with his hands in his pockets, easy, chummy. A deal maker more than anything, someone who knew his role and its parameters: to negotiate between the men like Charlie, who created software he couldn't understand, and the intelligence guys who let him understand only as much as they cared to, and not one jot more.

Price and Marshall, said McCraw, would be working directly with Charlie from now on: "The agency will want to use its own people to set up and run the system, which means you'll need to train them. We'll also need to mix some of our employees in with yours. To observe."

"I hope you won't have objections," said Price or Marshall, whoever was the older of the two. Charlie's gaze drifted for a moment to a row of photographs hung on the wall: McCraw shaking hands with various officials—George Tenet, Dick Cheney.

"It's for the national good, right?" he heard himself say. "Aren't we all on the same side?"

Handshakes were exchanged; McCraw would have their lawyers draw up papers. On the way out, McCraw spoke of the future, of the company whose existence Charlie hadn't dared believe in until then.

"You'll need a name—you got something in mind?"

He did: some weeks ago he'd mentioned his idea to Udi, an apt name for their system; three data streams analyzed at once, three races run by one machine.

"Triathlon."

As soon as Charlie returned to his hotel, he dialed Udi back in California. He knew that Udi had been catching flak lately for choosing him to represent them to investors, that others, including Doug Fincher, had been proposing they replace him. But however short his attention span, Udi proved enduringly loyal—he'd even passed on the news that Terrance Welch had been in touch with Doug two weeks before, suggesting that Charlie wasn't in a position to raise the capital that they required. "With Charlie out, we might have a conversation," Welch had offered. Charlie wasn't sure himself if Welch was sincerely interested in their project or was just intent on doing damage to him personally, but his opinion didn't matter; Udi's and Doug's did.

"I know what Welch is and what you are," Udi had assured him, as Charlie had assured him he would get them the results that they deserved:

"You won't regret your faith in me."

It was with great relief, then, that Charlie relayed his news: "We got it. Five million up front. Office, salaries, a staff of the best programmers: tell Doug and the other guys; it's *all* possible now."

Charlie's next call was to Welch, a few simple words left on his voice mail: "Nice try, you old fuck."

As soon as he'd hung up he dialed Roger, whom he meant to make an official partner in their company once he could offer him a salary comparable to what his firm was paying.

"You're in," he told him. "It's a done deal. They're working up the term sheet."

"You'll want my input—"

"Ultimately, sure. But could you stop talking like a lawyer? This is *huge*. A life changer. You're not excited?"

"I am. For you."

"For *us*."

Roger made no reply. This was not the first time Charlie had endured such silences; they'd been Roger's standard response to his recent complaints about the tone on Sand Hill Road. Roger, he'd discovered, shared in the misgivings about the current administration, especially on matters of defense.

"Look, I realize this isn't your ideal outcome. But In-Q-Tel's involvement won't affect your side of things." To insulate Roger from any dealings with the DOD, Charlie had proposed he be in charge of their private-sector clients. Their software had applications in a variety of industries; they could offer antifraud protection to insurance companies and banks, or develop research tools for pharmaceutical companies or investment firms.

"This money is only so we can get off the ground. Once we are, there's no limit to what we can accomplish."

We he kept insisting, though the one time Roger used that pronoun, it was in reference to Jasmine and himself.

"We just need a little more time to mull it over, the implications. I'm partner-track; Jasmine has her residency at Northwestern Memorial."

Of course what Charlie was proposing was a big adjustment for Roger, and for Jasmine, especially: moving out west from Chicago, away from friends, colleagues, and Jasmine's family. Probably, thought Charlie, if Jasmine had believed he might actually raise the millions he was seeking, she would never have let Roger agree to join him if he did.

He got off the phone with Roger, finally, reminding himself that his friend could be relied on for many things, but unbridled enthusiasm was not one of them. For that, Charlie would have better luck calling his mother, but if he did, he ran the risk that she would pass the news on to his father, who would inevitably say something bitter or belittling to spoil his mood.

His thoughts turned to Melissa. They'd been dating for two months; he'd met her at the offices of one of the investors that he'd courted. Smart, capable, attractive—she was precisely the kind of woman he should be nuts over, and yet their affair had been plodding along. He worked hard and she worked hard, and neither took offense if nearly every dinner, movie, or fuck they found time for was prefaced by the words: *I've got a meeting close by earlier, I'll be in the neighborhood.*

Maybe tonight was the opportunity he needed: a moment for a grand gesture.

"I want you here with me," he told her over the phone. "I'll get us a room at the best hotel; take the next flight and I'll pay. I'll pick you up at the airport."

"Charlie," she reminded him, "it's ten o'clock on a Tuesday."

"Planes fly on Tuesdays."

"I have work tomorrow."

"Call in sick."

"I can't, I have stuff to do. In fact, I'm in the middle of something right now."

She wasn't enticed; instead, he sensed irritation in her voice. Two months and he'd offered her nothing but takeout and cable and now she was expected to drop everything just because he wanted a witness to his accomplishment.

"Fine, we'll celebrate when I get back. At your convenience."

"We'll do that. And Charlie?"

"Yes?"

"Congratulations."

At eight o'clock Charlie went down to the hotel restaurant and ordered a steak that came out dry, a side of fries and spinach, and a chocolate soufflé, which he finished, although the cocoa was chalky and he'd lost his appetite. Toward the conclusion of the meal, the waiter came over to inquire whether he was Mr. Flournoy from room 9F. "I have some champagne ordered for you: a gift from Roger Waldman."

Champagne: just like Roger had given him their sophomore year, when Charlie lost his bid for Undergraduate Council—the same perfect, crystal fall day that Georgia Calvin came jogging up a Fresh Pond path to sit beside him on a blanket in the grass.

Ancient history for him, but reliable Roger was still the same man, stuck: still with the same plain girl and safe ambitions, the same unwillingness to skip out on routine, take a risk, have some fun—still offering the same hokey token of celebration—just a better vintage now.

The waiter left to bring the bottle and a bucket of ice: before he'd popped the cork, Charlie stopped him. Livelier, he decided, to drink among the crowd up at the bar. The place was bustling—a popular after-work hangout, from the looks of it, frequented by men similar to those he'd met earlier: slicked hair and suited, the most relaxed of them in blazers and pressed pants. The women matched them, in their fitted skirts and heels; Washington was an ordered, cliquish place, those of a common stripe predictably where they ought to be. Even seeking sex seemed a regimented business. People in this town respected hierarchy and were drawn to power, in rather obvious manifestations.

Charlie came to stand beside a brunette in a low-cut blouse and red lipstick; her long hair was blow-dried smooth. While he was thinking what to say, she was the one to address him first, observing that the bottle being opened for him was a good one.

He offered her a glass, as he imagined was the thing to do in such a case. Drinking with strange women in bars—this, Charlie felt, was behavior for a different man, the sort he'd served as a busboy at the Palm, men who flew in helicopters over traffic to make their dinner reservations, who felt entitled to skip the ordinary hassles and indulge in rarefied amusements. But next to this woman—Bethany was her name—and after the morning's improbable success, he could almost pretend he'd become one of them, while she was all the many women they attracted. He noted the same set of expressions he'd observed as a kid: shifting between greedy and coy.

"And what do you do, Charlie?"

"I'm in technology, or security, whatever you prefer to call it."

"Either sounds good."

After their first drink, she was the one to maneuver their exit, starting with complaints about the noise and then a draught coming from the door. When they left for the lobby, she was holding the champagne bottle by the neck; his hand grazed her waist as they started together for the elevator.

On the ride up to his room, he began to feel his nausea; the meal had been too heavy, and his beers at dinner didn't sit well with the champagne. In the sharper light of his hotel room, the woman's skin looked overpowdered; her bra was push-up, a pendant nestled in the cleavage. Crude seductions; he ought to be beyond them, would do better asking her to leave and calling Melissa to apologize instead. Maybe he and Melissa could become a proper couple, if he were to make an effort, take his romantic cues from Roger, whose relationship with Jasmine had lasted all these years. Already Roger and Jasmine were engaged; already they were talking about starting a family. He ought not ask his old friend to upset his life for his sake; he supposed he knew that Roger wouldn't do it, anyhow.

"Something bothering you, Charlie?"

"Nothing." He joined the brunette on his bed. They kissed a moment, then he unbuttoned her top; somehow she managed to slip out of her stockings. The sight of her tan hose, shriveled on the bedspread, made him stop and rise to open a window. "I just need a moment. I'm feeling a bit off."

She wrapped her shirt loosely around her and lay on her side across the mattress; her finger traced the pattern in the bedspread: "So tell me more what you do, Charlie."

"Like I said: security."

"That's a big category. You build bombers, you guard the corner store?"

He exhaled: *yet another stranger waiting for his pitch.* "I'm a war profiteer."

"Now you're just bragging." Her eyes were squinty; she was smiling. She stretched her legs out toward him. "You want me to think that you're a *bad* man, is that it?"

Bad men, good men—a distinction for the bedroom, merely. Out of the blue, it seemed, he found himself thinking of Luke. The army needed more "good men" so never mind that boy he'd beaten; they'd stick Luke in fatigues again and dust him off to dodge shrapnel in the desert. And for what? So that, if he weren't killed or maimed or otherwise destroyed, he'd earn the privilege of holding his head higher among the assholes in their town, or maybe so the girls who'd batted their lashes at him in school might do so again.

Charlie looked across at the brunette, her attention focused on the arrangement of her limbs.

"Are you married?" the brunette asked him. "Is that it?"

"No. Nothing like that."

"So what's the problem?"

He shouldn't be here. Instead of screwing around in a hotel, he should be on a plane headed home; he should be doing everything in his power to keep Luke from enlisting again, risking his life, getting torn apart by an IED—and for nothing—to soothe his father's wounded pride.

He had no doubt: it was their father behind Luke's decision; his father's vanity was so great that he would even sacrifice his eldest son, that once vibrant boy.

"Excuse me, Bethany, but I need to make a call. A private one. Downstairs."

"You're leaving?"

He grabbed his coat; his last glimpse of the woman was her reflection in the hotel mirror, looking perplexed to find herself alone on the bed.

The time was nearly midnight; far too late, Charlie realized, to start phoning his house, professing his objections to his brother's plans. Still, once he was out in the hall, he had no desire to return to his room; better to get some air, walk off his queasiness, and, with any luck, when he returned, the brunette would be gone.

He rode the elevator to the lobby, which was quieter at this hour; only a few people crossed his path on his way out, one of them a man—lithe and handsome, with a slender jaw, a high pale brow, and bold green eyes.

Charlie stopped short: Was he seeing ghosts now? This figure sprung from his addled, alcoholic nerves? The man's back was to him when Charlie turned; the clothes were nondescript—rumpled sweater, jeans—and the hair was brown.

It couldn't actually be Storrow that he'd seen. To be sure, Charlie thought to call out the man's name, but he hesitated, just an instant, long enough for the stranger to spin away through the revolving door. Charlie watched him cross through traffic, the side of his face red in the taillights.

21

Charlie's flight out of D.C. left in three hours; he'd pushed this visit to the limit, had just returned to his hotel, to pack his bags, after the sixth and final meeting arranged by Mike McCraw. From the hall outside his room, he could hear the phone ringing.

"Charles Flournoy. You know who this is?"

He knew the voice as well as any; not so many years ago, seated inside a classroom in Sever Hall, he'd studied its many inflections, taking in the pitch and rhythm, adopting some of its peculiar patterns. So it had not been his imagination: that dark-haired Storrow clone he'd glimpsed three nights before. It was the man himself, after all. A guest, it seemed, in this very hotel.

"Professor Storrow." He couldn't think how else to address him, though this way sounded much too childish; across the line, he heard a chuckle.

His throat felt dry; he was nervous. "How did you know I was here?"

"Five minutes ago, I saw you step out of a cab and I just had to ask reception. Charles Flournoy, in my hotel. Unbelievable."

"Unbelievable, indeed."

"How long will you be staying?"

"Checking out now."

"Now that's a shame," said Storrow, lightly, as if they were easy pals. "We might have met up sooner. Well, when's your flight? Want to grab a quick drink first?"

"No time, I'm afraid." In fact it was the truth: he'd yet to pack and needed to leave for the airport shortly; his morning meeting had been squeezed in at the last minute. All week, McCraw had been calling upon him, without warning, to perform for reps from the FBI, Homeland Security, and Special Forces. He'd been hustled from building to building, in and out of meetings with nameless men inside windowless rooms, encounters almost as incredible, and unnerving, as the one Storrow was proposing now.

"I can join you in your room, chat while you pack."

"At the bar is better." He'd spoken quickly, out of panic; instead, he should simply have told Storrow that he had no wish to meet. He'd need to learn how to say no; people were bound to ask for favors now that word of his deal was out. The quantity of In-Q-Tel's investment had garnered headlines in most of the industry publications. *Information Week*, *Mercury News*, and *Intel News* had each called or sent reporters by for comment.

Was he to believe it was an accident that Storrow, too, came calling now? Not since the man had shown up in his apartment back at school had they exchanged a word. Back then, Charlie had made it plain, moreover, he wanted it no other way.

Airline ticket, wallet, phone—Charlie gathered his essentials in his pockets and tossed the last of his belongings into his suitcase. He splashed cold water on his face and went downstairs to drop his luggage at reception and check out.

A few sips of club soda, a few civil remarks, and then he'd be free to leave Storrow and this hotel behind.

When Charlie arrived at the bar, Storrow was waiting. Almost unrecognizable, thought Charlie; he might have walked right past him if he hadn't spotted Storrow looking so plain three nights before. His hair was a dull brown, receding at the temples; he wore simple jeans and sneakers, clothes the old Storrow would have considered without style. His once military posture had grown stooped; he turned on his stool and waved, Kingfisher in hand.

"You don't drink," Charlie recalled.

Storrow broke into a broad smile. "It's awfully good to see you, Charlie. Awfully good. And looking so well, too."

"And you." Though, in fact, even in the dim light of the bar, the years showed on Storrow. His skin was no longer that smooth blushing white; it had grown rougher and more spotted, creased at the forehead and around the mouth. His jacket, tan corduroy, was faded and even dirty at the cuffs.

And yet, for all the wear and tear, Storrow still had an air of artificiality about him. Seated on his stool in that generic outfit, with that flat dyed hair, he seemed like an alien adopting local ways, like a visitor from someplace infinitely far away. And that was exactly what he must be, thought Charlie, wherever he'd set himself up recently: a pariah, a man living out of bounds.

Charlie cleared his throat. Already he felt the strain of conversation, hemmed in on all sides by the unmentionables—all the events and people that connected them—everything beyond the here and now.

"You're where these days?" he began.

"Virginia. But not for long. I've been in India the last few years—if you didn't already get the skinny."

Mumbai, to be precise: at least that was where Georgia had been when she'd called Charlie, frantic, to report a brush with Storrow. She'd been worried Storrow might be stalking her—the sort of thing he'd have expected to hear, instead, from Alice, still in the mental hospital then. But Georgia had run off. Whatever problems she was having weren't his to deal with; this sounded like a matter for the police, Charlie had told her firmly.

"India, that's something." He wasn't about to let on to Storrow what he'd heard or in any way allude to Georgia. Her name (along with Julie's) topped the list of unmentionables.

He thought back to that evening, before graduation, when Storrow was seated on his sofa, mute, unable to say Georgia's name or admit to what he'd done: succumbed to selfish impulse, broken his commitment to the school, betrayed Charlie's trust.

After that, even once Charlie was past anger, it had been impossible to swear by the man's innocence on anything. He'd clung to doubt, and did still, however inconceivable that he might be sharing a drink with a murderer this evening.

The bartender came by and Charlie ordered a scotch. Forget club soda; he needed something to settle his nerves.

"Over four years I've been away," Storrow continued, filling the silence: something, thought Charlie, at which he must have become expert. "I'd come to Mumbai for a short job, and then more work came up and, well . . . "

"Time does fly."

"Maybe it does—for *some*." Storrow raised his beer and took a swig. Neither the drinking nor the informality had been permitted himself by the old Storrow, but it seemed such sterling conduct had corroded. "When your whole life is about waiting, believe me, time is a rock. I spent years, Charlie, just waiting for people to forget. Foolish me—I see that now—not to recognize no one *can* forget anymore. Technology won't let you. It's all out there, every word ever written, every slander and speculation, there at your fingertips." Storrow paused and put up his hand, as if in modesty. "But what am I doing lecturing to you? *You* of all people ought to know."

What did he mean by that? As if the Internet with its vast trove of information was somehow Charlie's to account for—just because, broadly speaking, he dealt in technology. But perhaps he was reading too much into the statement; at that moment, Storrow's tone brightened.

"Anyway, the world turns and we struggle to keep up; that's how it's always been. And, in the end, it worked out. India suited me just fine." Storrow tapped the counter and clapped—more familiar again—the reliance on clichés, the old rallying gestures. A gold wedding band shone on his left hand.

"You're married."

"Two years." Reaching for his wallet, Storrow retrieved a pair of photos. The first was of him, also dark haired but slimmer then, with a very pretty Indian woman. It was a posed picture, taken at a formal function: the woman wore a sari and Storrow a white suit. The next picture was also posed: a studio shot of a baby girl.

"Linsey is almost a year now. She's the max. And there's a new one on the way."

"Beautiful family. Congratulations."

"Thank you, Charlie. Thank you. They're what's changed me most, you know. Head to toe." Storrow was pointing to his hair. "I dyed it there, so I wouldn't stick out, and now it's for them I keep it. This way I look more like Linsey's dad. They're a suspicious lot, the Indians, and always glad to think they got one over on us white guys."

Charlie forced a smile, reminded of similarly awkward remarks he'd tried to overlook before, remarks that students like Julie Patel had found so troubling.

Thinking of her then, the soft cheeks and mocha skin—a face not unlike that on the new Mrs. Storrow—Charlie felt his skin tingle. All of a sudden those pictures on the bar looked uncanny, this whole family exhibit perverse and contrived. He had the thought, however paranoid, that the wife and child just might be an invention.

"Are they here with you?"

"No, unfortunately I had to leave them back in Mumbai. It breaks me up each time I go away, but right now I've got no choice."

Insisting a bit too strongly, Charlie thought, on the settled man that he'd become. Happy in his life abroad, against all odds and with no help from the country he'd made it his life's mission to serve—so then, why was Storrow here, ordering a second drink in a bar in downtown D.C.?

"My mother," Storrow went on, though Charlie hadn't asked him. "She's been ill."

"Sorry to hear that."

"These last years have been hard on her."

That part Charlie *could* believe. He'd gotten an impression of the elder Mrs. Storrow from her brief statement on *60 Minutes*: a trim, well-dressed, silver-haired woman, with cool green eyes and a clipped voice: *I've always admired my son for being his own man.* The comment was apparently designed to absolve her of any share she might be allotted of his potential guilt.

"Leaving out what pain I've caused her, what responsibility I bear, I'm her only child; my father's gone. So her welfare, anyway, that falls on me." Storrow paused and stroked his chin, thoughtfully, manfully. "There are times like that, that bring home to you what your duties in life are: protecting the people in your care, above all, aging parents, children. You can imagine what I've felt then, sitting by my mother's bedside much of this past year, hearing the ghastly news from Mumbai. The bombings, I mean: I don't know if you follow what goes on over there."

"I read about them, yes." There had been a series of terrorist attacks that year, bombs planted on buses and trains and in parked cars: the worst, in August, had killed more than fifty people and injured hundreds. "Must have been a scare for you . . . and for your family."

"They've been all right. My wife doesn't worry the way I do; doesn't need to . . . to know the things *I* know." Storrow leaned in, his voice hushed. "I happened to have worked on a case involving a U.S. operative in Pakistan. The details, I'm afraid, aren't really something I can get into. Still, it's no secret terrorists are running the military over there and this much I will tell you—the Americans aren't innocent here, Charlie; there's blood on our hands, too."

Storrow's forehead had grown twisted, deep wrinkles appearing. He touched his fingers to the bridge of his nose, a sign of pain or tension that Charlie recalled from those interviews after the murder, one of those oddities that had made people suspect him.

"I'm not saying it's our fault, Charlie, those deaths, or even our job to prevent them. It's out of fashion, I know, jingoistic to think that way, especially these days—so I wouldn't admit such feelings except to somebody like you. Only you, you can understand it when I tell you, what keeps me up nights—something huge and awful happens again, 9/11 awful, and I know I didn't stop it."

Charlie took a sip from his glass, avoiding Storrow's gaze. He spoke carefully. "Well, I doubt one man would be equipped to prevent a thing like that."

"No, you wouldn't think so, would you? You're all about security software systems, isn't that right?"

So there it was: Storrow's first admission that he knew of Charlie's business. He must have read the recent news of his deal, just as Charlie had kept apprised of the man's activities. There had been one article, several years back, painting Storrow as a ruined man; no one would hire a suspected killer, no university, no law firm, and—despite Storrow's references to work with government operatives, despite his wish to place himself among the forces great enough to cause or prevent catastrophe—no military jobs had been offered to him either.

According to that article, at least, Storrow's former colleagues wouldn't even take his calls; all America had turned its back on him. *He*, thought Charlie, would be wise to do the same.

"I don't suppose you believe in karma, do you, Charlie?"

He shook his head: not in karma and not, Charlie was starting to feel, in the sincerity of this dark-haired reincarnation of the man he'd known at school; for that Storrow, good diet and steady exercise seemed philosophy enough. "Eastern religion was never quite my thing."

"Well, not mine, either, sure. I'm just playing around, son: you can't imagine I've gone *all* native?" Storrow let out a tight laugh and brushed a spot of foam from his lip. "My wife's family, though, they are believers; they take such notions rather seriously. But then, they're Brahmins and rich, so why not attribute one's fortune to the goodness of one's eternal soul? Do no harm, rise up the ladder of being. That notion, I suppose, might appeal to a guy like you."

"How's that?"

"Repairman's son. Blue collar made good."

No, actually the notion didn't appeal to him at all, nor did this line of talk. Storrow must be getting drunk, Charlie thought; his eyes were moist, his speech sloppier and more aggressive.

"To heck with all the pretense," Storrow barked. "You've made it, Charlie, let's just say it; you're going to be a very important man, and a very rich man soon, yourself."

Aha. *Yes, here it comes*, Charlie thought; philosophizing turns to more material concerns. He set down his drink and addressed Storrow crisply. "Whatever you might have read, you can see I'm still staying in midrange hotels, nothing is definite yet . . ."

"Relax, I'm not after your money." Storrow gave a haughty smile; Charlie could see him struggling, then, to ward off the offense. "Like I said, my wife's family doesn't want for money. I'm living like a king there. No need at all to work, but men like us—we must work, we must serve. I think—I *know*—that you believe in service, too. And that's why I always suspected that, of all my students, *you'd* be the one to make a difference, to achieve something truly exceptional."

"I wouldn't say I've done that yet."

"I would say that. I *have* said it. And it's given me some cause for pride, knowing that I had a hand in that. Don't you deny it; don't you take that from me, too." Storrow's smile quivered.

Pride, Storrow had said, but it was resentment Charlie felt lurking in his old professor. Storrow had lost so much after the murder, so much that Charlie had to boast of now: prospects; youth; the ordinary comforts, too, of living unharassed, of being admired by one's society rather than reviled.

Storrow raised his forefinger; it hovered in front of Charlie's face. "You don't even realize how good you have it. The future of defense, it's going to be based on guys like you: corporations, not government agencies. Those agency guys are afraid to let you see how much power you have—they're dinosaurs and they know it, so they mean to keep you down, long as they can, a beggar for contracts, but that's where I can help you."

"I see." Yes, he did see: too late, what a stupid coward he'd been to agree to this meeting. He'd known exactly how it had to end: Storrow would try to get in on his business, muscle for a position.

Storrow heaved himself up on his stool; he'd grown heavier, but no less strong. An athlete still, at his age.

"With someone like me to advise you, I'm telling you, you can be ten times what you are now."

"I'm not anything now, that's my point; I don't even have a staff or payroll yet. We're just at the initial stages—"

"Which is precisely when you need a strategy—a global one. America's just one player here; you know who the world's biggest weapons importer is? It's India. Military budget of over twelve billion this year, ahead of Russia. And they're only going to grow—they've got Pakistan to keep up with, and China, too. Spending's going to double and triple in the next decade, and I've got this on good authority, Charlie. I've got contacts; I've got experience, perspective. You need to consider this seriously, Charlie, what we could do together, you and me."

Impossible: there must not be a "you and me." No way he could bring in Storrow, even if he wanted to: the association to such an unsteady character, an accused murderer and professor publicly disgraced. Absolutely not.

"I'm afraid it's not my call."

"Dammit, Charlie. *Everything's* your call. That's just what I'm trying to show you. You can't let these agency guys bully you. You need to have other deals going; you can't let them think you need them too much. Forget loyalty; there's no such thing as trust with these people. They'll lie and call you crazy; they'll lie to *make* you crazy and then, when they have no more use for you, they don't know you anymore."

It might be true, what he was saying: at least as far as Storrow's story went. Charlie looked into the man's eyes, glistening, overbright. What had happened back at school, had it driven him over the edge or had his unraveling begun sooner—was there more to Storrow's history than Charlie knew?

"You listen to me, son: at our level, nothing is forgiven, no mistakes." Storrow was peering at him, sternly. "One shot and this is yours. Do you get me? This is it. You're *it* now. Or you can be, with me."

"I'm *it*?"

"It. *It.* The insider. The top. The new aristocracy."

He's serious, thought Charlie. *Mad, maybe, but serious.*

Storrow turned on his stool to face him. Despite his dishevelment, Storrow's features were perfect still: eerily symmetrical, with that neat blue line bisecting his forehead. Charlie recalled how much the man had once impressed him, those patrician looks and manners, the golden boy he'd been.

All at once it struck him, that Storrow's modified appearance might be about more than going incognito: the earlier model had proven obsolete. Before him sat a Storrow for the new millennium—jeans, worn jacket, almost like the one that Charlie owned, the one he'd worn that night he'd passed Storrow in the bar.

Could it be? Six years after he'd striven to resemble men like Storrow, Storrow meant to make some kind of model out of *him*?

Charlie stood, rather abruptly, and reached for his wallet to pay. "My flight, I'm sorry. We'll have to pick this up another time."

"Make sure we do." Storrow swiveled, rocking slightly; his head was heavy with alcohol. "I wouldn't have called today—I wouldn't be suggesting what I am, if I didn't know you want it too. *Triathlon* Technologies. I got your message, son."

"Sorry, I don't know what you mean."

"*Triathlon*, Charlie."

Only then did it dawn on him, the connection Storrow had made. Charlie recalled that first housemaster's dinner and the photograph on display in the living room of Apthorp House: Storrow, young, fit, among his West Point teammates in a moment of triumph.

"*My* sport, son. My bloody sport."

Storrow slid from his stool onto his feet; he drew back his shoulders and stood to his full height. Something familiar shone in his tense and reddened face, something of Charlie's own father: behind the paternal veneer, envy and contempt, the conviction that, however successful Charlie might become, he was a weakling, a worm that might be flattened without effort, without remorse, with only—from *real* men like them—a slight tremor of disgust.

"I'll see what I can do." He'd have said anything to escape from Storrow then.

"Good man." Storrow laid his palm on the hot nape of Charlie's neck.

A touch like that, so familiar—six years ago it would have pleased him.

PART

III

22

Georgia's dreams of India began after Mark's readmittance, for the second time since the surgery, to the cancer center at Mass General. Winter was encroaching, the brutal Boston cold unlike any she'd known in the desert and tropical countries where she and Mark had lived over the past four years. Her mother had been urging her to move to Santa Cruz, but Georgia was determined to remain where she was: in that heavily mortgaged, freshly decorated, South End bow-front row house, where, just that fall, she and Mark had brought their newborn daughter home.

Violet had been a quiet baby for the first month, but now, since she and Georgia were alone in that big house, she cried incessantly. Her howls reached across the walls into the adjacent buildings, brought neighbors knocking in the night on their front door. They even reached all the way to India, penetrating the marble walls of Georgia's dreams.

The dream was recurring, with slight variations, sometimes several times a week. Georgia would find herself walking down an opulent corridor, hung with chandeliers and flanked with large vases filled with flowers, white roses like those she sent each May to the Patels. Begging children pursued her, their clothes filthy and tattered. One girl carried a wailing infant; a boy was dragging something strange behind him on the ground. Straps and cords, a stethoscope, a tourniquet: a knot of medical equipment, tubes tangled like intestines.

A door opened at the end of the hall and Mrs. Gupta stepped forward; her face was full of pity; she placed a hand over her mouth.

Then came the dread, a sensation sharp enough to jolt Georgia out of sleep. Sometimes she would wake with a cry and disturb Violet. For the next hours, while she gave Violet her pacifier, stroked and rocked her, kicking her own shins to keep from falling back asleep and letting the baby drop, her thoughts returned to that brief nine days in India, to Nandi and to Storrow, and to the menace she'd felt then, before she'd left for Kenya where she'd gone on to find Mark, and her future.

She'd flown to Kenya that winter because she felt she had nowhere else to go: the only placement Global Aid could offer was assisting in the Marsabit Hospice, located in a remote, eastern province town. It was the same position she'd turned down from D.C. the month before, but this time, she took it; she had to get out of India, and she couldn't admit failure and return to the States so soon.

For three weeks she applied herself to her new job: she followed the nurses' instructions, performed every task they requested, however foul, and when there was nothing more for her to do, held the hands of withered patients who moaned to her in words she couldn't understand. She bore the heat and the mosquitoes, the flying roaches, the stench of the water in the bath and sink of her crumbling hut, until her body simply rebelled and she succumbed to fever.

She couldn't stir from her room; she struggled to leave her bed to call the hospice. Her sheets were soaked through with sweat, her teeth chattered and her throat was so parched she could scarcely eat or speak. These symptoms didn't much concern her new colleagues—standard, they said, for newcomers to Africa—but she'd never so acutely felt her own mortality. She lost ten pounds in as many days, until one of the doctors finally suggested she move into the hospice, where she could be supervised by staff, and where she began to suspect she'd meet her end among its patients, her short life a morbid, cautionary tale: run anywhere you like, away from troubles, fears, regrets—in the end, death will be waiting.

When she was at her sickest, Mark arrived: a young doctor radiating good cheer and competence. A fellow American come by chance to visit a French nurse he'd befriended the year before in a hospital in Jordan. There was, as Georgia came to learn, an active social scene among these young medical professionals abroad: a community of like-minded explorers, some of the most affable people she had yet to meet. None, it seemed, was more beloved than Mark, whom the French doctor had sent to her knowing that Mark, with his easy manner and his Johns Hopkins degree, would manage to reassure her when no one else could. There was something about his face—quietly handsome, topped with wavy light brown hair—and his voice, too, deep and steady, that allowed her to believe him when he repeated the prognosis others had given her ten times before: she'd caught a frightening, but far from fatal, local virus. In a week, she would be well enough to rise from bed and get the hell out of that place.

They'd joked about where she might go next—by now Global Aid owed her a trip to the Swiss Alps or St. Tropez—and then, on an especially sweltering afternoon, during one of Mark's longer and longer bedside visits, they resolved in earnest to set off from Kenya together. Mark was assigned for three months to a hospital in Marrakech—not the Riviera but a step up from the village where Georgia was staying. A whole house was waiting for him there, and she was welcome to share it while she figured out her plans. Never would Georgia have guessed that such a temporary arrangement would lead to marriage. But Mark proved her perfect companion: open to adventure, playful and kind. From Marrakech they moved together to a village outside Cairo, where he joined the staff at the local hospital and she took a position with a British NGO.

About two months into their stay in Egypt, Georgia's father phoned to announce his impending arrival. Georgia had been in touch with him from Marrakech and, since then, her father had arranged a lecture at the American university in Cairo that would cover travel costs. He'd fly in a week early, bring his latest girlfriend, take some photos, and drop by for a short visit with his daughter.

When Georgia and Mark came to collect her father at Cairo International, Mr. Calvin was alone; the girlfriend, he explained, had been unwilling to miss her first week of spring classes—she'd just begun her master's in film at NYU. No hardship, Georgia felt: she and Mark would be spared the awkwardness of sharing their house with her father and a lover even younger than she was. The three of them in three small rooms would be difficult enough, though Mark had quickly understood what the arrangement—and her father's ego—demanded of him: he spent long hours every day at work, so as not to intrude upon their time together.

Her father, for his part, chose to misread such thoughtfulness: Mark was avoiding him, he claimed—if not to conceal some major flaw then maybe to simply conceal how little self there was to hide. *Rather a lean personality* was how her father described him: confusing, Georgia felt, Mark's tolerance with blandness.

"You might try to get to know him just a bit," she suggested, "before you thoroughly dismiss him."

Afterward, she urged Mark to let her father join him at the clinic for a day. Her father went, toting his camera, and returned that night silent on the subject of Mark's talents as a doctor, but full of praise for the pictures he'd taken at the clinic—*remarkable stuff*—which he unassumingly attributed to the beauty of the Egyptian children.

"Probably it's hard to notice," he said to Mark, "while you're examining their bodies for infections and dysfunctions."

"I think I can see beauty, even so." Mark squeezed Georgia's hand under the table.

"Sure you can, but if you're taught to think of it in terms of rods and cones, even *seeing* starts to look different, doesn't it?" Her father smiled at her askance: a conspiratorial look that she recalled from dinners throughout her childhood, meant to exclude her mother and the larger world, to unite them in their singular perception.

Later that night, when she was getting into bed and Mark was in the shower, her father slipped into her bedroom to make her a proposition. Several galleries in Europe had been after him about a show; as long as he was taking a semester off from teaching, he might spend the next months in Rome or Barcelona and she could stay there with him. "I could insist you're my curator. You can get back to working in the arts again."

"And Mark?"

She'd given the guy five months, her father said: "Seems like more than enough."

Instead, it was her father she'd had enough of, she decided. Ten months later, she was hardly speaking to her father, while she and Mark remained very happily together: arranging a next move to Southeast Asia. After a year in Bangkok, they moved again, to Myanmar and then, eighteen months later, to Haiti.

She was drifting, according to her mother, who was in rare agreement with her ex-husband on the matter of Georgia's romantic commitment. Nothing against Mark personally, but no relationship was worth the sacrifices Georgia was making: she ought to return to her work at the National Gallery or else follow up on her plans to seek better prospects in New York or elsewhere. Love wasn't something to be relied on, said her mother; later, Georgia would regret letting a man keep her from developing her professional life.

But Georgia didn't care if, as her mother pointed out, she was already bound to be less successful than her overachieving classmates. Mark was good for her in a hundred other ways; beside him, she'd grown more loving and stable and responsible—perhaps even up to a responsibility as immense as motherhood. When she'd discovered she was pregnant, she could reasonably believe that this child also had a chance at happiness, that she'd found a father who could correct for every wrong her own father had done her and any harm she might do, too. Where she was lacking, Mark would compensate, and the child would be for him, above all, because he wanted one as much as, mysteriously, he wished to spend his life with her.

Nine weeks into Georgia's pregnancy, Mark announced he'd applied for a position at Massachusetts General. She hadn't been sure, at first, if returning to the States was what she wanted. For four years, she'd felt no longing for the country she'd left behind: not for its landscapes or entertainments or conveniences, nor for family or for friends. The only person she ever missed was Charlie, but their friendship had been damaged, it seemed, beyond repair. During the one nervous call she'd made from Mumbai, Charlie had been cold and dismissive; he hadn't answered her subsequent postcards, nor had Alice. Their silence only served to remind Georgia of the tenuousness of her closest relationships and recall the upsets she'd escaped, so it came as a surprise when the prospect of a child inspired in her a yearning to touch back on familiar soil.

In June, Mark was invited for an interview in Boston; Georgia flew over with him. She'd been apprehensive about revisiting that city, but the child she carried helped her to keep her thoughts fixed on the future. With her hand resting on her belly, and Mark holding her arm, she'd felt able to explore the neighborhoods south of the Charles, places she'd glimpsed only distantly on runs during her school days. A week later, when Mark was offered the position at Mass General, they went strolling through South End, looking at homes for sale among the blocks of bow-front houses. Georgia was taken aback by how joyful the scene made her: all those fresh green lawns with strollers parked out front. From there, she and Mark soon found themselves in meetings with a mortgage broker at the bank. The next month was spent installing a backyard garden and driving to auctions to select furniture charming and individual enough to make a home within those walls. They'd even gotten married in the house, with two neighbors as witnesses, and Mark's mother, in from Seattle, as the only family present.

Neither of Georgia's parents was invited. Their example, after all, had nearly been enough to spoil her on marriage, though Mark had managed to convince her to do it for the insurance: as a doctor, he knew well what childbirth could cost. It had been an antiromantic joke, a way of indulging her skepticism yet binding them together—a joke that seemed far less funny now that Georgia spent more time speaking to insurance representatives than to Mark, now that the hospital had come to feel more like their marital home than the one they'd so lovingly arranged.

Georgia had scarcely recovered from the birth, and Mark was only in his first week back at work, when he came home, midday, pale and stunned. He'd had an accident, thought Georgia, or else his mother had, or hers: a dozen awful possibilities sprang to mind, but he'd refused to tell her what the trouble was until they'd put Violet in her stroller and headed out. During their walk around the neighborhood, he'd admitted he'd been unwell. At first he'd only felt fatigued, but lately he'd had pains in his stomach and his back. He hadn't wished to say anything to Georgia while she was dealing with the pregnancy and birth, but he'd been examined by a fellow doctor at the hospital and had undergone some diagnostic tests: an MRI and an endoscopic ultrasound and biopsy. The results had come back that afternoon. Pancreatic cancer.

"The good news is, it's resectable," he said.

"Which means?"

In his most reassuring tone, the same he'd used to set her at ease in Kenya, years before, he let her know what the next months would require. He would undergo chemo and then surgery, a Whipple—to remove his gallbladder, bile duct, parts of the pancreas and stomach and intestine.

"And what," she'd asked him, her voice so weak it was as if *her* insides had been emptied: "What happens to the part of you that's left?"

The following week, Georgia's father called, insisting on coming to see his new granddaughter. "You wanted to keep me from the wedding, fine. Mark and I don't need to be close, but this is different, this child is my blood."

Georgia told him he was welcome to meet Violet, but the timing was not right.

"I haven't seen you in years now. I miss you. Don't you care?"

"At this moment, not especially."

"Georgia, I won't let you punish me forever."

"I'm not punishing you; this isn't about *you*."

At last, she'd felt she had no choice but to tell him what the trouble was.

"I'll pack a bag," her father said; he was dropping everything to join her in Boston. "Long as you need me."

"That's not at all what I need. Don't." It angered her to hear what sounded too much like excitement in his voice, to imagine the wish that lay behind it: Mark out of the picture, father and daughter reunited again. "I'm going to handle this myself. Mark and I. Please respect that."

Later the same week, a call came from her mother; her father had passed along word of Mark's diagnosis.

"William and I have discussed it," her mother told her, dryly, practically, "and we've both decided the best thing is for you and Mark and Violet to move here."

"To Santa Cruz?"

"The house is big."

"We have a house. A house we love."

"A house you can't afford. Certainly not now."

Easy for her mother to speak this way, about a home she'd never even seen, as she'd never set eyes on Mark, or Violet either, in the flesh.

"Think it through," her mother advised. "Whatever money Mark gets on sick leave, you need to be saving, preparing for all eventualities."

"I'm not going to discuss this with you."

"You need to. You have a child, and no career to speak of. The way William reasons—"

"What do I care how William *reasons*?" As if her family's upheaval were a problem to be solved, a matter of calculation, a chance for William to map out one of his "optimal solutions."

"It isn't just about what you want," said her mother. "I'm concerned about the baby. Money aside, you're under strain and she'll need more support than you can give her."

"And what? *You'd* be the one to help us, is that it?" This was rich; this was really too much for her to take. "You see this as your opportunity to prove your maternal muscle, after everything."

"Georgia, I realize your feelings for me are complicated."

"No, I think they're pretty simple." At that moment, she couldn't stand the sound of her mother's voice, let alone the thought of their sharing a home. Still, she knew her mother had a point. This month, next month, maybe, she had the means to pay the bills. Beyond that, she couldn't guess how she'd provide for her small family on her own. Those years traveling with Mark really had been the indulgence her mother said they were; she'd spent her adult life on the run and now her irresponsibility threatened to imperil the child she'd brought into being.

Mistakenly brought into being, it seemed now: she was not built to be a mother, even less a single mother. At twenty-five she'd known this about herself, so why had she thought otherwise at thirty? Too spoiled, too removed from reality, how could she be relied upon to guard another human being from pain?

She'd begun to scare herself, especially lately, during these difficult weeks, while Mark was undergoing radiation in the hospital. One morning when she'd gone for groceries, she'd forgotten Violet in the car and run back out to the parking lot in tears. Exhaustion was to blame: Violet was crying through the nights, and in the day, when the baby napped, Georgia lay awake. Sleep only seemed to visit her at the most dangerous moments, while bathing Violet in the evening or when she was behind the wheel. Finally, having veered out of her lane on her way to the post office—with Violet, sleeping in her car seat behind her—Georgia turned the car around and headed for the Mass General pediatric ward.

She needed to see a doctor, she informed reception. The nurse observed the baby—pink and crying, in a sling at Georgia's chest—and pointed to the waiting area. A TV screen hung from the wall, featuring an animated film: dancing fish and singing mermaids, seaweed swaying to the beat. Georgia swayed along, trying to calm both Violet and herself. Even on her feet, eyes open, she was half asleep; the voices in reception sounded themselves watery, submerged. The ringing of her phone roused her.

"Georgia? I didn't wake you, did I? Fuck."

"Alice?"

It startled her, this once-familiar voice, out of context and unwelcome. Whatever Alice wanted, Georgia was in no state to deal with her. She wasn't sure how Alice even had her number. In all the years following their encounter in New York, Georgia had heard nothing from her—no response to the postcard she'd sent her from Mumbai, nor to the next one she'd sent from Cairo.

"I wanted to let you know that I'm in Boston," Alice said. "Just for the week. I'd like to see you before I go. Maybe meet for lunch."

"I'm sorry, but this isn't a good time." The nurse was signaling Georgia to join her down the hall. "In fact, I'm going to have to go now."

"When you get a moment then, you can try me at the Charles Hotel. Please do. There's something important I need to talk with you about."

Inside the examination room, Violet's wails sounded twice as loud; Georgia paced the narrow confines, until the doctor entered, crisp and friendly. She looked fresh out of the classroom: moon-faced, with black hair swept into a ponytail.

"Dr. Yang. Good morning. Oh, poor thing. Not feeling well today?" She tapped the baby on the nose and pulled a pen from the pocket of her doctor's coat.

"This is how she always is, crying all the time. The other doctor thought it might be colic, but I don't think so; at least she's no worse after feedings."

Dr. Yang consulted the papers on her clipboard: "You were in two weeks ago. Dr. Arnold saw you."

"He did blood work, tested for allergies. But he found nothing wrong."

"Well, that's good news, isn't it?" The doctor offered her a placid smile, one that only added to Georgia's agitation. "I guess the other doctor told you then, there's really not much we can do in cases like this. Babies cry. So long as she's gaining weight, meeting all the markers, we consider the situation normal."

"Don't tell me this is normal."

"Newborns can drive you crazy." Dr. Yang smiled again, the smile of a young woman with no duties or misfortunes that she couldn't leave behind, in the examining rooms, at the close of every day.

"Right, newborns cry and new mothers are tired, but this, there must be something—because honestly, if I don't sleep—my husband's in the hospital and I'm on my own. On the drive here, I nearly crashed. I'm afraid something terrible will happen. Maybe it doesn't sound like an emergency, but it is, it *will* be."

"You're under stress." Dr. Yang made a note on her clipboard. "That could be a factor here. Babies pick up on a mother's anxiety."

Did this woman take her for an idiot? Did she think she didn't grasp that the child was in distress because *she* was? She didn't need this teenage doctor to tell her what she already knew—what she needed was for her to take out her prescription pad and *fix* it.

"Then give me something for the anxiety, how's that?"

"I'm not a psychiatrist, but I can refer you for another appointment."

"Look, I can't keep coming in here, waiting—I need this now. A simple script."

"I'm sorry."

"You're sorry." She felt the urge to slap the woman's face. Those sweet, earnest, young doctors, those people she'd counted as her friends for the last years, how she'd come to loathe them and their kindly uselessness, just as she'd come to dread these clean, bright hospital rooms, with all the vileness they contained. She didn't want another appointment, didn't want to pay one extra visit to these houses of illness, which she secretly blamed for Mark's condition: all those years he'd spent watching people's bodies fester and waste, death, as a concept, had been creeping in under his skin, taking root in his gut.

A male nurse escorted Georgia from the wing: Violet went on wailing; Georgia's cell was again ringing, while cartoon mermaids trilled above her head. As a precaution, for Violet's sake, Georgia caught a taxi by the entrance and left her car in the hospital lot. On the ride home, she listened to the messages on her phone: the first was older, from Mark's mother, in Seattle: *Mark suggested you might be feeling, well, a little under strain* . . . The last call had been from Alice.

I figured you might not get back to me, so I just thought you should know: Charlie's the one who insisted that I contact you. If you want to talk about it I'll be at L'Espalier, one o'clock, tomorrow.

Later that evening, Georgia made arrangements with a sitter for the next afternoon. She would meet with Alice, she decided: her immediate concerns left no room for old grudges and, besides, since Charlie was behind this invitation, it was really for Charlie's sake that she was going. That was the story she told herself, at any rate, though when she awoke the next morning, surprisingly undaunted by the prospect of facing another day, she had to admit the thought of seeing Alice roused her.

With her newer friends, those she'd made through Mark, she must always endure the same bromides—*he's strong; he has so much to live for*—but with Alice she might give voice to her true thoughts. Alice had lost a father as young as Mark. She was no stranger to suffering and senselessness and rage; foulmouthed Alice wouldn't flinch to hear her curse.

And what else was there to do but curse? What other language was a suitable response to the last months? Mark's painful surgery, followed by radiation and chemo, and, after that ordeal, his digestion was failing; to replace the hormones his body no longer produced, he was being pumped with insulin and still, in recent weeks, he'd developed diabetes. Dr. Poole, the man in charge of Mark's case, kept saying she should be grateful that Mark was doing *this* well. Pancreatic cancer was one of the most brutal types; she ought to form no expectations; she ought to be reasonable. But what was reasonable about any of this?

Mark was young and fit; he'd never neglected his health; he hadn't harbored secret hatreds, or indulged in any vices; he'd lived easily and decently and was, of all those she knew, the least deserving of this plight. What was a more suitable reaction to what he was enduring, than swearing at the top of her lungs, than wishing everyone who bid her be reasonable—these Dr. Pooles and Dr. Yangs—would have their peaceful selves deformed by pain until all they wanted was to shout obscenities, too?

L'Espalier was an upscale restaurant and Georgia had done her best to look presentable that day: she'd put on a skirt and proper shoes; she'd combed her hair and applied makeup. Still, she expected Alice would be a little shocked to see her; no amount of effort could hide her exhaustion or how very thin she'd become.

"There you are." Alice rose from her corner table to kiss Georgia, lightly, on the cheek. "I'm so glad you made it," sparing her, at least, a patronizing "you're looking well."

Alice, meanwhile, could truthfully be told that she looked good: she wore a short, tailored skirt suit, metallic tweed; her hair was shoulder length and she'd had the curls relaxed. This was a very different Alice from the last one she'd seen inside the ward, muttering incoherent confessions and laying her unwashed head upon Georgia's lap; this Alice more a stranger, less a companion in chaos, than she'd hoped to find.

Georgia began stiffly. "So what brings you to Boston?"

"Technology conference. I'm preparing the remarks for two presenting CEOs. That's the sort of writing I do now."

"Business writing?" It seemed that even Alice had joined the ranks of the reasonable. "When did this happen?"

"A few years ago." Alice turned to flag down a nearby waiter; her manner was different these days: impatient and assertive. "I had expenses and—well, actually, it was Charlie's doing. He threw some work my way, once his company took off. Maybe you've heard about it."

Only from her mother, who'd come across Charlie's name in the financial news. *And he was pretty smitten with you once, if I remember.*

"We haven't been in touch, not since I last saw you anyway."

She didn't want to be reminded of her New York visit: Alice's madness spurring her on to a mad act of her own, one that had cost her Charlie, the only true friend that she'd found outside of Mark.

The waiter was hovering. Georgia ordered a glass of wine, figuring that alcohol was her only means of relaxing into this lunch, her one shot at reviving that blunt communication she was craving and had always valued with Alice in the past. Today, though, Alice wouldn't join her in a drink. Alcohol interacted with her meds, she said, and so she asked instead for club soda and a shrimp cocktail—the one cocktail she was allowed.

"Charlie and I also had a falling out," Alice admitted. "It was the Patel fellowship that got us speaking again. I don't know if you're aware: we've set up a scholarship fund in conjunction with the memorial this May."

"No, I wasn't aware." Not that there was a memorial, let alone that Alice, of all people, was involved. "Charlie got you into it?"

"Other way around actually; I'd had the idea some time ago. It's a long story."

"It must be." Hard to imagine *any* series of events that could lead Julie's family to cooperate with Alice. Georgia had never met the Patels, but her one effort to reach them had been enough to dissuade her from trying again. *How dare she call this house,* she'd heard Mrs. Patel shouting in the background. *Where does she get the nerve?*

Well, Alice did always have nerve, whatever other qualities she lacked and made up for with those meds. "Sounds like a good thing you're doing."

Alice raised a brow, a hint of cynicism, of the less charitable spirit she'd been not so long ago. "Anyway, I'm much more interested in hearing about you."

"Nothing very interesting to say." She was married, a new mother: Georgia didn't wish to tell her more—the fantasy of speaking freely this afternoon had fast dissolved. Probably it was wrong to wish that Alice would be less self-possessed; probably she should give her old friend credit for her apparent transformation. But this meeting felt too much like a farce: Alice, newly reputable and constructive, offering hope to the Patels, sponsoring some other young girl who might give Julie's mother a smooth and eager face to look into, to mask the horrific feelings that ought to accompany her onto Harvard Yard.

"You look tired," observed Alice.

"Yeah, well, a newborn will do that to you."

The waiter returned, and Alice signaled for him to place the glass of wine before her friend. "Look, I'm just going to come out with it. You don't need to pretend. Charlie told me what you're facing."

"And what does Charlie know about it?"

"Husband in the hospital, bills you can't pay."

Georgia set down her wine and watched its wobbling reflection on the tablecloth. As far as she knew, Charlie hadn't even learned that she was married. On several occasions, she'd felt the urge to contact him, to tell him about her life now, especially to pass on the news of Violet's birth, but in the end she'd feared he'd respond with disappointment, or worse, not respond at all. "I haven't even spoken to him."

"Someone else has, on your behalf."

"Someone else?"

Alice's expression was one Georgia recalled from school: the small frisson that preceded a hurtful or humiliating comment. "A few weeks ago, your father called him. He was worried you were overwhelmed, making yourself sick."

"My father. He called Charlie? My fucking father—*he's* the one who's sick."

Alice leaned in, brushing back a lock of her smooth hair. "There's no reason to get upset, no cause for shame in needing help. We've all been in the shit, right? If it makes you feel better, there was a time when I also asked Charlie for a loan."

"I'm not asking. And I hope you haven't come here intending to persuade me." Bad enough Charlie and Alice were privy to her problems; she wasn't about to become their next charity case.

"No, that's not why I've come." Alice sighed and brought a chewed nail to her lips; her cuticles were raw and peeling, seemingly the one edge where Alice remained ragged.

Their dishes arrived: Alice's, a bowl of ice, ringed with shrimp; and, for Georgia, the soup, the cheapest item on the menu.

Georgia started in, though she hardly felt like eating; the faster this lunch was done, the better.

Alice laid her napkin gingerly across her lap. "What I wanted to discuss, it's connected to the memorial actually. The event will receive some attention in the press, which has prompted the police to reopen the case. Charlie already heard from the Patels that investigators have been in touch with them, and someone might try to reach you, too, maybe reporters. Whatever comes up, I felt we should speak first."

Alice left off, dragging a shrimp through a small dish of red sauce. She was waiting for her to speak, Georgia realized, though her thoughts were still stuck on her father's call to Charlie: a selfish manipulation, unsurprising. Her father inserting himself, yet again, unable to let her live her life with Mark.

"Honestly, Alice, I don't see why we have anything to talk about."

"Well, we never did properly address what happened. To start with, my illness." Bipolar disorder, Alice went on to explain, which she'd likely been afflicted by during college, too: "It wasn't diagnosed then, but in those weeks I stayed with you, and then, later, at Charlie's, when I wrote what I did about you . . . I'm not making excuses."

"Never mind: you weren't yourself, I get it."

"Of course, you know what a manic episode does to a person; you saw me at my worst." Alice bit into her shrimp and dropped the tail onto her bread plate. "We never properly discussed that either, your visit to the hospital in New York. Our heart-to-heart there in the ward. That you initiated about Storrow."

"*I* initiated?"

"For a while I was angry with you about it."

"*You* were angry with *me*?"

Alice seemed to be choosing her next words carefully: "I'm not here to apportion blame, or not to anybody but myself. One reason why I never responded to your postcard, though not the full explanation . . ." She left off, distracted, and pointed across the table. "You have something. On your shirt."

Georgia looked down. A wet stain had spread across the left side of her chest; she'd neglected to put pads into her bra, and her breasts were leaking. She dabbed at herself with a napkin while Alice set down her shrimp, quietly embarrassed.

"Why don't you just get to it," Georgia demanded. "Whatever it is you brought me here for, you want to clear your conscience, go ahead."

Alice offered Georgia her napkin. "There's another spot down there."

The right side was leaking now. The milk wouldn't stop flowing; it was feeding time, her body programmed, matched to the baby's needs.

A phone was ringing, the sound coming from her purse. The bag was crammed with items—a spare diaper, cream, extra formula. Unable to find her cell, Georgia tossed the mess onto the table. She'd missed the call. It was the sitter.

Violet must be causing trouble: refusing to take the bottle, screaming until the neighbors came knocking on the door again. And here she was, in a fine restaurant, waiting for Alice to muster the will to apologize—if that was what Alice meant to do, and not simply to enjoy the sight of her old friend coming undone before her—her shirt wet, her face red, her meager possessions in a heap—unable to keep up appearances even for an hour of pretend normality.

"I need to go; I don't have time for this."

"Georgia, please. Don't run away."

"You're telling *me*?" For ten years Alice had been the one avoiding her and any possibility that the matter of the murder or Storrow might be raised. Ten years since Alice had betrayed her and, in all that time, no sign of remorse, no sign that Alice gave a damn what had become of her. Only now that Georgia was, as Alice put it, "in the shit," did Alice care to face her, now that Alice was without cause for envy: independent, poised, and free.

"Why did you call me here? You want to know that you're forgiven? Fine. You're forgiven."

Georgia seized her wallet and placed a wad of bills, uncounted, on the table. Alice pushed the bills away.

"Let me. You came because I asked you to, and it was wrong of me. I shouldn't have forced my concerns on you."

"Anyway, I can pay for myself, thanks."

Alice nodded and slid the bills beneath a glass: "About the money issue: I'd like to say again, that's the last thing you need to worry about now. I realize we haven't kept up, but I still know you, I think. Hard reality is not for you. Take Charlie's help. Nothing's gained by punishing yourself with all of this."

This—meaning her life now; *this,* the family she'd chosen, the people she loved—these weren't punishments. "You have no idea what I need. Neither does Charlie."

"Actually I think I do know. I know when my father died—"

"For Christ's sake, Alice: nobody has *died.*" Georgia turned from the table. Her coat was at the front, her blouse soaked through. People in the restaurant stared. She wanted only to be home then, away from Alice and the strain of old suspicions and resentments, returned to her current and vital concerns: Violet. Mark. The small family she'd only just found and feared to lose.

Back to *punishment*, as Alice saw it—Alice who was finally, perhaps, groping toward concern for others, but had not yet, Georgia felt sure, made her own discovery of love.

23

Charlie parked his car—a Mercedes hybrid—in the back of the lot outside his office: no space reserved for chief executives, no privileges to reflect a hierarchy. Birds chirped in the trees along the pathway to the entrance, and the lingering smell of optimism greeted him inside—floor polish, paint. Triathlon's doors had opened just a year before: six thousand square feet, replete with stocked minifridges, movie screens, Razor scooters, all the amenities to satisfy employees average age twenty-six, dreamy kids whom he'd persuaded that Triathlon was less a business than an ideological mission: a means of making government more effective and accountable, a weapon for defense, and a tool for reform.

He greeted his staff by name, lingering among the rows of desks. Boys and girls in jeans and fleece spun on their chairs to ask about his weekend, or to wish him luck on his talk that afternoon. At three he was due to lecture at the Startup Conference at Stanford; people were surprised that he'd stopped in.

In the last few months, he'd been spending more and more time away from this office he and Udi had been so proud to create; either he was in Boston or New York, meeting with his next round of investors, or else he was appearing on campuses or at conventions, promoting their company, garnering positive press. Just that month he'd had invitations from TED and Charlie Rose. He was becoming a sought-after speaker, but not because people cared about the details of big data analytics; what they liked was his song and dance about a less invasive intelligence program. They liked to see a boyish, gentle face posing as the future of national defense, and to hear that security and liberty didn't need to be at odds.

Or they *had* liked it; lately, some of those who'd lavished praise had begun voicing suspicions. Triathlon, with its idealistic image, its freckle-faced CEO, was really a government PR tool: its much-touted privacy protections a mere distraction from the systematic agency abuses that were now coming to light; the last allegations, enumerated in the *Baltimore Sun*, relied on testimony from three ex-NSA employees.

Everyone within these walls—savvy, up-to-date young men and women—must be aware of the *Sun* reports, not to mention the rumors circling the blogs. Triathlon hadn't yet been directly implicated and McCraw insisted it would not be. Nonetheless, the main reason Charlie had come in that morning was to bolster confidence, so that his team could see him looking so deliberately carefree.

Gwen, his assistant, rose from her desk to greet him with a hug. Gwen was Triathlon's newest addition—only brought in reluctantly once Charlie had to admit the volume of his calls and e-mails, along with the intricacy of his schedule, were more than he could handle on his own. Gwen wore dreadlocks and wrote plays in the evenings. He'd hired her for all those ways in which she failed to resemble a career secretary; still, in such a progressive company, it didn't quite sit right, his starting his days like Welch and countless other professional white men over the past century—with a woman trailing him into his office to relay his messages.

The *Baltimore Sun* had called, she said, and handed him a stack of names and numbers.

"Anything from Roger or Shuster?"

For the last four months, Roger had been wooing JP Morgan Chase; they were on the cusp of a deal, and Shuster, their main contact over there, had agreed to send over a provisional contract. It hadn't yet arrived, a sign that Shuster, or whomever he took orders from, was skittish, reluctant to employ a company that might be tainted by scandal—no other explanation for Shuster's name being absent from the pile before him now.

All in his head, McCraw would say, if Charlie were to share such thoughts with him; McCraw insisted no one else was connecting Triathlon to the NSA rumors, rumors that, in any case, would never be confirmed. "Keep it cool, Charlie," McCraw had warned him, paranoia was an occupational hazard.

Gwen eyed him from the doorway; she was uneasy, fussing with the charm at her neck—if "charm" was the right term to describe a silver skull.

"Is something wrong?" he asked her.

"I thought you should know. A woman called for you, too, twice. She sounded upset."

"A woman?" He still wasn't accustomed to this arrangement with Gwen, a stranger so intimately entangled in his dealings. He hardly knew Gwen, really—couldn't say if she had a boyfriend or a girlfriend or name the subject of her latest play—and yet she knew far too much about him: that he phoned Chicago every evening to get Roger's advice; that he sent his mom checks and that she sent them back; that he kept canceling appointments to look at apartments with Melissa. She also knew when women who were not Melissa called him and which ones he hastened to call back.

"She left her name. Georgia Reese."

"I hope you're not too busy, Charlie."

It was so like Georgia to begin that way. She was well aware that he was busy—when *wasn't* he busy?—and aware, too, that he'd always make allowances to speak with her.

Her voice remained a rarity; it was just a month since Alice had persuaded him to phone Georgia and put an end to their long silence. Each time he pictured Georgia on the other end of the line, he had to remind himself how much had changed since they'd last met, that she was no longer the twenty-five-year-old semiprofessional who'd, miraculously, disrobed that single night in his apartment. For a while he'd sought to remember every detail of her body: the texture of her skin, the heft of her breast, the way her lower lip felt between his teeth, but memory always disappointed, proved so indifferent to one's wishes;

these sensations had been conflated with others he'd experienced in the years since. All of it faded.

No matter. Whatever he'd forgotten and whoever they were now, however freighted she was with cares—husband's illness, helpless infant—however importantly occupied he might then be, every time he heard her voice, she was again his airy fantasy and he a dreaming boy of nineteen.

"How are you, Georgia?"

"Me? I'm fine, fine. Honest."

"And Mark?"

"Mark, too, I'm afraid to say it." She laughed, a high, tight laugh he hadn't heard from her before. "Illness makes you superstitious. Mark came home from the hospital yesterday; sleeping in his own bed again. He responded well to the chemo. Exceeded expectations."

Of course, he would: heroic Mark. Under the circumstances, it would be awful to feel anything but pity for the husband, and yet Charlie couldn't help but be irked, a bit, each time Georgia spoke of Mark, the saintly, brave doctor who, before the cancer, spent his days tending to the weak and poor in the deserts of Mongolia or wherever the hell she'd met him. Feats of altruism to which his own efforts could not compare, though Georgia tried to make something grand of them: full of praise for his Patel Scholarship fund. *Really all Alice's project*, he'd replied. It was Alice who'd shown genuine concern for the Patels; his own intentions felt less pure, especially while Georgia expressed her admiration.

Just a month until the memorial, and still he hadn't asked Georgia if she planned on attending. Insensitive to even wonder, what with Mark so sick and so many concerns weighing on her then.

Georgia's father had laid out her situation for him—overcome by worry and exhaustion, she seemed bent on destroying herself, too, out of some mad guilt or pride. No doubt Mr. Calvin had taken artistic liberties; Charlie recalled the man's maudlin photographs, those care-lined faces. Probably, too, he figured that the boy his daughter had rejected must be a little gleeful to hear how she now suffered. Instead, Charlie found their talk depressing, disliked the chastened Georgia of her dad's description, with her worn-down, duller virtue. He preferred the vivid, thrilling Georgia of his memory: the source of his worst pains, but of his most intense excitements, too.

He heard a beep, another call was coming in: Roger this time, possibly with news from Shuster. He hesitated, kicking his foot against the leg of his desk, then let the call go, trying to concentrate on whatever had Georgia sounding so disturbed.

She'd had a visit, she was saying. A reporter. Come the day before to discuss Julie Patel. Had Charlie heard from him as well? Nat Krauss, was his name, from the *Crimson*.

For Christ's sake, it was a *student* reporter who had her so worked up. Meanwhile, the *Baltimore Sun* meant to reach him and over a matter of vital public interest. Not that Georgia was likely to be aware; people absorbed in their own crises tended not to be avid followers of national news.

Georgia *was* in a crisis, he must remember; given her condition, he'd be callous not to hear her out, not to offer reassurance.

Probably that was all she needed—simple comfort, since her husband, doped up on pain meds and whatever other chemicals were coursing through his veins, could provide her only greater cause for anguish. And so she'd turned to him, thought Charlie, as she'd have done at twenty, to help her feel calm again.

"I had this feeling when the reporter was talking—as if Storrow might be pulling the strings here somehow. Not that I have any idea what he might do, but you know, the timing seems dubious; the ten-year memorial, and suddenly Storrow turns up again."

He chose not to correct her, to inform her that Storrow had reappeared in his own life almost four years earlier. She didn't need to hear it: not about his brush with the man in Washington, nor about the harassment that had followed.

In his last call, eight months ago, Storrow had sounded so unhinged that Charlie felt compelled to involve one of his security consultants: Jarred Flynn, a retired investigator, brought in on retainer while Triathlon worked up software to sell to the LAPD.

Thanks to Flynn, Charlie knew more about Storrow than he had a right to—but there was no sense including Georgia in this mess. All she needed from him now were a few words of reassurance, to be set at ease by a man in the know. That was what he'd become for her, apparently—no longer an adoring, clumsy boy, but a man who could speak with authority.

"I'm looking after it. Don't worry. The Patels will have their ceremony, and everything will go perfectly smoothly."

"I hope so, Charlie. I'll worry less knowing you're there."

"Put it out of your head; you have Mark and Violet to think of."

Satisfied, she let him go. Mark would be up soon, Violet needed feeding, and he must be—of course he was—so very busy.

Busy, yes—with a lecture to prepare and a call from Roger that required his attention—but before he lost himself again in the business of the day, he dialed Flynn's office and told his secretary he wished to speak to him as soon as possible.

Flynn, Charlie believed, would make good on the promise given Georgia. After all, the man was trained to deal with threatening types like Storrow; that was why Charlie had chosen to consult him when Storrow's messages had become more frequent, his tone less controlled: *I know what lies you're facing, Charlie; you won't survive this without me—you know I'm right; it's happening just like I said; they'll lie and call you crazy; they'll lie and* make *you crazy.*

Of course, *Storrow* was the crazy one, his madness with deeper origins, surely, than double-dealing from men like Mike McCraw. Moreover, Charlie told himself, Storrow was the one who'd lie, who'd say anything to get what he was after: boasting and then fawning, imploring and then threatening: *Don't ignore me, Charlie. Don't forget who it is you're dealing with: I still have a few teeth left.*

"You're concerned he might come after you?" Flynn had been very direct at their first meeting. He had a scrubby, old Irish face, spotted in a way that also made him appear more frank than his slicker colleagues, though Charlie knew better than to judge by surfaces, or to trust a face that reminded him, he'd come to realize since, of home.

"Do you think I need to worry?"

"Is it advice you want? Or protection."

"Just advice. Unless your advice is that protection's necessary."

Flynn could only make his recommendation, he said, after conducting some research.

A nasty business, surveillance; it was the one Charlie was in, after all. If he'd managed to sugarcoat this for his employees and sympathizers, others inevitably found ways to remind him. There were always a few such unnerving e-mails awaiting him on his Triathlon account each day: *capitalist fascist—you hunt us, we hunt you*. As a result, McCraw and the board were pressing for a security detail to guard their offices. Charlie remained staunchly opposed: this would undermine the values Triathlon was meant to represent and now, more than ever, it was important to keep up company morale. He wondered what those kids, typing away outside his door, would think to hear he'd hired a PI.

"Let's try to make this quick and quiet," he'd told Flynn. Their following meeting had taken place in Charlie's apartment, a light-flooded condo on Alma Street in downtown North Palo Alto. Flynn had come bearing a twenty-page typed report, which, on principle, Charlie refused to read. "Just tell me if there's anything I need to know."

Flynn had obliged him, confining his remarks to the essentials: for the last five years, Rufus Storrow had been living mostly in Mumbai and Delhi, with occasional visits to his mother in Great Falls. Great Falls was where Storrow resided currently, in a boarding house ten miles away from his family home. According to the owner of the house, Storrow seemed a solitary type, keeping to himself. He'd alluded to a wife and children, but none had ever accompanied him to Virginia. About his current business, Storrow was tight-lipped; the story going around Great Falls was that he was employed as a legal consultant for the U.S. embassy, but no one at any of the embassies in India, said Flynn, had confirmed his employment. Instead, Flynn had found a paper trail linking Storrow to a Mumbai law firm, one with a rather shady reputation, a history of defending local mafia, dealers in blood diamonds and opium.

If Charlie wanted details of Storrow's professional activities, Flynn offered to pursue this, but Charlie's instructions had been to focus on the matter of his personal security. As far as that went, Storrow hadn't reached out to any of Charlie's contacts; he hadn't followed him to Palo Alto or made signs that he would come. The last call he'd made to Charlie was three weeks in the past and so it didn't appear as if Charlie was the object of any pressing obsession. Flynn's recommendation—rest easy, expel Rufus Storrow from his thoughts.

So Charlie had tried to do, but still, on nights when he lay awake in his big, empty apartment, he sometimes let his imagination get the better of him. From the moment the bullying calls started, from the first evening, when Storrow phoned to invite him to that D.C. hotel bar, he'd had fantasies of Storrow coming upon his name in the paper, some account of his success, and, in a fit of jealousy, the blurriness of an ego in decay, mistaking his former protégé for some self he might have been, resolving to end it all and take Charlie with him.

Yes, these heroic types were just the sorts to go for a bloody ending, to think in terms of grand, trite, final acts. For all Charlie knew, moreover, Storrow had been capable of extreme violence once, even if this fact was never proven, and even if Charlie had preferred to doubt his guilt before.

On the message Charlie left for Flynn, this morning, he tried to make the worries sound like Georgia's: "A friend asked me to look into Storrow again: with the Patel memorial approaching."

May was just about four weeks away; the notice of the memorial event had already gone out to members of their class, his own name listed among the program's speakers. The Patels had insisted he offer a few words, as the fund's biggest patron, though he couldn't fathom what words these would be. For a speech like that he'd rely on Alice, he'd decided: let her fret over what to say about a girl they'd hardly known, let her hang pretty phrases on such a grisly matter as violent death. He was preoccupied enough by his own impossible subject, "Sensitive Surveillance," the title of his talk that afternoon.

The time was nearly twelve; he'd do well to get on the road, to call Roger from his car. Inside his hybrid, he rolled down the window, turned the stereo up high, and tried to banish all negative thoughts: Shuster, the *Baltimore Sun*, Rufus Storrow.

He had reason to be glad this afternoon: it was a sunny, brilliant day and in a few hours he would appear before a room full of young, talented entrepreneurs who looked up to him—even with a few critics and spoilers, there were plenty who would see him as a champion, as he'd once seen his beloved professor. Somewhere in the audience might be a girl as pretty as Georgia had been back then: a bold, ambitious girl who'd follow him out to the halls. He could always find an excuse to linger, let her find a way to lead him to her bed, like Storrow had done with Georgia, and all the while, he could flatter himself that he deserved her adoration, that she'd sleep safer at night on account of him.

I worry less knowing you're there.

Did Georgia really? Did she really believe he could keep Storrow from causing harm if that was what he wished to do?

Storrow wasn't a grave threat, Flynn had assured him, though Charlie couldn't pretend he'd been too thoroughly persuaded. Nor could he pretend there weren't days that he rethought his refusal to McCraw; maybe Triathlon *could* do with a security detail, or maybe he could. Maybe there were worse calamities than having men with earpieces and black gloves paid to look over your shoulder, trained to see the things you missed.

24

Mr. Friedlander would be meeting her at Friedlander Park. From the airport in Baltimore, where she'd flown in first class, Alice had been chauffeured by Mercedes into Laurel, Maryland, on her way to visit the nearly completed, two-acre public garden that was Maurice Friedlander's first vanity project, the second being the mayoral campaign he planned on launching the next year.

He had an unusual job to offer, Friedlander had explained over the phone the month before. His park would be opening in May; there would be press coverage, and this would be his chance to make the round of talk shows, and so forth, to introduce himself, Maurice Friedlander, to local voters.

He was aware, he said, that Alice hadn't worked in politics before, but after meeting with advisers and pollsters, and more experienced speechwriters, he and his wife believed that they could benefit from the services of someone such as Alice, with a gift, as Mrs. Friedlander put it, for moving ordinary people to care about the privileged. What they needed was a narrative to make Friedlander, eldest son of the hugely wealthy hedge fund manager, as sympathetic as Alice had made late Lady Di and John John.

Death had made them sympathetic, Alice had replied; she really couldn't take the credit. But Christine Friedlander wouldn't be dissuaded. It had been her idea, too, for Alice to get to know her subject better by spending most of April as a guest at their estate. Three weeks, ten thousand dollars. For this sum, Alice had agreed to abandon her quiet Manhattan studio/office and her good espresso pot; she'd even abandon her biweekly salon and psychiatric treatments, the pivots of that very ordered routine it appeared that she required, along with five bottles of pills, now secured inside a locked pouch in her suitcase (so that it rattled like a maraca when it was lifted by the driver) to keep her existence manageable and her behavior, more or less, under her control.

Friedlander was waiting for her at the fountain by the park's main entrance; he jogged up to the car, bald and stocky, with a full mouth and a beaked nose. He carried a yellow straw sun hat; his shirt was pink: pastels that matched the flowers in the garden around him, but would be better suited to a man twice as tall and half as wide.

"Hope you don't mind that I dragged you here straight from the airport."

"Not at all." Given what she was being paid, minding of any kind was out of the question; she must, instead, pretend as if she'd much rather stand under the noon sun than unpack and wash her face and maybe even rest for a few minutes after her travels. She must pretend that she adored these gardens, the baroque arrangement of roses that recalled her uncle Vasily's front yard and now resembled, she imagined, the elaborate gravesite she hadn't cared to visit.

"Christine did the landscaping," Friedlander informed her, pointing out the trellis roses, whose varieties he'd obediently memorized: "New Dawn Rose, Eden Rose." As they toured the grounds, he dabbed at his face and neck with his handkerchief; such a profusion of sweat, even on this mild April afternoon, seemed to her enough to disqualify him from a future in elected office.

A decent, modest, plain sort of man, he seemed to Alice, despite his family's success and these recent fantasies of political influence. She'd quickly come to suspect that such fantasies belonged less to him than to his wife.

"I personally never saw myself as a politician," he admitted, not long into their chat. "I've always stayed behind the scenes, at the company, too. But different times call for different men. Christine has a sense for these things. She thinks I might have a chance now; in a time of recession and war, what people need is stability, sound management."

"Your wife sounds like a clever woman."

"She is. And she thinks—well, I'll let her tell you what she thinks of you. Christine's read all your work. Every last word. You're her favorite writer."

As if familiarity with a few fluff magazine pieces was an achievement on par with reading all of Proust in French. As if the sort of brief, narrow career Alice had once established could qualify her as anybody's "favorite writer."

"I'm flattered."

"You're the key to this campaign, she says. It's not the issues, it's the man, his story and how you tell it. Christine has a great respect for writers; she always says, language is power."

And there Alice stood nodding, trying to stay alert in the midday sun, agreeing that what this man's wife said was true, and for the simple reason that money, as everyone without it knew, was truly power. Money could buy language; it could buy, even, forgiveness, which was what that ten thousand the Friedlanders would pay her would finally do. With this last imbursement, she'd be cleared of her debt to society (specifically, to one Miss Mary Wittmer, whose settlement demands continued to haunt her), and no amount of rhetoric, no profound apology or proof of moral improvement could accomplish that.

"I'm very eager to get started."

"Then we'll go now; Christine has prepared lunch."

Friedlander's wife was waiting for them at a table down by their artificial lake, where she'd arranged a three-tiered platter of *fruits de mer.* Upon being asked, Alice had said she liked shrimp cocktail, so Mrs. Friedlander had assembled this gruesome pile of raw oysters and clams, tentacled crayfish and barnacled snails, along with two old vintages, red and white, each of which Alice felt obliged, despite contraindications, to sample.

Christine had already been drinking before Alice arrived. She was a nervous, pert-featured woman in her late fifties, dieted flat, eyebrows orange wisps, bony arms stacked with bracelets; they clattered as she fidgeted at her neckline or with the silverware. *How do you feel about leaving New York? You won't be bored here with us, will you? I'll do my best to prevent it: we'll keep each other busy . . .* She prattled on, irritated, overwhelming with her many questions, her bottomless need sadly apparent.

After forty minutes in the sun, an ocean graveyard piled upon each of their plates, Alice felt compelled to begin making arrangements for her exit.

"I should mention in advance, through April is as long as I can stay; I've made other commitments starting the first of May."

"What sort of commitments?"

An event for a foundation, she explained, "Something to do with a former classmate."

"From Harvard, you mean? Not that murdered girl, is it?" Mrs. Friedlander sat upright, sharply enough to give Alice a start.

Her mistake—the mix of wine and meds—to forget the husband's warning: This woman had read every piece she'd ever written.

"Your first story, years ago. A master was implicated. Young. Dashing. Starling, was that his name?" Mrs. Friedlander fingered her pearl earring, turning it, like the screws of memory. "His family was from Virginia, Great Falls."

"Amazing how much Christine can remember," put in her husband. "Especially if a handsome man's involved."

"Oh stop, Maurice, it was in all the papers ten years ago. And Great Falls, the family practically lived next door. Paula knew them: I'm really not so up on all that story, not in comparison to Paula."

"Maybe not in comparison to *Paula*." Mr. Friedlander winked Alice's way, dabbing sweat from his upper lip.

Mrs. Friedlander swiveled from her husband, who turned away then, too, to lie back in his chair, hat tipped over his face.

"It is true though," she addressed Alice, leaning forward, wine glass in hand. "I do like stories about people, their personal lives. I don't see what's wrong with that. You understand, a writer like you, how fascinating a peek into others' lives can be."

"Can be."

Mr. Friedlander sneezed, and his hat fell to the grass.

Mrs. Friedlander eyed her husband, rapping her nails on the edge of her glass. "He was so impressive, the young master, that was the sad thing: athletic, clever, a person with ambition and charisma. Paula told me, she knew the man. And you, too, you must have known him."

"No, I didn't really."

"To write that article, to describe him as you did, you must have."

"All I really did was question what others *thought* they knew."

"Right, that's right, we never really do know about people, which is what—for those like us—keeps us so fascinated." Her hostess drained her glass and dropped back, clinking, in her chair. "Though in this *particular* case, well, when you think about it, it really was a shame that Sterling man wasn't more the way he seemed. He had so many attractive qualities . . ."

Alice's head had begun to ache behind her eyes. The setting was much too bright: the sun, glinting off the china and the implausibly still lake. "If you'll excuse me, Mrs.—"

"*Christine.* Please. We're going to share a house for practically a month."

They were, yes, and if she meant to last that long, she would need to restrict her exposure to this woman. "If you'll excuse me, it's been a long trip and I'm afraid I need a rest."

Alice lay down in her new room—one of the guest beds of an elaborately restored Colonial Revival, a room formerly occupied by two Siamese cats. Lunch had tired her too much to begin the work of unpacking, which she'd insisted on doing herself. She didn't want the Friedlanders' maid handling her luggage. However common it might be to find a stash of Paxil or Zoloft inside the cabinets of the most outstanding families, the sight of five such bottles tended to erode people's confidence in one's reliability.

While Alice was stretched out on the plush duvet, the *Crimson* reporter called her; Nat Krauss he'd said his name was, this kid who'd left multiple messages for her back in New York and whose visit she'd only narrowly escaped by coming here. She turned off the ringer on her cell. It would be punishment enough to be held captive, in this synthetic landscape, by a woman so torturously curious as Friedlander's wife; she didn't need to be pursued here, too, by an ambitious young writer like she'd been once herself.

Though not really so like her: at twenty she'd already known better than to talk like Nat Krauss did, as if revealing the truth was an obvious good. Far more good was accomplished through tactful lies and elisions; there would be no Patel Fellowship, for instance, had she informed the Patels that *she*, their daughter's libeler, was the one to bring the idea to Charlie. If Mrs. Patel had suspicions, she'd chosen not to press for the full story, and Alice had known better than to force the truth upon her. She'd reached a similar conclusion after her meeting with Georgia: their lunch had made plain to Alice what an act of self-indulgence it had been to try to clear her conscience, to inflict a confession upon her friend over an overpriced shrimp cocktail.

That was a scene to suit a woman like Christine Friedlander, with her taste for cold shellfish and steamy scandal. Christine, she imagined, would be in raptures to hear the answers to those questions the *Crimson* reporter had been asking: whether Storrow's car was parked outside Georgia's dorm on the night Julie was killed, about a neighbor hearing voices inside Georgia's room.

According to Ms. Calvin's police statement, you were living with her then, isn't that right? But Lombardi never followed up on that fact, did he?

Silence, Alice thought: *this* was her real gift to the Patels and to everyone who would gather for the memorial next month. Even if Charlie had enlisted her to provide a speech, she would accomplish less through what she said than what she left out—the uncertainties and complications, the many figures of corruption, investigators who'd been, it seemed, willfully negligent, politicians less concerned with seeing the case solved than protecting their positions. None of that had to do with honoring a murdered girl, not any more than a crude encounter driven by vengeance, a reckless knock upon the window of a black BMW that she'd observed from Georgia's window on the fourth night of May.

Storrow had already been a mess before anything went on between them. When he'd rolled down his car window, she could smell the liquor on his breath. It must have been a moment of panic that sent him seeking Georgia, and then there was the shock of being spotted by Alice, the prying friend, instead. *Come on up, it's all right. Georgia should be back soon.*

What was he doing, entering a dorm filled with students who might spot him, traipsing after the mad roommate of the girl he'd really come to see? Alice had sensed the question arising in his thoughts more than once; first when he'd stumbled, wild-eyed, into Georgia's living room, and then again, when he'd followed her up the stairs to Georgia's bedroom.

But even if she wasn't the one who Storrow wanted, seducing him hadn't been hard: from Vasily she'd learned how to master an egotist, those most desperate to escape humiliation, to accept adulation. *I don't judge you for falling for Georgia, anybody would, and I don't blame her either about you. I was the one who pointed you out to her to start with. I was the one who'd noticed you first . . .*

In bed, Storrow had refused to look at her; instead, she caught him eyeing Georgia's things: a bra left on a pile of newly washed clothes, a necklace on the bedside table. His touch was cold; his performance ruined by vanity: he pushed himself up to seem taller and, to prove his strength, he pinned her legs down under his knees. A man so superior, he seemed almost ashamed to be with her, and couldn't have imagined that she found him loathsome too, with his antiseptic smell and that brutish vein running down the front of his skull. Once she felt him losing potency and was sickened to recall her nights with Torsten. But while Torsten had been indifferent and lethargic, Storrow was obliged to make a display of his prowess—so he pressed on through to the end, athletically, dutifully, and mutely, letting out short bursts of breath.

You'll say nothing, he'd warned her afterward, trying not to sound alarmed.

Of course I won't.

I want your word.

A man innocent enough to believe in oaths, whatever he might have been guilty of next. And whatever she'd wondered about him, over the next weeks and months and years, she'd nevertheless kept her promise to him to stay quiet. No good would come from piling on the shame: no one would be spared one jot of pain, not then and not now, not Storrow and not Mr. and Mrs. Patel, who deserved better than to have remembrance of their daughter despoiled by crude revelations. It was for their sake she was avoiding Krauss's calls, for those mild, decent people who would assemble in three weeks to receive, if she could manage it, a small message of comfort from her.

Sounds to satisfy a need, this was her trade—to offer up some kind of rousing statement about Julie Patel, one that would distract from the fact that the event everyone was there to mark was, in reality, a senseless death. Words *in place of* sense, *in place of* truth—very little to do with what this *Crimson* editor still believed he might wring from her. Such revelations would only please people like Christine Friedlander. Gossip for old vampires: nothing to bring rest for the living, nor justice for the dead.

25

When Georgia returned from the hospital at three, grocery bags in hand, Violet babbling in the sling beneath her chin, a new message was flashing on her answering machine.

I'm trying to reach Georgia Calvin: I hope this number is correct.

The voice was a man's, the accent Pakistani or Indian. Not a nurse from the hospital or an insurance agent (always her first assumptions): to these people, she was known exclusively as Reese. This was someone who'd known her in the past.

Mr. Patel, was her next thought: thanking her for the donation she'd made to his daughter's foundation, calling either as a matter of course, without knowing who she was—the girl who'd sent his family flowers for nine years—or else, knowing full well, as a gesture of appreciation.

My name is Mr. Kadam. This is regarding an associate of mine, Rufus Storrow. . . .

She set the groceries down onto the table. Violet clamored at her chest; she placed a hand, half consciously, over the baby's mouth, and stepped closer to the phone.

I'm very sorry to bother you, Miss Calvin, but the man left India suddenly; we had some business unresolved, and I'm unable to contact him. He let me know of your relation and I wondered if he might be staying with you. If you'd be so kind as to return my call.

The baby's mouth was wet against her palm; coming back to herself, Georgia lowered Violet into her playpen and took the groceries to the fridge.

Storrow in the U.S. She'd learned as much two weeks before from that *Crimson* reporter, but the rest of this message was perplexing:

Might Storrow be staying with *her*? the man had asked. God knows what Storrow had said to lead to that conclusion: that they remained involved, emotionally, romantically? The last she'd heard from him, Storrow had been intending to marry. Vaguely, she recalled a photo he'd presented inside Mrs. Chandar's Mumbai flat, the pretty figure posing beside him. What had become of the future Mrs. Storrow? Was there such a woman out there in the world, wondering, like this caller, where her husband might be?

That she could allot a moment to such considerations, that she could find room for concern for *anyone* but Violet or Mark, this was a sign of progress, surely. More than all the trembling efforts at normality—leaving Mark alone long enough to buy groceries for dinner, pick up a movie for the evening at Blockbuster—this was a sign that she was almost back to functioning as a human being again.

She could permit herself some cautious optimism, Poole had told her, when, for the second time since Mark's last adjuvant chemo treatment, his blood work had come back clean. Though Poole still felt obliged to offer warnings at each checkup—Mark's immune system hadn't yet recovered; the cancer could recur at any time—he'd been encouraged enough to allow Mark to return home. For the past fifteen days, she'd been blessed to wake to the sight of her husband's clothes lying on a chair, to the sound of him humming in the shower, or muttering nonsense to Violet in the next room.

Now that their lives no longer revolved around that hospital she loathed, Mark meant to keep it that way, going so far as to insist she leave him behind with Poole that morning, for the time required to run the several tests he needed, including a glucose exam that could run up to two hours. *We're out of food and Violet needs her nap*, he'd told her, an excuse, as much as anything, for her to go home until four thirty, when he'd be through with being poked and bled and inspected, and she could find him dressed in his own clothes again and munching a stale muffin in the main lobby café.

When, by 4:45, Mark still wasn't where he'd promised to be, Georgia returned to the cancer center and searched the front desk for

Ginette. Of all the nurses, Ginette was the one on whom she'd come to depend, the one Georgia could count on to make certain Mark had that extra blanket or pillow that he needed, or that no one kicked her out of the doctors' lounge when she went in to nurse Violet. Ginette was a mother six times over, born in Haiti, where Georgia and Mark had spent ten months through *Médicins sans Frontières*. It was the basis for a bond strong enough to compel Ginette to put aside her other business and go find out right away what might be holding matters up.

"The doctor's in there now," Ginette informed her and didn't try to stop her when Georgia headed for Mark's room. To hell with it: she was a doctor's wife and had long established herself here as impatient with the rules.

Inside the room, she found Mark as she'd left him, still in that hospital robe that seemed an insult to a grown man, that made him look—made all those bald and shriveled cancer patients look—so much like the babies they'd begun as, like Violet, helpless in her arms.

"There's been a delay," Mark explained. "I just got word, I'm sorry, I'd have told you to stay home."

"What sort of delay?"

"They pumped me full of sugar, so now my temp is up half a degree. It's nothing; they'll keep me here until it goes back down."

"What did Poole say about it?"

"Exactly what I told you."

"This couldn't be an infection?"

"Just an excuse to spoil the day."

"And you don't feel sick?"

"I feel perfect."

Even in that robe, it was true he did look healthy: his weight was up, his color returning; brown bristles darkened his skull and jaw.

"What movie did you get?" Mark asked her, though they both knew Poole well enough to know there would be no movie later; Mark would end up held for observation overnight.

Of course, that didn't mean she ought to worry. Dr. Poole preferred to be prudent, even discouraging—uneasy with that whole messy, stubborn condition known as hope. But it was also true that Mark had a habit of understating his problems, sparing her what fears he could.

For Mark's sake, she matched his cheer, but privately, she sensed a panic coming; the prospect of another night in an empty bed made her breath weak. She resolved to find someone to watch Violet and to spend the night right here with Mark on one of those awful hospital recliners.

On the return drive, she tried calling Mrs. Leahy, the home-nurse who'd assisted her for a few days after Violet's birth. Leahy was out of town, visiting her sister.

"It's Friday evening," she reminded Georgia, which was probably the reason the other sitter wasn't answering her phone. A weekend night, on such short notice, no one would be free to come, even if she were willing to leave Violet with a stranger, even if Mark would forgive her if she did.

At six thirty, after she'd fed Violet, Georgia called to check on Mark again; when he wasn't picking up his cell, she grew nervous enough to phone Poole on his private line. Interrupting him at home, she received word that Mark's fever was coming down when Poole had left him in another doctor's charge.

"Call and ask for Dr. Brant," Poole instructed. "I'm assuming Brant meant to release him."

But Dr. Brant was with a patient, according to the unfamiliar nurse Georgia was forced to deal with this time: Ginette, like Poole, had gone home for the day.

"My husband was supposed to be discharged; I'd like to speak with him. The name is Reese, Mark Reese."

Ten minutes later, she was told that Mark was napping. "Do you want me to get him up?"

She considered it: nothing, she felt, could calm her down except Mark's voice. But Mark had to be tired; with Violet crying in the night he couldn't get the rest he wouldn't admit that he still needed. "Don't bother him," she said at last. "When he's awake, though, please tell him to call me and let him know I'm on my way."

As soon as she'd hung up, she dialed a number she hadn't used in months, and never to request the favor she required tonight.

"Dad, it's me. Any way you could drive in? Mark's in the hospital again and I'd like to be there with him."

"I'll be over in an hour."

"Thank you. Thank you, Dad." Not since childhood had she felt such appreciation for her father: for the man's long-standing refusal to be banished from her life, for his arranging to be close by without the least encouragement from her. Two months before, he'd moved to Providence, where he was living with a young RISD professor—near enough to help out, he'd let Georgia know, though she hadn't accepted his offer before. Officially, she was still angry over his calling Charlie—the humiliation that he'd caused, not to mention the implicit insult to Mark—but, truth be told, she didn't regret her father's intervention. As a result, she and Charlie were back to speaking and the voice of her old friend had been a recent source of comfort.

The time was around seven when Georgia finished giving driving directions to her father. Over the next hour, she bathed Violet and put her down to sleep. At eight, when her father still hadn't arrived, she cleaned the kitchen and changed the sheets on her and Mark's bed; by eight thirty, the house was all in order and her overnight bag was packed and leaning by the door. She phoned her father, who was now officially late, but got no answer.

At nine o'clock, he called her back.

"Sugarplum, I'm sorry. I was almost there."

"What do you mean? Where are you now?"

"The hospital."

"With Mark? Is something wrong with Mark?"

"No, no, not Mark. It's me. I'm at McLean. A fender bender. Nothing to worry over, but I've got a concussion and they won't let me out of here without someone to take me home."

On the ride to the hospital, with Violet, who was enraged at being woken, wailing in the seat behind her, what Georgia most wished to do was laugh. Anger was pointless, as it was pointless to blame a man who was so desperate to be loved—as Mark sympathetically described it—that he'd run his car right off the road, derailing himself and his daughter both. It was slapstick, finally: her father's manipulative antics had moved beyond merely annoying; they'd become absurd.

Mark would see the humor in the story, she was sure; on her way to McLean, she'd resolved to make a pit stop, to keep her father waiting a while longer so that she could drop in on Mark and relay events first-hand: let him know why, instead of staying with him, she was needed to look after two babies tonight.

Entering the cancer ward for the second time that day, she heard her phone ringing again.

"Hello, Miss Calvin? This is Raj Kadam."

The accented voice was the same she'd found that afternoon on her answering machine. "How did you get this number?"

"It was left behind in Mr. Storrow's office, among his things. He'd spoken of you, too. As I mentioned, I'm sorry to bother you, but it's important that I reach him."

Already she regretted getting caught on the line, felt a foreboding, a desire to steer clear. "Storrow and I, we're not in touch. I'm afraid he gave you a very wrong impression."

She left off, no longer listening to whatever the stranger had to say: Dr. Poole was standing ahead of her, past reception, in the hospital hall. Poole, who was supposed to be home with his family, was here instead, without his doctor's coat, dressed, disturbingly, in ordinary clothes. He was speaking with another doctor and they were standing only a few feet from Mark's door. She snapped her phone shut and called out Poole's name; at the sight of her, he cringed—scarcely perceptibly but she had seen it and so she smiled, not because she felt like smiling, not at all, but as a test. When he failed to smile back, her knees wobbled and she clutched Violet so tightly that the baby squealed.

"It's an infection," she told Poole, as if *she* were the doctor, *she* the one who knew.

"Yes. But we're treating it. Let's not get alarmed."

It was this reassurance that she found most alarming.

What had happened to the Dr. Poole she'd come to know and trust, ever-pessimistic Poole: *It's progress, yes, but keep in mind, the odds are poor . . . pancreatic cancer is among the hardest types to treat . . . we still have a ways ahead of us, let's not forget.* Had Poole now told her Mark was in peril, that she was facing one of those horror stories where a man comes into the hospital healthy and contracts some fatal disease, if he'd told her this, she might have been able to catch her breath. It was Poole's refusal to present bad news that came as the most fateful news of all.

"He's going to recover from this," Poole assured her, and already she could predict the outcome of the next thirty-six hours, up to the moment when Ginette drew her into her arms to inform her that her husband was dead.

26

His parents' van was parked in the lot beside the dock: *James Flournoy, Delivery and Repair*, painted in neon orange. A brand-new van, his mother claimed, by way of refusing Charlie's offer to buy her one that would be only for her, as an investment in her business. *We've got everything we need, really, Charlie; it's good enough.* Even from a distance, as he drove his rental Prius into the spot beside it, he could see a dent across the van's back bumper, rust above the wheels.

His mother didn't stir when his car pulled in: she was seated in the van's driver's seat, head tilted back, catching a nap. He hoped she hadn't been waiting here too long. From the airport, he'd called to let her know his flight had been delayed, but then roadwork on the highway cost him another hour, and now hardly twenty minutes remained before he'd need to board the ferry. No time to fulfill his promise: to take his mother out to brunch, at whatever barely decent restaurant they might manage to find here at the tip of the North Fork.

He stepped from his car and over to the van's window. His mother's head was tilted toward him; her eyes were closed, her mouth open, her breathing deep. A sign of depression—wasn't it—to sleep like this in the middle of the day? If not depression then exhaustion, or perhaps it was just age: her auburn hair was clouded with gray; tiny red veins bloomed among the freckles on her cheeks. An old woman's complexion. But his mother wasn't, really, so very old. In Manhattan and Palo Alto, women her age still attended yoga and Pilates classes; they flirted with valets and waiters and walked around in strappy heels. Even at twenty, his mother hadn't done these things.

He rapped on the window and his mother gave a start.

"Charlie!" Grappling with the door handle, she tried jumping down to meet him, but her seat belt strapped her in. She seemed puzzled at finding herself stuck.

"I'll come around." He boarded the passenger side, and she freed herself and caught him in a hungry, bony hug. The bar of the brake kicked his shins as she rocked him back and forth. Three years had passed since he'd seen his mother, since he'd smelled her still-familiar smell, mixed with the reek of ammonia and grease inside the van.

He apologized for being late. Up ahead, beyond the guardrails, he could see the ferry passing back across the sound. Ten minutes to dock, fifteen more unloading, and then the boat would be shoving out again. "I should have taken an earlier flight. We'll just have time for a short walk."

The sky was gray and the air heavy; rain might be coming, but it hadn't started yet. He'd have liked to stretch his legs, after the six-hour flight and two-hour drive, but his mother was tired and preferred to sit. A small patch of rocky beach stood beside the asphalt lot. They climbed down and settled together, on the stones, to watch the ferry make its way up to shore.

"Can't you take a later boat?" his mother asked him.

"Cutting it close as is."

"Close for what?"

He was sure he'd told her before about his speech at Harvard, but he reminded her again—"another university engagement"—he left it at that, omitting all references to the memorial, the matter of Julie Patel. His mother had never learned about the murder or his relation to anyone involved. So many events intervened that she knew nothing of either, and a ten-year-old story seemed too irrelevant to tell.

"Will it be like the talk you gave on TV? The Barnetts said their son saw you on a few months ago."

February: his proud debut on Charlie Rose. He hadn't bothered to inform his mother of any of his TV stints, for which he now felt a pang of regret. "It was nothing; it all is, really."

"Well, I know Chip was impressed anyhow. You remember Chip

Barnett? He's in business school now. His mother told me he tried calling you a few times."

"I must have missed it."

"Yes, I explained that, but they keep insisting how much he'd like to speak with you."

"All right, you let them know I'm sorry and I will. I've just been pretty busy these days."

His mother studied him; a frown puckered the loose skin around her mouth. He wasn't the only one disturbed by the figure he'd encountered on this dock, by what changes the last three years had wrought.

"Are you sleeping enough?" she asked.

"I'm fine, just took a red-eye last night."

"A red-eye—is that some kind of pill?"

He smiled, choosing not to correct her, not to sound like the smart-ass his father made him out to be. Her concern for him was unaffected and uncomplicated; his response should be the same. "Mom, you don't need to be worried about me."

She had enough to worry over, after all, with a husband who was an endless source of strain and a son on active duty overseas. Luke, whose appeal to reenlist had been granted two years earlier, had since been stationed at Al Udeid Air Base in Qatar. From what little Charlie gleaned from his mother, Luke was doing well there: the discipline of service had rid him of those troubles, which, until then, his mother wouldn't admit that he'd been having. Well, if his brother had righted himself again, Charlie was glad to know it, though the military was a dangerous cure. Luke could always be called into a war zone, a fear his mother never voiced, but that must haunt her still.

The last thing Charlie wished, at any rate, was to have her learn about the storm he was facing now. Even before the accusations, even in the days when Triathlon was a media darling, he'd been disconcerted by the thought of his parents reading about his company, the sizes of the contracts that were mentioned, numbers sure to make his father fume. Possibly that was why his mother kept herself in ignorance, or maybe his professional life was simply not her great concern.

"I know you're working hard, but are you also having a good time out there?" she asked him. "Are you seeing anyone?"

"Still Melissa."

His mother gave no sign of recognition.

"*Melissa.* It's been three years."

"Three years? With the same girl?"

Was his mother's memory starting to fail her? She was too young for that, but people with little to keep them occupied, people who found more use in shutting out thoughts than staying sharp, could deteriorate early. He ought to be keeping better track of her; he ought to dedicate more time.

At least they might have this day together. He had the impulse to take his mother up to Harvard with him. "That restaurant we went to at graduation—you liked it, remember? When I'm through, we could have dinner there again."

But as soon as he'd asked, he knew that it would be impossible for her to agree. His father must be awaiting her at home; he probably had no idea she'd gone to meet her youngest son.

For two years now, he and his father hadn't been on speaking terms. That blowup Charlie had spent his youth avoiding had finally erupted, just after he'd received word from his mother that Luke was reenlisting. The next day, he'd given his brother a call and tried to convince him to back out. "Join me, help me instead. You'll make more difference in this war and, really, I could use your input as someone who's been there, on the ground."

Luke had promised to get back to him, but it was their father who dialed Charlie up instead.

"Your brother won't be bribed."

"Sorry, is this about you? *You* want to get yourself killed, I won't try to stop you."

"You know what your trouble is, Charlie?" His father's voice was thicker than he remembered it—from age and added pounds and pent-up bile. "You sit in your office and you think you're better than a soldier, that you're doing more for this country—Luke told me what you said. Well, let me tell you, courage and sacrifice don't have a thing to do with it. I know it and Luke knows it, too. It doesn't take a genius to figure it out: want to know if you're in it for yourself? Check your wallet."

Useless to even try, Charlie had realized: he had no say in family matters anymore, had been too distant for too long. For a decade he'd let his father poison Luke against him. By now, only his mother cared to sustain any relationship with him, and he'd just managed to make this harder for her: obliging her to take his calls on the sly, and to pretend the situation at home wasn't as soured as it was.

Brightly, his mother turned to him, shifting her weight on the sharp rocks: "I don't think I can get away today. But you should come back soon, and bring her too, Melissa, you said?"

"If it gets to that point."

"You mean to say it hasn't already, in three years?"

A legitimate objection: this was a long time to invest in anything, business or personal, without something to show for it.

"How old is this girl?"

"The same as me." No longer a girl, in other words, just as he was no longer a boy. Thirty-one was an age, he could see his mother thinking, for a man and a woman to be raising boys or girls of their own.

"Probably she's waiting for you to bring up the future, family and so on; she's just afraid to say."

He didn't wish to contradict her, to explain that Melissa had ambitions greater than being knocked up by Charles Flournoy. Even if he could, possibly, bring Melissa home to meet his mother, it would not change how far apart they were.

In that moment, he felt he understood what he was doing with Melissa, with her MBA from Wharton and her hectic schedule—Melissa who needed nothing from him, not his approval, not his support, who already owned her house without the assistance of any man, and wasn't convinced yet what the presence of a man would add. He was with her precisely for her difference from this person—glancing at her watch, wondering if her husband would be enraged at her brief absence—he was seated next to now.

The boat was at the dock and the guardrails had been lowered; the first cars were driving up the ramp to take their places in the hull. Charlie stood and kissed his mother good-bye, glad to have his exit arranged for him and feeling, after just twenty-five minutes, that he had nothing left to say to her, and no desire to stay.

He walked her to her van, that piece of shit she'd never allow him to replace.

"I'll call you, Mom. If you can, we'll meet again on my way back." With that he got into his own car and drove ahead to take his place among the other vehicles on board the ferry, lined up five across.

A relief to be alone again inside his rental, with its reassuring strangeness and its new car smell. A relief to be moving again, to hear the engine of the boat humming below. He looked around him, at the expanse of gray water ahead, then at a blonde exiting the next car. A young girl, ponytail, pretty; two boys tagged along after her. His stomach lurched. He thought of Georgia, of the chance she might be waiting on the other shore.

Not likely. Georgia wouldn't be up for a memorial, not with Mark's funeral only weeks behind her. And even if she were to be there, she would not be the girl he still stubbornly imagined: the blithe, blond co-ed, striding coolly in suede boots. *That* Georgia would not be appearing anywhere again.

Still, whatever had become of Georgia Calvin—Georgia Reese, he must remember—the real change was in him. At nineteen, he could be brought into raptures just by picturing her sprawled, as she sometimes was, across his dorm-room bunk. Today, no woman had this effect. He'd been with too many, though probably fewer than most: some beautiful, some not, and the difference between them had practically collapsed. This was maturity, a process he ought to welcome, but it was also one to mourn. And maybe it was not maturity either, not progress, but a sign of his diminishment. Of something in him that had arrested, withered.

What a passionless longing to long for passion. If he could write poetry, he would write a poem about this. He would write like Eliot or Larkin, a poetry of quiet loneliness—the sort of poetry he hadn't begun to appreciate when he was just a kid first drawn to study by the words of wiser men.

But for God's sake, he wasn't old yet; he was only thirty-one, and there were men of forty, fifty, and sixty who fell madly in love. Forty-five was the age that Storrow had been when he'd jeopardized so much—more than he ever could have realized, even—for a few stolen afternoons with Georgia.

An attendant rapped on Charlie's windshield. "Fare, please."

Charlie paid him and watched the attendant turn to the next car, to collect cash from the shy-looking boy left behind, by his friends, to pay.

As soon as the attendant had moved on, Charlie followed the shy boy to the roof deck and watched him take his place with the blonde and other boys. All of them college age, probably heading back to campus after a weekend romp: the boys were rowdy, clowning for the blonde's attention. One jumped up onto the ship's rails, another made as if to push him; the girl let out a shout of alarm that trailed off into laughter.

Charlie moved to the other side of the deck. The water that day was choppy; the boat rocked. Though sons from old fishing towns were meant to inherit sea legs, Charlie was prone to getting sick. Better to stay outside then, where the breeze was sharp, vitalizing.

Fresh air. Fresh scene. Maybe Roger was right; he needed to get out of Palo Alto to clear his head, take some distance from work. Soon, perhaps, he'd be in a better frame of mind to accept Roger's decision; he'd given Charlie the news the week before, wanted him to be the first at Triathlon to know of his plans to resign.

"You can't possibly leave now," Charlie had replied: the deal Roger had been working on all spring had just come through: a four-million-dollar contract with JP Morgan; others like it were bound to follow; Roger would be more essential to the company than ever.

"Come on, man, a hundred guys could do my job." He had no illusions, Roger said: Udi had only brought him in to begin with to satisfy Charlie, and McCraw and the board believed the company had since outgrown him (Charlie had no doubt they'd said the same things about himself). But if Charlie meant to cling to his position, Roger preferred to walk away. Nothing against Udi and the other programmers, but he wasn't excited by the technical advances they were making and he wasn't able to bracket the political context like they were; reports of warrantless wiretapping had headlined in all the major papers, the board was introducing larger numbers of agency people to ensure loyalty, and the more conscientious employees at Triathlon were leaving.

Public sentiment had turned against them: Charlie knew this as well as Roger; he'd felt it firsthand. At his last campus appearance, student protesters had broken into the auditorium where he was speaking. McCraw had been advising him to bring a security detail to all such future events, but Charlie wasn't afraid of his critics, he was afraid that they were *right*.

Don't concern yourself with the side of the story you don't know. That had been McCraw's advice: Charlie would never learn whether Triathlon software had been tampered with or if it had been put to illegitimate use; in a sense, such details hardly mattered. Theirs wasn't the only data mining system on the market, as McCraw had pointed out; IBM or Lockheed would provide the same tools if he didn't.

How like McCraw: consolation that doubled as a threat.

"So you think the best thing is to leave guys like McCraw in charge?" Charlie had chosen to make an ethical argument to Roger. "What do you imagine Triathlon will become *then*, without people like you looking out? It's precisely because we're in such morally complex territory, and because the stakes are so high, that we need to stay involved. It's a matter of social responsibility: a company like ours needs men of conscience at the helm."

Roger hadn't disagreed, but he wasn't thinking about what was best for society right now: Jasmine had been terribly upset by all the news that spring and he didn't like to see her under pressure, especially not when, as he'd recently learned, she was pregnant.

"I have to think about my family," Roger told him.

"Well, that's you. This company is what *I* have to look after."

"How about yourself for a change, buddy? *Your* happiness."

"I didn't do this to be happy." He'd wanted to be admirable. Plenty of people were happy, but who the hell was there out there to really admire? The last person he'd admired was Storrow, and he'd done about all he could to correct for that mistake.

Storrow's deceits, his humiliations, his burdens: each carefully documented, cataloged, for Christ's sake, as per Charlie's request—all part of the twenty-page report that Flynn had insisted Charlie keep in his possession. *Read it or not, it's yours; you paid for it.* As if shelling out ten thousand dollars gave him any true share in Storrow's secrets.

After his last meeting with Flynn, Charlie had tucked the report away in the top drawer of his bedroom desk; there it remained, untouched, until, in April, a call from a man claiming to be Storrow's business partner provided an excuse to pull those pages out again.

"I'm trying to contact Storrow's associates in the U.S.," the man explained. "Three weeks ago, we had an important meeting with a client. Storrow never showed; I've looked for him; I've called Mumbai police."

"I'm sorry, who are you?"

"Raj Kadam. Storrow has done some work with me."

"What sort, if you don't mind my asking?"

"Legal consulting," said the man, evasive. "I guess you have an idea about his business, since he had dealings with you, too."

Storrow had no business with him, Charlie had made clear, disentangling himself from Storrow's issues—thorny and unpleasant ones, he sensed—with this cagey stranger. He didn't have a clue about

Storrow's activities or whereabouts, he told Kadam, speaking almost honestly, as it so happened; even *after* reading Flynn's report, he knew little that might be of help in tracking Storrow down.

The twenty pages Flynn had left him were composed almost entirely of current records—travel, bank, and phone—that had led Flynn to draw the conclusions he'd shared with Charlie at their meeting. The only information that was new to Charlie was contained in transcripts of interviews that Flynn had conducted, the most revealing of them with a longtime friend of Storrow's mother.

This old Great Falls companion, Paula Moreaux was her name, was the one to provide stories of Storrow's past, stories Flynn, justifiably, hadn't found relevant to Charlie's concerns, or fit to mention at their appointment.

Paula Moreaux had known Mimi Storrow sixty years; she'd grown up alongside Mimi, née Warber, and run in the same circles—the Moreaux family of the same status as the Warbers—not that people besides Mimi concerned themselves with such things these days. The Warbers had less money than the Storrows, but Mimi could—and did—boast of the three generals in her family, which was more impressive, in her opinion, than the fortune made by her husband's great-grandfather, culled from copper mines in Arizona.

Rufus Storrow Sr. turned out to be less wealthy than Mimi must have expected; whatever he'd inherited he hadn't increased, and his career proved modest. After failing to make partner at a prestigious Virginia law firm, he moved to a smaller firm; twice he ran for local office but lost by a wide margin each time. The opinion among those who knew Mimi was that she was disappointed in her marriage and sought distraction in frequent visits from her youngest and much-admired uncle, Thaddeus Warber, a decorated field marshal. Later, she found more steady consolation in the presence of her handsome only son, Rufus Jr., whose great promise she never tired of proclaiming. Moreaux remembered the young Storrow as very striking, with flaming hair and green eyes, a boy devoted to his mother, indifferent to his father, and severe with himself.

When Rufus Jr. was fourteen, his father died of pneumonia. Mr. Storrow had been sick all winter, without, so it was said, once setting foot in a hospital. Possibly some suspected Mimi of negligence in her husband's care, but the widow put on a dignified show of mourning and never remarried. Instead, she invited her uncle Thaddeus to live with her son and her—an arrangement no one could call improper, though in a town as quiet as Great Falls, there was bound to be some conjecture about the bachelor uncle's secret interests in his attractive niece or—some did wonder—in her equally attractive son.

Why, after all, did Thaddeus Warber never socialize with any of the local single women? And why were his hands always on his nephew: fixing his clothes or posture, giving teasing taps or sparring? They often practiced sports together—boxing, wrestling, football—and some people didn't find it right: a grown man and a boy rolling around together on the grass. The chatter only increased when word got out that Rufus Jr., then fifteen, had cracked his uncle's jaw one summer. A football accident, Mimi claimed, never once behaving as if she had something to hide. On the contrary, she'd bragged about the incident—the two men such avid sportsmen that they'd kept on playing while she phoned the ambulance.

When it came to her family—Warber blood—Mimi never displayed any sentiment but pride. In this, Rufus Jr. soon came to resemble his mother: as a teen, he held himself above his classmates, who considered him arrogant and strange. Kids didn't conceal their judgments, after all, said Ms. Moreaux, the way polite adults knew how to do.

For her part, Paula Moreaux wouldn't stoop to speculation. All she would tell Flynn definitively was what she'd observed of Rufus Jr.: that, in all the years he'd lived in Great Falls, and on all the occasions he came home to visit, he'd never seemed to have any friends, or girlfriends either, despite how good-looking he was. *I almost doubted he had a romantic life, until it came out in the paper, the pictures of that pretty college girl.*

Georgia—again Charlie felt the sickening jolt of nerves. He leaned down, over the rails, letting the cool spray brush his face. He ought to have outgrown such symptoms, the butterflies of a love-struck boy—what could it mean to feel the same way now, and over a woman he hadn't seen but once in a decade? It couldn't be love—if he was moved, he reasoned, it wasn't by Georgia, but by the reminder she offered of his younger self, who had been ardent, who still believed in great loves, great deeds, and great men.

The boat was halfway across the sound, the facing woods made lusher by the cloudy sky. A fresh shore ahead, another left behind: a symbol, if not of hope, then at least, of forgetting.

Forget the boy he'd been when he made this crossing before, better not to be embarrassed by the faith he'd carried in the future and in others, not to recall feelings stronger than he could contain now. Forget Storrow as he'd first known him: handsome, eager, and punctilious, cheeks rosy, smile pristine, looking as he had the night he'd welcomed Charlie into his home.

Better to have the past a blur so he could stand before a hundred people whose names he didn't recall and read empty words that would vanish as soon as they were spoken. He'd delivered dozens of speeches, without one line that remained memorable, and why should they be memorable? What was worth memorizing but private scenes of love and, for those who didn't have them, poetry?

There, standing on the bow of the ferry, Charlie was reminded of a poem about the river Lethe, a poem he'd discovered as a boy—obscure, mostly forgotten—whose best lines he'd committed to memory once.

O Lethe, what ruins thou holdest of body and soul!
Of the greatest of masters, and of wrecks and disasters.
Thy sweet forgetful flood sweeps over us all . . . the
living and dead . . .
and them that live on . . . after honor is fled.

27

It was on the final day of her service to the Friedlanders, as Alice was already on her way out, that Christine announced they'd be making a small detour on their way to the airport.

"Just over to Great Falls for a quick brunch."

Alice warned her there really wasn't time. Her flight left in two hours and she couldn't miss this one; as it was, she'd barely make it to the campus for the memorial at four.

"We'll have to be quick then. What else can we do? Paula Moreaux insists on meeting you. You really can't say no to Paula."

She might have guessed Christine would spring something like this on her, Alice thought: the woman couldn't simply *let her go*; for three interminable weeks, she'd been the Friedlanders' prisoner, along with the Siamese cats and trellis roses. Kept for the wife's benefit rather than the would-be mayor's, it turned out, to provide conversation throughout the unbroken chain of breakfasts, lunches, teas, and dinners underpinning Christine's days.

Brunch with Paula Moreaux was one final torture Alice could have done without, and would have, if Christine hadn't found a means of holding her in her power for just a while longer: the payment from the Friedlanders still hadn't come through.

"I'll phone the bank again, from Paula's," Christine promised; meanwhile she was sure Alice wouldn't find the visit boring. Paula was always good for an amusing anecdote; her family went back two centuries in Great Falls, and she knew anybody of interest within a hundred miles, including details about that unfortunate young master, Storrow, whose name Christine had, apparently, had occasion to recall.

Paula Moreaux wasn't what Alice had envisioned as the dear

friend of frail, high-strung Christine, nor as the owner of the restored plantation house where she greeted her guests at the door, dressed in overalls—her "work clothes," she proudly called them. She was older than Christine, past sixty, but robust: tall and lumbering, about Alice's own height, and nearly twice as wide.

She lived on her own in the huge house, she and her pretty maid, Maria: there were no traces of another presence—no man's jacket on the hook, no children's or grandchildren's pictures on the mantel—little to fill the seven bedrooms, except for numbers of large, brightly painted pots and vases. Her creations, Paula announced, as she dragged her guests on a tour through her potter's studio and up and down the stairs to view its issue. Only then came brunch, served on the back porch by Maria, during which Paula poured out tall glasses of mimosas, and Christine raised the subject they'd all gathered to discuss.

"Alice was the expert on Storrow herself once. Not to mention that she's attending the memorial for that poor girl today. She wrote the speeches."

"Just one," Alice corrected. "An introduction."

"Such a funny thing, your turning up now, Alice." Paula smiled, slowly pulling open a brioche. "You're not the first person this year to come to me asking about Rufus Storrow."

"Funny," Alice agreed, neglecting to point out that she *hadn't* asked about him, nor been the one to in any way suggest this meeting.

"I don't think I even mentioned it to *you*," Paula went on, leaning toward Christine. "The investigator who came by this fall."

"No, somehow you neglected to," Christine said, chiding.

"Because, you know, it didn't seem like such a big thing then." Paula placed a morsel on her tongue and paused to chew. "But that was before those strange calls started coming. Did either of you hear about this? A month ago, almost exactly, a man starts calling people here in town, inquiring after Storrow: some business partner in Mumbai, I guess he was. I'm almost sure he must have been the one who hired that detective—not, as I'd imagined then, the wife."

"Storrow was *married*?" Christine's wispy brows furrowed.

"There's another question, really—to hear Mimi tell it, no, he couldn't possibly have been. Not to an Indian girl, anyway. But I'm getting sidetracked. How are we on time? Alice, how much longer are you mine?" Paula dropped the brioche and reached out to clutch Alice's hand. The woman's skin felt dry, and there was clay under her nails and in the wrinkles showing at the edges of her palm.

"I can stay a few more minutes." In fact, she should be on her way already; instead of lingering over rumors and mimosas, she should be pulling up to departures, picking out her seat at check-in.

A clock stood on one wall of the porch, half concealed by immense hydrangeas, planted in stout, pink pots of Paula's making. Alice had to force herself to keep track of the time while Paula finally told the story that Christine had vowed, that morning, would be well worth the trip.

The crowd gathered behind Thayer Hall filled just the first few rows of chairs. The gates onto the Yard were open. Security stood quietly by; no curious onlookers, no crush of press to manage, only a single cameraman leaning against the back wall of Holworthy and a student reporter, standing a few feet off, scribbling into a pad.

Nat Krauss—Alice was sure it must be him: greasy haired, jittery and self-serious. If she squinted, she might mistake him for the editor who'd published her in the *Crimson* ten years before. She passed behind the boy and around the corner of Canaday Hall, choosing a spot nearly out of sight of the crowd. The reporter wasn't the only one she didn't wish to see her. From a distance, she regarded her former classmates, clustered on the green; some hairlines had receded, some cheeks had thinned, others grown rounder. They looked adult, if not yet old, chatting soberly in suits and skirts, turning their faces up to scan the clouds. The air was damp, the strong breeze threatening rain: no provisions had been made for bad weather, no costly tent erected on the grounds, just a platform in front of Bradstreet Gate, where a small plaque had been hung ten years before.

On the platform sat the speakers and the family. Alice had arrived late, spared the difficulty of avoiding the Patels, who were already removed from the audience and set out on display. Alice observed them from the side: Mrs. Patel, surveying the sparse gathering ahead; Mr. Patel, preferring to study his hands, or gratefully exchange a few words with the first fellowship recipient, seated on his left. Darlene sat at the end, scarcely recognizable, stripped of combat boots and nose ring, resembling her late sister in a modest gray dress and a braid. The next row contained the speakers: the Quincy dean, the university's chaplain and president, and, on the far right, an empty chair that must have been reserved for Charlie. Fifteen minutes before the start of proceedings, Charlie was nowhere to be seen.

Somewhere in the crowd, a baby cried. Alice searched the courtyard, studying the several women leaning over carriages, arranging shades and blankets to protect their little ones from any pending drops of rain. Georgia wasn't among them—she'd no doubt had enough death to commemorate this month—though Alice did recognize two of these new mothers: friends of Julie's. Julie's former boyfriend was here too, Lucas Parker; he'd grown a short beard, but looked otherwise the same. His arm was around another woman, a trim brunette who stood with a fixed smile, pretending to be listening to whatever it was Lucas was saying, and not to notice Mrs. Patel staring at her, sadly, from the stage.

The microphone let out a screech; a technician stood over the dais, fiddling with the wires. The first raindrops were falling. Time to begin; the crowd grew quiet, obedient students once again. The president eyed the empty chair at his right.

It was then, while the president sat, craning his neck, and people lifted their jackets up above their heads, that Alice heard a woman's laughter behind her and turned to see a couple passing: Charlie and Georgia, her baby in a sling across her chest, crossing through Meyer Gate to enter the Old Yard.

They hadn't seen her, caught up in their own dizzy absorption with each other. Georgia was wiping the cheek beneath one eye: either tears of laughter or else she'd been crying. Her nerves were frayed, of that much Alice was sure; Georgia's hands kept fluttering up to her hair and even that laugh of hers, though still husky, aware of its own charm, sounded unsteady.

Alice's experience with loss, at the age of twelve, remained enough with her to identify what she was seeing: Georgia wasn't yet among the living; she'd been married to death for the last year. Perhaps, here, today, revisiting her past, she hoped to be revived a little, to think back on afternoons such as she and Alice had spent together: running, stealing lunches from the dining halls, picnicking on the grass.

Brilliant days because of Georgia, who'd had such a gift for being young. She'd understood so much better than most others—better than Alice, herself—how to be agile and audacious and unencumbered by ambitions or the weight of great affections.

So Georgia had come, thought Alice, to a memorial of all occasions, to recall life and freedom, and her own simple glory, and to be looked on again by Charlie, who'd always adored her.

Charlie walked beside her, stiffly, staring at her, then lowering his eyes; his face was drawn, his complexion yellowed. At the platform he stopped and reached out a tentative hand to touch the baby. Georgia squeezed his arm, and a small flush colored his cheeks.

The speakers looked on, waiting; at last Charlie stepped away to mount the platform. The university president nodded to him, no longer free to scold, not the young man who'd financed these proceedings. He stood, instead, to offer the opening remarks.

A quotation stands on the opposite side of Bradstreet Gate, by its namesake, Anne Bradstreet, America's first published female poet: "I came into this Country, where I found a new World and new manners at which my heart rose."

Julie Patel was also a newcomer to this country; her parents moved here when she was two, and instilled in her appreciation for the unique opportunities afforded her here. . . .

Ten years before, this same man had stood in the same spot and offered similarly bland and careful remarks. Alice had listened to his words from the sidewalk, standing on the other side of Bradstreet Gate. She meant to go unseen that afternoon, to avoid the dark glances from Julie's friends. The only classmate who'd ever known she'd come to hear the speeches on that day was Charlie.

He'd spotted her on his way out and paused to say good-bye, feigning cheer and looking mournful in his black and gaping robe. Then he'd left her, to meet his family, she'd supposed, like all the others clustered inside the dining halls to grow dull with food and sentiment. Not her; she'd skipped the family and the formal meals; her robe and cap lay in a pile at her feet. For her, the finest celebration was to enjoy a cigarette and the relative quiet on Cambridge Street.

Across the road, a car was parked, engine idling. She wasn't sure when it had appeared, or how long she'd failed to note the man, watching her, it seemed, from the driver's seat. He might have been anyone: some father waiting for his son or daughter to come down with a last piece of luggage. But something in this figure—his straight posture, his stillness—made Alice suspect otherwise and cross the street to the brown sedan: a deliberately nondescript replacement for the black BMW Storrow used to drive.

She'd guessed what Storrow meant to say before she'd even reached the car: she should tell the police he'd been with her on the night Julie was killed. Already he'd approached her once to ask this impossible favor; four days before, he'd come to Charlie's room at night when Charlie and Roger were both out. She'd have gone out, too, if she'd guessed that Storrow would dare to find her, would risk anything so foolish, with police watching him the way they were—they'd tapped his phones, he said, using this as an excuse, also, to appear this way: they had to speak in person.

Through the door would have to do. Just his voice in the night was enough to make her think about calling the police herself.

She wanted to be left out of it, she'd said; there was nothing she could do to help him anyway. Her story would only make him more detestable—a serial lecher—besides, the timing of his alibi was off; he'd left Georgia's apartment at midnight, not at one, and so what he, with his talk of honor, required, was a lie.

She made the same point that afternoon, taking her place beside Storrow in the passenger-side seat. She couldn't do it; she couldn't change the facts to suit his interests. "It's a crime, what you're asking."

"It's an act of mercy."

From outside came the sound of young voices; two students in graduation gowns were crossing in front of Storrow's car. He dropped his head, not to be seen, and waited for them to pass.

"I can't teach; I can't go out. They've taken my life away. One hour, that's all it comes down to. If I'm innocent, what does it matter? I'm innocent, Alice. What's one hour, for a man's life?"

It was terrible—and wonderful—to hold the fate of another person in one's hands. Of course, she didn't *really*. Two facts were already becoming clear—to her if not to Storrow yet: Storrow would *not* be arrested, nor would he ever, no matter what she might say, be cleared of suspicion.

"You're still a free man. Consider yourself lucky."

Storrow's eyes narrowed, his looks grew sharp, anger enlivening that blandly handsome face. He thought her remark glib, but in fact she'd been sincere; he *ought* to have been grateful, not only for being spared prison, but for being released from that burdensome idea he maintained of himself, from the whole antiquated and exhausting effort of being Rufus Storrow.

"I'm going to go now," she announced. "You should, too; you shouldn't even be here." She pulled the handle on her door, but Storrow reached his arm out, pinning her to her seat.

"I *am* here, dammit."

One hand gripped her arm; the other clenched into a fist. His whole face was like a fist then: strained and blank. His anger filled that tiny space of the car, flooded it, robbing her of breath.

"I *am* here," he repeated, through pursed lips. "I have plans. I have ambitions. I will not just disappear because *some* people would prefer I don't exist."

Storrow endured and would continue to endure—whatever the hell anybody wished—this, at least, was one heartening way to interpret the account produced by Paula Moreaux that morning, over the last warm sips of mimosas:

"Simply disappeared is what I've heard. Two months he's been gone. And before that, the last day anyone saw him, it seems he was clearing out a bank account in Mumbai. A business account that he'd been sharing with his partner, one of those criminal lawyers who's half a criminal himself. It must have been a considerable sum Storrow went off with, too—enough for this partner to mount an inquiry, come and beat the bushes here.

"Of course Mimi's been mortified; in public, she's done her best to hold herself above it, not to acknowledge this shady partner or dignify his complaints. I can tell you she's the *last* person to bear a scandal, so to be put through yet another, after everything: first her boy's an alleged killer and now he's a thief among the lowest kind of thieves. Not to mention that Indian family that some claim he's left behind—little brown Storrows running around—this is *Mimi's* view, not mine, obviously. She'd prefer to deny the possibility of such creatures: if they're out there, better they stay hidden. I imagine she must feel the same way about him. No pity left. That son, she must be thinking—wouldn't it be the best thing for everybody, really, if Rufus Storrow never showed his face again?"

Standing in the shade of Canaday Hall, beside the gate that now stood open, Alice could hear Charlie's voice through the microphone, his tone measured, meant to reassure the several dozen people gathered on the patch of grass inside that they were still among the sheltered, favored

vored and secure. It was up to him to introduce the fellowship recipient being honored on that day and to enumerate her many virtues: daughter of immigrants, like Julie, valedictorian of her public high school, like Julie. A young woman possibly as good as the other one buried in the Pittsburgh earth, good enough to inspire clapping, though nothing thunderous enough to block out the ring of a cell phone.

Alice took the call, which was from her lawyer, letting her know that the last payment to Mary Wittmer had been made, reminding her that, with enough money and luck, sometimes, one could receive a second chance and that she, Alice Kovac, was, officially, forgiven of her debts. Thirty-one, alone and broke, not a young woman to inspire applause, but innocent, at least under U.S. law, the surest innocence there was, either in heaven or on earth.

Acknowledgments

For their wisdom and vision, I'm indebted to Adam Eaglin and Elyse Cheney, Alexis Washam, and Molly Stern. For their dedication to getting this book made and read, thanks to the rest of the marvelous team at Crown. For his expert advice, thanks to Barry Carr and, for their generosity and insight, to Jon Dee, Debbie Cohn, and Diane Greco. Finally, I'm grateful to my family, for inspiration and encouragement.

A Note on the Type

In 1902, Linotype produced a Transitional typeface named Old Style No. 7 that was based on an early 1870s font from The Bruce Type Foundry (New York, 1813–1901), which had based its version on a design from the Scottish foundry Miller and Richards.